Advance praise for

BREATHLESS

"If you're looking for a book to thrill and transport you, then *Breathless* is the read for you! Set high in the chilling Death Zone, this thriller had me on the edge of my seat. I loved being immersed in the competitive, high-stakes world of alpine climbing, and Amy brilliantly evokes how risky this setting is, a setting that can only get deadlier with a murderer on the mountain. . . . A must-read for 2022."

—Sarah Pearse, *New York Times* bestselling author of *The Sanatorium*

"*Breathless* is a high-altitude, high-stakes thriller that combines fascinating, authentic mountaineering experience with pure thriller entertainment. The suspense rises like the Nepalese mountain it is set on. Reminded me of the best of Michael Crichton, where indepth knowledge and a masterful plot work together to create a tense adrenaline-fuelled ride. I loved it."

—Matt Haig, *New York Times* bestselling
author of *The Midnight Library*

"I climbed Manaslu with Amy—she is the real deal."

—Nirmal "Nimsdai" Purja, author of *Beyond Possible*
and star of the Netflix documentary *14 Peaks*

"Chilling, vivid, and entirely unique."

—Abigail Dean, *New York Times* bestselling author of *Girl A*

"Nail-biting, chilling, totally exhilarating—a true triumph."

—Stacey Halls, bestselling author of *The Familiars*

"Tense, chilling and terrifying with unforgettable characters and an unpredictable and atmospheric plot. One of the most original thrillers I've read. It deserves to be huge!"

—Claire Douglas, bestselling author of *Last Seen Alive*

BREATHLESS

BREATHLESS

Amy McCulloch

VIKING

VIKING

an imprint of Penguin Canada, a division of Penguin Random House Canada Limited

Canada • USA • UK • Ireland • Australia • New Zealand • India • South Africa • China

First published in hardcover in the Great Britain in 2022 by Michael Joseph,
an imprint of Penguin Random House UK
Published in Viking paperback by Penguin Canada, 2022
Simultaneously published in the United States of America by Anchor Books,
a division of Penguin Random House LLC, New York

www.penguinrandomhouse.ca

*Publisher's note: This book is a work of fiction. Names, characters, places and incidents either
are the product of the author's imagination or are used fictitiously, and any resemblance to
actual persons living or dead, events, or locales is entirely coincidental.*

LIBRARY AND ARCHIVES CANADA CATALOGUING IN PUBLICATION

Title: Breathless : a thriller / Amy McCulloch.
Names: McCulloch, Amy, 1986- author.
Identifiers: Canadiana (print) 20210231378 | Canadiana (ebook) 202102313862 |
ISBN 9780735242852 (softcover) | ISBN 9780735242869 (EPUB)
Classification: LCC PS8625.C86 B74 2022 | DDC C813/.6—dc23

Book design by Christopher M. Zucker

Cover design by Ervin Serrano

Cover images: (woman) © FotoDuets/Shutterstock; (mountains) © Skazzjy/iStock/
Getty Images; (snow) © rolfo/Stocksy; (landscape) © Michela Ravasio/Stocksy

Printed in the United States of America

10 9 8 7 6 5 4 3 2 1

Penguin
Random House
VIKING CANADA

For Angus—
the best dad, my number one reader
and my biggest fan

PROLOGUE

SUMMIT DAY

Breathe, Cecily.

Cold air filled her lungs. It was strange. When she'd pictured breathing up here, she'd assumed it would feel like suffocating. Choking. Maybe, in a way, like drowning.

But it didn't.

She could feel the sting of the wind on a tiny bit of exposed skin on her cheek, between her buff and her sunglasses, and then a stronger gust against her body, threatening to bring her to her knees.

The air was there. It just wasn't doing what it was supposed to.

She was so tired. Her muscles struggled to work as she pushed through the snow. Not just her muscles. Her blood. Her lungs. Her brain.

It was simple, really—there wasn't enough oxygen in the air, less than a third of what her body was used to. The altimeter on her watch read that she was still up above eight thousand meters. In the death zone.

Her heart raced. She looked over her shoulder. *Was he following?* She stopped in her tracks. A hulking silhouette a few meters above her, his ponderous steps breaking fresh snow, stalking her, chasing her. But no . . . She blinked and realized it was only the shadow of a cloud on the mountainside.

Without enough oxygen reaching her brain, not even her eyes could be trusted.

So is he coming? Or is he waiting below?

She didn't think it was possible for her heart to beat faster, but it did, galloping inside her chest. Her breath sped up too as she gulped down the thin air. She swooned, her head spinning.

What did it matter if he was above or below her?

Worry about *him* later. Worry about survival now.

She moved as fast as her body would let her. A thousand-meter drop was one misstep away. Meanwhile, phantom footsteps haunted her from behind.

She had to get down the mountain.

And she was going to have to do it on her own.

MISSION: FOURTEEN CLEAN—A PROFILE OF A MOUNTAINEERING LEGEND
By Cecily Wong

At sea level, Charles McVeigh is a man like any other. But take him into the death zone—above eight thousand meters—and he becomes superhuman.

When he stood atop the summit of Manaslu on [insert date], he achieved what many had deemed impossible: summited the fourteen highest mountains in the world in under a year, with no oxygen and no ropes—cementing his position as the world's greatest living alpinist.

Yet perhaps even more inspiring than his mountaineering feats are the daring rescues he's managed along the way. On Dhaulagiri, the third mountain on his list, he led the attempt to rescue two Italian brothers who were stranded above camp four. While he was able to save one of the brothers, the other sadly succumbed to his injuries.

That he managed to save even one life after the pair had spent a night exposed to the ice-cold temperatures and thin air is something of a miracle. Neither man would have survived had Charles not been strong enough to turn around in his descent and return from camp three. It took almost fourteen hours for the rest of the rescue team to meet them. They would have been too late.

This rescue—along with lives saved on Everest, Broad Peak and Cho Oyu—thrust Charles into the world's media spotlight.

But what drives a man to go to such extremes? I was fortunate enough to climb with Charles on his final mountain, Manaslu, to find out. [Insert interview when I get it!]

CHAPTER 1

IN A CRAMPED HOTEL room high above the prayer flag–strewn streets of Thamel, the main tourist district of Kathmandu, Nepal, Cecily snapped her laptop shut. The opening to her article wasn't right, but getting *something* down early soothed her jangled nerves. Far easier to whip a weak lede into shape than face a blank page.

She used to think a blank page was her greatest fear. Now, thanks to Charles McVeigh, she was about to face something far more terrifying.

The death zone of the eighth-highest mountain in the world.

Her head pounded after her excursion to Tom & Jerry's the night before. She hadn't intended to drink much, but one of her new teammates—Zak, the American—had been buying, and a hangover seemed like a small price to pay for the bonding she'd done with him. She needed to be on her game for this expedition, yet already she was starting off-balance.

A sharp knock on her hotel-room door brought her to her feet. She opened it, allowing her expedition leader, Doug Manners, and head guide, Mingma Lakpa Sherpa, to enter. They'd met her at the airport the day before, Doug instantly recognizable by the shock of silver hair against his mountain-tanned skin. Yet today, his shoulders were hunched and he seemed tired . . . not like the bold pioneering mountain man, legend of the British alpinism world she had pictured. She'd read a lot about his accomplishments in the high peaks: five Everest summits, from both the south and north side, along with numerous first ascents on some of the lesser-known peaks in the Karakoram and in the Andes. He'd spent many years guiding for one the world's premier high-altitude commercial expedition companies, Summit Extreme, before leaving to branch out on his own with Manners Mountaineering. He was known for his no-nonsense approach and his high regard for safety.

Mingma next to him was a slip of a man, and yet she knew he was a fifteen-time Everest summiteer. Cecily could barely wrap her head around the steel and bravery it would take to accomplish such a feat.

"All set?" Doug asked.

"I think so." She flipped to the gear list printed and glued into the front of her notebook, and allowed them in to inspect the gear laid out neatly on the double bed. She'd already checked it a dozen times that morning, carefully marking off every item she'd been asked to bring. Nothing forgotten. Nothing left behind.

This time, on this mountain, she was determined to be prepared.

"Feeling all right this morning?" asked Mingma, a twinkle in his eye. He'd helped her make her way back to the hotel last night, providing directions to the Nepali taxi driver.

"Yes, fine!" She forced a grin, and he patted her on the arm, not pressing further.

She watched as Doug cast a critical eye over her gear. He lifted a piece of footwear, inspecting the sole. It was one of her enormous triple-layer, eight-thousand-meter-ready boots, wrapped in wasp-yellow gaiters that came up to her knees. Hers were pristine, unworn. They would be critical in protecting her toes from frostbite in the extreme cold, but hers were so big, she'd had to layer the inside with extra insoles. Almost all the high-altitude mountaineering gear—summit suits and boots—was made for male bodies. She had to adapt it all to fit.

"Thank you both again for having me on this expedition," she said. "It must be strange having clients with you—I know you've been supporting Charles alone on his mission so far."

"It is our pleasure," said Mingma, his sparse mustache tickling the underside of his nose as he smiled. His warmth was a stark contrast to Doug's grunts. Doug's frown deepened as he moved on from her boots to inspect her orange-handled ice ax and harness.

"I hope that one is OK," she said. "I googled the best harnesses for mountaineering and it had good reviews."

"It'll do. One that clips around the legs would have been better."

Her cheeks reddened. "Oh. I didn't know."

"You should have asked—Google's not going to save you at eight thousand meters." Doug placed the harness back onto the bed, careful not to tangle the loops. "Normally when I run an expedition, I only take climbers with the right experience. You never know when a mountain will turn on you. It's not just your own life you put at risk up there."

"My last summit attempt taught me that," she said, suppressing a shudder. "I actually wrote something about it online. I don't know if you saw . . ."

Doug looked blank. "I don't really keep up with the internet."

"Oh, of course you don't. I only thought you might've seen it because Charles says it's the reason he invited me on the expedition . . ." She was embarrassed to have brought it up, but pleased at the same time. At least one person on the trip hadn't read her now-infamous viral blog post "Failure to Rise"—all about her total *inability* to reach the summit of the mountains she attempted. Once Zak had realized who she was, he'd insisted on buying another round of shots.

"Looks like everything is in order here. I need to check on the others," said Doug. "When you've packed up, leave your duffels in the room and Mingma will bring them down. Meet in the lobby at eleven hundred sharp, then we'll head to the airport."

Cecily straightened. "Got it." She surveyed the vast amount of gear to pack up. This was her life savings. Everything she owned was on this bed. She caught Mingma's eye. "Do you think I've brought too much?"

Mingma laughed. "You should see Mr. Zak's list. I think he is bringing a photo album of his children to the summit. What are you taking to the top?"

She chewed on her bottom lip. "To be honest, I haven't thought that far . . ."

"You haven't?" He blinked, taken aback. "They sell flags all over in Thamel. Why don't you see if you can get one? You have a bit of time."

"Really? Great idea. Thanks, Mingma. I'll go once I've finished here."

He bowed his head before following Doug out of the room. Cecily folded her clothes into packing cubes, stacked them inside the duffel bag, and checked each item off her list again.

"Summit flag" wasn't on it. Of course she should have something to take to the top, to hold up in a photograph. Why hadn't she thought about it before?

As she made her way out onto the bustling streets, the answer was obvious.

Because you don't think you're going to make it.

CHAPTER 2

POCKET-SIZED UNION JACK SECURED, Cecily made her way back to the guesthouse. The moment the doors slid open, she found a phone thrust in her face. "And look, here's one of my teammates now!" exclaimed Zak.

She'd googled him as soon as she'd returned to the hotel after the bar and discovered that he was the CEO of TalkForward, some kind of high-tech communications firm based in Petaluma, California.

"Say hi, Celia!"

"It's Cecily," she said, raising a hand to wave at a gaggle of blond, beaming kids on the wide screen of his phone.

Zak threw his arm over her shoulder, pulling her close so they were both visible in the frame. "Still suffering from jet-lag brain over here. Kids, this is Cecily! She's a world-class journalist writing a story on Charles."

She winced at the description of her job title—hardly accurate—but she didn't correct him, and Zak didn't seem to notice her discomfort.

"The mountain man!" shouted the youngest boy.

"That's right, buddy, our hero of the Himalayas. OK, guys, love you so much, but I gotta run. The mountains are waiting for me!" He ended the call and exhaled loudly. "Strange to think that might be the last time I talk to them like that for a while. You called any family yet?"

"I think they want to hear from me when I'm back and safe, to be honest."

"I hear ya. Oh, look who's just arrived!" Zak pointed over her shoulder at the lift doors. "Isn't that Charles?"

Cecily turned to look and felt a fluttering deep in her belly. "That's him."

Of course it wasn't hard to spot Charles McVeigh in any room. But even here, in a hotel packed with climbers about to embark on their expeditions, he stood out. He was muscular and tall—unlike most mountaineers, who were rangy. He wore a sky-blue puffer jacket, with the TalkForward logo emblazoned on the arm, along with his initials—CM, with the M a stylized mountain range—embroidered over the breast and on his baseball cap.

Beside her, Zak drew himself up to his full height—which wouldn't even bring him to Charles's shoulder. Still, she understood the impulse to impress. In the world of mountaineering, Charles McVeigh was already famous. Soon he would be legendary. He was on the brink of becoming the first person to complete an unprecedented, near-impossible feat: climbing the only fourteen mountains in the world that stood taller than eight thousand meters without using supplementary oxygen, alpine style—and all within a single year.

He called it Mission: Fourteen Clean.

Most mountaineers—like Cecily, Zak and the rest of the team—climbed expedition, or "siege," style. Their way meant using every advantage possible—porters, fixed lines, ladders, dining tents, oxygen tanks, an intense acclimatization routine, one-on-one climbing Sherpa attention—to get up the mountain and down safely. *His* way shed all that support. Climbing in its purest form.

Charles was the whole reason she was there, in Kathmandu. He'd promised her an exclusive interview once his mission was complete. The article would easily be the biggest story she'd ever written. A career-defining piece.

Seeing him, she fumbled in her daypack for her notepad and pen. She thought back to her editor Michelle's rush of excitement when she told her she'd scored the interview. It would be a huge boon for *Wild Outdoors* magazine to run an exclusive with the world's most famous mountaineer.

Then Michelle had seemed to have second thoughts.

"Do you actually think you can do this?" she had asked. Cecily was sure her editor was thinking she would've much rather had someone like James, Cecily's then-boyfriend and a renowned adventure travel journalist, writing the story. Instead Cecily—the person who was best known for *not* summiting mountains—had been commissioned, and Charles had tacked on a significant condition.

She had to reach the top of Manaslu with him first.

No wonder Michelle had her doubts.

"I'll try my best," she had replied.

Michelle sighed. "Trying is good but . . . look. I've spoken with the team here. We want the article, but we can't pay you until you deliver."

The news was a gut punch. "Are you serious? Then there's no way I can afford it. I need to pay for the flights, the training, not to mention all the gear and the expedition costs." There was more, but Cecily was wary of sounding too desperate, wanting to maintain some semblance of professionalism.

"I can maybe get you travel and a bit extra if you provide expedition reports. But the rest . . . I'm sorry, Cecily. You'll have to figure that out on your own."

"You covered all James's costs to Antarctica! And this interview will be much, much bigger than that piece. You said yourself it's the profile of a lifetime."

"James is one of our top journalists. He's a proven entity. Whereas you . . ."

"Whereas I'm not."

There was an awkward pause, as Michelle didn't rush to correct her. Cecily's mind was in overdrive. She needed the interview to launch her career. But it sounded like she was going to have to put everything on the line to make it happen. "But if I do it?"

"If you do it, we'll pay. And you'll get more commissions. Trust me, the more women of color I can get on my staff, the better. Honestly—get this right, and I believe it would mean more than just an article for *Wild Outdoors*. It's a book deal. A movie. This is the break that could define your career. They don't come along often."

Cecily's breathing returned to normal. It was good to know Michelle would be rooting for her, even if it was because her white-passing face accompanied by her Chinese father's surname made her the most readily accepted version of diversity.

Still, her editor's words rang in her ears. Not just because of the opportunity. But because of the unspoken flip side. The fact that if she messed it up, her career as an adventure travel journalist was over. She'd be back at square one, competing for pieces that barely paid enough to cover her groceries. If she couldn't do this, it would be more than just a failure to summit.

She would fail at yet another career.

She would fail to get a deposit together to rent her own place.

"Failure to Rise" would turn into failure to live at all.

Charles strolled over to a collection of leather armchairs in the lobby. "Come on, let's go say hi before he's mobbed by fans." Zak started walking over before he had even finished his sentence. Cecily lingered behind, still searching for her pen. Seeing Charles in the flesh for the first time in months brought home what she was about to attempt.

Her first eight-thousand-meter peak. One of the highest summits in the world.

One of the most deadly.

She shook off the grip of fear that had started to take hold, and followed in Zak's wake.

"It is *so* great to be here, man." Zak shook Charles's hand with vigor. He seemed starstruck. "I'm honored to be on the team, really."

Charles put his hand over his heart. "The honor is all mine. Please, sit. Cecily, it's good to see you again."

"You too. Hard to believe this is finally happening." She held up her notebook. "Do you mind if I ask you a few questions while we wait for our flight?"

He laughed. "Trying to get an interview in, are you? That isn't what we agreed . . ."

She attempted a winning smile, hoping to change his mind. "I thought since we're technically not on the mountain yet, a few pre-trip questions might be allowed?"

He shook his head, unmoved. "Put the notebook away. I brought you here to experience real expedition life." He leaned in, lowering his voice and raising his eyebrows. "Enjoy it."

"Excuse me, Charles?"

An older woman, with a vaguely Germanic accent, approached them. Charles stood up and gave her a kiss on each cheek. "Vanja! How are you? Vanja, meet Zak Mitchell—he's the CEO of Talk-Forward, a pioneering tech firm—and Cecily Wong—she's the journalist I chose to accompany me to Manaslu. She's going to climb it to get the whole picture. No interview until you summit, right, Cecily?"

Her smile faltered, and she took a beat before replying. "Right."

Vanja appraised Cecily. "Impressive!"

"This is Vanja Detmers—she runs the Himalayan Database here in Kathmandu. She's been the one verifying all my Nepali summits for me."

"And it's been a pleasure, Charles."

Cecily shook the woman's hand before jotting her name down in her notebook.

"I've come to take down all the team details, so I can verify your summits later on. I can start with you, Cecily?" Vanja sat next to Cecily, perching her laptop on the low coffee table in front of them.

"Oh, I'm not sure . . ."

"You want your name in the history books, don't you?"

She paused. "If I make it."

"No doubt," said Vanja. "You're with Charles! You couldn't be in safer hands. And if you get into any trouble, he'll save you."

Charles smiled. "That's kind of you, V. I'd rather get through this mountain without any more trouble, after Cho."

"Ah, Charles, you are too modest. Nothing sells a story like good old-fashioned rescue, hey?" the woman replied, all but winking. She opened her laptop, her hands flying across the keys. Cecily leaned over, curious. The Himalayan Database aimed to catalogue everyone who attempted to summit an eight-thousand-meter peak in Nepal. "British woman?" she asked Cecily, who nodded. A few more key-strokes brought up on-screen the list of British women who had summited Manaslu since the first in 2008. Cecily blinked rapidly, shocked at how short the list was. If she made it, her name would join only a handful of others. Another reminder of the enormity of the challenge ahead.

"What does the asterisk mean, next to some of the names?" Cecily asked.

"Ah, that is to mark the years climbers only made the fore sum-mit, not the true summit, of the mountain," explained Vanja. "Some years it is too difficult to fix a line to the true summit."

"We'll make it this year," said Charles. "Don't you worry."

"Cecily?" Mingma caught her eye and gestured her over. At his side was a young woman in a strappy neon-yellow sports top and purple leggings, a swipe of bright red lipstick the only trace of makeup on her face.

To Cecily's surprise and delight, she recognized the woman: Elise Gauthier, a French-Canadian influencer and mountaineer she'd fol-lowed on social media for ages, ever since she'd first started research-ing the climbing world. She was known for wearing bright colors and bold jewelry on the mountain. Her photographs and videos were eye-catching, highly saturated and well composed. She had a great eye.

Cecily couldn't stop the smile from spreading across her face. "Oh my god—Elise?"

"That's me!" Elise pushed her sunglasses into her hair and beamed back. "Do I know you?"

"I'm sorry—I'm Cecily Wong, I follow you on Instagram. You're a huge inspiration to me. Are you climbing Manaslu?"

"I'm climbing with Charles—aren't you as well?"

"I am—what a great surprise to have you on the team."

"For me too!" She leaned in, giving Cecily a kiss on each cheek. Then she took Cecily's arm, squeezing it. "I thought it was just going to be me and the boys, like it normally is in the hills. We can stick together."

"I have something for you both," said Mingma. He reached into his bag and pulled out lengths of orange fabric covered in Buddhist symbols. He wrapped a loop around Cecily's neck. "This is a khata. To wish you a safe journey on the mountain."

Cecily ran the silky fabric through her fingers. The thought of meeting the other team members had worried her on the flight over. But last night, Zak had seemed friendly enough, if a little arrogant. Now Elise was a ray of bright sunshine, and she basked in her presence. If this was her team, she could do this.

The doors to the hotel slid open, and Doug stepped through. "Cars are here," he said. He raised his hand, doing a silent head count. Then he frowned. "Mingma, he's not down yet?"

"I haven't seen him."

Doug glowered, staring at his watch. It was a few minutes past eleven.

"Is someone missing?" Cecily asked Mingma.

"Yes, we have one more on the team. A last-minute addition. His name is—"

Before Mingma could finish his sentence, the elevator pinged and a man in mirrored sunglasses stumbled out, a fancy-looking DSLR camera hanging around his neck. He made a beeline for the coffee station in the corner of the lobby, but Doug intercepted him. "No time for that, Grant. We have to go. Now."

"Seriously? Just one cup of coffee and I'll be sorted . . ."

Cecily raised her eyebrows. It looked like another Brit was joining them on the team, probably around the same age as her, if not a bit younger—though the man's cut-glass accent was at odds with his dishevelled appearance. He looked like he had just come in from a bar. Grant's mouth twisted, but his expression changed as he spotted Charles. "Oh, there you are, brother! Good to see you. I was beyond blotto last night; I lost you in the club and woke up in a momo restaurant. Classic. Ready for the mountain?"

"As I'll ever be." One of Charles's eyebrows quirked. He didn't step forward and shake Grant's hand, as he had with Zak. Grant didn't seem to mind. They had obviously met before. The feeling of comfort she'd had with her teammates wavered. Grant's posture and demeanor reminded her of the arrogant posh boys who swanned around her university, acting like they owned every place they entered. Maybe she was just feeding off Doug's disapproval, which was radiating from him—not that Grant seemed to care.

"Can't wait to get it all on camera. I'll be capturing every moment." Doug coughed. "Right, team. Let's go."

"Just a second!" said Elise. "Vanja, can you take a photo of all of us?"

They squeezed together as a team, and Mingma handed out the rest of the orange khatas. Charles stood in the center—head and shoulders above the rest of them. Seven virtual strangers thrust together for the next month, attempting to climb one of the biggest and most dangerous mountains in the world.

Cecily could only hope she was ready.

CHAPTER 3

CHARLES STRODE OUT OF the line once the moment was over. "So, see you soon! Have a safe flight."

"You're not coming with us?"

"No, I'll be there later. I have a few administrative things to take care of here in Kathmandu—and besides—I'm already acclimatized."

The others were heading out to the waiting cars, but Cecily felt rooted to the spot.

"Come on, Cecily—we have to get going," said Doug.

Her gaze darted between Doug and Charles. Charles seemed to sense her concern. He stepped toward her, clapping her on the shoulder. "Don't worry," he leaned in, speaking into her ear. "There will be plenty of time for us to talk on the mountain."

She nodded, taking some reassurance from his touch. It was hard for her to believe that the first time she'd heard of Charles McVeigh had been less than a year ago.

She remembered it all too well. It had been a frigid morning last October. The wipers swept furiously across the windshield of the car, the rain lashing down.

"You can see it in his eyes. He's going to do it. As long as he can raise all the funds by the time he launches next spring, he'll break the record, easy," James said.

She and James had been driving up from London to Fort William to attempt the famous National Three Peaks Challenge to climb the highest mountains in Scotland, England and Wales in only twenty-four hours. Well, his friend and fellow journalist Ben was doing the driving, as they had to conserve their energy for the climb. Cecily was a bundle of nerves, worrying about the weather, her fitness, the monumental task ahead, and James was trying to relax her. Only he would think that the way to make her less anxious was to tell her about some man attempting a near-impossible mountaineering feat. It was sweet, but not doing anything to ease the tightness in her chest.

"And he has to get the permits. The Chinese government have cracked down on Shishapangma recently," said Ben, jumping into the conversation. He was so tall he had to hunch down over the steering wheel to fit. It didn't look comfortable.

"He'll get it. They'd be idiots to turn him down; the publicity he's bringing to the big mountain industry is incredible."

Despite her concerns about the challenge, Cecily loved seeing James so animated. It was rare that he was so effusive in his praise—he was normally the first to be critical about these high-profile alpinists. She had to admit she was intrigued.

"What's so special about this guy . . . ? What's his name again?" she asked, leaning forward from the backseat.

"Charles McVeigh," said James.

"Aren't people breaking records in the mountains all the time?"

James scoffed, catching her eye in the rearview mirror. "Are you kidding? Not like this. If Charles completes his mission, it will be game changing—and not just for the mountaineering world. He's pushing the limitations of the human body. He's showing the world what humanity is capable of. It's next-level shit."

"Sounds cool," she said.

James grimaced, and Cecily knew "cool" was an understatement. "I covered his Fourteen Clean announcement for ClimbersWeb but he deserves much more attention. Really hoping I can get *Nat Geo* or *Wild Outdoors* interested in a big article about it. No one's been able to score an exclusive with him yet."

As James and Ben continued their discussion of Charles's prowess, she sat back and googled Charles's social media, intrigued by James's passion and admiration for the man. She was awed by Charles's photographs of vast mountainscapes and terrifying pathways through towering seracs of ice. She'd only been on one mountain in her life: Kilimanjaro in Tanzania. That had been hard enough. And it wasn't nearly as high in altitude as the peaks Charles was attempting.

"So why these fourteen mountains in particular?" she asked James.

"They're the only mountains in the world above eight thousand meters, and they're all in the Himalayas. The 'death zone' peaks. Literally every minute you spend above that altitude, your body is dying. Most people carry supplementary oxygen tanks with them, but not Charles. He's a purist."

"How come Charles is able to do it?"

James's jaw tightened. "I don't know. I'd really like to ask him that. He's dodging all my emails at the moment."

"Maybe I should send him one," said Ben.

"You fucking dare," James growled.

Ben lifted both hands off the steering wheel for an instant, in a gesture of surrender. "Just joking, mate! You'll get the interview. You know these mountaineering types, really superstitious. Probably doesn't want to talk to anyone until his mission is completed."

"Like you, Jay—aren't you wearing the same socks you wore to Aconcagua?" she teased, lightening the atmosphere. James and Ben had always competed for stories, but they'd also gone on many adventures together. She'd had an anxious twenty-four hours waiting for news when they had attempted the highest mountain in South America. They'd made it, and she'd shared their elation even though she'd been safe and sound at home in their London flat. She'd got a window then into "summit fever." That drive to reach the top no matter what.

"My trusty summit socks." He winked. "Work like a charm."

"Except for on Kilimanjaro." She rubbed his arm. "I still feel bad about that. I hope I don't let you down this time."

He reached behind and grabbed her hand, squeezing her fingers tight. "That was different. There's no altitude to deal with here, baby. You've done the training. You'll be fine. Nothing to worry about."

Except she hadn't been fine. On the third mountain, Snowdon—Yr Wyddfa—she'd been delirious and exhausted after having been on the move for over twenty hours straight tackling Ben Nevis in Scotland and Scafell Pike in England, unable to properly rest or sleep on the long car journeys in between. Battered by fierce wind and torrential rain, shivering with cold, she couldn't move any farther. They were halfway up a knife-edge route known as Crib Goch, scrambling on rocks slick with running water.

"I'm not going to make it," she told James. "Honestly, you should go ahead. You can still do the challenge in under twenty-four hours if you leave now."

"Cecily, I'm not abandoning you." He stopped at the top of a pitch, looking down as she struggled to climb her way to meet him, unable to get a grip on the boulders.

She shook her head. "It's no use. I can't do any more. I'll go back to the car—it's not far. Ben has a thermos of hot tea. Please, I can't take another Kili situation."

She saw the decision warring on his face. He'd turned back with her on Kilimanjaro. But now he could complete the challenge. "If you're sure . . ."

"I am. Look—the rain is stopping, I think. I'll be fine." She was drenched to the bone, her fingers frozen and cramped.

He blew a kiss down to her. "Head straight to the car, OK? Signal's a bit intermittent out here so I won't be able to call and check on you. I should get to the top and back in a couple of hours."

"Got it. Now go!" she said. He'd gone.

She hadn't made it to the car. After he left, she witnessed something that would stay with her for the rest of her life.

A woman had slipped off the rock in front of her eyes.

It had been the most terrible few hours of her life. She waited for mountain rescue, blowing a whistle to alert them to their location.

"You're a hero," James said when he'd caught up with her, holding her tight to his body. She didn't feel like a hero. All she'd done was wait for help. She couldn't save her. Couldn't stop what had happened.

When they got back to London, James had written an article about the accident, dubbing her the "Hero of Snowdon."

She wished he hadn't. Shame gnawed at her. So she did the next thing that felt natural to her. She wrote, putting her experience—her story—down on the page. The result was a raw, visceral blog she called "Failure to Rise." She wrote about her shock at what she had seen. Her sadness. And her deep and abiding sense of failure—that she'd failed to summit Kilimanjaro, failed to complete the Three Peaks Challenge, failed to save a woman's life.

She sent it to Michelle, who ran the blog online for *Wild Outdoors*. To everyone's surprise, it went viral—racking up hit after hit, their most popular piece of the month. Thanks to James, readers already saw her as a hero. But the blog seemed to resonate with an even wider audience, especially her unflinching honesty about her inability to summit. What she kept out of the piece was just how deeply she grieved for the woman she'd met so briefly on the mountainside. It was too raw.

Still, she'd taken a risk—opened up and poured her story out. And it had paid off. For the first time, she found herself on a launching pad to success. She just needed something to blast her career off.

Then along came Charles.

An unexpected side effect of her traumatic Snowdon experience was a new appreciation for Charles's challenge. When, the following spring, he set off for Annapurna, the first mountain of his mission, she and James tracked his progress online. James's write-ups grew more and more vehement in their praise. On Dhaulagiri, his third summit, Charles rescued an Italian climber from certain death—and that story touched her. Here was someone who was not only striving to achieve something for himself; he was willing to put it all at risk for a rescue attempt. He was a real hero. Not like her.

She wasn't the only one. The story of Charles's dramatic rescue spread to mainstream media, and now the world was watching. The pressure was on, but Charles took it in his stride. With every mountain he conquered, the buzz around him grew.

She was shocked, then, when she was the only journalist invited to hear him speak at a fundraising event in London after his successful summit of K2. He was then over halfway through his mission, but needed a fresh injection of cash to make the final mountains happen. James had bristled with jealousy, but she'd assuaged his feelings by taking him along. At the event, Charles made a controversial announcement: he was going to take a team with him on his final mountain of the mission, Manaslu. It only added to his legend. *Not only can I do this, but I can do it while leading a team.*

Charles sought her out at the party following the event. They were in a grand room at the Royal Geographic Society, filled with people lingering with one eye on Charles's back, desperate for a moment with the man of the hour. Yet his attention was solely on her.

"I've been looking for a journalist to come out with me to my final mountain. I want you to do it, Cecily," he said.

She almost spat out her champagne. "I'm sorry, what?"

Beside her, she felt James stiffen, shifting his weight.

If Charles noticed James's discomfort, he didn't acknowledge it. "Come with me to Manaslu. It's a good mountain, achievable for a first-timer, stunningly beautiful. The only way to do my story justice would be to witness it from the mountain itself. Document it by my side."

She shook her head, chuckling, but Charles wasn't laughing. She swallowed, glancing at James. "Wait, seriously? I couldn't . . ."

"You could. And after you and I *both* reach the summit, you'll get the interview," Charles said.

"And if I don't?"

Charles smiled, his ice-blue eyes flashing. "Not an option."

That had been it. The career break she'd been waiting for. It was decided then. She was going to the mountain.

Doug coughed from behind her, staring pointedly at his watch. Not a patient man, then. He caught her looking and gestured for her to follow before walking out to the cars himself.

"Have fun in Samagaun and at base camp," Charles said to her.

"Concentrate on getting ready. Do your rotations; get comfortable on the mountain. Make this expedition yours. I know you can do it. When I arrive, we can head straight up to the summit together. And then we can talk properly."

"Thank you, Charles. Good luck with your admin." Cecily took a deep breath before following her expedition leader. The automatic doors slid open, and a blast of warm, sticky, humid air hit her face. It felt like a storm was about to break.

She glanced back over her shoulder for one last look at her interviewee. His arms were folded across his chest, watching them leave. She slid into the backseat next to Zak and Grant, the cars ready to whisk them away to the helicopter pads for their flight to Samagaun at the base of Manaslu.

She was excited to be heading deep into the heart of the Himalayas, but couldn't ignore the hard ball of anxiety in her stomach.

She was here to cover a story, and it seemed to her like that story was staying in Kathmandu.

EXCERPT FROM CECILY WONG'S BLOG
"MANASLU: THE FINAL MOUNTAIN"

September 3
Samagaun, Gorkha, Nepal
3,500m

Hello from the beautiful village of Samagaun! We made it.

Well, all of us except for the main man—Charles McVeigh. Don't worry; he hasn't given up his mission. He's stayed behind in Kathmandu to complete a few remaining administrative tasks. Between the paperwork, bureaucracy and fundraising to climb these big mountains, the logistics of the mission seem to be an even bigger challenge for Charles than reaching the summits themselves.

So much about mountaineering is about luck—even getting to the mountain. Heavy rain threatened to strand us in Kathmandu but thankfully we caught a break, and the weather held long enough for us to get a helicopter. Trekking from Kathmandu to Samagaun, the village nearest to Manaslu, would have taken us a week (although our Sherpa team can reputedly do it in a couple of days), so Doug decided it made sense for us to fly.

And what a flight. Just after two p.m., we took off and soared low over the sprawling city of Kathmandu. The jumble of buildings soon gave way to rippling green terraces and dense jungle as we followed the meandering river below, dodging clouds and rain. Every now and then, the sky-blue tin roofs of isolated dwellings punctuated the green—it wasn't exactly clear from the air how people accessed those remote homes. After a brief pit stop to refuel, the scenery shifted again; this time to stunning pine forests and mountain ridges headed higher in altitude, waterfalls cascading from the rocks on either side of us. Honestly, I think the views from that helicopter alone were worth the price of admission for the expedition.

Samagaun sits at the base of Manaslu, but the mountain hasn't shown its face just yet, as it hides stubbornly behind a bank of cloud, this being the tail end of monsoon season. Still, the anticipation is building.

I'm writing this in a local teahouse, next to a roaring wood fire. The guesthouse owner, Shashi, has provided us with warming milky coffee from her kitchen and I've already dived into my stash of snacks. The wooden tables are crowded with other mountaineers from all over the globe, and we're all about to embark on an adventure of a lifetime.

As many of you reading this will know, I made my name by failing to summit mountains. But Charles has the remarkable ability to inspire confidence in even the most insecure individuals. Under his leadership, I know I can do it. He exudes success from every pore. Even in the brief time I spent with him in Kathmandu, it's clear he's inspiring a whole generation of climbers. And this is the type of person we should be celebrating. Every step he takes on a mountain takes him closer to changing everything we know about what is possible for the human body to achieve—in the most inhospitable environments on Earth. And I'm privileged to be along for the journey.

What are our next steps? Since we're already at altitude here, we'll spend a day getting used to the thinner air. That's going to be a common theme of this adventure: abiding by the old mountaineering maxim of climb high, sleep low, so our bodies can acclimatize to the higher altitudes. This means heading out on a series of rotations, up and down the same paths, each time facing the same terrifying obstacles: looming seracs, deep crevasses and near-vertical ice walls.

Of course, Charles faces everything without oxygen and with no fixed lines. Yet he is famous for how well he can handle the altitude, moving with near enough the same ease at eight thousand meters as he does at sea level.

As for me? Even with supplemental oxygen, I have no idea how

I'm going to cope. There's no way to find out beforehand, no way to truly prepare your body. All I can do is keep putting one foot in front of the other, until either I reach the summit—or am instructed to turn around.

And, of course, getting to the top is only half the battle. Many mountaineers say that going down can be just as much of a challenge as summiting.

So wish me luck! I might need it. Anything can happen on the mountain.

CHAPTER 4

THE SUN BROKE OVER the mountain, bathing the terrace of the teahouse in light and warmth. Hot tea steamed in Cecily's hands, her notebook and pen abandoned on a side table. She leaned forward against the wooden railing, and it creaked ominously but held. In the courtyard below her a goat bleated. The rest of the place was quiet. Too early for most people.

She had the view to herself. Her first time taking it in. Her phone was charging back in her room, her camera buried deep in her bag. So instead of documenting the moment, she took another sip of her tea and stared.

The razor-sharp double peaks of the summit and the east pinnacle pierced the sky, the tail of a leviathan diving into a deep blue ocean. By comparison, she was so small. A minnow. It seemed impossible that she was going to be up there.

She wondered, not for the first time, about the arrogance of even trying.

Everything was on the line for her. Her career. Her finances. Her home. So she had to focus now, on the mountain in front of her.

The smell of puri, the traditional Nepali fried bread, wafted up from the kitchen. More people stirred from their rooms, and the teahouse came alive with activity. Across the way, on the terrace of another blue-painted guesthouse, more hardy souls emerged, stretching and breathing in the fresh Himalayan air.

"Magical, isn't it?"

Elise climbed the stairs to the terrace wearing a hot pink soft-shell jacket and knitted beanie, accompanied by a couple of French mountaineers from the Summit Extreme team whom they'd met the night before. Cecily glanced down at her notebook, recalling their names—Alain and Christophe. Now she remembered. They'd just completed their trek in on foot from Kathmandu and were spending a couple of nights in Samagaun acclimatizing before continuing on to base camp.

"Doesn't quite look real," Cecily replied.

One of the men—she thought it was Alain—stood close to Elise. Over coffee around the teahouse stove, he'd regaled them with stories of where he'd been climbing last. Somewhere in Afghanistan? She hadn't recognized the name of the mountain. It had sounded impressive and terrifying. A first ascent of some sort.

So many mountains, so many stories, so many egos, so many beards. It was hard to keep them straight.

"This is going to be a piece of cake," said Christophe, as he snapped a photo of the view with his phone.

"What?" Cecily blinked, staring at the man in disbelief.

He shrugged. "Come on. Manaslu is not a difficult mountain. Two hundred and fifty people are set to climb it this year. The fixing team's already at camp two. It's like a high-altitude via ferrata."

Cecily felt insulted on Manaslu's behalf. She'd done a via ferrata in the Lake District—an "iron path" of metal ladders and wire bridges that turned difficult routes into protected, safe ones. Even with ropes, this was going to be a thousand times more challenging. "It was once known as the Killer Mountain," she pointed out.

He snorted. "Every mountain is a killer mountain in the right year. Manaslu is almost as commercial as Everest now."

"So why have you come?" she asked. Clouds had already started to gather around the summit again, drawing around it like a shroud. The wind up there must be intense.

"Because, why not?"

She opened her mouth to answer, but his companion, Alain, jumped in first. "Ignore him. He's a joker. You are right—Manaslu is dangerous. All the big mountains are. I've stayed away from the eight-thousanders for years because of the risk."

She glanced over Alain's shoulder. Elise and Christophe were moving farther down the terrace to take photographs from a different angle. "What changed your mind?" she asked.

"I've come here to honor one of my friends. Pierre Charroin." A shadow of pain flickered across his face. "He died on Everest this year."

Cecily gasped. "I'm so sorry. What happened?"

"We don't know for sure. It seems he disappeared on his way back to camp four. He made the summit." As he spoke, he pulled up a photo on his phone of a young man in a pair of reflective blue sunglasses, kneeling by the jumble of prayer flags on Everest's summit plateau. "His climbing Sherpa took this photo. Pierre was such an experienced climber . . . it was a shock."

"It must be so hard to lose a friend like that."

"It's more than hard. It's inconceivable." He sighed. "In the death zone, it is impossible to conduct a proper search, let alone an investigation. I have come here to leave a flag for him on the summit, in his memory."

"That's really moving, Alain. But wait . . . an investigation? Why?"

"It's difficult for me to talk about it." His voice cracked, and he turned his face away, looking up at the mountain.

She wanted to reach out, offer some small measure of comfort. She sensed his grief was a chasm a simple touch wouldn't span, but she had to do something. "Of course. How about some tea?" Cecily asked, with a soft smile. She reached for the flask Shashi had brought to her, and plucked one of the overturned cups from the stack on a nearby table. She filled it for Alain before topping up her own on the table. After a moment, he accepted the steaming liquid with a tight smile, then took a sip. His shoulders released some of their tension. Tea always helped.

She followed his gaze to the summit. "I hope we are luckier on our expedition," she said, trying to contain the tremor in her voice.

"Mountaineering's dangerous by nature. Anyone who spends time in the high peaks knows that." Alain exhaled a long, slow breath. "But some accidents shouldn't happen."

"Are you talking about what happened to Pierre?"

He sighed again and turned his back to the mountain.

"I'm sorry," she added quickly. "You don't have to tell me about it."

"It's not that . . . I just wish I knew more myself. His climbing Sherpa claimed he must have unclipped from the fixed rope to relieve himself, and then he fell. But Pierre would *not* have stepped off the line. Of that I am certain." His eyes flashed, an anger in his tone that took Cecily by surprise.

She leaned in. "Could he have been suffering from altitude sickness? Maybe he got confused . . ."

"Possibly."

She searched his face. "But you don't think so."

He hesitated, blowing on his cup of tea. "No, I do not." He turned to face Cecily, lowering his voice so she had to lean in to hear. "For good reason: I spoke to him. Just after he reached the summit, via satphone. It wasn't the excited call I had been expecting. He said to me that he was alone, separated from his climbing Sherpa, and that someone had been stalking him. Someone he was afraid of, who wanted to hurt him. At the time I thought: 'Oh my god, he has altitude sickness; he's hallucinating on the mountain.' Yet I've never heard him like that before. His voice. It sounded like sheer . . . terror. Before I could say anything, the line cut off." He sucked in a deep breath before continuing. "And then I found out he never arrived at camp four. Just like that." He snapped his fingers. "Gone. A brilliant climber, lost."

"What are you saying? Do you think someone did something to him?"

He placed his cup down on the table with deliberate force. "Something doesn't add up. It's why I've come here. Yes, I want to leave a flag but I also want to ask some questions. That's why I'm using the same company he climbed with, the same guide."

"Who is that?"

"Dario Travers. I just want to know what really happened up there. A climber as good as Pierre wouldn't slip." He clenched his jaw, and when Cecily glanced down she noticed that he was gripping the railing so hard that his knuckles had turned white. She knew what she should do. She could practically hear James—the *actual* professional mountain journalist—screaming at her to ask more questions. He'd be sniffing out the story, pressing Alain for details about a suspicious death at high altitude. Yet in Manaslu's shadow, she couldn't help the fear that clenched her belly. Death stalked even the most experienced mountaineers. She was a novice. She didn't want to ask questions. She needed to cling to the idea that everything was going to be fine.

Still, she had a job to do. Maybe focusing on that would be a distraction from the dangers up ahead. She swallowed her fear.

"Alain, I don't know if you remember me saying this last night but . . . I'm here working for *Wild Outdoors* magazine, covering Charles's story. Pierre shouldn't be forgotten, and if something did happen to him, I want to make that known. Would you be willing to answer a few more questions for me?" Even if Pierre's death was indeed the result of a tragic accident, she could see how she could weave Alain's words into her article about Charles. It would help to explain what drove people to climb these big peaks. The risk and the sacrifice. The lives lost in pursuit of lifelong goals. Give context to Charles's achievement.

"You are a journalist?" He arched an eyebrow.

"Don't worry—I won't use what you've said now. But we could do a more formal interview?"

After a few tense moments, he nodded. "Come by the Summit Extreme base camp and we can talk properly. I have a few more photographs of Pierre; maybe you could use them?"

"Of course," she replied. "I won't get to speak to Charles until after I summit, so I'll have plenty of time to devote to your friend."

"What do you mean 'until after I summit'?" Alain rubbed at the rough stubble on his chin.

"My interview with him is conditional on my reaching the top."

He frowned. "Look, I am not your team leader, and I am certainly not as strong as Charles. But I don't like that. There should never be pressure to reach the top. Climbing a mountain, especially one of these gigantic peaks, is one of the hardest things you can put your body through. The attempt is just as valid as the achievement."

"You don't think I can do it?"

He shook his head. "It's not that." He reached out, placing his hand over hers. "It's just—the mountain will always be there. Don't take any unnecessary risks for the sake of a summit."

"And a story."

His eyes searched her face. Maybe her desperation was a little too close to the surface.

A clatter of pots and pans broke the moment between them. "Breakfast, team!" shouted Doug from the entrance to the teahouse dining room.

"I'd better go," Cecily said. She looked back toward the mountain. The peak was now fully hidden behind a thick bank of cloud. She blinked. The change had happened so quickly. She put her other hand on top of Alain's, squeezing his palm between her own. "I'm sorry again, about Pierre. I hope you get the answers you're looking for."

"So do I," he replied. His voice softened. "Be safe up there."

"You too." She smiled.

In the dining room, Grant, Zak and Mingma sat together at one of the long wooden tables. Other teams mingled in the room too, the air alive with different languages and accents. Everyone had their own reason for wanting to summit. Everyone had a story.

Elise emerged from the kitchen at the far end of the room, one arm around Shashi, the teahouse owner, the other carrying a large canister of hot water, which she placed on their team's table before sitting down.

The only free seat was next to Grant. He seemed hungover for the second night in a row, a baseball cap pulled down low over his head.

She chose not to sit next to him straightaway, but instead plopped down on a seat beside an iron stove that was emanating gentle heat. The wall above her head was plastered with photographs of famous Sherpas and climbers, some of them signed. Of course Charles was up there—or rather, his promotional poster for Mission: Fourteen Clean was.

Suddenly, an impossibly tall man appeared and stooped over in front of her. "Cecily?"

Her mouth dropped open, her fingers flying to her lips. "Oh my god. Ben?"

CHAPTER 5

EVEN CROUCHING DOWN, HIS head touched the beams of the teahouse. Ben Danforth. Their Three Peaks chauffeur, a rival adventure journalist, and one of James's oldest friends.

"What are you doing here?" she asked, standing up to give him a hug after a few stunned seconds.

"I could ask you the same thing! I'm here to climb; didn't James tell you?"

"No . . ."

"Shit, sorry." He slapped his forehead with his palm. "I knew you two had split up. I'm such an asshole."

She shrugged. "Split up" seemed kind of a casual way to put being dumped and kicked out of her home for the crime of landing a big interview. She looked over Ben's shoulder to try to attract the attention of one of her teammates. Anyone to divert this conversation. But they were chatting among themselves. She swallowed. "You here working?"

"Nah, it's been a big dream of mine to climb all the eight-thousanders. So I'm here on a solo trip. But using Summit Extreme logistics."

"I had no idea you were such a strong mountaineer." Using only the "logistics" of a company like Summit Extreme meant Ben was making decisions about the climb by himself—arranging his own acclimatization plan and summit attempt. He'd be carrying his own oxygen and food too, although he would use the tents set up by

Summit Extreme, and a climbing Sherpa would accompany him on his summit push. Even he wasn't experienced enough to attempt it completely on his own. That was reserved for the climbing elite.

He slumped down onto the bench, and she tentatively sat next to him, still recovering from the shock of seeing him there. "Cheaper this way," he continued. "Since James and I climbed Aconcagua, I caught the climbing bug. It's like an itch I have to scratch. This is the first peak I've been able to get to in a while, though. Having a family makes it tougher to travel." He brought out his phone and showed her his screen saver: a photograph of two gap-toothed, ruddy-cheeked kids. She gave an appreciative sounding "aww," though her mind still raced. He said he wasn't working but . . . would he tell her if *Wild Outdoors* had sent him? Was he here as her possible replacement? Or was he working for a rival publication?

She needed to say something; she'd been quiet too long, and if he was here as a rival, the last thing she wanted was for him to realize she didn't trust him. She dragged the name of his wife from her memory. "So . . . Mel's OK with you being here?" she asked, as Ben swiped to a photo of him with his wife.

He gave a small smile and shrugged. "She's handling it. This is my dream. It might keep me from my family, wreck my body . . . but it's a compulsion. I thought I was done when my son was born but—here I am. And I figured if I was ever going to achieve my dream of standing on top of the world, I had to start while I'm still young and dumb enough to do it." He laughed. Somehow, Cecily didn't think Mel was laughing back in England, "handling things" (like their two children) as Ben put it. She hoped he knew how lucky he was. "So, what brings you to Manaslu?" he asked her. "Big step up from Snowdon. Glad you've recovered from that, by the way." He nudged her shoulder.

She stiffened, her jaw tensing. It had always annoyed her how flippant Ben could be, some kind of twisted macho defense mechanism, minimizing the impact of such a horrible incident. He'd been there; he'd seen firsthand how it had affected her. She cleared her throat. "I'm covering Charles's final mountain for *Wild Outdoors*."

His eyes opened wide. "Bloody hell! You scored the elusive interview? Incredible. Charles is like the modern Mallory. Nice to have a
Brit on top."

"I think so too."

He rubbed at the side of his nose and sniffed. "That's very cool.
Big job, too. Does James know?"

"Yes," she said, through gritted teeth.

"Bet he's gutted to be missing out." She could almost see him
putting the pieces together in his head—her landing the biggest
story of her career ahead of his friend, and now the two of them were
separated. "Say—maybe you can introduce me to Charles?"

A glint in his eye caught her off guard. A look she knew all too
well from her time with James. It was the one he got when he sensed
a story.

The blood in Cecily's veins turned to ice. She glanced over her
shoulder, glad when Doug signaled her over. "I'm sure Charles is
going to be really busy when he gets here, so we'll have to see. I'd
better go join my team." She stood up, almost bashing her head
against the arching chimney of the stove.

"Wait a sec. Can we catch up at base camp?"

"I don't know. I'll be with my team . . ." She took a step away.

He reached out, grabbing her hand. "Cecily, please. I'm alone up
here." He tried to laugh, but the sound strangled in the back of his
throat.

She swallowed. Maybe it wasn't that he wanted to scoop her. It
had to be hard coming to a place like this, isolated, facing death,
without a team around you or a guide to trust. He could just be
pleased to see a familiar face. Or he could be a *really* good actor.

She couldn't risk letting her guard down either way. "I'll try to
find you," she said, with a tight smile.

"That means a lot. Thanks, you're a mate." He released her hand.
She edged over to her team's table, sliding onto the bench next to
Mingma.

She took a breath. Ben was here. Whatever his motives, he would
be watching. Reporting back to James at the very least, if not to a

rival publication. Was he waiting for her to fail, expecting her to turn around? She lifted her chin, holding her head up, and took in her teammates. Doug, Mingma, Elise, Zak, Grant . . . they were her team, along with Charles and the climbing Sherpas. She could take confidence from them, until she found her own.

"Tea?" Mingma asked, nudging her shoulder.

"Absolutely," she replied. Out of the corner of her eye, she saw Ben get up and leave the dining room—and finally the tension eased from between her shoulder blades.

Shashi walked over to their table, her arms laden with plates. Last night, Cecily had put in a tired order for banana pancakes. Grant, sitting opposite her, had pancakes, eggs, bread and oatmeal. Her meal looked tiny by comparison.

Doug leaned forward, propping his elbows on the table. She moved her plate aside to make room for her notebook, pen poised as Doug spoke.

"Today is a rest day, as we're already at three thousand five hundred," said Doug. "Take it easy, eat lots, drink lots. If the weather holds, we'll head up to base camp tomorrow."

Mingma nodded beside him. "If you need anything—water, or more food—please ask Shashi inside the kitchen."

"I know for some of you this is your first time on such a big mountain," Doug said, "so we'll do some skills training at base camp before starting our acclimatization routine. Our aim is to spend at least two nights above six thousand meters before descending back to base camp to await our summit window. We'll need at least four days of good weather, with the right wind conditions and temperatures, to summit and return to base safely. Safety is of the utmost importance."

"Do you even schedule our bathroom breaks?" Grant asked.

Zak chuckled, but Doug didn't crack a smile. He continued: "If all goes well, we'll be back in Kathmandu in three weeks' time, all with successful Manaslu summits, celebrating the completion of Charles's mission. But"—he snapped, preempting another Grant interruption—"do not underestimate this mountain. Manaslu is dangerous: not only is it high, but heavy precipitation—whether that's rain or snow—can make conditions tough. Avalanches will be our major concern, but snow could conceal deep crevasses, we could have problems in the icefall, there could be storms higher up. If the window creeps too close to winter, it will be too cold and unstable for us to continue."

"Jesus, now you're making it sound impossible," said Zak.

"No, not impossible. But I don't want you to go into this without being aware of the risks."

Elise let out a squeal of excitement and beamed. "This is so exciting! I can't wait to get to the hill."

"Any other questions?" continued Doug.

"Where are the other climbing Sherpas?" asked Zak.

"They are already on the mountain, setting up base camp."

"Oh, is Phemba on the team with us?" asked Elise.

Doug nodded.

"Yay! We had such fun in Pakistan. He's one of my favorite people—and the best dancer," she said, shimmying her shoulders. "I love the climb, but I love the party just as much."

"I'll drink to that," said Grant, draining his coffee.

Once they finished their breakfast, they settled in for a day of acclimatization. "Any chance of Wi-Fi?" asked Zak, pulling out an ultrathin tablet. "I wanna send a video of the mountain to my kids. They'll be psyched we've arrived."

"Shashi turns it on at five p.m.," said Doug. "Can you go without until then?"

"I guess so," Zak grumbled. But then he grinned. "Hey, it's not like I have a mega following to please or anything, like Elise here. A hundred thousand followers and you're, what—twenty-five?"

"Twenty-two," she said, with a small smile.

"Just a baby!"

"Speaking of your Instagram, Elise . . ." Grant leaned back against the bench, lacing his fingers behind his head. He whistled through his teeth. "Nice photos. I especially liked your picture on, what was it, Broad Peak? I bet Pakistan didn't know what hit it when you arrived. Going to take any shots like that on Manaslu?" He waggled his eyebrows.

"Not in front of you, beauf." She pushed his arm playfully, but Cecily thought there was an edge to her voice. She knew the photo Grant was talking about. Elise was topless, her naked back to the camera, her arms spread wide. It was the kind of attention-grabbing shot that her followers ate up. "Anyway—if you'd read the caption rather than just perving on me, you'd know I only did that because I was celebrating being alive. Broad Peak almost killed me. I don't plan that here."

"Is that the most dangerous peak you've climbed?" Zak asked.

"No—that was the north face of the Eiger. That is the only time I called m'man to say goodbye, thinking I was done for."

"And she still lets you climb after that?" said Grant.

Elise shrugged. "She doesn't have a choice. I go anyway. The mountains are my life."

"I know what you mean," said Zak. "What I went through in Alaska, on Denali . . . let's just say, it changed me. And yet I keep coming back for more."

Cecily shifted in her seat. She wasn't in the mood for more stories of death and misadventure in the mountains. It seemed the only thing mountaineers wanted to talk about, constantly one-upping each other in the danger stakes.

A hand brushed her arm. It was Mingma. "Feeling OK?"

She blinked and forced a smile. "Is there anything to see in the village? I'd love to walk around."

"Yes, there is a monastery a few minutes away. And if you want a bit longer walk, there is a lake not too far called Birendra Taal. It is fed by the Manaslu glacier."

"Sounds like exactly what I need."

"Take a left out of the teahouse and follow the trail," he said. "You won't miss it. But take care: it's easy to slip when the rocks are wet."

She finished her pancake and excused herself from the table. Only Mingma's eyes followed her as she left. The rest were too busy swapping big-mountain war stories.

CHAPTER 6

OUT IN THE COURTYARD their duffel bags were being weighed, so they could be distributed between the porters and donkeys. Mountaineering was about so much more than daring adventure. It took military-level planning to handle the logistics involved.

She followed Mingma's directions, passing brightly painted houses with low walls, along a ramshackle path paved with smooth, flat stones. The weather had cleared, and although the summit of Manaslu was still shrouded in cloud, other mountains stretched up around her. These peaks were too small to be of interest to mountaineers—most were unclimbed—but still impressed Cecily with their height and the sheer beauty of the striated rock formations. What must it be like to live in the shadow of such giants—and especially of Manaslu when it was in view? To be constantly reminded of your place in the world?

The path was flecked with mud, and she stopped to pet a few small fluffy dogs that trotted at her heels as she walked up the hill away from the village. A stream flowed down a gulley alongside the trail, the trickling sound a peaceful accompaniment to her hike.

Before long, she reached a series of mani prayer wheels, bronze metal cylinders embossed in mantras that spun on spindles. A nun dressed in a rust-brown shawl, her back stooped with age, walked clockwise around the wheels, spinning each one in turn. Cecily hesitated. She wanted to copy the woman but wasn't sure if that was respectful or not. Or would it be disrespectful to walk past, without acknowledging the wheels?

She felt the safer option was to spin. She walked up to the one nearest and spun the little wooden handle, turning the wheel above. It rattled, but didn't topple. She moved on to the next, and then the next, until they were all spinning. She sent up a prayer as the final mani wheel slowed: for a sign she was doing the right thing by choosing to come here.

The nun turned and smiled at Cecily. Cecily bowed her head in greeting, struck by how much the woman's wrinkled face reminded her of her grandmother. She hadn't been able to visit her grandmother much since she'd moved back to Suzhou. It remained the biggest regret of her life that she hadn't been able to see her at least one more time before she'd passed away.

Of all the people in her life, her grandmother had been her main source of comfort and love. When she'd messed up her secondary-school exam results, her dad had given her a lecture, her mom had set her to writing letters begging universities to give her a place, and her grandmother had sat with her and taught her how to make jiaozi, her favorite meal. *You might as well learn how to cheer yourself up*, her nai nai had said.

She'd taken a degree in English literature, but after graduation flitted from one job to the next, never quite finding her place. As a result, she made herself a lot of dumplings over the years. Interview-rejection dumplings. Breakup dumplings. Out-of-money-till-payday-but-luckily-she'd-remembered-to-freeze-some-dumplings dumplings.

She smiled, thinking about it. Her grandmother would have been so proud to see Cecily take on Manaslu. She had been a tough woman, making her way as an immigrant in the UK with less than ten pounds to her name, barely able to speak any English. To see her granddaughter in a position to attempt a summit of one of the highest mountains in the world—she would have loved that. *You must stand on your own, Ceci.*

The nun spoke to her—Cecily wished she understood. It was

accompanied with a warm smile, however, so she bowed her head. "Monastery?" she asked. The nun waved her hand in the direction of a somewhat derelict-looking building. "Danyabad," Cecily replied, in faltering Nepali.

The monastery was locked, the building under renovation. Just off to one side, though, she spotted a sign for the lake: BIRENDRA TAAL.

She had plenty of time. She decided to head up there.

The trails around the monastery were overgrown, deep holes gaping in the ground, likely the foundations for future buildings. For now they were traps for mountaineers terrified of twisting an ankle before the trip had even begun. She thought of Mingma's warning, and stepped extra carefully.

The path curled through the forest and became more peaceful as the village bustle disappeared behind her. She crossed several babbling brooks, stepping on strategically positioned logs as she made her way higher and higher through the trees.

The forest thinned, giving way to bare rock and scree. She crested a small pile of boulders, and suddenly the lake appeared in a basin below. The scene made her gasp with pleasure. Birendra Taal sparkled bright teal, the mountain climbing behind it into the clouds. Waterfalls cascaded from the cliffs on the far side, and she could hear the Manaslu glacier crack and rumble. She scrambled down chalky-gray boulders to reach the shore, navigating around stacks of pebbles left by previous travelers, minding her footing on the uneven terrain. Shards of debris, dislodged by her movement, tumbled down after her, narrowly avoiding her head.

Even the lower reaches of the mountain had its perils.

As she approached, the surface of the water shimmered, calm and inviting. Contrasted against the white stones under her feet, it was an even paler tranquil blue. She knelt down and dipped the tips of her fingers. Ice-cold.

"Going in?"

The deep male voice from behind her made her jump out of her skin. Yet, as she spun around, scrambling to her feet, she was relieved to see it was Alain. His sleek sunglasses reflected back the teal water, a backpack slung over his shoulder.

"Ach! I didn't mean to scare you," he said, offering her a helping hand.

She took it with a smile, regaining her footing on the loose boulders by the water's edge. "It's fine. I wasn't expecting anyone else to be here."

"It is quite a sight, isn't it? So . . . are you?" He gestured at the rippling surface.

She shook her head. "I don't think so. I'm not exactly equipped for wild swimming."

"Shame! Nothing better to help prepare for heading up there, than a freezing-water dip."

"I'm not sure anything will make a difference if I'm not ready now," she said softly. "Are you not worried about catching your death?" She averted her eyes as he dropped his backpack and slid his trekking shirt over his head, exposing a well-muscled body for someone who must be approaching sixty.

"I have been practicing this for many years now. Immersing my body in the cold helps awaken my senses, readying my body and my mind for what is to come. Keeps me sharp. You need all your wits about you for an eight-thousander." He tapped at his temple.

"Maybe after we summit, I will feel brave enough to join you," she said. There was a loud bang from the far end of the lake, and more shards of ice and snow tumbled into the water. Cecily shivered, taking a step farther back from the shore.

Alain smiled. "You are here, Cecily. You have all the courage you need." He waded into the water, and she gasped for him as he ducked his head under. He came up whooping, shaking his head like a dog and sending spray up onto the shore. Cecily felt the icy sting of it on her cheek, but she smiled. It was infectious, seeing his connection, his passion, for the wonders of the natural world.

It annoyed her that she couldn't bring herself to join him, even though—with no towel, no swimsuit and no experience swimming in cold water—the sensible option was to remain warm and dry. James would've been in there like a flash. Of that she was sure.

"I'll leave you to it," she called out to Alain. He lifted his hand to wave in reply before launching into a sweeping front crawl stroke.

Cecily picked her way back through the boulder field, leaving the serenity of the lake behind. She chose a different trail, one that peeled off to a high viewpoint, and when she reached the top she took a panoramic photo of the view with her phone.

She tried to spot Alain in the water, but he'd either finished his swim or dipped beneath the surface.

A sound caught her attention.

A whistle echoing off the rocks, a few notes: low, low, high, low.

Her breath caught in the back of her throat, her heart racing. Another wild swimmer? She waited to see if the whistler would make an appearance.

But no one came. The moraine around her was still.

She found her voice. "Hello?" she shouted to the empty rock.

The whistling stopped abruptly.

No answer.

She stood stock-still, listening, waiting. Goosebumps rose on her arms and across her back. It was the same shiver that made her cross the street at night, that had her lace her fingers around her keys as she picked up her pace, the same shiver that caused her to run across a busy road rather than brave a darkened underpass.

Her gut urged her to move. She scrambled back to the main trail, her heart hammering. Beneath her feet, a rock wobbled. She stumbled, slipping, falling hard on her knee. She winced in pain, and with it came the memory of debilitating vertigo—balancing on a tiny ledge narrower than the width of her foot, nothing but a sheer drop beneath her, rain and wind hammering at her back, gripping onto the ledge so tight that her palms bled for weeks.

There was another sound—but not a whistle this time. This sounded more like a low buzzing, like the approach of a swarm of bees. She tilted her head, searching the sky for the source of the noise.

A small drone whizzed above her head, disappearing off over the lake. She stood up cautiously, rubbing at the side of her knee where she'd bumped it. She waited for the operator to appear. But whoever it was, they didn't make themselves known.

Dread trickled down her spine. She picked up her pace and headed back to the village.

CHAPTER 7

BACK IN SAMAGAUN, SHE debated telling Doug about the incident, but all she had was a bad feeling and the drone. She was sure there were plenty of legitimate reasons people were taking aerial photographs of the lake. She didn't want to come off as paranoid.

That evening, the team feasted on noodles and momos, delicious Nepali dumplings filled with chopped meat and vegetables. The neat folds in the dough reminded her so much of the time she spent making dumplings with her nai nai. It felt like an answer to her prayers at the monastery. A touch of home, even though she was thousands of miles away. The unsettled feeling that had enveloped her near the lake dissipated, eased by the warm, jovial atmosphere of the teahouse.

There was excitement in the air too. New groups had arrived throughout the day and settled in—some of them mountaineers like Cecily, others simply hiking along the lower trails. Every table was full.

"How was your walk?" asked Mingma, when she had finished eating.

She smiled. "The lake is astonishing. The water is so clear and fresh. The village was very peaceful, even with all the work going on."

"Ah, maybe not for long. With all the tourists coming in, the village is growing every year. Soon it will be like Namche Bazaar!"

"Is that where you're from?"

He shook his head. "No—my village is in the Khumbu region, but higher up than Namche. My wife is there now."

"Oh! I didn't realize you were married. You must be missing your family."

He placed his hand over his heart. "Every day." He slid over a piece of paper to her. "I think you might need this? It is the Wi-Fi code. But there are many people using it, so it might be slow."

"Mingma, you are a legend." Cecily typed the code into her phone.

She logged in and a stream of emails arrived in her inbox, two of them from Michelle. She opened up the first one.

> *Cecily! Are you on the mountain yet? Make sure you get your next trip blog over to me so I can get it up on the website ASAP. People want to hear about your journey! Your first blog has had a ton of hits—I think our readers are really intrigued by your trip reports. Your perspective as a first-time climber is introducing big-mountain climbing to a whole new audience.*

She smiled. More views meant maybe Michelle would have more confidence in her ability to see this through. It also meant the pressure was on: people were watching, waiting to find out if she would summit. She clicked on the next, sent a few hours later:

> *Hi Cecily,*
>
> *I hope you know how important this story is to the magazine, but also for your career. I had a slightly worrying email though from James. Can you let me know you're OK, and that you still plan on continuing? If not, we will have to move quickly . . . Personally, I hope you stay, but I'm not going to force you.*
>
> *Let me know.*
>
> *Michelle*

She reread the paragraph several times. Michelle sounded like a completely different person in the second email, more formal and guarded. After all the work that Cecily had put in to build Michelle's trust, she couldn't understand what had changed. What did Michelle mean about James? He hadn't been in touch with Cecily for months. She'd half thought he'd get over himself and apologize—if for no other reason than to try to get the inside scoop on Charles. But . . . radio silence. Why was he emailing Michelle about her?

She fought the urge to respond straightaway. She needed time to compose a reply. Instead, she opened an email from her mom.

> *Honey, I've been doing even more research about this mountain. I don't like the idea of you being out there on your own. We read on your blog that Charles isn't even with you right now? So why are you there? It was different when you were doing these adventurous things with James and he could look out for you.*
>
> *Don't be angry with us, but we spoke with him. He said he's been training, and if you wanted to swap, he was willing to go to Nepal and take over your assignment. That way, you can come back home. No silly article is worth this, is it?*
>
> *We miss you and just want you to be safe.*

She'd included a link to an article about the 2012 Manaslu disaster. Cecily didn't need to click on it. She'd read it before.

So, mystery solved. Her parents had contacted James. That was the problem, wasn't it? Any of the "adventurous things" she'd done before, she'd always been with someone stronger to prop her up, to protect her, or—in some cases—to rescue her. Their expectations defined what she was capable of.

Their *low* expectations.

They never believed she could do it. And so far, she hadn't surprised them. She was no stranger to failure. No wonder they tried to get James to take her place. And she bet he felt gallant for agreeing.

Coming here alone, seizing this opportunity, was all about proving she was more capable of more than they thought. It was following the spirit of her blog post "Failure to Rise." Knowing she might fail again, but trying anyway.

She remembered what Alain had said: *You are here, Cecily. You have all the courage you need.* She'd taken a huge step already. Now she was going to show everyone—her parents, her editor, her ex—just what she was capable of.

She sent a reply to Michelle:

> *I'm not going anywhere—except to the top of the mountain. Another blog coming very soon!*

Next, she opened her WhatsApp to send a message to Rachel, her closest friend. The only person in the world who knew the whole story. Cecily had been crashing on her sofa since the James breakup, and Rachel had witnessed firsthand how her parents' overbearing nature undermined Cecily's confidence at every turn.

> *I've traveled thousands of miles but my parents are still trying to control me,* Cecily wrote.

A reply appeared straightaway, making Cecily smile.

> *You're there! I've literally been watching my phone for a message from you.*

Then, a few moments later:

> *Forget about them. You can do this. I believe in you. Screw your parents, and screw James.*

Of course, Rachel had guessed that James was involved. She could always read through the lines of Cecily's texts that way. Cecily quickly responded:

> *You're the best! Thanks for always knowing what to say.*

A series of heart emojis followed.

Cecily scrolled through her list of contacts and stopped at James's picture. She wondered if he was waiting for the call to fly to Kathmandu, to take over her gig. She caved and clicked his photo. Maybe she should let him know she'd met his old pal Ben. Her heartbeat sped up. He was "online."

His final text glared at her. Taunting her. *Good luck. You're going to need it.*

It was so tempting to message him, to open up that line of communication again, to show him what she was doing . . .

DON'T MESSAGE HIM!

Rachel's next message popped up at the top of her screen, breaking her out of her spiral. Her best friend was reliably reading her mind. Cecily sighed and—before she could think more about it—deleted the thread between her and James.

Rachel again:

> *And any moment you have a sliver of signal, you'd better tell me you're OK. I'll be waiting.*

Cecily composed a gushing email back to her parents about how much she was enjoying the experience so far, how prepared she was and how safe she felt as one of the team. They wouldn't believe her, but that didn't matter. They couldn't stop her now.

She ignored their reference to James.

Next, she logged into her Instagram. It was painfully slow to load, but eventually the images appeared. Elise had posted already, documenting her own hike around the village, and the likes climbed up into the thousands. She'd posted a selfie with Birendra Taal in the background. Had Elise flown the drone? Was she the mystery whistler? If that was the case, Cecily was extra happy with her decision not to tell Doug—she really would have come off as unreasonable.

Elise had put a link to Charles's fundraising page in her bio. Cecily clicked through and saw how the donations spiked with every post.

"Have any of you seen Alain?" Christophe stood at the end of their table. He was twisting his crocheted beanie in his hands.

"Not since this morning, sorry," Cecily replied, with a small frown.

"Me either," said Elise.

"Who's Alain?" asked Zak, removing one of his earbuds.

"He's my teammate. He went for a walk, but I don't think he's come back yet. Bit strange."

"Have you checked the other guesthouses?" Mingma asked. "There are climbers staying across the road."

"Ah yes, that makes sense. Maybe he decided to eat there. Merci— sorry to bother you." Christophe walked away, not looking entirely convinced.

She thought of Alain diving beneath the icy waters. He was probably by a roaring fire somewhere, warming up. Cecily opened her laptop and started writing her next blog for Michelle. She'd decided on a profile of the team Charles had put together:

> Zak, the CEO;
> Elise, the influencer;
> Grant, the filmmaker;
> And her. The journalist.

A curious group. All under the care of their mysterious guide, Doug. She needed to learn more about him.

She had numerous tabs open on her browser from all the research she had been doing for her piece. While Doug's mountaineering feats were well documented, when it came to his personal life, Google was very unforthcoming. She couldn't find any mention of a family. No permanent home. There also wasn't much about why he'd left Summit Extreme to start his own company. On the Summit Extreme website, though, one name caught her eye: Dario Travers. Not only had he been a colleague of Doug's, but he'd also been mentioned to her by Alain. He'd been Pierre's guide on Everest. Worth doing a little more digging on him. She typed his name into the search bar, and *plenty* popped up—he'd done interviews with every major outdoor magazine and forum available. He seemed to be a trusted guide and an experienced mountaineer, from a small town in the Austrian

Alps. A bit of a mountain playboy, by the sound of it—she noted his arm around a different woman in each of the pictures accompanying the articles throughout the years.

One paragraph in his most recent profile stood out to her:

> I'm grateful to Summit Extreme for allowing me to turn my passion into my work. Guiding clients up these beautiful peaks is very rewarding. But my favorite part of this job is scouting other mountains as potential new destinations for the company. That's when I realize how lucky I am to do what I do.

Even she could read between the lines from her experience of mountain guiding with James. It was a hard way to make a living. The people who loved the mountains enough to want to support themselves from it longed to break the mold, travel off the beaten path. Yet the money drew them back to the same routes over and over again, with no say about the clientele. Dario clearly felt stifled by commercial guiding on the well-known peaks. Of course, Charles's way of doing things wasn't without its challenges; he had been open about how difficult it was to raise the funds and work through the logistics of his mission—the multitude of paperwork, visas and permits required. But the freedom to choose your own routes, to make your mark on these wild frontiers—he was living the mountaineer's dream. She was sure there would be plenty of envious eyes trained on his back.

The Wi-Fi switched off just as she sent her blog to Michelle, and the electricity wouldn't be far behind. According to her watch, it was only just past eight p.m. But she was ready for sleep now. She wasn't the only one—the teahouse had emptied around her while she'd been writing.

Outside in the courtyard, Cecily heard the low murmur of voices. Up on the terrace, Elise lounged on a wooden chair, her feet balanced high on the railing. Someone stood over her, swigging from a flask. Grant. And a group of young female gap-year hikers were gathered around them, drinking beers.

"Cecily, come and join us!" Grant called down.

She climbed the rickety steps, pulling her jacket tight around her body, huddling into the collar to ward off the chill.

"Are you climbing with Charles too?" asked one of the girls in a strong Aussie twang, wrapped in a North Face–branded jacket.

Cecily nodded.

"You are so brave. I could never climb one of these big mountains. Aren't you terrified?"

She glanced at Elise and Grant. "I have a good team—that's who I have to trust. But Elise is the true brave one. She's not even using any oxygen for the climb."

Grant snorted. "Fuck me. You're not?"

Elise swung her legs off the railing, crossing them underneath her. "Nope."

"Does Doug know? He didn't give me that option."

"Why don't you ask him?" Elise said, sipping her tea.

"Are you using oxygen?" Grant turned to Cecily, setting down his flask on the railing with a thud.

"Definitely. I wouldn't stand a chance without it. This is my first time on a mountain like this."

"Seriously? What's the biggest climb you've done?"

"I went to Kilimanjaro last year. But I turned around before Stella Point."

"Hang on, you didn't even summit Kili?" Grant barked a laugh. "And now you've come to an eight-thousander . . . are you mad?"

Cecily felt color rise in her cheeks. "Charles invited me. I've been doing the training and done a lot of research."

"Don't worry. Doug won't let anyone climb who is not ready. We are all on our own journeys," said Elise.

"Well, I'm in awe of all of you," said the hiker. "I hope you all make the summit."

"We will as long as we don't get a repeat of what happened on Cho," said Grant. "One person's mistake ruined it for everyone. My team got turned around when some climber from India got in trouble."

"You were on the mountain when that happened?" said Elise.

"Bloody right I was. Our climbing Sherpas got diverted to the rescue, so the rest of us had to turn around. If it hadn't been for Charles, things would have been a lot worse. To be fair, all I could think was that it would make a brilliant film. So that's why I'm here. To capture on camera exactly what Charles is capable of. Our version of *Free Solo*. Hoping I'll come away with an Oscar at the end of it too."

"Sounds epic!" exclaimed another of the hikers, leaning in closer to Grant. "I bet a million filmmakers wanted that gig."

"A million and one," Grant said, picking up the flask again and clinking it against the woman's beer bottle. "I'm just the lucky bastard who found the way to get Charlie boy's attention."

Cecily's temples throbbed. The altitude was taking its toll. "I'm going to head in. Good night, all."

"Need to recover from your slip?" Grant asked.

Her mouth went dry. She hadn't told anyone what had happened to her on the rocks above the lake. Had he been there? Was he the whistler? She bowed her head, pretending she didn't hear, and returned to the courtyard.

To her surprise, Elise followed her down. "Don't worry about him," she said. "We all have to start somewhere. I have been climbing my whole life, yet I still feel a beginner."

"Are you kidding? You're already a legend." Cecily sighed. "I just don't want to let the team down."

Elise scoffed. "Not a chance. By climbing without oxygen, I am the one putting the team at risk. But if I don't make the summit, I try to be relaxed. It will be there still next year. *It's the mountains themselves—not the summits—that teach me so much.*"

Cecily blinked. "Is that from my article?"

Elise smiled. "You see? I am just telling you what you know already." She patted Cecily on the shoulder before heading to their shared room.

Cecily sat down on her bed, pulling out her notebook. She wished what Elise had said was true.

This chance at the summit would *not* always be there. The

attempt didn't matter. Ben's arrival was a stark reminder of that. She'd been brought here for one reason: to get a killer story. And for that, she had to make it to the top. Charles had been clear about that. Nonnegotiable.

She wrote down as much as she could remember of the conversations she'd had that day, by the light of her headlamp. She couldn't get the conversation she'd had with Alain on the terrace out of her head. *I just want to know what really happened up there. A climber as good as Pierre wouldn't slip.*

She hoped he'd find the answers he was looking for. But somehow, she wasn't so sure. The mountains knew how to hold their secrets.

Elise was already fast asleep when Cecily prepared to turn her headlamp off. As she reached for her water bottle, she realized she'd left it in the dining room. She was tempted to leave it, even though her throat was parched and she knew she'd suffer in the morning.

Be bothered . . . The mantra floated to the front of her mind. A reminder to tackle small issues before they became big ones. Another female mountaineer had passed it to her, a pearl of wisdom from one climber to another. It propelled her out from under the heavy blankets and into the cool, dark night.

In the center of the courtyard, she stopped, tilting her head up toward the sky. Her breath caught, but it had nothing to do with altitude. The sky was filled with stars, more densely packed than she had ever seen before.

There, in front of her, was Manaslu.

The peak stood out, its enormous bulk an ominous black mass against the sparkling night sky. It dominated the horizon, stretching up into the heavens, and the summit wore the stars like a crown.

CHAPTER 8

SHE WOKE TO SUNSHINE streaming onto her pillow. Elise was creeping back into their room to grab her backpack. "Sorry for waking you—I hoped you were already up."

"I should be." Cecily pulled down her sleeping bag, and then blinked, registering the grave expression on Elise's face. "Are you OK?"

Elise paused, then shook her head. "You better come outside."

Cecily dragged her down jacket from the window ledge and zipped it over her thermals, then pulled on her boots. She followed Elise out.

A large crowd was gathered in the courtyard—Cecily spotted Doug, standing with Mingma and Zak. Christophe was slumped on the low stone wall in front of them, with Ben's arm slung around him. Today was the day they were moving to the mountain, and it should have been the most exciting moment yet. But a somber cloud hung over the group that even the bright sunshine couldn't penetrate.

"What happened?" Cecily asked.

Elise sighed. "They found a body by the lake."

Her heart jumped into her throat. "Oh my god. Who?"

"They think it is Alain."

"What?" Cecily's mouth gaped open. "It can't be. I—I just spoke to him yesterday. We were setting up an interview. I saw him there, at the lake. He went for a swim . . ." Cecily trailed off. "What do they think happened?"

"Sounds like he had a bad fall on the rocks. Apparently one of the locals spotted him as they were carrying supplies up to base camp early this morning," Elise said. "I hiked halfway toward base camp yesterday and saw the lake from above but checked my photos already—I didn't catch sight of him."

"He was fine when I left." Cecily's mouth went dry. Was she the last person to have seen Alain alive? "Wait—I saw a drone flying in that direction, and I thought I heard someone whistling. Maybe someone saw him after me?"

"I am sure we will find out. So, so sad." Elise shook her head, then took a sip from her water bottle.

Cecily glanced at the younger woman. While Cecily felt like her throat was closing up, her mind picturing the horror of Alain wounded, dying by the lake . . . Elise seemed more detached, as if she had already processed the news and moved on. Cecily knew death was a part of a mountaineer's reality, something they faced head-on every day. Maybe compartmentalizing it was the only way they could reasonably continue.

But Cecily wasn't there yet. "Who will notify his family? His wife?"

"I'm sure Christophe and the Summit Extreme team will handle it," said Elise.

Cecily nodded. Christophe seemed in shock, hanging his head. She couldn't imagine what he was feeling. Alain had come here to honor a friend who'd passed away in the mountains, and now he was the one who was dead. He had been searching for answers, clearly in distress. He'd gone to the lake for the same reason she had—to clear his mind, prepare for the journey ahead. Except she'd come back. And he would never take another step.

Someone tapped her shoulder, and she flinched. She didn't realize how on edge she was; her hands were shaking. Doug stood behind her, looking solemn. "Team meeting inside. I'm gathering everyone."

"Whoa, who died?" Grant emerged from one of the rooms, raking his hands through damp hair, one of the Australian hikers from last night pulling his puffer jacket close around her body.

"Épais," snapped Elise, as she pushed past him toward the teahouse dining room. Cecily raised her eyebrows. Maybe Elise *was* feeling on edge too.

"What?" Grant put his hands up. Zak went over to explain, leaving Cecily standing alone. She wanted to ask more questions, to reach out to Christophe, but didn't want to interfere. Mingma gently touched her on the arm, guiding her into the teahouse. She walked, feeling numb and helpless.

There were large flasks full of sugary black tea on the table. Cecily poured herself some, holding the ceramic cup tightly between her fingers until it almost burned. It was the only thing stopping her from shaking.

The last time she was on a mountain, someone had died. And now Alain was dead too. She knew it was irrational, but she felt like the common denominator. Like a bad omen.

And now it looked like the expedition was over before it had even begun.

Doug rubbed at his temple, waiting for the team to settle around the table. "Mingma and I were in touch with base camp this morning."

"Great!" said Grant. "When we moving?"

Cecily looked aghast at her fellow Brit. "Surely we can't continue? A man *died*."

Grant shrugged. "So? It's not like it was someone from our team. You can bet this won't stop Charles. And I have to be on the mountain and acclimatized before he arrives."

"Are you serious?" But when she looked at the rest of the team for support, she noticed no one would catch her eye. Not even Elise. "No one seems to know what caused this accident. Shouldn't we at least wait for a bit while someone investigates?"

"It was an accident, Cecily. But if anyone is uncomfortable continuing and wants to leave, I wouldn't blame them," Doug said, his voice quiet. "We can arrange a helicopter back to Kathmandu. No questions asked."

No one spoke. After a moment's pause, she gave a small shake of her head. She thought the right decision—the one that honored Alain—was to leave the mountain. But she seemed to be the only one feeling that way. She knew she was in shock. Maybe that was affecting her decision-making.

"All right. I'm going to find out if Summit Extreme need support after the accident. We'll head to base camp at nine, as we planned. See you outside and ready in an hour."

Cecily and Elise headed to their room to pack.

"Do you think we're doing the right thing?" Cecily asked, sitting down on the edge of the bed.

Elise stopped halfway through stuffing her sleeping bag into its sack. She came and sat next to Cecily. "I trust Doug, and I trust Charles. I texted him what happened, and he replied saying he thinks we should continue."

Cecily's eyes widened. "Charles said that?"

"It's always hard when there's an accident like this. A tragedy. Even when it's not your team, you know? But we have to keep going. Alain wouldn't want you to give up your dream."

Cecily picked at a thread on the bedding. "I'm not sure it is my dream, exactly."

"But you do want to summit?"

Cecily nodded. "I want to try. I have to, if I want this story."

"Then I am glad you're staying. We will honor Alain on the mountain. We can't do anything by going home."

Cecily thought of Alain, wanting to pay tribute to Pierre by leaving a token at the summit. Maybe she could do something similar. "Thanks, Elise."

They double-checked their room for a dropped glove or any forgotten cables. It would be a difficult journey back if they left something behind. When Cecily emerged with her daypack thrown over her shoulder, the atmosphere in the courtyard had changed once again. Porters were loading donkeys with bags and drums full of gear, the bells around their necks jangling. She lingered by the entrance to the dining hall, watching the activity.

"What a morning." Ben strolled toward her from the other side of the yard.

She straightened. "I saw you with Christophe—how is he doing?" she asked.

Ben shrugged. "He's staying behind in Samagaun, making sure Alain's body gets back safely. I don't think we'll see him at base camp. It's mad, isn't it? I just met the guy a couple of days ago and now he's dead."

Cecily tensed. She still felt uneasy around Ben, and she didn't want him to see her vulnerability. "It's awful."

Ben leaned in. "I've been asking some questions. It sounds like Alain walked up to the lake for some extra acclimatization. Then he might have lost his footing on the rocks up there—a freak accident kind of thing."

"He went for a swim. Said that it helped to ready his mind for the task ahead."

"You were at the lake too?"

She nodded. "We spoke briefly, but I left while he was still in the water."

"OK, wow. So did you see anyone else up there?"

"No one. I saw a drone, but I didn't see who was operating it."

"Interesting . . . there are only a few people with drones, that I've seen. The permits are expensive. When you were up there, did you find it dangerous?"

"The rocks were loose underfoot, but nothing an experienced mountaineer like Alain couldn't have handled." Cecily frowned. "You're asking a lot of questions. Do you know something?"

"Actually, yes. I spoke to one of the villagers who found him." Ben lowered his voice. "Alain's injuries were bad. He had pretty severe head trauma, apparently."

"Really? Oh my god." She paused, and took a breath. "Do they think he hit it when he fell?"

"Maybe . . . Did he tell you about his friend Pierre Charroin?"

"The one who disappeared on Everest? Yes, poor man. Sounded like another tragic accident."

"Well, between you and me . . . ?"

Cecily nodded. Despite her distrust of the man, she wanted to hear Ben's theory.

"I'm not so sure about that," he continued. "It seems suspicious to me. Alain came here asking some serious questions. Now he's dead. That doesn't seem like a coincidence."

Concern grew in the pit of her stomach. She itched to dig out her notebook and look over her notes on the conversation she'd had with Alain.

"You seriously believe this wasn't an accident?"

"I'm just saying maybe it's not all as cut and dry as it seems."

"So what's going to happen now?" she asked.

"The Nepali authorities are getting involved. There'll be an investigation."

"Good," she said. "But as tragic as an accident would be, I hope they don't find any reason to suspect someone else was involved."

The rest of her team entered the courtyard, all ready to begin the trek to base camp. Ben shook Doug's hand before quirking his eyebrow at Cecily and disappearing inside.

A cold shiver traveled down Cecily's spine. Ben had dropped a bombshell, and as much as she hoped it wasn't true, her mind was turning his words over and over. She stared up at the mountain one final time. Even the most experienced mountaineers died on peaks like the one she was looking at. The one she was about to climb.

One slip, and that could be the end.

Or one push . . .

The thought slid into her mind unbidden. She swallowed, and hurried to catch up to the others.

CHAPTER 9

THE ROUTE FOLLOWED HAND-PAINTED metal signs pointing to Manaslu base camp. They fell into single file, with Doug up front, followed by Grant and Elise. Doug's hands were buried in his pockets as he walked, his shoulders slumped. Zak and Mingma came next, while Cecily brought up the rear. She gripped the straps of her backpack as she walked, trying to focus on the task at hand: getting to base camp.

A light, misty rain fell as they hiked up out of the village. They walked through a forest thick with lush rhododendron, peeling white birch and Himalayan blue pine. It was so much greener than she had imagined. But as they climbed higher, the path beneath their feet grew heavy with mud, made slick by hundreds of heavy hiking boots tramping up and down in short succession over the tail end of the monsoon season.

At higher elevations, the trees thinned and the countryside around them spread out into glorious alpine meadows, long grasses interspersed with clusters of tiny pink and purple flowers. She wished she could appreciate how scenic it was. Her mind was still clouded by thoughts of Alain.

Zak was tracking their gain in altitude. "Just passed four thousand meters." He paused, waiting for Cecily to catch up.

"Only a few hundred meters to go," she replied, stopping to take a sip of water. She gestured to his expensive-looking computerized watch. "That looks fancy."

"It's one of my TalkForward prototypes. We're hoping to launch to the public next spring."

"Oh, wow, I didn't realize it was one of your company's products. Amazing. Have you always worked in tech?"

"Yup. I studied at Caltech, then settled in Petaluma to start my company and haven't looked back since. It's been my mission to bring world-class communications equipment to the most remote corners of the world. We want to rig out the pioneers, the guys taking the biggest risks. Give them secure satphones, GPS devices, cameras they can rely on even in the worst weather, deepest cavern or densest jungle."

"Or tallest mountain?"

"Right! TalkForward is my baby. I work with the smartest people on the planet, honestly. They're all rooting for me out here."

She smiled. He sounded so earnest and engaged—she could see how he'd make an inspiring CEO. His employees seemed more like his family. "Sounds like a worthy goal."

"It means a lot to me, and I've been driving that mission hard for the past fifteen years. Back in 2010, I took some of my engineers to Mount Rainier to test some equipment and for some bonding, and even though it was one of the most difficult things I'd ever done in my life, I just fell in love with it all—the challenge, the scenery, that immense feeling of reaching the summit and pushing harder than you've ever pushed before. At the Rainier BaseCamp bar afterward, the guide mentioned to me about climbing the Seven Summits and from that moment I was like a dog with a freaking bone. I couldn't get enough. It just synergized perfectly with my TalkForward mission: technology without limits. When I heard about Fourteen Clean and how Charles was struggling to get the finances together, I knew we had to get involved. I said we'd sponsor the final part of his mission, in exchange for bringing me along and testing out some of our equipment. Now here I am! Climbing with a legend in the making."

"Your family doesn't mind?"

"Hey, I'm doing it *for* my family. To give them a legacy other than my company. Something real. Personal. I want my sons—Josh and

River—to look at me and be blown away, you know? Show them life's not all about making money. What about you? Have you always wanted to be a journalist? Maybe after you're done with Charles, you could do me next."

She shrugged. "I sort of fell into journalism, really. I wanted to be a doctor growing up. Like my brother and my mom—a family of medics."

"So what happened? Couldn't hack it?"

She almost choked on her water. She caught the twinkle in his eyes, though, and her shoulders loosened. She smiled. "Something like that. I guess I lost my way for a while. I studied English at uni, and ran a lifestyle blog while working various retail jobs. But then my boyfriend—well, ex-boyfriend now—showed me how to turn my blogs into pitches, connected me with editors, that sort of thing, so I could turn my articles into paid freelance work. He's an adventure travel journalist—he covers Everest and the high mountains."

"You're kidding? He must be jealous you're getting to do this."

"Yeah . . . hence why he is an *ex*-boyfriend."

"No need to explain. I get it. So how did you train?"

She laughed. "There was a *lot* of climbing up stairs."

"You're telling me. I spent a month exercising in a hypoxic chamber to help me pre-acclimatize. Slept in there too. It simulates oxygen levels up to eighteen thousand feet."

"That's high-tech!" *And costs a fortune*, she thought. "Did it help?"

"Oh, for sure! Those chambers and high-altitude tents are game-changers for the mountaineering industry. I tried to revolutionize my prep at every stage, to make it as efficient as possible. Shame you're not a doctor—you could've checked my oxygen stats."

She hadn't thought about being a doctor for a long time. In secondary school, she'd taken all the right subjects for a career in medicine, like her brother, Alexander, had done before her. Alex was the overachiever, the person who ran marathon after marathon, even completing an Ironman in Mallorca (and if you spent more than fifteen minutes in his presence, he would tell you about it). He was also her idol—until she realized she had to find her own path in life, not just follow in his footsteps. She'd hated seeing the disappointment in his face—and on her parents' faces—when she told them about her change of direction, choosing to study English instead. Alex wanted to understand but couldn't. He'd always known his purpose in life; she felt stuck. Caught between two paths—appeasing her family and pursuing her growing passion for telling stories. She longed to see more of the world, yet felt too afraid to seek it out alone.

Then along came James. She'd been awed by his dating profile. He was a true adventurer—he didn't just ski, he skied *backcountry*, he didn't just go cycling, he mountain biked in the remote Carpathian Mountains. He was a trained mountain guide and proficient rock climber, with a gift for writing that made him an in-demand outdoor adventure journalist. Add to that a chiseled jawline and warm honey-brown eyes—Cecily couldn't believe her luck.

Her profile had seemed ultraboring in comparison to his—her photos showed her sipping cocktails in Brighton, in front of a mural in Shoreditch, on the dance floor at Rachel's wedding. He told her he'd swiped right because he'd been attracted to her smile—and the touch of wit and warmth that came through in her writing, even just in the small paragraph about herself she'd composed for the dating app. And while some men lied about how adventurous they were to attract women, James was the real deal. From their wobbly first-date paddleboarding on the River Thames, he'd pushed her far out of her comfort zone. He had been the one to encourage her to look beyond the crowded field of "luxury" travel writing and join him on writing about more off-the-beaten-track adventures. Not that he'd imagined his encouragement would lead to her poaching his biggest story. He might not have been so pushy otherwise.

For a while, they'd existed in a happy bubble, full of adventure and spontaneity, and she missed it so much she ached—even though she could see now that it hadn't been real. He'd had a vision of her, of who he thought she could be. When reality sank in, she'd felt him pull away.

Probably Kilimanjaro had been the beginning of the end. He'd come back from Aconcagua and suggested the tallest mountain in

Africa would be the perfect challenge for them to take on together. She'd been apprehensive, but she hadn't wanted to disappoint him.

So, Kilimanjaro it was.

She hadn't trained much, even though she'd never done any sort of mountaineering before—she wouldn't even climb the three flights of stairs to their flat. But it was the kind of climb that thousands of tourists did every year; she figured it wouldn't need any special preparation.

The reality had been far more intense. She'd puffed and panted her way up to each camp, suffering from the altitude and the cold. Even though porters were carrying her gear, she'd stopped on a plateau a short distance from Stella Point, unable to take another step toward the summit.

James had stayed with her, holding her hair back as she vomited up the rich food the expedition company had cooked for them. Pole-pole, slowly, slowly, her Swahili guides had told her. But there was no way she was continuing—and so neither did James. She'd felt both grateful and guilty. He'd blamed the altitude, but she wasn't so sure. It felt deeper than that. Some kind of fundamental flaw, her lack of resilience built into her DNA.

Then the National Three Peaks Challenge happened. On the car ride home after Snowdon, she felt like a complete failure. Writing the blog had been cathartic, but James hadn't understood why she'd want to publish it. He'd already called her a hero. Why would she want to define herself as a failure?

Hero and failure. Brave and cowardly. Adventurous and homebody. She wondered if duality had always been a part of her, ingrained at birth. Both Chinese and white, never quite finding her place in one world or the other. Mixed race? More like mixed-up.

"Jesus, is that the lake . . . you know, where it happened?" Zak asked.

Now that they were far above the tree line, Birendra Taal was visible below them, shimmering turquoise blue, like a tranquil paradise. Except, at the edge of its calm surface, tragedy had struck.

"Poor Alain," she said.

Zak adjusted his TalkForward-branded baseball cap. "Unreal. That someone could slip like that and be a goner." He snapped his fingers.

She thought back to Ben's theory. "Maybe he didn't slip."

Zak frowned. "What do you mean?"

She swallowed. "One of the other Summit Extreme climbers, Ben—he's a friend from back home, another journalist—said a local told him Alain had been found with a suspicious head wound. I guess the authorities are looking into it."

"Robbed?"

Cecily blinked. That motive hadn't even occurred to her. "No idea."

"You never know with all the tourists and hikers about. God, I'll be glad to get to base camp. Last thing we need is to feel like we have to watch our backs for opportunistic thieves. Between the Talk-Forward gear I brought, all Grant's camera stuff and Elise's tech, we're like walking targets."

"Nonsense," Doug said, a scowl on his face. He was waiting for them to catch up. Cecily hadn't realized he'd overheard. "It was a terrible accident, that's all. There are no thieves here. You better keep moving. You're lagging behind."

She swallowed.

"Maybe your journalist 'friend' was trying to throw you off your game," said Zak, arching an eyebrow before following Doug up the trail.

Cecily paused, taking another sip from her hydration pack. She couldn't tear her eyes from the lake, its soft and shimmering water, the rocks around it that had proven deadly.

Snowdon had demonstrated all too clearly how fast the situation on a mountain could change. She could only hope, as they climbed higher, that now they were leaving tragedy behind.

CHAPTER 10

THEY PAUSED AT A makeshift "teahouse"—a lean-to shelter propped up against the cliff side—where some local villagers were stoking a fire under a corrugated-tin roof and boiling large pots of water for tea and momos. The momos here were stuffed with potato and dipped in a fiery-hot dipping sauce, which Cecily learned was particular to the Gorkha region. She greedily stuffed the little parcels into her mouth. They provided the perfect mountain snack.

"The glacier used to come a lot farther down," said Doug. "A few years ago, it stretched right into this valley."

"Climate change," huffed Zak.

She was surprised at how Zak had been coping—or rather, not coping—with the journey so far. Over the past half hour, he had been sucking down air and sweating profusely, looking as tired as Cecily felt. The hypoxia tent might not have worked as well as he'd hoped.

She felt Doug's eyes appraising them all. "We're about halfway now," he said. "Take your time."

She was glad for the moment of rest. She thought of her preparation, the miles that she'd put in on Box Hill—the steepest place she could find close to London. Up and down, up and down. She appreciated every step now.

Elise stood off to one side, taking photos. Zak slumped down on the log beside her. After eating a couple of momos, he fumbled in his pocket for a small, shiny, black electronic device about the size of a credit card. When he flipped it around, she spotted a big round lens on the front.

"Is that a camera?" she asked. "I've never seen one so compact."

"Neat, huh? One of the new TalkForward SatCam prototypes I want to test at altitude. The camera uses satellite technology to upload footage directly to the cloud. That way my team—and my family—can experience the journey along with me."

"Livestreaming an eight-thousand-meter peak? Makes writing a blog seem so old-fashioned."

"That's the idea! It's still in trials, but the quality is insane and could revolutionize adventure photography if it works, especially in super-remote areas. But our main goal is to help isolated communities if a disaster strikes and they need aid. That's part of my 'limitless' mission, anyway. I wanted to give Charles one, but he said he wouldn't climb with a prototype."

"Don't give him a camera; filming him is my job," interjected Grant, strolling over to them.

She squinted. "What about when he's not on the main route?" she asked. "How can you film him if he's off climbing alpine style?"

"That's what this baby is for." He patted a bag at his side. "High-altitude drone. Got it flying over seven thousand meters on Cho, and hoping for higher here."

"You have a drone?" Cecily's eyes widened.

"Of course I do." Grant all but rolled his eyes at her question. She wanted to ask him whether he'd flown it over the lake, but he was already bounding up the trail, as Doug gestured for them to continue.

"Looks like we're moving," said Zak. "Onward and upward!" He clipped the camera onto the zipper of his jacket and pressed on the tops of his thighs to stand.

Above the momo station, they left behind the meadow and spindly trees for the rocky foothills of the mountain itself, followed by their first steps on the desolate glacial moraine. Every so often they had to step aside to allow a small train of donkeys to pass, each one carrying two large duffel bags balanced across its back.

After several hours, the novelty of the walk wore thin. She kept telling herself that camp must be *just* over the next ridge. But it never came. This high up, there was less visual interest to distract her mind: thick gray fog had closed in on them, obscuring the view, and underfoot there was only rock, mud and ice.

So the sight of the first bright yellow tent was a beacon. A relief. Soon even more tents popped out of the gloom, little jewels in the mist, and Cecily thought there had never been a more perfect place in the entire world than that neon-colored plastic-sheet city. It meant that home camp couldn't be far away. Over the course of four and a half hours, they'd climbed to just under five thousand meters, taller than any of the mountains of the Alps, and yet still they weren't quite at the day's finishing line.

Doug pointed at a narrow path. "We're a bit farther."

Cecily was panting, her hands resting on her knees. She really thought they'd arrived. She felt Mingma's hand on her back. "Think of it this way: it will mean less walking to reach camp one when we set off next," he said.

"I suppose so," Cecily said. She forced a smile, even though she felt as if her feet were about to drop off.

Base camp was massive. Rows of tents, divided by team, stretched across the rocky glacier, rolling in sync with the terrain. Most of the tents were small, meant for only one person to sleep in. But within each cluster there were larger tents too—for cooking, dining, communications equipment and gear. Some of the bigger teams had luxurious living rooms inside clear-plastic domes—like igloos—and she spotted porters carrying up armchairs and tables for the mega-wealthy clients. The Everest effect, with clients demanding more and more lavish accommodations. The biggest operators were Summit Extreme, and by the look of it, they were the slickest too.

Every group of tents was adorned with flags bearing the name of the expedition, its sponsors and the nationalities of the climbers. So many people from across the world came together for this one adventure. A miniature international city in the heart of the Himalaya.

Her heart lifted when they arrived at the Manners Mountaineering base camp. An MM flag marked the entrance, alongside a banner for Charles McVeigh's Fourteen Clean mission.

She'd made it.

CHAPTER 11

A DOZEN SMILING FACES gathered around to greet them, like the receiving line at a wedding. She shook hands with each member of their base camp crew and all the Sherpas.

"Welcome home," said the final Sherpa. He had a strikingly handsome face, sharp jawline, dark tanned skin and serious deep brown eyes. He draped a wreath of bright orange marigolds around her neck. He was the same height as her but compact with muscle. "I am Galden. Congratulations on making it to base camp."

"I'm Cecily. I can't really believe I'm here," she replied. All the aches and pains of the past few hours caught up with her, and she winced as she shifted the weight of her backpack.

Galden's eyes widened. "Let me take that!" He took hold of the straps of her bag as she staggered free.

"Thank you," she said, with a grateful smile. He slung the pack over one shoulder with ease and began his orientation.

"Come with me, I will show you to your tent and you can relax. Over there is the dining area," he said, pointing to the largest tent, on the edge of the camp. "The one you can see behind is the kitchen, and then those two small ones are the toilets."

Cecily grimaced, as reality of life on the mountain sank in.

Galden showed her which was Elise's tent next, as it was closest to the dining area, then Grant's and Zak's were side by side a few steps behind. Hers was the farthest away, a bright yellow limpet clinging to the rocky ground. Behind it, a pile of boulders hid a steep drop into the valley below. At least she wouldn't be bothered at night by the noise of people coming and going.

"Here you go," Galden said. Her duffel bags were already stacked outside. "I'll let you get settled."

She knelt down and unzipped her tent. She sighed happily—it was already furnished with a single mattress and pillow. She crawled in, lying back on the soft foam. It was hard to believe she was here. At the base of the eighth-tallest mountain in the world.

She closed her eyes, the effort of the day catching up with her. Everyone else seemed so confident and strong, unshaken by Alain's death. She wanted to relax, but couldn't shake the feeling that something wasn't right. Doug had dismissed outright the idea that Alain's death was suspicious, but her worry—her fear—wasn't so easily set aside.

Action. Action would help. First, she sat up and dragged her bags into the vestibule. She unzipped the first duffel and started unpacking. In this, she wasn't particularly careful—she prioritized getting her lighter-weight sleeping bag out, along with some clean underwear and socks. Within minutes, her tent was filled with stuff—her long lists come to life.

There was a rustle of fabric as the flap opened. She scrambled backward, colliding with the far side of the tent, her heart beating wildly. Yet it was only Galden's smiling face that appeared. "I brought you a drink, didi. You must stay hydrated."

She laughed to cover her shame at her terrified reaction. She hadn't realized quite how on edge she was. She was glad Galden was concentrating too hard on not spilling the cup of tea in his hands to have noticed.

"Didi? Oh, but my name is Cecily," she said, when she could trust her voice not to wobble.

"*Didi* means 'big sister' in my language. You are on the mountain now. We are a family."

She took the cup from his hands, her fingers still trembling.

Now Galden frowned. "Are you OK?"

She shook her head. "A man I met in Samagaun died yesterday.

We found out this morning." The words tumbled out before she could stop them, but when she looked up, Galden was nodding, his lips pressed together. He didn't seem to think she was overreacting or paranoid.

"Ah, I heard about that. He was with Summit Extreme, yes?"

"I guess I'm a bit shaken by it."

"I understand. But you are here with us now. You are safe."

Cecily's throat tightened. "I might have been the last person to see him alive."

Galden's frown deepened. He cast an eye over the explosion of her belongings, but didn't say anything. Instead he reached over and grabbed her khata—the orange scarf that she'd received at the beginning of her journey. "Let's hang this here. A good-luck charm to ward away any evil," he said, and tucked it into the roof of her tent, so it hung over the entrance. "Please, drink your tea. You can rest and relax now. We will have dinner at six p.m. You will be OK until then?"

"Yes, thank you, Galden. You've helped a lot." She mustered a smile, which seemed to satisfy him as he left her alone. Yet anxiety lingered in her belly.

Rest *did* sound good. But there were other tasks to be getting on with. She needed to charge her phone, the battery was dead from the long journey up. She needed to talk to Grant, to see if he had been the one flying the drone she'd seen at the lake. She wanted to find Ben, to find out if he'd heard any more from the authorities.

And she had a blog to write, to do the job that she'd come here to do. She couldn't let one sad, but most likely accidental, death derail her from her purpose.

She had to find a way to let go. Allow the authorities to deal with it.

Galden was right; she was safe here.

Her mind was set. She just had to convince her body that was true.

September 5
Manaslu base camp
4,800m

In Sanskrit, *Manaslu* means "mountain of the spirit." It's a peaceful name that belies the many dangers ahead. Sadly, we have already experienced tragedy in Samagaun. A member of the Summit Extreme team, Alain Flaubert, suffered a fatal accident on the rocks near a glacial lake. My heart goes out to his friends and family in Chamonix.

Our expedition, however, continues, and we made our way up to base camp this morning. The shark-like fin of the east pinnacle hides the mountain's true summit, and our camp has an unbroken view across the glacier. I am writing this from a small tent, and if you'd told me a year ago that I'd be spending a month living on a glacier in one of the most remote places on Earth, I never would have believed you. Yet here I am.

But what amazes me most is just how many people there are here. Apparently over two hundred permits have been issued for Manaslu this season, making it a very busy mountain indeed.

All this has me asking: Why?

It's much easier to understand why people climb Mount Everest. It's the tallest mountain in the world—a reason in itself, instant kudos, universal recognition. But why climb Manaslu, or the other lesser-known eight-thousand-meter peaks? Is it purely to gain experience for the big E?

And what's more, while Manaslu might not be as famous as Everest or notorious as K2, it is properly dangerous. The fourth-most-dangerous eight-thousand-meter peak, in fact, by death rate. Manaslu has a reputation for avalanches. The instability of the route, the relative "warmth" of the mountain, the amount of sun on the face, and the heavy precipitation that falls during monsoon season all mean it's impossible to find a truly "safe" place to camp, unlike say on Everest, where the Western Cwm is mostly protected from avalanche risk by the width and depth of the valley.

Manaslu requires its climbers to go fast, take every precaution and pray. Not long ago, it was known as the "Killer Mountain." It seems . . . unlucky.

Yet now that I'm here, staring up at the beautiful eastern pinnacle, there is something alluring about it too. It is certainly impressive to look at. And if the conditions are perfect, it is supposed to be a challenging yet achievable climb even for novice mountaineers like me.

As Doug outlined for us in Samagaun, this expedition follows the northeast ridge. A team of highly skilled climbing Sherpas will "fix" the route, anchoring thousands of meters of rope onto the mountain. Once we've acclimatized at base camp, we'll start moving up, following the path they've laid out. The route to camp one is supposed to be quite straightforward, crossing rocky slopes and a wide glacier.

The journey from camp one to camp two will be the most difficult, as we encounter the Manaslu icefall. This is the most dangerous part of the glacier, where it flows the fastest—a literal waterfall of ice. This is where we are most likely to encounter the widest crevasses, crossing them on a series of ladders set up by the fixing team. We'll also encounter the "crux" of the expedition: an enormous wall that allegedly requires more technical climbing than any obstacle in the Khumbu icefall on Everest. Its steepness means we'll have to deploy our ice-climbing skills—and we have to move quickly. Speed is of the essence, as you don't want to linger under the hanging seracs—columns of ice that could break off and crash on our route.

Beyond camp two, the climb is more straightforward again—

although we have to be constantly alert for falling debris, especially from other climbers—or slips that could easily trigger an avalanche.

Camp three is considered the most dangerous. Huge cliffs of ice loom over the tents. Yet the terrain becomes easier to manage all the way to camp four: a long, slow slog up a steady slope.

Above camp four: our goal, the summit. Controversy swirls around Manaslu's true summit. Some years—depending on weather and snow conditions—the highest point of the mountain is too difficult to access, as you need to cross a precarious, heavily corniced ridge. If the ridge is covered in unstable snow, the fixing team establishes the traditional prayer flag marker on the "fore summit" of the mountain—a few meters below the apex. Those years are marked down in the Himalayan Database with an asterisk and mean that season's climbers have not really reached the highest point. Everyone hopes the snow will be right this year. As for Charles, since he's climbing alpine style—without the need for fixed lines—he should be able to summit no matter what the conditions.

We have a month to complete our expedition before winter sets in and the weather makes it too treacherous to continue. It should be plenty of time for us to acclimatize, do a couple of rotations, and make it to the summit and back safely. We just have to pray for the right weather window—and to the mountain gods for safe passage.

In the meantime, I am going to double-check that my carabiners are locking smoothly and the points of my crampons are sharp. My prayers might not be granted, but I'm going to do everything in my power to make sure I'm ready if they are.

CHAPTER 12

SHE EMERGED FROM HER tent, feeling disoriented after falling asleep at her laptop.

"Didi, over here." Galden waved her over to the kitchen tent, and she could hear pots banging inside and smell lentils cooking in spices. Her stomach rumbled. She'd had plenty of dal bhat since arriving in Nepal, but somehow she never got bored of it.

She followed Galden inside. All the climbing Sherpas, and some of the porters who had helped to transport their bags, were there, digging into plates piled high with food.

She felt as if she were being allowed into an inner sanctum. This was how you made climbers feel special: not by giving them their own tent for their "luxuries," but allowing them to feel like part of the Sherpa family too.

"Here, try some of this." Galden dipped a metal spoon in the nearest pot, then passed it to Cecily.

Even before she had tasted it, the pungent hit of chilies and vinegar hit her senses. "Oh my god, that's hot!" she exclaimed.

"Too much?" Galden's brow knitted together in concern.

"No, it's delicious!" she added. Her mouth burned with spice.

"Glad you enjoy it, didi. This is our traditional mountain food."

"Well, sign me up."

"This is our cook, Dawa." Galden gestured at a man who turned toward her and bowed, one hand on his chest.

She bowed her head in return. "Lovely to meet you. I can't wait to try more of your dishes," she added.

"And our other Sherpa brothers—Tenzing and Phemba—you met them earlier." Cecily smiled at them both, glad for an opportunity to get to know them better. She'd been too flustered and anxious on arriving at camp to truly take in all the names and faces.

Tenzing looked to be the oldest. He had a calming presence—probably confidence built from a wealth of experience in the mountains. Phemba and Galden, by contrast, seemed closer in age to Elise. She remembered that Elise had said Phemba was one of her favorite people, and she could see why—he had a cheeky grin and an infectious laugh as he joked with the cooking staff in Nepali. Galden was downright serious by comparison.

"Didi, it is time to head next door. You will have dinner soon."

"Thank you, Galden."

In the dining tent, she chose a chair next to Elise and opposite Grant. She thought this might be the moment to ask her questions about the drone, but Doug strode in through the plastic vestibule. He did a head count and gave a sharp nod. "Good. Let's eat."

As if waiting for his cue, Dawa walked in carrying an oversized saucepan filled with a watery vegetable soup. He gave them all a huge spoonful, and Cecily drank down the entire bowl.

The next course was pizza, made with homemade dough and topped with a mountain of roast chicken and vegetables. Considering she thought they'd be subsisting on dahl bat, it was a surprise.

"This is better than the food on Broad Peak," said Elise, reaching for another slice of pizza.

"How was that?" Cecily asked. She'd read Elise's captions about the expedition, but it was different hearing it in person. "It was your second attempt, wasn't it?"

"Yeah. The first time I went was also my first time in the death zone with no oxygen." She puffed out a blast of air. "Nothing could have prepared me for how tough it was going to be. When I got to eight thousand, it was like BAM!" She slammed her palm on the table. "I hit a wall. I was woozy—I even told Phemba I thought I saw aliens coming toward us! Turned out it was just another team . . . Never in my alpinism career have I experienced that. Seeing things that weren't there. No energy. My legs wouldn't move. Phemba saw how

I was struggling and we turned around. I didn't want to. It was the hardest decision of my life, and that was why I was so happy to come back again this summer and do it. This time, I took it slow. But I made it to the top." It was hard to imagine the little powerhouse on a remote peak in the Karakoram, but Elise had all the photographs and stories to prove it.

"So why not use oxygen?" asked Zak. "Then you could've checked off a different mountain rather than have to do the same one twice."

"For me, it is not about the 'check.' It is about seeing what I can achieve. It is important to me to make these climbs without oxygen. If that stops me, I will try again another time." She flipped her long hair off her shoulders. "Like Manaslu and Cho Oyu, they say Broad Peak is one of the 'easier' mountains. But tell that to Dorje who died when a snow bridge collapsed . . ." Elise's voice trailed off.

The skin on the back of Cecily's neck prickled. Yet she was beginning to understand now. If these alpinists weren't able to move on from death, they'd never last long in the mountains.

"Cho *is* easy," muttered Grant, oblivious to Cecily's discomfort. "Just not when some wanker decides to keep going instead of turning around when he's told." He popped the top off a bottle of Coke and swilled it.

"What happened?" Zak prompted.

"I'd been at camp two, getting some wicked drone footage for my client when the news came over the radio. There was a huge Indian team in front of us, maybe twenty guys in total. Most of them made the summit, but one guy never made it back to camp. Lucky for us, Charles was higher up the mountain. We all had to huddle around this one radio as he reported in on his search. When I realized he was over the ridge from where we were, I took my drone out to see if I could spot them."

"Wow, any luck?" asked Elise.

Grant gave an exaggerated wink. "You'll have to wait for the feature film to find out, baby."

She grimaced.

"What happened to the climber?" Cecily asked.

"Charles found him inside a crevasse. He had to prusik down to him and haul him out. Hell of a job. Trust me—you wouldn't want anyone else other than Charles doing that move."

Cecily took a small spiral notepad from her jacket pocket and jotted down "prusik," circling the word. She needed to look it up later—she wasn't keen to demonstrate even more ignorance now.

Grant continued: "Anyway, the guy was a goner if it hadn't been for Charles. When they were clear of the crevasse, our team's climbing Sherpas went to help take the guy back to base camp—which meant the end of my summit attempt. As it happens he'd been told to turn around hours before but had ignored it. Some people don't know their limits."

"That sucks," said Zak.

"Tell me about it." Grant glowered. "But, man, when Charles walked into our camp, parting the fog with the Indian climber in his arms, it was like a superhero had arrived. Some kind of mountain Avenger. At least it gave me the chance to film him in action." He reached into his jacket and pulled out a thick hard drive, wrapped in a rugged orange plastic case, tapping it protectively. "The footage I have on here convinced him I was the right chap to shoot the last phase of his mission."

"Don't you have it backed up on the cloud somewhere?" asked Zak.

"Have you seen the upload speeds in Kathmandu? It would take me years. No, these things are bombproof anyway. It's like my baby. Never leaves my sight."

"So, Grant, about the drone—" Cecily began to ask, but Dawa entered with an enormous "welcome to the mountain" sponge cake laden with cream. How he had managed to bake a cake up here, she had no idea.

As they tucked into a slice each, Doug leaned forward, lacing his fingers together.

All their eyes were drawn to him. Doug carried himself taller at base camp than in Kathmandu or even Samagaun, the hunch in his shoulders rolled back. "Team. Welcome to your new home. Because we'll be here for the next month, we all need to do our best to keep it tidy and respectable. You can charge your electronics while the generator is running in the evenings. We'll do dinner here every night at eighteen hundred, and that will include a briefing for the next day, so don't be late.

"We're going to rest tomorrow as there's less than half the normal oxygen here compared to what you're used to. Your bodies are going to need time to adjust." He threw a little device onto the table. "This is a pulse oximeter. Clip it onto your forefinger and wait for a few seconds. Take a reading at the same time every evening. We're looking for an increase day by day—if you notice any sudden dips, or if you're failing to get above eighty percent by next week, you must let me know."

Cecily clipped the device onto her finger and frowned when the reading showed sixty-eight percent. If she were in the hospital, she'd be on supplemental oxygen by now. But this was to be expected up here, considering they had climbed over a thousand meters in one day. Her heart rate was also abnormally high, racing at over 80 bpm despite the fact that her normal resting heart rate was much lower.

She took a note of the reading on her notepad and passed the oximeter on to Zak.

"Hydration is the key to not getting sick up here. And for the first few days you have to *take it easy*. I mean it. When we're ready to start our acclimatization routine on the mountain, you need to be fit and healthy. Otherwise you will have all wasted your money. That also means no showers for the next few days. Nothing that might shock your body or prevent it from recovering in these temperatures and conditions."

Cecily grimaced. It wasn't exactly like she'd expected a nice hot shower, but hearing it was still uncomfortable. She'd already tied her hair back in tight braids to keep it under control.

Doug continued. "We've had word that the rope-fixing teams are already at camp two on the mountain and making good progress. So we should be on track to start our rotation in a couple of days. We'll climb to camp one, drop some of our heavier gear for higher up the mountain, and sleep there. You'll all be sharing tents—Cecily with Elise, Grant with Zak. If everyone is feeling good, we'll continue on to camp two. Once everyone here has spent at least one night at camp three and made it safely back to base, we'll wait for a summit window. Patience is the key."

This was one aspect of climbing mountains Cecily had never understood before she'd followed James's climb on Aconcagua. Rotations were key to acclimatizing for the altitude, even though it meant climbing up and down the same route on the mountain several times before an actual summit attempt.

Of all the dangers of the mountain, altitude was the one that scared her most. Its effects were impossible to predict. Impossible to cure. Descending was the only way to improve. Even a prior trip to altitude was no indicator of how you'd fare up there.

It would start with a headache. Stuffed nose—potentially with a little blood. Fatigue. Those symptoms were inevitable—manageable with time, hydration and painkillers. If it progressed to AMS—acute mountain sickness—she could expect loss of appetite, nausea, dizziness, low oxygen-saturation levels . . . for which stronger medication might be required. She had a prescription for altitude sickness medication in her bag, just for that purpose—although it was better to acclimatize naturally, as pills could obscure the symptoms. Beyond *that* the body rapidly worsened. HAPE and HACE would come next. High-altitude pulmonary and cerebral edema.

Hacking cough. Shortness of breath. Hallucinations. Delirium. Fluid leaking into the lungs. Fluid leaking into the brain.

At that point, a summit would be impossible—the only option would be to turn around and descend.

Refusal would mean death—and it could happen in a matter of minutes.

"Just remember"—Doug's tone was grave—"you need to take care of the small stuff: making sure your water is always full, you're applying and reapplying sunscreen, you've got a spare pair of gloves. Don't rely on this team to carry you. That's not what the Sherpas are here for. The only person who can get you up the mountain is you."

Silence fell. The task ahead was so big—monumental—and yet could be undone by the smallest of mistakes. Experience helped to mitigate that. But that was the one thing she didn't have.

"*Be bothered*," Cecily whispered.

Doug was visibly startled. "What?" he asked.

Cecily shook her head. "Oh, it was just something another climber told me once. *Be bothered*. Like a mantra for mountaineering."

"Right." He cast his gaze down, his jaw tightening.

"I've been thinking about it, and I'm going to climb without oxygen," said Zak. He waited a beat, but Doug's stony expression didn't change.

From the far side of the table, Elise stifled a laugh.

"Yeah. I don't want to use Os either," Grant added.

Cecily stared from one man to the other, not quite believing what she was hearing.

"No," Doug stated. His jaw twitched, his nostrils flaring. The change in his demeanor came on quickly: no calm before the storm, just the wrong words and his expression boiled over with anger, barely concealed beneath a veneer of civility he had to maintain for the sake of professionalism. "Do you understand how much danger you would put us in? Every time we accompany you up the mountain, we put our lives in your hands. You want to go without vital life support? Not on my watch."

To her surprise, Zak actually protested. "But Elise . . ."

"Elise has proven herself beyond a doubt that she's capable. That's more than I can say for you. Just because you've done a couple of climbs in the past means nothing at eight thousand meters. You have no fucking idea. None."

He stormed out of the tent, the zips flapping in his wake.

"Guess that's a no, then." Zak laughed nervously.

"So, now can we celebrate? I brought my customary bottle." Grant smirked like a naughty schoolboy as he reached under the table and pulled out a half-empty bottle of Captain Morgan, placing it down with a clink.

Elise did an exaggerated eye-roll and Cecily suppressed a laugh, then winced as pain shot through her skull. She couldn't believe Grant could contemplate alcohol at this altitude.

She was even more surprised when Zak rubbed his hands together and said, "All right!"

"Cheers, mate," Grant said. He poured a generous amount into his coffee and did the same to Zak's. He then waggled the bottle in the direction of the rest of them. Cecily shook her head. From the Sherpas, and Elise next to her, there were only polite coughs of refusal.

"More for me," Grant said, gulping his coffee.

Cecily's head throbbed, and she almost couldn't see straight. She took a large gulp of water.

"Altitude," said Elise, patting her leg. "Do you have medicine?"

"Back in my tent."

Elise dug into the bag around her waist and pulled out a blister pack of ibuprofen. "Here."

"You're a lifesaver. I think I need to go to bed," said Cecily. As she stood up, she swooned, gripping the edge of the table. She squeezed her eyes shut and pinched the bridge of her nose.

"Pass me your Nalgene." Elise took the bottle from her and filled it with hot water from the canisters. "Put this in your sleeping bag with you. Helps to sleep in the cold. And then you have extra water, so you won't run out."

Already the warmth of the bottle radiated through her body as she hugged it against her chest. "Thank you," she said, but it came out as barely a whisper.

"Don't mention it." Elise smiled.

Cecily hustled out of the dining tent and into the frigid night air. She unzipped her tent flaps, tossing the warm Nalgene inside her sleeping bag. Crawling inside, she barely had the energy to take off her boots.

The enormity of her experience hit her. She had at least three weeks to go of sleeping on ice and snow, far from the warmth of her own bed. She was thousands of miles—in almost every direction—from anyone she knew. She thought of Alain, his body wrapped into a bag, left out in the cold, waiting who knows how long to be bundled into a helicopter and flown home. His teammates continuing their expeditions, leaving him behind in the pursuit of their goals.

She thought of Pierre, a man who simply . . . disappeared, quite literally, into thin air.

Anything could happen to her, and who would care?

CHAPTER 13

SHE AWOKE IN THE middle of the night to blinding pain. Her head felt as if it were being sawed in half. She fumbled at the pockets of the tent, searching for her flashlight. She needed medication, fast.

Order. Order would have been helpful. But the Cecily of earlier that day hadn't *been bothered* enough to unpack in an organized manner. Her watch face glowed way too brightly. 23:03. Had it really only been a couple of hours since she had crawled into bed? She must have been out cold from the moment she shut her eyes.

In the beam from the flashlight, she spotted her red first-aid kit. She sifted through it for ibuprofen and popped two of them dry before remembering the Nalgene. The water was still warm, and it made sliding the pills down easier.

Still sitting up, she closed her eyes and took some deep breaths. Her leg muscles were tight and stiff from the walk to base camp. She grimaced, her mind turning—as always—to the most negative scenario: that she was too unfit to continue and Doug was going to put an end to her expedition before it could begin. She forced herself to take another sip.

A sound outside made her heart skip a beat.

A stone rattled along the bottom edge of her tent. Moved by a gust of wind, she told herself.

But when she dared to breathe again, she heard something else—a whistle from outside her tent. Four notes. Low, low, high, low. Then footsteps. Slow, ponderous steps, edging closer.

Now her heart was racing.

She clamped her hand down over her watch, not wanting any light to reveal her in the tent—even though whoever was outside would know she was in there already—and awake. She was suddenly very aware that all that lay between her and whoever was outside was a thin sheet of nylon.

There it was again: the whistle. It was the same sound she'd heard at the lake.

Right before Alain was murdered.

She hadn't allowed herself to think that word before now. The heightened unease of being out here, alone, made her think the worst. Someone had hurt him. It wasn't an accident.

Now they were coming for her.

Another step closer to the tent, another rock skittering against the entrance. Just someone out for a stroll . . . surely? But what reason would they have to come all the way out to her tent? It wasn't on the way to anything. Whoever was out there had to be coming to her deliberately.

Low, low, high, low.

Leave me alone, she begged in silence. She squeezed her eyes tightly shut, wanting to disappear inside the cocoon of her sleeping bag, pretend she was anywhere else but here.

The whistling faded quietly into the night. But the dread clung on, her body twitching at every sound. Eventually she fell asleep, exhausted by the effort, a rabbit cowering in her darkened den, wondering if a fox was outside, waiting to pounce.

The next morning broke bright and clear. Under such serene blue skies, her fears from the night faded, and she tried to dismiss the whistling sound as a figment of her imagination, an innocent noise twisted into something sinister by her pain-racked brain.

Instead, she stretched and stared at the mountain. A strange lens-like cloud hung over the peak, a mountain wave. An indication of just how fierce the winds were blowing higher up. The top of the east pinnacle looked an impossible distance from where she stood. The thought that soon she would be even higher than that? It was unfathomable.

Her headache had subsided to a dull throb, but she popped more ibuprofen and paracetemol for good measure. Before pulling on her boots, she surveyed the explosion of mess around her sleeping bag, vowing to give it a spruce before someone else saw it and judged her.

After a quick visit to the toilet tent, she brushed her teeth in the remnants of her water, spitting the residue out onto the rock. It was then that she saw it. A boot print in the muddy ground by the entrance to her tent.

It was much bigger than her own.

Someone *had* been right outside last night.

The whistler was real.

CHAPTER 14

SHE CHARGED OVER TO the dining tent.

Zak was the only one inside, sipping his morning coffee. He put his cup down as she entered. "Whoa, what's going on?"

"Someone was stalking my tent last night. I wasn't sure, but then there was this boot print in the mud right outside . . ."

"Hang on, take a breath." He took her by the shoulders and guided her to a chair. "Look, someone probably got lost or something. No need to freak out about it. I bet they were looking for the bathroom. It's so easy to get turned around on these rocks."

His hands were warm and reassuring. Cecily felt the surge of adrenaline rise and fall within her. Still, she shook her head. She couldn't explain it, but something wasn't right. Zak was looking at her like she was talking gibberish, but her gut sounded alarm bells.

"Hey, didn't you say there was some other journalist on the mountain?" he continued. "A rival?"

"Ben?"

"Yeah, him. Ever think he's trying to scare you? He put the idea in your head about that guy who died."

She frowned. She thought of the flash in Ben's eyes when he realized she was here on a big assignment. How he'd told her he wasn't working, but then he'd been going around the villagers, asking questions, digging into Alain's death. "I suppose he did tell me about the suspicious head wound . . ."

"I bet he's trying to get in your head. So what if someone was hanging around your tent? Who's going to try anything up here, with all these Sherpas with ice axes around?" Zak clapped his hands together decisively, as if he could clear the mood. "I'll make you a coffee," he said.

She took a deep breath. Maybe Zak was right. Ben had been the one to plant the thought that Alain's death was something *other* than a tragic accident. But to go so far as to scare her? It seemed a stretch, but it reminded her of the stories James used to tell her about how he and Ben would battle it out for the big exclusives.

This interview could change your whole life, she reminded herself. *Maybe Ben thinks it could change his too.*

She could speculate all day, but it was obvious what she needed to do. She had to speak to Ben. He might have more information about Alain's death. And if he had just been trying to scare her, she'd show him she wasn't going to be intimidated.

Dark thoughts plagued her mind all the way through breakfast. Dawa brought them bowls heavy with porridge, sweetened with Nepali honey. She pushed hers around the bowl, only looking up when Doug entered the tent. Cecily tried to catch his eye to ask him how to get to the Summit Extreme camp, but he didn't look at her.

He placed his hands on the back of a chair at the head of the table and leaned forward. "All right, team, here's the plan. I know I said to rest today, but since the weather is better than expected, we're having a training day."

Cecily's stomach dropped. There went her plans. She'd also wanted to find out how to access the internet to send her latest blog to Michelle. She wasn't ready to hit the mountain yet.

"Let's meet back here in half an hour, gear on and ready to go."

Once Doug had left, Grant signaled the chef. "Dawa, any chance of a couple of fried eggs, mate? I'm famished."

She swallowed down the rest of her porridge and walked back to her tent. But she scolded herself. She wasn't here to investigate Alain's death or worry about a mystery boot print. She was here to summit the mountain and write an in-depth exclusive profile of the most exciting adventurer on the planet. If she didn't want to get scooped by Ben, then she needed training.

She pulled on her harness, double-checking she had all the required equipment in her bag. She looped her ice ax through the straps, then stepped outside, ready to go.

Doug walked over to inspect her. He rubbed at the wiry gray hairs on his chin. "Where's your knife?"

She examined her harness, despite knowing full well there was no knife there. "I don't have one. It wasn't on the list . . ."

He huffed, removing a folding blade from his harness and hooking it via a carabiner onto one of her harness loops. "The list said 'fully equipped harness.' Take my spare. It could save your life."

"Wait, Doug . . . just one more thing." She paused, seeing if he'd allow her to continue. When he lingered, she launched into her question. "If I wanted to find the Summit Extreme team, how could I get there?"

There was a moment of silence between them. "Why?"

She didn't want to explain about Ben. She already knew Doug thought Ben's theory about Alain was nonsense. "Um, I want to talk to one of the guides, Dario Travers. Alain mentioned him to me the morning he died. He told me this terrible story of what happened to his friend Pierre on Everest this year. Dario was the guide on the expedition. I want to ask him a few questions."

Doug's dark eyes searched her face. "He won't be able to tell you much. I was on Everest that day too. Pierre fell—it was an accident. Just like Alain. I wouldn't look into it anymore."

"Why not?" Cecily's heart beat faster, the tips of her fingers tingling. "Ben said . . ." She trailed off as Doug began shaking his head.

"Listen, Cecily—I understand Alain's death has hit you hard. But you have so much to learn if you're going to reach the summit and come back safely. I need your focus here. I need you to be one hundred percent with me in the moment. Not worrying about investigating deaths you consider suspicious. The mountain is dangerous enough, without inventing problems." He stalked off.

She felt guilty for making him so grumpy with her. An interview with him would be crucial for her piece. He was the closest person to Charles on the mission. He'd been there for every summit. Every rescue. Every step of the way. If anyone could give her some insight into Charles's mind, it would be Doug. She needed to get him on her side.

Mingma waved her over, and she followed him out of base camp, across the glacial moraine. After an hour's walk, they detoured off the route that would eventually take them to their first camp and stopped at a steep slope of ice and snow. Phemba waved at her from the top, where he and the other climbing Sherpas had clearly been busy for much of the morning, fixing lines to re-create the conditions they would face farther up the mountain.

"We've chosen this wall for training as it's steeper than anything you'll encounter on the route," said Doug, dropping his backpack at the base of the ropes. "It'll be good practice for the whole team. Even for you, Elise—a chance to refresh your skills."

"Looks pretty basic to me," said Zak, leaning back with his hands on his hips to examine the wall. "Nothing compared to what we had to do on Denali."

"So, rope up and show us how it's done. Galden, you watch Grant and Zak. Elise, Cecily, come with me and we'll train walking in crampons and using ice axes."

The temperature was mild, and her hands sweated inside her thick gloves. She pulled them off with her teeth, then tied the fussy straps of the crampons to her boots. It was important to get the perfect snug fit.

Soon Doug's looming shadow crossed her path. She looked up at him and caught the deep frown on his face.

Give me a break, she thought. She examined her crampons but she was quite proud of the job she had done—the flat wide ribbons were secured tightly across the toe and heel of her boots, and they were on the right feet, the ends tucked away neatly, so there was no stupid mistake that she could see. She shrugged and thought maybe she'd imagined his disapproving expression.

"I would never do that on the mountain," he said, as she stood up.

"Do what?" She leaned down, swinging her backpack over her shoulders.

"Leave your gloves tossed to one side like that."

His words were a gut punch. *Of course.* She'd made a huge error. One of the first things James had taught her on Kilimanjaro was *don't leave shit lying around*. If she'd been higher up the mountain, a gust of wind could have sent her gloves flying. And the consequences of that would be fingerless hands for the rest of her life—or, more likely, death.

She swept the gloves off the ground and hugged them to her chest.

That was the thing about mountaineering. It tested every single one of your faculties, in a place that was depriving your brain of oxygen. That's why it was all about putting actions into logical steps, a series of checks, making steps so foolproof that even when you were being a fool, you wouldn't get it wrong.

Be bothered.

Keep your gloves tethered to your body. She tightened the straps attached to her gloves around her wrists. She felt like a toddler, with mitten strings running up through the back of her jacket so she wouldn't lose them. But she needed it to be toddler-proof.

Keep applying sunscreen. She removed her lip salve, slathering it not just on her mouth, but over her nose and the exposed parts of her cheeks too.

Keep drinking water. She took a sip from her Nalgene.

Thank you, Carrie, she whispered.

She followed Doug and Elise off up the side of the hill.

They trained for half an hour, practicing how to walk on the steep ground. They sidestepped up the slope, forcefully digging in the teeth of the crampons and making sure they were secure before taking another step. She took extra-large steps to avoid tripping over her own feet or snagging the teeth of the crampons in the tall gaiters of her boots, a major hazard.

When they reached the midway point, she took a breather, resting almost doubled over, her palms on her knees, trying to catch her breath.

Doug shook his head, but she didn't understand. What was she doing wrong now? Surely it wasn't bad for her to take a small rest?

"Many times on the mountain you'll be forced to stop," he said. "A queue to cross a ladder, say. You might think a break is a good thing. But you have to rest properly. Don't underestimate the stress on your body of wearing all this gear, of the heavy backpack you'll be carrying, of the weight of the boots on your feet. You need to take the stress off your joints. So even if you're standing still, try taking a rest on a straight leg. Lock out your knee. Your bones are stronger than your muscles, so although it might feel strange, it will help. Then relax the weight of your other leg on top, and lean into the slope of the mountain ever so slightly."

It took some practice to get the move down, but once she did, the weight lifted off her legs.

"Next, if you're stopped for any length of time, I want you always to do one thing. Any guesses as to what that is?"

He left a pause.

"Breathe," said Elise.

Doug nodded. "Exactly. Breathe." He took a deep breath in, the type that swelled his chest and his belly, held it behind his lips for a second or two, then released it in a long, deliberate exhale. "Get oxygen to those blood cells. You'll be so busy concentrating on moving that breathing won't be as second nature as you imagine it to be. It will help with everything: staying alert, tired muscles, acclimatization, blood-ox levels. Breathe."

She did as instructed, inhaling fresh mountain air deep into her lungs. He was right; she instantly felt better.

They made their way back to the ropes. Zak was at the top of the cliff already, clipped in next to Phemba. His face was pink with the effort of the climb, but he reached out to give the Sherpa an enthusiastic high five.

Grant was almost finished with his rappel back down the slope, so Elise and Cecily could climb. Elise clipped in, and within moments she was speeding to the top of the wall.

Then it was Cecily's turn.

She tried to control her racing heart. Could they all tell that this was her first time using an ascender device on a mountain? Sure, she'd practiced a bit on a small slope in Brockwell Park, rigging a line between two trees, but she hadn't been wearing her full gear. It had seemed easy then. Looking up at the cliff face now, it seemed anything but.

"Ready, didi?" asked Galden. She nodded, unclipping the ascender from her harness. The device worked by allowing rope to slide through smoothly while moving uphill, whereas little metal teeth would catch the rope if it started moving backward—stopping the climber from falling. That was the theory, anyway. She fumbled with the intricate clips as she tried to align the rope with the inside of the ascender. Finally she got it into place. She prepared to take her first step. Galden stopped her with his hand, and used his other to release one of the lengths of rope from the harness at her side, and clipped it in above the ascender. "Your safety line," he said, nudging her shoulder. She'd forgotten about that. A backup even for her backup. But he didn't berate her. He took a step back and allowed her to take the first tentative step up the mountain.

The ascender was magical. She pushed it up the rope, but not too far. She needed to be able to reach it if she slipped. Then, once the teeth gripped the rope, she could step up with confidence, without worrying about sliding backward. When she felt tired, she could lean back, allowing the teeth to sink deeper into the rope and hold her in place. Even on a steep slope, she could rest.

The fixed lines would lead her all the way up the mountain to the summit.

Water flowed down the cliff next to her boot, gritty gray where the mud had merged with the ice. It carved gullies out of the ice, trickling down. Just a few final steps forward and she was up, over the edge.

"Well done, Cecily," said Phemba at the top of the cliff. He grabbed her arm, helping to unhook the ascender and secure her safety line to the anchor. She punched the air, elated. She'd made it to the top of the first cliff. All the terrifying anticipation melted away, like the glacial waters beneath her boots.

"OK, now it's time to rappel down. Do you feel comfortable doing it?" Phemba asked.

"Could you show me one more time how to attach the belay device properly?"

"Sure," he said.

She detached yet another of the contraptions hanging from her harness—a small piece of orange metal in the shape of a figure eight—and handed it over to Phemba. He bent the rope in half, threading it through the larger "bottom" of the eight, then hooking it back over the top of the smaller circle. That way, the rope would run smoothly around the metal, but catch if she pulled the tail end of the rope around her body. The brake line.

Then he undid it so that she could practice. It took her a few attempts, but finally she managed to get the rope in the right position. She leaned back and felt her weight catch, the rope tightening around the circles of metal. Then, once she felt secure, she took a first few steps backward down the cliff, allowing the rope to slide through her gloved hands. The heat from the friction of the rope was intense—she was grateful for the leather pads that protected her palms. Already it had seared the bright orange color off her device, leaving stark shining silver metal in its place. Her right hand was her brake hand—the farther out she kept it from her body, the faster she went. But the instant she moved it behind her back, she came to a stop. She tried to keep her steps smooth, to remain in control.

But she shut her eyes for a moment, and she was back on the Crib Goch ridge on Snowdon. Stuck.

Crag-fast, they called it. She knew that now. Unable to move up or down, she was paralyzed with fear, staring at a two-hundred-meter drop that would mean certain death. Shivering in her soaked-through sneakers and lightweight poncho.

She heard a woman's voice call down to her. A fellow walker, but one who was much more prepared—with rope and harness, proper boots and wet-weather gear. Her rescuer.

No. She couldn't think of that now. She tried to bring her focus back to the ice wall, to the glacier, to Manaslu.

But it was too late.

Her body hadn't listened back then; now that same fear returned. It slid into her muscles, causing everything to stiffen like lead. She stumbled, her crampon catching in the fabric of her trousers. She heard an awful rip, and in looking down lost her footing completely. She just about held on to the rope as her shoulder slammed into the side of the cliff, getting a mouthful of snow in the process.

Her vision swirled, her fingers trembling as she tried to maintain a grip on the rope. If she let go, she would crash down.

"Cecily!" she heard Galden shout from the ground below.

She didn't look. Instead, when she stopped spinning, she took a deep breath. She dug her crampons into the snow. Only then did she slide the rope through her palm again, and make her way down to the ground.

CHAPTER 15

"OK GUYS, THAT'S ENOUGH for today. Let's pack up," said Doug, once she'd reached the base of the cliff for a third time without incident.

She removed her helmet, sweat gluing strands of her hair to her forehead. She wiped her face with her glove and packed everything away into her backpack. Her shoulder ached in protest as she swung the pack up, but she clenched her jaw and jogged a little to catch up with Elise and Doug, who were making their way back to base camp.

Snow crunched beneath Cecily's boot, and Elise turned around. "You did well today! I know you haven't done much ice climbing."

"Thanks. Yeah, I felt pretty OK by the end . . . just that first slip was a bit dicey. Hang on a sec, Doug?"

He was already striding ahead of them, not even turning around to acknowledge Cecily's call. She frowned.

"He's in a bad mood," Elise said.

Cecily squirmed. "I think I annoyed him yesterday."

The younger woman shrugged. "He has a reputation for being the grumpy grandpa of the mountain. Always aware of every danger. Always alert. And always frowning."

"Have you climbed with him often?"

"Not really. I've been at other base camps while he's been there. Like at Broad Peak a couple of months ago with Summit Extreme; Doug and Charles were there, of course. I was surprised when Charles mentioned to me he was putting a team together for his final mountain. I hadn't planned on climbing another eight-thousander this season, but when he asked I thought, why not?"

Cecily tugged at the end of her braid. "Oh, I didn't realize you had climbed with Summit Extreme. Does that mean you know Dario Travers?"

Elise looked at her sharply. "Why?"

"I was hoping to get an interview with him at some point. His name has come up a fair bit in my research."

Elise paused for a bit, then nodded. "I know him. He was the team leader on Broad Peak. I can introduce you."

"That would be great." Cecily watched Doug's back as he speed-walked away from them. "Seems a bit strange to be so grumpy when you guide clients for a living."

For a moment, Elise was quiet. She removed a small tube of lipstick from her breast pocket, reapplying the bright red color using a small mirror she had pasted onto the back of her phone case. It was one of the things that Cecily had admired most about Elise from Instagram; she didn't see the need to change herself to be taken seriously. She saw no need to diminish herself or play down her femininity to gain respect in this male space. She belonged just as she was, makeup, jewelry and all.

Her accomplishments spoke for themselves. She had more endurance, more power at high altitude, bigger lung capacity than men—athletes—twice her size. She chose not to use supplemental oxygen. That's where the respect came from. That she did it while wearing lipstick and with a perfectly styled braid, well—that just made it Elise.

Elise was at the forefront of changing the preconceived notions about what it meant to be an alpinist. A new wave of young women pushing themselves, and their bodies, to the limit.

Cecily herself was also part of a new wave—an even larger swell—of people who probably had no business in the high mountains. Novice mountaineers, who wanted a taste of rarefied eight-thousand-meter air. Tourists in the death zone, reliant on climbing Sherpas. Or maybe that was harsh. Climbing big mountains was so much more accessible now, with better equipment and the highest safety standards. Why should it only be the domain of elite athletes, if the opportunity existed?

"Guiding is one of the few ways to earn a living in the mountains. And from what I heard, Doug is a very good guide—people skills aside. I don't know why he left Summit Extreme exactly," Elise said. "It was all very . . . hush-hush, but when Charles announced he was going to use Doug's new company for his mission support, I think a lot of people were surprised."

Cecily took a mental note of Elise's curious expression as she said the words "hush-hush." It definitely seemed like there was more to that story. "Because Charles didn't choose an established company?"

"Exactly. But I think it's nice of Charles. By hiring Doug to do all the mission logistics, it's given him a way to work but not worry too much about clients until he is ready. Since his wife left, the mountains are all Doug has."

"He was married?"

"Yeah, and he had a child, I think, though he doesn't see them now. Typical mountain guy—loved being out here more than being at home. But he is one of the best guides out here. I don't judge." As they walked through the boulder field close to base camp, the sun broke through the clouds. Elise stopped to tie a loose lace on her boot. As she leaned forward, the pendant of her necklace fell from beneath the collar of her jacket.

"Wow, that's beautiful," said Cecily.

"This?" She lifted the pendant up so Cecily could see. It looked like a chunky piece of Lucite jewelry, in the shape of an old-fashioned camera. It had a small array of stars decorating the back. "It was a gift from my papa. He had it made specially. The front is a camera, because it's my business, and on the back are stars in the shape of a mountain." She winked at Cecily, then tucked it back inside her jacket. She released her hair from its ponytail, shaking it out. "Speaking of which, will you take a photo of me?" Elise handed Cecily a slim black rectangle.

"Is this one of the TalkForward cameras?" It had the same profile and slick black body that she'd seen Zak with earlier.

"Yes! Zak asked me if I'd try it out for his company. Seems pretty cool!" She scampered up the side of an enormous boulder, as easily as if it had a built-in staircase. She posed on the top of the rock, the cliff they had trained on in the background behind her. Cecily kept her finger on the button, taking multiple photos from multiple angles.

Elise jumped back down again. "Thanks! For my socials, you know?"

"Hope I took one that will work."

"I'm sure you did! I will tag you," she said.

"I'm not brilliant with social media." Cecily smiled. "But I think the following you've built is amazing. It's so great to see a woman kicking ass in the mountaineering world. I'd love to interview you. Maybe when we get back to base camp if you're feeling up for it?"

"Bien sûr!" She clipped the camera to her zipper and they continued down the trail toward their camp.

September 6

Elise Gauthier mixes her drink of choice on the mountain: a blend of malted milk, hot chocolate powder, coffee and several heaped teaspoons of sugar. She takes a photo of the brew, steam rising, sharp against the blurred landscape of the mountaintops behind.

Almost a quarter of a million people check in for these posts from Elise, snippets of high-altitude life, curated by mountaineering's most stylish influencer. Her social media profile attracts big-name sponsors who fund her lengthy expeditions to the remote corners of the world.

But Elise isn't style over substance. Her alpinist profile is seriously impressive—she was the youngest Canadian woman to solo-climb the north face of the Eiger at just seventeen years old, and at twenty-two, she's making a mark as one of the world's top female mountaineers. She's already summited Broad Peak without oxygen, which she managed this summer on her second attempt—and now she's come to Manaslu to claim her second.

With the mountain behind her, legs crossed at the ankle, balancing up on a rock, she looks completely at home. She's released her wavy, near-waist-length hair from its braids, a wide sports band—printed with a geometric neon pattern—holding it back off her face. She has the typical mountaineer's tan, with pale circles around her eyes the perfect imprint of her sunglasses.

CECILY: First question—how did you get into mountaineering?

ELISE: My parents have been taking me to the mountains ever since I was a little girl. My papa was a ski instructor at Saint-Sauveur, a little ski resort in the Laurentians, and I learned to ski before I learned to walk. Then I used to follow him everywhere in Europe, on all the famous routes in the Alps, Mont Blanc, Matterhorn and the Eiger.

CECILY: You were the youngest Canadian woman to climb the north face of the Eiger? What was it like facing that at just seventeen?

ELISE: They say so, for a time perhaps, but honestly . . . being 'first this' or 'youngest that' doesn't matter to me. Still, the Eiger has been my most challenging ascent, and is my favorite mountain of all. So technical and just . . . delicious.

CECILY: And now you're facing Manaslu. What do you think drew you to the Himalayas?

ELISE: I first came to Nepal two years ago with my boyfriend at the time. I climbed Ama Dablam and stood at the top, looking out at Everest, Lhotse and Makalu. I decided I wanted to climb them all without O^2. I know it will take years to accomplish, but in my heart that's my dream.

CECILY: Why take such a big risk—especially to climb without supplementary oxygen?

ELISE: A couple of reasons, I suppose. One is boring—I don't have the money that some climbers have, so I need to attract sponsorships to commit to this goal. Climbing without oxygen gives me something unique. I still had to sell my car, sublet my condo and do a lot of corporate fundraising to get here, but without sponsorship money I'd never be able to climb at this level. Next, everyone has a different standard. There are a lot of politics on the mountain. Who uses oxygen, who uses fixed lines, who opens new routes, et cetera . . . For me, it is all personal choice. I am interested in what my body can achieve. Using oxygen would be like doing the Tour de France on an electric bike, you know? Still, as long as you have integrity, I am one hundred percent behind however a person would like to climb.

CECILY: Does that mean you believe there are mountaineers who don't have integrity?

ELISE: Of course, like with every sport, there are those who cut corners, lie, cheat. Mountaineering has always been—how do you say— *self-regulated*? You take people at their word that they reach the summit, that they don't use O^2, or touch a rope on a risky ascent. With so much pressure, so many eyes on you and new technology to log progress, it is more difficult to cheat now, maybe. But come on. In a place with so many egos as this? It is natural . . . But as long as it's just bragging and they are not claiming something—a first ascent or a world record, then it is not my business.

CECILY: I suppose one reason Charles has brought the team here is so we can all regulate for him—witness his feats and testify to his integrity. Tell me, how did you meet Charles?

ELISE: I think it was two years ago, in Kathmandu. Yes, it must have been. It was after the avalanche in Tajikistan. You heard about that, right? He lost both his teammates on Peak Lenin but he survived, totally uninjured. A wild story. When you go through something like that, you reach a crossroads: either you must quit or you must keep going. For him, the choice was to continue— and maybe also he needed to do something bigger. For the sake of his fallen comrades. The idea for his mission was just forming, but when he shared it with me, it seemed impossible. Which I suppose is the point!

CECILY: Is it the fact that he is not using ropes that makes what he is attempting sound so impossible to you?

ELISE: Yes, exactly. Alpine style is the purest form of mountaineering. No one can criticize you if you climb that way. I don't have the experience or the skills yet. Maybe one day—but I'm not sure I am cut out for such enormous risk. I don't want to be a legend. I just want to be able to spend every day living in the mountains. It is my passion.

CECILY: Still a very worthy ambition! But when it comes to Charles, I'm curious . . . as someone who clearly has such insight into this world, do you have a theory as to what drives him?

ELISE: Bof, well, there is always pressure to do more, to create headlines, to push boundaries in alpinism, you understand? Charles—he is the type who wants to be *known* as the best. He wants the recognition. And he deserves it! He might be the strongest climber I have seen in the mountains. I climbed with Dario on Broad Peak this summer and we saw Charles there, of course. It was a difficult expedition, with many challenges.

CECILY: Yes, I remember you saying something about a Sherpa who died? What was his name?

ELISE: Dorje. Dorje Norbu Sherpa. Yes, what happened to him was very unfortunate . . . Charles, Doug, Dario and a few others did their best to rescue him but he could not be saved. After that, when I heard Charles was setting up a team for Manaslu, I said I would be interested. Later, I got the call from him inviting me. Seemed like the perfect opportunity to climb with him once again, watch him, learn all I can. If I am not learning, I am not improving. And if I am not getting better, then what is the point?

CHAPTER 16

CECILY HAD BEEN EYEING dark clouds rolling up the valley from Samagaun over Elise's shoulder, and, sure enough, the heavens opened above them and they were forced to shelter in the dining tent. Grant and Zak were already inside, both transfixed by their devices. She was annoyed at having to stop the interview, as she'd only been able to squeeze in a few questions about Charles and there was so much more to learn about Elise's mountaineering journey, but the noise of the rain on the tent roof made continuing any conversation a challenge.

Elise had already put her headphones on anyway, setting about darning a tear in the sleeve of her fleece. In light of what Elise said about how difficult it was to finance these expeditions, Cecily understood why. Every penny counted.

Cecily took the opportunity to type up her notes while everything was still fresh in her mind. Something Elise had said niggled at her. About how many big egos there were in the mountains and how it might lead to cheating . . . She rewound the phone recording and listened to it, wishing she had the interview on video. There had been a flash in Elise's hazel eyes, a twitch of her red-painted lips, which had given a different timbre to the words. And yes, when she listened back, she thought she heard a shift in her tone of voice. A slight hardening.

Also, Dario Travers's name had come up again. It reminded her that she had to get to the Summit Extreme camp, not just to talk to Ben about Alain's death. It sounded like Dario would be a good person to interview about Charles. Doug was top of her list, of course, then Mingma and the other Sherpas, Galden, Phemba and Tenzing. Neither Grant nor Zak had climbed with Charles before, so they were lower on her list of priorities.

Grant had all his camera equipment spread out on the dining table, checking his various lenses and charging the batteries, hogging all the sockets.

"How does your gear handle the cold?" Zak asked.

"Honestly, mate, it's a nightmare," Grant replied. "That was by far my biggest issue on Cho. I keep the batteries inside my suit but otherwise you just have to keep backups after backups. But this drone is amazing." He reached under the table and pulled out a black case. He unclipped it to reveal a small spider-like piece of equipment.

When Cecily saw it, she recalled the lake. She might have been the last person to physically see Alain alive, but maybe the drone she'd seen had caught sight of him too? She asked before she could overthink or be interrupted again, the words tumbling out. "That drone—did you fly it the day Alain died?"

Grant leaned back in his chair. "I did a test flight in Samagaun, I think. Can't remember."

Cecily felt a tingling in her fingers. She wasn't going to be fobbed off so easily. "How can you not remember? It was only a few days ago. Did you fly it over the lake? Did you see anything?"

Grant put his hands up in the air. "Whoa, what's with the third degree, Poirot?"

"Still wondering if what happened to Alain wasn't an accident?" asked Zak.

Cecily nodded. "I'm not ruling anything out. Maybe you caught something on video . . ."

Grant arched his eyebrow. "You can check all my footage if you want. I just flew it over the village but it might have caught the edge of the lake."

"I would like to see it, if that's OK," she replied.

He gestured to his laptop. "Knock yourself out."

She moved her chair next to Grant's. He shifted so his leg bumped up against hers, and when he lowered his hand, she felt him graze her lower back. She inched away, under the pretense of adjusting her chair on the uneven ground.

"Let's see . . . Oh no, let's not click on *that* folder, that's got my private videos. You know, only for late-night tent viewing." He smirked, and Cecily rolled her eyes. "Here we go. Footage from two days ago." He double-clicked on the file name and Grant's face appeared, close-up as he adjusted the camera, and then the drone flew up over the village. The shot must have been taken from the terrace of their teahouse; she recognized the painted railing.

Samagaun spread into view, but the drone didn't have the range to reach the lake from there. The filming wasn't always so smooth, with the drone jerking and spinning under Grant's control. He didn't seem to her like the most proficient operator—but then, maybe a lot of work could be done in the editing suite later on.

"May I?" she asked, gesturing to the keyboard.

"By all means," said Grant.

She clicked forward in the footage, but there didn't seem to be any of the lake. She exited the video.

She double-clicked the next one on the list.

The turquoise blue of the lake appeared. "You were there!" she exclaimed.

He tilted back on his chair. "Guess I was."

She couldn't tear her eyes from the video, scanning every frame. The surface of the water was still, no sign of anyone near the lake's edge, but she didn't know if this footage was from before or after her visit. She tried to judge by the angle of the sun in the film, but the video ended abruptly, and no one appeared.

"Satisfied?" Grant asked. "No Alain, nothing suspicious."

She sighed, disappointed. Although one thing irked her—the video on the lake was a lot shorter than all the others on the list. Had he already edited the footage? Why would he have done that?

"Anyway, that guy was nuts," he muttered.

"What do you mean?" Cecily asked. "I didn't realize you knew him . . ."

"I didn't, but I'd heard of him. I follow the mountaineering sub-reddits, and he'd commented this wild conspiracy theory on a post about some guy who died on Everest. I mean, it's Reddit so you expect some crazy people posting. But Alain made out like it was deliberate or something. He seemed unstable. Not surprised he had an accident. Probably out of his mind."

Cecily instantly reached for her phone to google what Grant was talking about, but there was still no internet connection. Frustrated, she scribbled it down in her notepad instead, as a reminder to look it up later.

"Do you remember anything else? How did people react?"

Grant waved his hand, dismissively. "It was all bunk, of course. I'd better get this stuff back to my tent." He gathered up his equipment, sweeping out of the dining area.

She bit her lip. She wasn't any closer to having any answers about Alain. It was all just speculation, wasn't it? She remembered Doug's stern advice to keep her focus on the mountain. Yet Ben had theorized that maybe Alain's questions had led to his demise . . . and Grant had clearly known about Alain before coming to the mountain. Then there was the length of the video. It seemed very much like it had been cut short. She didn't dare think beyond that, but moved her chair back to the opposite side of the table. She needed to keep an eye on Grant.

"Anyone know when the internet is going to work?" Zak lifted his phone as if to catch some imaginary signal.

Doug entered the tent in time to hear the tail end of Zak's question. "Delayed," he replied.

"For how long, do you know?" she asked. Not only did she have a list of things she wanted to look up; she was desperate to send her next blog to Michelle.

"If there's no signal in a few days, we can head to Samagaun," said Doug.

Zak dropped his phone down on the table. "A few days? Hang on, buddy. Charles said there would be internet at base camp. How am I supposed to connect with my engineers? Or my family? I can't be the only one who needs it. What about Elise and her social media? Cecily and her work?"

Doug glowered. "This is the Himalayas, not the Hilton. Elise gets that. If we get Wi-Fi, we're lucky."

The tension broke as Mingma walked into the tent, Grant following behind. Mingma beamed at them all, shaking his radio in their direction. "Good news. The fixing team have already made it to camp three."

"Right. So, if the weather improves, we'll start the rotation in the next couple of days." Doug tapped his phone, pulling up a screenshot of the weather app. "I got this forecast this morning. The rain is continuing today and tomorrow, but after that it looks pretty good. Although"—he gestured to the entrance to the tent—"the best indicator of mountain weather is to stick your head outside and take a look."

He swiped the screen, showing the long-range forecast. "This is a lot less accurate, so take it with a pinch of salt. But, all being well, we're in for a decent spell of weather at the end of next week. If we do a rotation by then and the ropes are fixed to the summit, we might have a window."

Zak put his phone down. "Excellent! That's way faster than predicted. On Denali we had to wait for what felt like weeks for a window. Definitely the worst part of the whole experience."

"We could be on the summit before we know it!" Elise exclaimed.

"What about Charles?" asked Cecily. "Will he be able to get here in time?"

"Don't worry about that. While the rain might delay him in Kathmandu a bit longer than expected, if *we* have a weather window, it means he'll be fine getting a chopper up here."

"Oh good," she said. Doug made her feel ignorant for asking the question, but she couldn't help fretting about the interview. She didn't want all her worry and fear and work to be in vain.

"Also very important, we will have our puja tomorrow," said Mingma.

"What's a puja?" asked Cecily.

"It's a blessing. Two lamas from the monastery in Samaguan will come and ask the mountain for permission to climb and bless some of our equipment to help keep us safe."

"Other people from around base camp will come and join us," said Doug. "There'll be a party," he added.

"All right!" said Grant, and Elise snapped her fingers in the air.

More people coming to the Manners Mountaineering camp? The thought filled her with unexpected dread. Or maybe it wasn't so unexpected. Until she knew for sure Alain's death was an accident, there was a chance someone dangerous was on the mountain.

And now the mountain was coming to their camp.

CHAPTER 17

DOUG LEFT THE TENT, and Cecily saw her opportunity. She slipped out behind him, following him into the comms tent, which also doubled as his sleeping quarters. A copy of Joan Didion with a cracked spine lay next to his neatly packed sleeping bag, along with a leather-wrapped journal. Before he realized she was there, he closed his eyes, rolling his shoulders and releasing a long, slow breath. She was interrupting his moment of peace. She tried to back out without disturbing him, but her thigh bumped against a table, rattling the mound of equipment on top.

Doug wheeled around, his face tightening when he spotted her. Cecily swallowed. He seemed to dislike her for reasons that far exceeded her misstep earlier. Was it because she was a journalist, always asking questions, probing, not letting things drop when she was told? But he knew why she was here. She had a job to do.

"Is this a good time to do a quick interview?" she asked, her throat suddenly dry.

"Your story is on Charles. I don't see why you need to talk to me." He shuffled some of the paperwork on the desk.

She inched forward. "Just a couple of questions? You know Charles better than anyone. You've been with him every step of the way, arranged the expedition logistics . . . and it's gone so smoothly. I know he couldn't complete this mission without you."

He paused for a moment, staring at a piece of paper with a complicated-looking chart on it. "Fine—a couple of questions."

"Great." Cecily pulled out her phone but grimaced as she saw it was out of battery. She'd have to rely on the old-fashioned methods instead. Doug sat down in a camp chair, and—not seeing any alternative—she perched on a nearby table. "How did you and Charles first meet?" She was poised, pen and paper at the ready.

"We met in Scotland. At Glenmore Lodge. He was just a young lad on my winter mountaineering course."

"They say if you can survive a Scottish winter, you can survive anything," she said, tilting her head to the side.

That elicited a small smile. "That's true." He sighed, scratching the graying stubble on his chin.

"How old was he then?" she asked, leaning forward.

"Oh, maybe seven?"

Cecily raised her eyebrows. "His parents allowed him to go off into the Scottish wilderness at seven?"

"It was part of a program I was running at the time. For children with . . . difficult home lives. Even back then, he showed a lot of promise. Quick to pick up the skills, more grit and endurance than anyone else. I've never met anyone so at ease in the mountains—he's more mountain goat than human. And he had that hunger that you rarely see. He came back every year after that. He learned his alpinist history, too. He impressed me. I was going out to Ama Dablam one autumn after he'd turned eighteen, and I invited him along on a Summit Extreme expedition."

"What an experience for him."

"He didn't have much money, so he helped with the expedition in exchange for a heavily discounted fee."

"Is that normal? Seems very generous of you."

He shrugged. "Mountaineering is a sport that thrives on mentorship. It's part of my duty to give back."

Cecily watched his expression as he spoke. He had a tender, faraway look in his eye as he talked about Charles as a boy. He clearly cared a lot for him. It felt like more than mentorship. "Sounds like you were more of a father figure to him."

"Maybe," Doug replied.

"So did you climb together a lot after that?"

Doug shook his head. "He went off on his own, ticking off the big peaks around the world while I guided clients. Learning his craft, becoming more self-sufficient. When he summited Everest, I was so proud. We always kept in touch."

Cecily tapped the end of her pen against the paper. "So tell me, when did he start breaking records and really making a name for himself?"

Doug was quiet. "It was never about that. But something changed for him, after the avalanche."

"The one on Peak Lenin?"

"Yes."

Peak Lenin again. Elise had mentioned it too. Apart from a few translated lines on an Austrian news site, there wasn't much information about it online. All she knew was that the other two climbers on Charles's team had been from Salzburg. "What happened?"

"They were on their summit push and an avalanche triggered under their feet. All three of them were buried, but only Charles managed to dig his way out. He spent all night searching for his teammates. When he made it back to base camp, he barely had a scratch on him. It was a miracle."

Cecily wrote as fast as her pen would let her. The ink didn't flow so easily at altitude and it kept clogging. Eventually, she had to give up. "How come this wasn't a bigger story? It sounds devastating."

"Unfortunately, while every death in the mountains is a tragedy, they are also commonplace. It doesn't create much media attention, especially on the smaller peaks. And Charles wasn't so interested in the global spotlight back then."

"Lucky for me he's a media darling now. Maybe I can bring some attention to what happened on that peak."

Doug's frown deepened, and he gave an almost imperceptible shake of the head. She needed to bring him back into the conversation before she lost the thin thread of connection they'd developed. "So that experience changed Charles?" she pressed.

There was a long pause—Cecily wondered if the moment had

passed. But then he continued, and she could breathe again. "After that, he was no longer satisfied with just climbing. He wanted more recognition. Acclaim. He approached me with his Fourteen Clean idea, and, I'm going to be honest, I laughed."

"You did?" She couldn't imagine Doug laughing at all.

"On paper, it looks absurd. All fourteen eight-thousanders, no oxygen or fixed lines, in under a year? But when I realized he was serious, I got serious too. We started planning. And you've seen him . . . he's checked off every mountain, one by one. Now—here we are."

"That's a pretty succinct way of putting it."

He grunted. Maybe that was a laugh? "Let's just say, it's been the longest and shortest eight months of my life. But Charles has paid back my mentorship now in spades."

Cecily's eyes grazed over all the communications equipment, a tangle of wires. Blocky black battery packs and satellite phones were charging, a radio receiver and several laptops with heavy-duty covers were stacked up on the desk. There was a small generator in the corner, powering it separately from the team's charge points. All this so that Doug could analyze weather forecasts and stay in touch with the outside world. "How does your family feel about all this climbing?"

He paused. "I thought this interview was about Charles."

"Yes, but—"

"I'll talk about Charles, but nothing else."

She nodded. "Well, one common thread seems to be that Charles has done a number of daring rescues on this mission that you've helped coordinate. What goes through your mind when one of those calls comes in?"

"In the mountains, we're all one team. If someone is in trouble, and we have the means to help, I believe it's our duty to try. Anyone on the mountain who doesn't feel the same way isn't a true mountaineer in my books."

"That's very honorable. Is there a particularly memorable rescue?"

"Memorable? Every life we save is memorable."

She winced. "Poor word choice then. Any that stood out to you?"

"You and I have already talked about it, but Everest was sad this year. The sheer amount of people on the mountain. We've never received so many distress calls; one almost every hour during the summit window. Some were fine—others, not so much. Fifteen deaths in one year is too many. That's what you get when you have too many unprepared climbers. I don't think I'll go back. No matter how much money is offered."

"I guess Pierre was one of those deaths." She put the pen to her lips. She was both fascinated and horrified by what Doug was saying. *Fifteen* deaths in one year, on one mountain. It turned her stomach. She wondered if she wouldn't be so affected if she wasn't about to face a similar challenge to Everest—with similar risks—herself.

"Yes, that was particularly unfortunate."

She looked up, intrigued by his tone. "What do you mean?"

"I thought Charles had found him. There was some mix-up in communication. It happens. He came across someone else in distress along the way, and by the time he had sorted that situation, there was no sign of Pierre. He had been the last person on the summit and must have fallen."

"So no one was higher on the mountain than Pierre? No one that could have been following him down?"

Doug shook his head. "No. Everyone else was accounted for."

"What about his climbing Sherpa?"

"He was at camp four with us. You'll have to ask their expedition leader why."

Doug's story was convincing. He'd been there. It seemed most likely that Pierre *had* been hallucinating when he called Alain—a symptom of cerebral edema.

Cecily bit her lip. "How about on Dhaulagiri? That rescue of the two Italian climbers sounded very daring, but sadly Charles couldn't save one of the men. You went up too . . ."

He sighed, rubbing his brow, and she trailed off. When he lowered his hand, his eyes were glazed over.

She'd lost him.

"I've got some planning to do for the puja tomorrow. Do you mind?" His voice was soft, tired.

She nodded.

Her notes were a mess, the ink had dried up halfway through, but she'd got more than she anticipated. Doug's face was tight and drawn. He spent his life escaping people, in some of the most remote and dangerous parts of the world. He was not used to being bombarded with questions.

"That's fine. Thank you for the time you've given me. I'm looking forward to the puja." She flipped over her notebook and jumped off the table.

"Cecily?" Doug piped up as she was about to leave the tent. She turned back. "Preparation is the key to success. What you said before . . . *be bothered.* It's a good thing to remember. Galden spoke to me about your tent."

"I'll sort it out," she said—and then quickly left the comms tent. She didn't want Doug to see the tears that pricked her eyes as she thought about the woman who had passed that mantra on to her. She felt exposed enough as it was.

CHAPTER 18

HER DREAMS THAT NIGHT were hyperrealistic and discomforting.

She was back at the lake, in it—to be precise. Freezing water lapped at her neck. Alain approached the shore and she shouted to him to turn back, but no sound came out. Blood dripped from his temple, creeping down toward the edge of his mouth. He reached out toward her, pursing his lips.

And from those lips came a whistle. That same tune. The discordant combination of notes.

She opened her eyes. She heard it. The whistle wasn't in her dream. It was coming once again from outside her tent.

There was someone there.

She wasn't going to remain paralyzed this time. She had to find out who was behind it. She pulled on her down jacket, unzipped the entrance as quietly as she could, and slipped out into the night.

It took a moment for her eyes to adjust. But then she saw him. Tall, muscular, his face shrouded in darkness.

The whistler.

Grant? His physique was closest.

She frowned. The man stood beyond her tent on the rockfall, staring out at the mountain. His body was a silhouette against the pale light of the moon, his face pointed away from her.

He shifted his weight, looking as if he was about to turn, and she ducked down—she didn't want whoever it was to catch her watching in the middle of the night.

But instead, he dropped—disappearing off the edge of the boulder and into the abyss.

Cecily clamped her hands over her mouth, suppressing the urge to cry out. There weren't any camps that way. No reason for someone to head in that direction. If it was Grant, what was he doing?

She fought down rising panic and a sudden yearning for James—he would know what to do. He'd stride over there and confront the man, find out what he was doing in the dead of night. But James wasn't here. She was on her own.

Knowing was better than cowering with fear, her imagination conjuring up possibilities. She took a deep breath, held it between her lips and scrambled across to the boulder. She released the air in one long stream; she'd made the first move now. Lifting herself up so she could see over the ledge, she spotted a little path along the rocks. The drop down to it was steep, though, and without a headlamp it was tricky to tell just how far the fall would be. Still, if the whistler could do it . . . Without giving herself time to second-guess her decision, she lowered herself down.

Her toes fought for purchase against the rock, and her fingers couldn't take her weight for long. They slipped, but the ground wasn't far. She fumbled along the path, keeping one hand on the boulders in case she lost her footing.

If it was raining, this would be just like . . .

No. Don't think about it.

She breathed a sigh of relief when she rounded a corner and the ledge widened out to a small plateau. She crouched down, hiding behind a rock. Peering around it, she saw the man again.

He had his headlamp on now, his back turned to her. She still couldn't catch a glimpse of his face, but she could see what he was looking at.

A tent. Much smaller than ones used by Manners Mountaineering, and a different color—red, with navy accents, unlike the bright yellow tents they were sleeping in. In the brief flash of light from his headlamp, she spotted some duct tape in the shape of an X holding together some of the plastic outersheet. The outside of the tent was littered with trash.

Crouching made her tired legs twitch, and a small stone skittered down toward the mystery whistler.

The figure looked up sharply. Cecily hid behind the rock, leaning her head back as if she could melt into the shadow. The beam of his headlamp lit up the wall of boulders in front of her.

She waited a few agonizing seconds. But she didn't hear the crunch of rocks underfoot. In fact, the beam dipped, and she heard the tent zipper growl.

A couple of more breaths, then she risked another glance. The man was inside, light from his headlamp filtering through the plastic. She took her chance and ran back along the trail, no longer so cautious of every step. She wanted to be back in her tent, in the Manners Mountaineering camp, where people would come running if they heard her scream.

Who had camped out all on his own? Did he have something to do with Alain's death?

She thought of the boot print outside her tent. Too close to be an accident.

She thought of the whistle. The man wanted her to know he was nearby.

But if that was true, what did he want with her? And why?

CHAPTER 19

SLEEP DIDN'T COME EASILY after her excursion. She took more painkillers, swallowing them down with the lukewarm water from her Nalgene. When she woke up, her stomach was still tied up in knots.

She had to tell Doug. If someone was hiding out near their camp, then their team leader needed to know about it. She walked down to the comms tent. It was early; no one else had stirred yet. But she was certain he'd be awake. "Doug?" she called through the plastic doorway.

After a few moments, he appeared, his eyebrows raised in question.

Cecily swallowed. Seeing his face made her doubt herself, wonder if once again she was blowing things out of proportion. She lifted her head. *Not this time.* "I know this sounds strange, but I think there's someone camped out behind my tent."

"Another team?"

She shook her head. "No . . . a single tent. One man."

Doug crossed his arms, burying his hands underneath his armpits. "Unusual. But some guys climb without support."

Cecily tugged at the end of her braid. She needed to redo it at some point; it had become frayed and loose from tossing and turning on the mattress. "I don't like the idea of some unknown person walking past my tent at night . . . Would you mind coming with me to find out who it is?"

He sighed. "Really?"

She didn't answer. Doug was used to camping in remote areas and probably never worried about who might be lurking nearby. What that might mean for his personal safety. But for her, the unknown was too close for comfort.

To her relief, he stood up. "OK. Let's go."

He followed her to the edge of their camp, up past her tent. In the cold light of day, it seemed irrational to be venturing into the rockfall—the drop looked even more precipitous, and the path that had been visible to her last night now seemed a jumble of boulders. Impassable.

"You're sure there's a tent that way? Doesn't look safe to me." Doug craned his neck over the edge.

"I crossed it last night. I saw the tent." She clambered over the ledge and dropped down. She heard Doug follow her. She picked her way through the maze of rock, hoping to come across the plateau again. Otherwise, she really would look the fool.

"Watch your step," Doug said, grabbing her arm as a stone wobbled beneath her foot. Finally she saw something she recognized: the boulder she had hidden behind.

"It's just beyond here," she said. As she predicted, the plateau appeared next.

But it was empty.

No sign of a tent.

She half slid down the slippery scree that led to the plateau. "It was here last night, I swear. Right here." The rock stared back at her, gray and empty. Unyielding.

Doug sighed. "I have a lot of work to do."

"It was a red tent, with navy blue accents. Or at least, I thought that in the light of his headlamp—they might have been black, or dark green. And it looked well used."

Doug halted in his tracks, almost sliding on the scree. He stared down at the ground, his expression neutral. "Sometimes we can have vivid dreams at altitude."

"It *wasn't* a dream . . ."

"Well, there's no one here now. No one to pass your tent. You're safe in our camp."

She frowned, kicking at one of the stones. Doug coughed. "Cecily, I'm worried. The incident while we were training, the suspicions around Alain's death . . . Zak mentioned to me something about a boot print?"

"You know about that?" she asked.

"He told me, out of concern for you. To climb these big mountains, you have to have a positive attitude. You need to have respect for the mountain and the people around you. We're such a small team, one negative attitude affects everyone. If you can't contain your paranoia . . . it might not be wise for you to continue."

Cecily reeled back like she'd been slapped. "Doug—a man died. Am I not allowed to have concerns about that?"

"My advice to you remains the same. If you're not one hundred percent focused, I won't send you up." He strode back toward their base camp.

She clenched her fists hard, her nails digging into her palms. She scoured the ground for some clue, remembering the trash that had littered the outside of the tent. Something glinted under a rock, at the far end of the plateau. She knelt down.

The cap of a bottle, the jagged edge upturned. She picked it up. It wasn't concrete proof, but Cecily knew what she had seen.

Someone had been there.

CHAPTER 20

WHEN SHE GOT BACK to the Manners Mountaineering camp, it was filled with people she didn't recognize.

Puja day. She tried her best to shake off the events of the night, massaging the tension out of her shoulders. She wanted to be present for this; it had been one of the moments she'd been looking forward to, before Alain's death had thrown her anxiety into overdrive. Plus, she needed to send Michelle more content—in her position, even the token amount she got paid for the expedition reports was vital. The puja would make for a great blog. She needed to concentrate, putting the mysterious tent, and the possibility of someone dangerous on the mountain, to the back of her mind.

You won't be able to investigate if Doug kicks you off the team, she rationalized. She needed to at least appear levelheaded, even if her mind was doing somersaults.

Doug disappeared into the comms tent, avoiding eye contact with all the newcomers. Mingma was greeting everyone instead, smiling as a group wearing matching T-shirts approached, and he gave their head guide an enormous embrace. They smacked each other on the back.

"Good to see you, dai."

"And you." The man had a heavy Russian accent, and looked different from other mountain guides she'd met—stockier, his T-shirt stretching over a little pot belly. He wore a bandanna over his thinning hair, advertising a soft drink brand in Cyrillic letters. He caught her eye over Mingma's shoulder and stepped back to take her in. She wondered what he saw when he looked at her. Someone ready for the mountain?

She grew uncomfortable under his prolonged stare, and decided to introduce herself. "I'm Cecily Wong," she said.

"Andrej—I am the guide for Elbrus Elite." He shook her outstretched hand. "First time in the big mountains?"

"Yes, my first eight-thousand-meter peak."

He nodded, a small smirk on his face.

"Are you bothering this young woman, Andrej?" A woman in her late thirties, maybe, with shoulder-length blonde hair, heavily tanned skin and a curled-lip smile, stepped up beside him, clapping her hand on his shoulder. She leaned in toward Cecily. "Excuse him, he doesn't get to see too many female faces out here."

Andrej muttered something in response Cecily didn't understand. Still, he seemed to take the jibe well enough, his eyes crinkling with good humor. His attention moved to Grant, who had emerged to introduce himself.

"I'm Irina," said the woman, leaning in to give Cecily a kiss on each cheek. "You said your name was Cecily, right? Wonderful to meet you. Is Charles here? We are all dying to meet the British legend of the mountains."

Cecily shook her head. "He's still in Kathmandu, but should be arriving soon," she said. She hoped that was accurate.

"Another time then!" The woman turned next to Grant, her eyes lighting up as she took in the tall rakish Englishman. As a smile crept onto Grant's face, Cecily thought the feeling might be mutual.

"Their group has serious cash," said Zak, his voice low so only she could hear. Cecily hadn't realized he'd come up to stand beside her. "Irina is a former Miss Russia."

"You're joking?"

He shook his head. "Nope. Galden told me. He climbed with her on Makalu and she wants to check off more of the big peaks."

"Wow, that's incredible."

"Even more people are arriving now. This is going to be some party."

Cecily scanned the faces, wondering if one of the newcomers was Dario Travers. She also looked to see if Ben had come, but she couldn't spot him.

She drew herself up tall, preparing to introduce herself to the new group, when a curious sound reached her.

A drumbeat. Low at first, then rising gradually. She turned toward the sound. A pair of monks sat on a small pile of rocks just above their camp. Phemba and Tenzing bustled around them, building a fire on a small pyre. The smoke wafted down toward camp, lightly fragrant.

The puja was starting.

Galden passed them, carrying a bundle of juniper branches. He lightly touched her forearm. "You should take something for the lamas to bless, didi."

"What do you suggest?"

"Most people choose an item that will touch the mountain. Your boots, or trekking poles—something of that nature."

She nodded, and she and Zak detoured to their respective tents. She pondered over her gear, but the item that caught her eye was her ice ax. It would be critical: if she found herself sliding down the mountain and needing to stop, she could dig the ice ax in to self-arrest. It could do with a blessing.

She picked her way up the pile of rocks to the altar. Behind her, Elise was narrating to her camera, ready to stream to her followers. She had her crampons in hand. Together, they laid their items at the foot of the pyre.

Two lamas sat cross-legged on a blown-up air mattress. A few other foam pads had been spread out in a semicircle around them. Cecily chose a position directly behind one of the lamas. Over his shoulder, she could see the long scroll of parchment that he was reading from, the beautiful intricate characters crowding the page. The chanting was hypnotic and relaxing, accompanied by the consistent drumbeat and occasional smash of a cymbal.

She closed her eyes and she was back in her nai nai's living room, staring at a small altar in the corner, the white Buddha always pristine while the rest of the bookshelves gathered dust. The little gold bowls on either side held offerings for the Buddha. She'd once been caught stealing one of the sugared fruits. She'd received a slap on the wrist for that.

She hadn't thought of that shrine in a long time. She'd never found a place for religion in her adult life. But now, in the shadow of the highest mountains in the world, she felt her heart lift and her mind open.

The lamas sent up their prayers, and the clouds cut open to reveal Manaslu's jagged eastern pinnacle, framed by the intense blue sky. As incense and juniper fumes from the small ceremonial fire reached her nostrils, she felt transported up to the summit itself. This was what they were praying to. Not to God, but to the mountain, asking permission to climb her, to crawl on her shoulder just for a few weeks, a mere blip on her life span.

While Manaslu looked serene, the shark's-fin peak was a reminder of the danger. She thought of Alain, how he wouldn't be making this journey. She hoped he was at rest.

Fear, anxiety and eventually a kind of calm acceptance swept through her. It made her think of why she was here—why she was *really* here. When Charles invited her to join his team, she agreed because she was buoyed by his belief—his utmost confidence—that on his team she could do it, but she also wanted to overcome the trauma of Snowdon. Then, when James had dumped her, she wanted to show him what she was capable of. But every step she took toward the summit—from the days spent training on Box Hill, to the flight to Kathmandu, from the hike up to base camp, to the time spent on the training wall—she was shedding her spite.

The puja swept the last of it away.

She was grateful to give it up, an offering to the mountain.

Stand on your own, Ceci. Her nai nai's advice. Cecily knew she should take it. And that meant shedding the props that had held her up.

Every step she would take now would be for her and her alone. To show *herself* she wasn't a failure. That everything she had been through was going to be in service of the moment she made the summit and clawed her own way out of the deep pit of doubt she was in.

At a signal from Doug, she crept forward and took her ax from against the altar, where it lay next to Elise's crampons, Zak's boots and Grant's camera. Hopefully the lamas' blessing would be another level of protection on the mountain.

She would take everything she could get.

Before long, Galden and Phemba raised a pole above the pyre. It was covered in long strands of prayer flags, the bright strips of blue for the sky, white for the air, red for fire, green for water and yellow for the earth. The wind picked up the flags, adding fluttering to the heady mix of chants.

Then the atmosphere changed from peaceful to exultant, and the Sherpas grabbed small pots of tsampa flour that had been sitting in front of the altar. They smeared the flour on each other's foreheads, and then, one by one, they went around the climbers.

"What's this for?" Cecily asked Galden, as he dabbed streaks of flour on her cheeks.

"A wish that you will live until your beard turns gray!" he said, with a laugh.

"Better sprinkle some on my hair too then," she said, bowing her head, and Galden obliged.

One of the lamas tied a bright yellow string around her wrist—a sungdi, or thread of protection. Mingma passed her a bowl of rice, and she took a handful to toss in the air. The atmosphere was joyous, the excitement of the impending climb palpable. Soon shots of whiskey were passed around. Cecily worried for a split second about imbibing at altitude, but then tipped the fiery liquor back before she could overthink. She was here to write about the experience of being on a mountain expedition. So she needed to live it.

The party moved from the puja back down to the campsite. More booze was brought out of the cook tents and Phemba produced a large portable speaker from his tent, setting it up in the middle of a circle of chairs. Nepali music blasted out across the moraine, and Phemba was the first one to start dancing. Elise joined him, and together they clapped and moved. Cecily and the others formed a circle around them, drinking and swaying to the beat.

Galden took her hand and dragged her into the center, teaching her and Elise some dance moves that went with the songs—tales of unrequited love, hit theme songs from Nepali movies. It reminded her of Bollywood music, the same catchy rhythms and expressive choreography. Even Tenzing, the oldest Sherpa, got up to dance, shaking his hands to the sky. Some western music was mixed in too, anything with a catchy beat. Whiskey flowed through her veins, eased through her bloodstream by the altitude. Her limbs loosened, her smile widened. She already felt like she'd risen to a transcendent plane during the puja itself, and now this was a different sort of release.

From Dawa's kitchen, platters of food streamed out: momos, little fried sausages, cubes of dried meats and cheeses, packets of chips, bars of chocolate—all the high-carb, high-fat delicious fuel that they would need for the weeks ahead.

Zak danced with her, putting on goofy dad moves that she filmed for the benefit of his family. She threw her hands up and let the music take her, swaying and jiving, the smile on her face impossible to wipe away.

"Someone's found a friend," Zak said. He gestured with his head to Grant. Cecily moved so she could dance and watch him at the same time. Grant had his arm around Irina. He didn't waste any time.

Zak leaned in. "Looks like he might prefer to share his tent with someone else other than me . . ."

She laughed.

She hadn't expected the expedition to have such moments of *fun*. She expected it at the end, a celebration of a mission accomplished, but this was a different kind of energy. Everyone here knew they were about to embark on a dangerous adventure. Something potentially fatal. They needed to release all that pent-up anxiety and fear.

Then she caught Doug's eye. He was staring at her. Yet just as quickly his gaze passed on. Had she imagined it? Or maybe the drink was casting a hazy glow over her judgment. But she wasn't having it this time. If this was supposed to be bonding time, well, she was going to bond with the most important member of the team: their leader.

"Come on, Doug, aren't you having another drink?" Cecily asked, sidling up next to him.

He shook his head. "I don't think so. I've had more than enough. We are planning on climbing tomorrow." He surveyed the crowd— the dancing hadn't died down. "Maybe the day after tomorrow."

"That puja . . . it was so moving. What an experience. I think I would have benefited from one of these before my other climbs."

"I've sat through so many of them now; I forget what it's like to have your first one. How do you feel?"

"I feel . . . ready."

"Good."

"Sure I can't entice you to a dance?"

"No." Something caught his eye over her shoulder. "Shit, what's he doing here?"

She hadn't heard Doug swear before. She followed his gaze, and Doug stalked off in the opposite direction. Now she was intrigued. The man in question was wearing a Summit Extreme–branded down jacket, with a wicked scar on his cheek. Elise must know him—she was greeting him with a familiar double kiss on each cheek.

Cecily walked over, emboldened by the drink. "Who's this?" she asked.

"I was just about to come and find you," said Elise. "This is Dario. Didn't you want to talk to him?"

"Yes! I know you," said Cecily, before she could stop herself.

"Oh? I had no idea I was so famous," he replied.

Elise put her hand on Cecily's arm. "This is Cecily Wong. She is on Charles's team as well. She is a super-successful journalist, writing for one of the top adventure magazines, is that right?"

Cecily shifted on her feet. "Well, I write for *Wild Outdoors*."

Dario lifted his sporty sunglasses, revealing pale green eyes. "A journalist! Interesting. Like our Ben was."

"Where is he, anyway?" Cecily asked, once again scanning the crowd.

Dario took a swig of his beer. "He is no longer a member of our team."

"What?"

"That is what happens when you cannot pay your expedition fees."

"Oh, that's such a shame," she said, stroking the back of her neck. She had never been Ben's biggest fan, despite his closeness to James, but she knew he would be absolutely gutted to leave the mountain. She could relate to his money woes—she was teetering on a knife's edge herself. But part of her was relieved, too. At least she didn't have to be worried about her story being scooped anymore. Or word about her progress getting back to her ex. She cleared her throat. "But listen, Dario, I'd love to talk with you if you have some time?"

"Right now?"

"Why not?"

He didn't need to reply. Doug interrupted them, his fists clenched. "What are you doing here?" he asked Dario.

"Krass! There is no need for such hostility, Doug. I came to pay my respects to the great Charles McVeigh." He held up his hands as he spoke, not sounding altogether sincere.

"He's not here."

"So I can see. Why is that? Hiding from me after Broad Peak?"

"Leave it alone, Dario." Doug's voice had a dangerous edge.

The skin around Dario's eyes tightened. "Not using the fixed lines is such a joke. We know that he used our ropes."

Cecily wondered if she misheard. Dario thought Charles had cheated on Broad Peak? She stared from one man to the other, wanting to ask for clarity but her mouth had gone dry. Dario was tall, rail-thin and sinewy, his hands on his hips. But Doug—shorter, graying and wizened—stood his ground. Elise shifted from foot to foot beside her. Cecily tried to catch her eye, but the younger woman's gaze was fixed on Dario.

"Do you have proof?" Doug asked. He didn't seem surprised by Dario's question. It made her think this wasn't the first time it had come up. Now Doug's hostility made more sense.

Dario did not reply.

Doug folded his arms across his chest. "Your accusations are out of line, baseless and malicious. You're not welcome in my camp. Leave."

"Oh, come on . . ."

Doug gestured for Mingma to escort Dario away from the party.

"I'm going, I'm going," Dario said.

She watched Dario walk away, and finally found her voice. "What was that all about?" she asked Elise, but the other woman had gone.

Cecily downed her drink for extra courage, then crept away from the festivities, following the path toward Summit Extreme.

CHAPTER 21

THE SUMMIT EXTREME CAMP was eerily quiet, especially compared to the party she'd left behind. Far more tents were set up here than at their team's camp, each one spaced with military-style precision.

The igloos were even more luxurious than she had imagined. As she passed one, she stuck her head inside—shocked by actual sofas, a projector, an espresso machine. Doug had joked to Grant that base camp wasn't the Hilton. Well, this was pretty fucking close.

"Want to switch teams?"

She jumped as Dario spoke close behind her. "Oh my god, you shouldn't scare people at altitude."

"Maybe you shouldn't be sneaking around other people's camps?"

Dario was even more striking away from other people. A raised scar, pink at the edges, cut across his cheek, speaking to a life lived on the edge.

"I actually came here to find you," she said.

"I'm flattered. What can I do for you?"

"I was hoping that we could talk a bit more. I have a few questions, if you don't mind."

"Persistent, aren't you?" He paused, his eyes searching her face. Then he gestured for her to step into the igloo. He sat down cross-legged on the sofa, Cecily choosing one of the camping chairs opposite. She felt in her jacket pocket, glad she'd remembered to stash a small notebook and pen inside. "What do you want to know?" he asked, lacing his fingers around his knee.

"Well, first of all, what did you mean when you spoke to Doug about Charles using the fixed lines on Broad Peak?"

"Diving right in there, OK. Well . . . you understand what 'Fourteen Clean' is all about, right?" he said, making air quotes.

"I do."

"Right. His claim is very specific. Alpine style means not using any of the fixed lines on the mountain. I don't believe him. I think he's using the ropes."

"Why do you think that?"

"One of my team saw him."

"So you didn't see him."

"I was too busy looking after that team."

Cecily kept her expression neutral, wanting to hear Dario's version of events in full. But it felt flimsy to her. And she wondered if Dario would be so brazen with his accusations if Charles were on the mountain to defend himself. "OK . . . did that teammate take a photograph? A video?"

"If I had the evidence in my hands, you would know about it," he said, testily.

Cecily chewed on the end of her pen. "So if you didn't see it, and your client didn't have any proof, why do you believe it so strongly?"

"Did I say it was a client? I said it was one of my team. Someone I trust very much."

"So can I talk to them?"

Dario shook his head. "All I will say is—they were not the first to say such a thing. Someone said the same thing on Everest."

"How come I've never heard any of these allegations before? I feel like I've read every article about Charles on the internet and no one has even hinted at that possibility. What you're saying is very serious."

Dario threw his hands up in the air. "Because look at him! The media is going crazy for him. He's handsome, charismatic, charming, clearly a very, very talented alpinist . . . No one wants to cast doubt on the hero. But I believe in the integrity of our sport, so I am not letting it go."

"Can I speak to the person who saw him on Everest?"

Dario sighed. "That man can't offer proof either. He died, coming down from the summit."

"Hang on—you're not talking about Pierre Charroin?" Cecily blinked. "He believed Charles was using fixed ropes?"

"How do you know about him?"

"I spoke to the man who died in Samagaun, Alain. He told me he'd come to Manaslu to honor Pierre, who had been one of his close friends. He also wanted to ask you what really happened on Everest, face-to-face."

Dario sighed. "Scheiss. It has been a difficult season. Lots of deaths. Too many, in my opinion. I am sorry for what happened to Alain and to Pierre. In the latter case, I wish we could have done more to save him."

"Alain told me that he received a call from Pierre right before he fell. He had said it felt like someone was behind him. Stalking him."

"Impossible. No one was on the mountain behind him."

"Doug said the same thing."

"On this, Doug and I agree."

She nodded. "So you don't think Pierre's death was suspicious."

"No. Unfortunate, sad, but not suspicious."

"That does bring me to my next question. Have there been any updates on the investigation into Alain's death?"

"Investigation? There was no investigation. He fell and fractured his head on a rock."

"Oh. But Ben . . ."

"Ben is a liar. He wasted our time and resources coming here, without adequate funds. I would not trust him."

She sensed Dario closing down, so she steered their conversation in another direction. "Have you been mountaineering for a long time?"

"After my time served in the military, I knew I wanted to spend my life in the mountains. Lots of great peaks in Austria."

"And what about Summit Extreme? When did you start guiding for them?"

Dario let out a long stream of breath. "*Oof*. It's got to be fifteen years now?"

"It's quite the outfit. Don't you think companies like yours have contributed to the popularity of mountaineering? Not just the publicity around Charles and other famous alpinists?"

Dario tilted his head to one side. "You are probably right. But still, we take everyone's safety very seriously." He stood up. "You should be at your puja. Celebrating. Charles really will not be happy if he finds out you have been talking to me. Nor Doug. You do not want to get on the wrong side of him—but I am sure you know that already. He cannot keep that famous temper of his under wraps for long."

"That was the last thing I wanted to ask you about. You must have worked with Doug closely. What do you think of him? Do you know why he left Summit Extreme?" she asked, her fingers tingling.

"All I will say is that Doug is one of the most cautious individuals I have ever met. To a fault, maybe. As for why he left Summit Extreme, I will allow Doug to tell you himself."

She knew the conversation was over. She tucked the notepad back in her pocket. Dario's green eyes appraised her as she stood. She jutted out her chin ever so slightly.

He smiled. "I think Charles chose wrong when he invited you to write this article. He might have more than he bargained for."

"What do you mean?" Cecily asked. Her breath hitched in her throat. She wasn't sure if he was paying her a compliment or not.

Infuriatingly, Dario shrugged. He pointed her back in the direction of the Manners Mountaineering base camp. Not that she needed the help. The sound of the party—still ongoing—echoed all the way to her.

As she picked her way carefully back across the stony path, she thought about what Dario had said.

Why *had* Charles chosen her to write the article? Was it really because he'd liked her work? Or was it because he thought she wouldn't be savvy enough to ask the right questions? That she would be so overwhelmed with the experience of climbing the mountain that she wouldn't probe into the controversies, the allegations?

To be fair, she hadn't even known there were any controversies until she got here. All the research she'd done, all the previous press about him had been almost universally positive. The golden boy of the mountains.

Maybe he wasn't so golden after all.

CHAMPION OR CHEAT? FOLLOWING MISSION: FOURTEEN CLEAN—THE STORY OF CHARLES MCVEIGH

By Cecily Wong

It takes nearly five kilometers of rope to fix lines on an eight-thousand-meter peak. Five hundred ice picks. Two hundred ice screws. And a team of climbing Sherpas—icefall doctors—to expertly plot the route, avoiding crevasses and navigating seracs, breaking the trail through waist-deep snow. For the vast majority of mountaineers, whether using oxygen or not, these ropes are a literal lifeline.

What sets a climber like Charles McVeigh apart is his decision to climb alpine style. Not using the fixed lines on the way to the summit.

Not even for a moment.

If he touches a rope, he might save his own life. But he won't accomplish his mission.

Mountaineering is a sport with no regulating body. Even the Himalayan Database, the most comprehensive compilation of eight-thousand-meter summits, states that they are a "trust-based" service. There is big money on the line, in terms of sponsorship, media attention and even calls from Hollywood. The stakes are higher than ever. And with high stakes come doubters and skepticism.

I ask Charles if he feels the eyes trained on his back:

[Insert Charles's response to the rumors.]

CHAPTER 22

BEFORE BREAKFAST THE FOLLOWING morning, Cecily sat, curled up in her sleeping bag, reading back the new introduction she'd written. She'd searched for Doug at the puja to no avail. He wasn't in the comms tent either. She'd lingered for a while, observing the ongoing festivities, before collapsing in her tent. It had been a long day, her mind as exhausted as her body.

Dario's words had disturbed her. She'd never considered that Charles might have cheated on his mission. His reputation was pristine. He was such a strong, talented mountaineer; there was no question about his *ability* to climb alpine style. But if he thought no one was watching, and a rope was there . . . would he use it?

Wouldn't anyone, if their life depended on it? Surely that would be the only reason.

Integrity warring with safety. If *Wild Outdoors* wanted an attention-grabbing story, that might just be it. Better, even, than one about his record-setting attempt.

When she left her tent, the camp was quiet—in stark contrast to the night before—but her teammates were up and about. Zak was wandering around at the edge of the camp with his phone held high in the air, trying to catch a signal. Grant was doing push-ups outside his tent. Shocking that he had so much energy at this altitude, but as she rounded the corner she understood why—Irina was sipping coffee in a camp chair in front of his tent.

She must have spent the night there after all.

Doug and Mingma exited the comms tent, Doug balancing a laptop on his forearm. He spotted Grant working out, and his brows
knitted together. Mingma whispered something to him, and Doug
gave a sharp nod, before disappearing into the kitchen tent.

"Grant, dai—please, you need to rest," Mingma said.

"Just trying to keep strong. I want to be ready for when we head
up." Grant continued to press as he replied.

"I don't think it's a request," said Irina, before standing up to
stretch. "I should head back to my camp. Nice to meet you all."

"Finished," Grant said, leaping to his feet, his cheeks red with
exertion. "See you on the mountain, Irina?"

"Undoubtedly," she replied. As she made her way out of the Manners Mountaineering camp, Galden passed her coming in.

"Who was looking for Wi-Fi?" The young Sherpa stood at the
edge of camp, his hands on his hips.

"Me!" said Zak. But the reality was, they *all* wanted access to the
internet. Grant clapped his hands together, and Elise popped her
head out of her tent. Galden should have known it would be all of
them. They were meerkats on alert for connection.

"Follow me."

Cecily raced back to her tent to grab her laptop, and thoughts
of breakfast disappeared as Galden led them through the Summit
Extreme camp to a small outcrop of rocks, a triangular antenna built
on a stone plinth at its highest point. Already a few people were
milling around, some seated on foldaway camping chairs, their faces
intent on their screens.

"We call this Wi-Fi mountain," said Galden, with a chuckle.

The Manners Mountaineering team scrambled up, and Galden
relayed the password to log in. Cecily typed as quickly as she could,
sighing with relief when her phone connected, and a stream of messages began to download.

She opened up her laptop browser and typed PIERRE CHAR-
ROIN into the search bar. She was desperate to find the Reddit
posts Grant had talked about. Between Alain being more vocal than
she'd realized about his conspiracy theories, and now learning Pierre

might have started a rumor about Charles cheating, it was all too coincidental.

A link popped up to a post in a mountaineering subreddit titled "MAN DISAPPEARS ON EVEREST." She clicked. No wonder it hadn't come up in her research; it didn't mention Charles anywhere. Instead, it was text copied and pasted from a news story detailing Pierre's disappearance. The main article didn't mention any possibility that it was anything other than a tragic accident, and it was presumed he'd fallen off the mountain and died.

Then she saw what Grant was talking about. A comment, massively down-voted, that appeared to be from Alain, under the username AFlaubertChamx. He wrote a long post about the strange phone call he had received from Pierre. He was much less circumspect in writing than he had been to her on the terrace. He wrote outright that he thought Pierre had been killed by someone on the mountain, his body pushed off the edge so it wouldn't be discovered.

The thread was hundreds of replies long, some commenters dismissing Pierre's words as hallucinations from hypoxia. Others pointed to the numerous statements taken from other Everest climbers. There was a consensus: Pierre had been last on the summit. No one could have been behind him, stalking him. She found it fascinating that even the conspiracy-loving users of Reddit believed his death to be an accident. But it matched what Dario and Doug had told her.

It meant Alain hadn't been killed for asking the wrong sort of questions—because there was no mystery. Alain wouldn't have found any other answers. His death was unfortunate, unnecessary, unthinkable—but not a murder. She'd allowed herself to be distracted by Ben's theory, by the mystery whistler, by the accident. It was unsettling, but Doug was right. She needed to focus.

Email notifications popped up at the top of her screen as she scrolled. One from Michelle caught her eye, and her heart leaped into her throat.

CALL ME it read in huge bold letters—marked as urgent.

She had no idea if the signal could handle a phone call, but she put in her earbuds and dialed. In a couple of rings, Michelle picked up.

"Hello from base camp!" Cecily said, trying to keep her tone bright.

"CECILY! Thank god. Where have you been? I haven't had an email from you for ages."

"I'm sorry, Mich. We got to base camp, had a training day, then a puja—and no signal at all until now."

"I hope you have a blog ready to go? We're desperate to update people over here. Especially since someone died already? Did you know him?"

"Yes, I did. I talk about it in my blog. But wait, how did you know?"

"I take it you haven't seen James's story?"

Cecily's heart sank. "No . . ."

Exasperation laced Michelle's voice. "He's got a source on the mountain."

Cecily sighed. "Oh my god. It must have been Ben."

"Ben Danforth? He's there? So he's the one feeding James material for *Nat Geo*. They not only had updates from your expedition, but James published a pretty damning exposé on your guide, Doug Manners. Something about how your team are his first clients since he was spectacularly *fired* from his last guiding job?"

As Michelle talked, she desperately searched for James's article, her fingers flying across the screen of her phone. "I know, I just heard about the story last night and I was going to ask some more questions . . ."

"A bit late now, isn't it? What are you doing up there? James is in London and he's been able to uncover a bigger story than you—and you are the one on the bloody mountain! Come on, Cecily—you have to do better. Do you have anything else for me?"

"You don't have to worry about Ben. He's been kicked off his team for not paying his fees."

"Well, that's something. But it sounds to me like you might be missing the stories happening right under your nose."

She thought back to her new introduction. She didn't want to give too much away, not before Charles arrived and she'd given him a chance to respond. But she could tease . . . "I do have something.

A new angle on Charles, but it needs more work. And I'm sending you a blog right now, plus I'm doing a series of interviews with my teammates . . ."

"You'd better—"

The signal died.

Zak roared with frustration. "Damn! I wasn't finished. I was trying to take a meeting with my company. I didn't even get to video-call my kids."

Cecily was annoyed too. She wouldn't be able to send the blog as she had promised, and James's article had only half loaded. All she could read was the headline and subheading:

BAD MANNERS
By James Clifford

Doug Manners, 54, founder of Manners Mountaineering, was once one of the most sought-after guides for Summit Extreme—until his explosive temper led to a canceled expedition and major lawsuit.

Rule number one of guiding: don't punch a client . . .

James never was one to bury the lede. Shit. Cecily wasn't quite getting to the story fast enough. Dario had mentioned something about Doug's famous temper, but she hadn't got around to looking into it between Alain's death and the allegations against Charles . . .

"I will see you back at camp, guys," said Elise. She slipped her phone back into her pocket and ducked into one of the nearby Summit Extreme tents, presumably visiting other friends on the mountain.

"Well, I'm not going anywhere. I'm going to wait right here for the internet to come back." Zak paced around the antenna, staring up at it, as if he could will the signal back into existence. "This is so weird. Even my sat devices aren't connecting. That's not normal. I got a note through to my team. I'll see if they can sort it out on their end, but Jesus."

"You two really need to learn how to relax," said Grant, leaning back in his chair, stretching his long arms over his head. "Look where we are! Take it all in."

Cecily eyed them both. "Maybe you can help me . . . While we wait, do you mind if I ask you a few questions for my piece?" she asked.

"Sure, I'll do it," said Zak.

"Only if you make me look good," said Grant.

EXCERPT FROM CECILY'S NOTES: INTERVIEW WITH GRANT MILES-PETERSON AND ZACHARY MITCHELL

September 8

MEN WANTED: for hazardous journey, bad wages, freezing cold . . . constant danger. [Note to self: google exact wording before sending.]

While it's unlikely that Ernest Shackleton really placed this advertisement in the *Times* for his voyage to Antarctica, it's true that it takes a certain type of person to take up the challenge of an expedition. For a month, you're thrown together with virtual strangers, often in the most isolated places in the world, facing dangerous terrain and unpredictable weather. You have to be able to work as a team, but ultimately only you are responsible for getting yourself off the mountain. Collaborative yet capable.

Each one of us on the Fourteen Clean Manaslu expedition was personally invited by Charles to join him on this final phase of his mission. We have all come together to support him in our own way—through sponsorship, social media, film or journalism.

My interview with teammates Zachary Mitchell, 42, and Grant Miles-Peterson, 29, is taking place at a rival base camp, on a perch known as "Wi-Fi mountain"—the only place where there seems to be internet access. It's intermittent at best, with the same strong winds and rain that are preventing the helicopters from flying and delaying Charles's arrival also affecting the signal.

CECILY: Thank you both for talking to me. I'd love to know more about how you came to be on this expedition?

ZAK: TalkForward is Fourteen Clean's key sponsor, and as the CEO I wanted a front-row seat to the action. It all comes back to our mission matching up with Charles's objectives: *technology without limits*. Charles's ambition is limitless too.

GRANT: Zak's the money, and I'm the camera. I saw Charlie boy on Everest, but I was only filming clients at base camp. Then I actually got to climb Cho, while I was documenting some Saudi bloke's summit attempt. Obviously, Charles was there too, and I was keen to meet him. Tons of filmmakers I know have pitched to him, because everyone is going to want the movie of his mission. I'm hoping to sell it to Netflix personally, but loads of networks will be gagging for it. The competition is intense. Probably like for your article, right, Cecily?

CECILY: Well, it is the story of a lifetime.

GRANT: I would have done literally anything to get this gig. On Cho, I just happened to be at the right place at the right time to convince him.

CECILY: You must be quite experienced behind the camera. How did you get started?

GRANT: I got my start on YouTube, shooting stunts and pranks, that kind of thing. But I've left all that juvenile stuff behind now. Now I've filmed all over the planet, wherever I can make my mark.

CECILY: And what about you, Zak, how did you meet Charles?

ZAK: I went to a fundraising event in San Francisco, thinking it was going to be so boring. Probably my most hated part of the job, you know? It's so damn hard to find the right project that will fit with TalkForward's mission statement and ethos. People throw pitches at us left, right and center—most of them wildly off base. Waste of their time and ours.

But this guy got up onstage—dominated the stage, really. I've never seen anyone hold an audience like that. He flashed a photo of K2 in his presentation and started talking about what he intended to do with Fourteen Clean. It sounded completely impossible. And I thought, shit—this is the guy. If anyone on the planet is going to wear the TalkForward logo, I want it to be him. He so totally epitomized the limitless mindset that TalkForward is all about. The battles I had with my insurance guys after that . . . You have no idea. But I got it through.

CECILY: Charles does know how to make an impression.

ZAK: I guess it's because I'd already had this dream of doing the Seven Summits, and Charles showing up at this event . . . it was like destiny. I immediately knew I wanted to climb with him. Learn from the best. Like my business and personal goals aligning. The dream. For me, it's worth all the risks. This is mountaineering history in the making. Without Charles—

Just then there was a crash of thunder, a rumbling in the earth. Zak shot out of his chair, knocking it over. "What the heck was that?"

Galden stood on the edge of the rocky ledge, watching the mountain.

"Incredible, isn't it?" he said.

"Is it an earthquake?" Cecily asked. She was perched on the edge of her stool, ready to run.

"No need to worry—just an avalanche," said the Sherpa.

There was another sound, like a gunshot. Zak yelled as he spotted snow and ice tumbling off a nearby cliff.

"Shit, where's my camera?" Grant scoured the ground around him before snatching his DSLR up off the rocks. He stood next to Galden, muttering about how he should have changed his lens, filming the plume of powdery snow that swelled and grew as it cut through a gap in the rock.

They stood shoulder to shoulder, watching as the avalanche gradually subsided. Cecily was the last to turn away, transfixed by the scene.

"That was amazing!" she said to Galden, when it was clear they were safe from the avalanche debris. "Say, do you think I could interview you as well for my piece?" she asked. "I'd love to know more about why you climb mountains, and how you know Charles."

He nodded. "Yes, of course. But I think we should head back to camp now. It looks like bad weather is coming in." He pointed at dark clouds on the horizon, over Samagaun.

She checked the signal again in a last vain effort. Nothing. Michelle would have to wait. She knew that no matter what James wrote for *Nat Geo*, the interview with Charles was the prize. And to get it, she needed to concentrate.

"Holy crap!" Zak cried out, as another chunk of ice cleaved from the glacier, echoes of its crack resounding in the valley. After the puja yesterday, it felt like a warning, like maybe the mountain had rejected their plea.

Galden read her mind. "Don't worry. Avalanches are good. We want the unstable ground to fall."

"Why is that?"

"Because tomorrow, we will be walking on it."

CHAPTER 23

THE WI-FI SIGNAL NEVER returned, and the satellites were down too, so she couldn't send her work to Michelle. She added that to her list of things to worry about, along with the identity of the creepy whistler, how to dig into the cheating allegations, and the case of Doug's unpredictable temperament . . .

That and the mountain itself, of course.

At dinner, Mingma had announced they were going to start their acclimatization routine. So when she woke up the next morning, Cecily packed her sixty-liter backpack ready for the journey up to camp one.

Lots of teams were making similar moves. Cecily watched as climbers moved single file past their camp and began to climb the rocks above, framed by the mountains behind. Small waterfalls breached from the cliffs and tumbled over the rock.

"Cecily, I saved you one of the best food packets." She turned at the sound of her name, and Zak chucked a bag of freeze-dried food her way. "I tried every one I could find before I came out here and the only one worth eating is the spaghetti bolognese."

With some trepidation, she opened her already very full pack and stuffed the spaghetti into the top. She staggered as she attempted to lift it.

"Here, let me help." Galden took the weight of the bag, then removed her bulky, heavy sleeping bag from where it was clipped on the outside.

"No, Galden—I can carry it," she protested.

He shook his head. "Don't worry, didi. I have it."

Galden knelt on the compression sack until it squished down as small as it could go. The addition of her sleeping bag meant his backpack became comically large, straining at the straps. When he swung it onto his back, it increased his height by half again. Mingma threw a plastic sheet over the top to protect Galden's pack from the rain.

"Thank you," she said, her hand over her heart. Galden replied with an impish smile.

"Must be nice to be a woman," grumbled Grant from behind her. His pack was enormous too—but mostly because he had packed it strangely. It bulged in the center, throwing him off-balance. Maybe it was all his extra camera equipment. She'd already seen him tuck his orange hard drive into his jacket.

Zak stood out in his shiny jacket, fitted and made to order, the kind of expensive gear she could only dream of.

Even without the sleeping bag, the weight of the backpack pulled at her neck. Still, there was no time to complain. Doug took the lead, his hands buried in his pockets, heading past the puja site and on toward the mountain itself.

Drizzly rain fell, and Cecily pulled the hood of her jacket over her hair. They took extra care as they crossed rock slabs slick with running water, the small streams flowing toward Birendra Taal.

After an hour and a half of walking and scrambling across large boulders, tricky in eight-thousand-meter boots, they came across another group sitting on the ground, tearing into their snacks. Bright blue barrels with waterproof seals were dotted around the rock, and, just beyond, a vast field of snow was steadily rising toward the icefall. They had reached the glacier.

"OK, this is crampon point. Take a break," said Doug. "Eat something and get your crampons on. The rest of the journey is on snow."

When he was in full guiding mode, Doug was the model of a cool, calm, efficient leader—no sign of rage simmering under the surface. She knew she should ask him about Dario's allegations, as the closest person to Charles on the mission. Yet if he was as volatile as James and Dario had suggested, not only did she feel it was a risk to anger him, but he might not be honest about Charles either. Maybe he was indebted to Charles, if he'd been spectacularly fired and starting his own company was his only option . . . Elise had alluded to that too, on the way back from the training wall.

She slumped down onto the nearest boulder, grateful to slide the backpack straps off her aching shoulders and give her racing mind a chance to rest.

"Sweet?" A woman in sleek sporty sunglasses and bleached-blonde hair tied back with a scrunchie held out a bag of sour candy toward her.

"Oh, Irina!" Cecily smiled and took one gratefully. "Are you recovered from the puja?"

"That was a fun party." Irina was fierce looking, her suntanned skin tight across the bones of her face. Although she was on the Russian team, her voice had a tinge of London accent.

"Do you live in England?" Cecily asked.

"Yes, central London. I work in fashion now. Boring, actually, but it pays to get me out to the Himalayas!" She laughed. "You hear about above camp one? Big queues to get up the crux; apparently it's very tough this year. It'll be fine. It'll be fine," she repeated, like she was trying to convince herself. Cecily was about to ask for more details but the rest of the Elbrus Elite team were moving, so Irina heaved herself up. "You can have the rest of these."

"No, thank you . . . ," Cecily replied, but Irina had already dropped the bag into her hands and walked off—but not before blowing a kiss at Grant.

Cecily tucked the sweets into the side pocket of her backpack and finished tying on her crampons. Doug called for their attention. "All set, team? Let's keep going."

They set off across a serene snowy plain; the slope gentle to start off with. This was it. Her first few steps on Manaslu proper. She was excited, invigorated by the brief rest and snack. She paid close attention to every moment, listening to the snow crunching underfoot and breathing in the crisp mountain air.

"Up there is camp one," said Galden, as he passed her. She followed the line of his arm and finger, but couldn't quite make out what he was pointing at. Was there a tinge of orange and yellow on top of that rise? Were those the tents? If camp one was in sight, that meant it couldn't be too far. She clung onto that thought. She could do this.

Only a few steps onto the snow and she encountered her first proper fixed line, a bright blue snake against the white snow.

"Everyone, clip in," said Doug. "It might seem like easy walking and a tedious task to clip in and out every few steps. But there are deep crevasses across this glacier, and it's good practice. The habits we embed now will become second nature."

They nodded, but after a couple of anchor points, Grant huffed with irritation. It did seem a little pointless, since the path was flat, clear and well trodden.

Still, Cecily didn't take any chances. Two carabiners hung off her harness, with arm-length strips of cord attaching them in a knot to her belay loop. Both needed to be clipped in, so that when she reached an anchor point and needed to change to the next length of rope, she was always attached by at least one point—preferably two. The rule on the mountain: never be detached from the line.

For the next few hours, the route was monotonous. Walk a few steps, approach an anchor, clip in the new safety line, unclip the old one, keep walking. She had to make sure the screws on her carabiners were locked each time, but even in thin gloves, it took some fumbling to get it right. She tried to get into a rhythm, but the movement was so unnatural. Every time she messed up, a queue of climbers would form behind her. A few times they asked to overtake her, and she had to grind her teeth, swallow her frustration and allow them to clip around her, glad that her buff was pulled up to her cheekbones to hide her embarrassment.

They walked for so long that she fell into a kind of stupor, and camp one didn't seem to be getting any closer. They crossed the glacier in a zigzag, rising slowly. Her steps were to the beat of the carabiner click. Walk, bend, clip, unclip, walk. Grant had given up clipping in completely.

Doug stood, arms folded, waiting for them to catch up. He stared, unblinking, at Grant. "What did I say about using the lines?" The tone of his voice made Cecily shiver.

"Oh, come on, mate. We're walking on packed snow here. It was like this on Cho and it was fine."

"Is that what you think?"

Doug kicked his foot down in front of him. The sound was hollow. The ground beneath his boot collapsed. He grabbed his line and took a deliberate step backward.

A deep, yawning crevasse gaped at his feet.

If Grant had carried on walking, his leg would have disappeared straight down it. Maybe this one wasn't wide enough to have swallowed him whole. But the next one might be.

"Fuck," Grant muttered, before fumbling at his harness for his safety line and clipping onto the rope.

"Snow bridges," said Doug. "One of the most terrifying dangers on the mountain. You can't anticipate them. Clip in."

Cecily gulped. Doug took an extra-large step over the crevasse. Grant followed, then Elise, Zak and finally her.

As she glanced down, all she could see was darkness. She took a deep breath and leaped. The ground on the other side was solid, and she pumped her fist at her side in quiet celebration.

The crevasses became more commonplace after that. Most could be stepped over, though the fixed lines weaved around to avoid them as much as possible, which was why the route was so circuitous. Then they came to their first ladder.

Anticipation mixed with dread. There was always that epic shot in any Everest documentary or movie—of people making their way across a yawning crevasse, on a flimsy ladder that seemed barely supported on either end by thin shelves of ice that could collapse at any moment. And if you fell off the ladder? You'd be dangling in midair—your entire body reliant on whether the fixed lines were anchored securely enough into the ice to catch you.

It was a huge, dramatic risk. One of those moments you would talk about when you got home . . . if you managed to survive.

"Come forward, Cecily," Doug said, before the others. Galden was already across. He knelt down, holding the far end of the ladder steady. Mingma took her hand to guide her for those first tentative steps. Why had she had been called up first? Maybe Doug wanted to make sure she could get across and to show the others that if she could do it, then they could too.

She clipped onto the lines and held the thin cord in her gloved hands. She tried to "catch" the rungs of the ladder between the front and end points of her crampons. She took it one step at a time, slowly lifting her foot and placing it carefully. But every time her crampons caught on the rungs of the ladder, making it shake, her heart caught too, sticking in her throat.

At one point, her crampon lodged between the rungs. She glanced down at her boot, but instead of seeing that and the ladder, she ended up staring deep inside the crevasse. It was a wound in the snow, a slash of deep blue in the endless white. It disappeared into the earth, the bottom not visible.

There would be no way out.

CHAPTER 24

THE MANNERS MOUNTAINEERING FLAGS fluttered in the wind. Camp one. The emotion of finally arriving almost brought her to her knees. She was exhausted, tears staining her cheeks. For the last hour of walking, her mind had been in overdrive, wondering how much longer she could keep taking steps before her legs would simply stop working.

She stumbled into the largest tent, which stank of gas but was warm from the fire.

Doug stood inside, his back to her, his head bent over his phone. She decided she should give him a chance to explain what had happened with his last expedition, but Mingma popped his head into the tent. "Ah, Cecily—you've arrived. Shall I show you where you'll be sleeping?"

She glanced sidelong at Doug. He'd moved even farther into the tent, discussing something with Phemba. She wrinkled her nose, frustrated that her moment to speak to him had been thwarted. Still, she nodded to Mingma. "Yes, please. Lead the way."

She followed Mingma back out into the snow. It was about four p.m., meaning it had taken her a good six hours to hike to camp one. Clouds hung tightly to the campsite, obscuring any view. She waved at Irina, who was sipping tea outside her tent with the rest of her Elbrus Elite teammates, only a few meters from where the Manners Mountaineering tents were clustered. Just beyond, the Summit Extreme flag was planted. She craned her neck, scanning for Dario, but he wasn't around.

"Your tent is over here. Elise has already been unpacking but there should be plenty of room."

"Thank you, Mingma."

She ducked into the tent.

Her first night on the mountain proper. After a full belly of fried rice, more tea and the promise of an early wake-up call, Cecily was so exhausted that not even worries about the mystery whistler could keep her from sleeping.

She woke congested and groggy, every muscle throbbing. She ground her teeth, forcing down painkillers in a bid to dull the ache throughout her body. She absolutely did not feel in the right shape to face the crux of the mountain: the formidable ice wall that she had read and heard so much about.

She glanced at Elise, who was preparing for the next stage of the climb with a cheerfulness that seemed almost unnatural. The influencer—her lipstick expertly applied even at almost six thousand meters—packed up her belongings twice as fast as Cecily did. It was an obvious difference between them. Elise had plenty of experience. Cecily had none.

By the time she got outside, Zak was also ready to go, his harness, boots and crampons on. He was sharing a tent with Grant, and wasn't happy about it.

"That guy spreads his shit out everywhere," Zak muttered as he passed her. "Never known someone to take up so much room. I barely got any sleep."

She grimaced. "Poor you. Sleeping on the mountain is hard enough already."

"Don't even get me started on his snoring . . ."

He stalked off toward the toilet area, shaking his head. There were some deep grumblings from within the tent, and Cecily skittered away.

Galden filled her Nalgene bottles with hot water, and she dropped some energy tablets inside, listening as they fizzed up. She slipped them into their insulated covers and tucked them inside her backpack. She double-checked the laces of her crampons, the fit of her harness, making sure it was comfortable and there were no twists in the leg loops. Everything had to be perfect today, for the crux.

"Can you see up there? That's our route."

She followed Galden's arm and saw some Summit Extreme climbers setting off for camp two.

Doug trudged past her on the way to Grant and Zak's tent. "You ready? Get going," he said.

Cecily raised an eyebrow at Galden. "What's with him?"

"He hates lateness and Grant hasn't moved in a while."

"Whoa!" Zak had returned, staring wide-eyed over Cecily's shoulder. "Do you need a hand with that, man?"

Tenzing was lifting an enormous ladder onto his back. He balanced it horizontally and half stooped over with the effort.

"Oh my god, what are you doing with that?" she asked.

"One of the ladders farther up is broken—crushed by a serac fall. So I am taking another." He paused for a moment, checking the stability of the rope bindings around his arms. Then he started walking—as smoothly as if he was wearing a normal backpack.

She'd never thought about how the ladders got up the mountain. She watched him in awe. Although he wasn't part of the main "fixing team," all the climbing Sherpas did their part to maintain the route, and so much of what they did was taken for granted. It hadn't even occurred to her that someone had to carry those ladders to install them. But now she was watching a man with a ladder on his back, six thousand meters above sea level, lifting it across crevasses and up steep cliffs. She couldn't complain about her backpack now.

Straightaway, it was a very different climb from the day before. It was much steeper, for one. She needed to put all her training into action, starting with hooking her ascender onto the fixed lines.

It was gritty, focused work that required brain power along with physical strength. But she preferred it, because there wasn't room to ruminate over her worries or think too much about how far she had left to go.

"What the heck is that?" said Zak from behind her. They had been keeping pace with each other all morning. She turned around, and he gestured ahead of them with his ice ax.

She'd been staring at the ground—and the rope—for so long that she hadn't noticed what was going on up ahead. A large group, maybe fifteen people, were all waiting on the fixed line. Queuing. And the reason? A sheer wall of ice, stretching high above their heads.

The crux.

She'd read online that it was nicknamed the "Hourglass," and now—standing at the bottom—she could see why. The wall narrowed where the two lines hung down—one for climbing up, the other for rappelling down. It was intimidatingly steep—far more challenging than what she had practiced on.

She swallowed, shuffling forward until she caught up with Galden at the back of the queue.

"What's taking so long?" Zak asked.

"Only one person can be on the wall at a time," he replied. "And some teams are coming down the route, on that second line. There is barely enough space to pass, so it takes a long time."

"Jesus, we can't be waiting here for hours on end. Is this what it's going to be like all the way up the mountain?" Zak asked.

"No idea," Galden said, with a shrug.

"Now I can see what those people on Everest were moaning about. This is as bad as Bay Area gridlock."

"Or the lineups at Tesco on Christmas Eve." Cecily laughed.

"Don't just stand there and moan," said Doug. He'd come up behind them without Cecily realizing. "Think about what else you could be doing in this moment. What are you missing? What do you need?" As if to demonstrate, he swung his thermos out from the side of his pack and took a swig.

He was right, of course. This was the perfect opportunity not just to rest, but to breathe, to hydrate, to refuel. He just didn't have to be so grumpy about it.

Every few minutes or so, they moved closer toward the wall. It was tough watching people struggling to climb, and so she sat on her backpack, reserving as much energy as possible.

Only when she was next in line did she crane her neck to watch. The wall showed signs of heavy use—crude steps cut into the cliff from the force of hundreds of crampon stabs.

To reach the base of the wall, she needed to cross one more crevasse. The remains of a broken ladder hung halfway down into its depths, Tenzing's new one laid afresh. A reminder that the ice was ever shifting, flowing like a river. The path laid out today might well be gone and buried tomorrow.

Once the line went slack and she heard a shout that the person before her had reached the next anchor point, she hooked her ascender onto the line and took a few tentative steps toward the wall.

"Cecily, move!" Doug shouted. She barely had time to react, taking a large leap to the side, crashing into the snow, her knees banging against a hard block of ice.

A gust of wind zipped past the back of her head. There was another shout, and she turned to look. A bright orange blur hit the ground and then disappeared—straight into the crevasse.

CHAPTER 25

DOWN IN THE ICE, a man lay faceup, flailing his arms and legs.

He'd rappelled straight into the fissure in the ice, saved purely by the fact that his backpack was so wide that it had caught on either side of the crevasse walls.

Galden and Doug moved like machines. Doug lifted the coil of rope from around his body and unwound a length. He threw it down to the man, who clipped it onto his harness with shaking fingers. They tried to lift him out of the crevasse, but his backpack was jammed. It had saved him, but now it threatened him. He was going to have to ditch the pack.

What made it harder was that this guy didn't speak English. He was from a Chinese team—Cecily spotted the badge on the breast of his coat—and no one nearby spoke any Mandarin. She only knew enough to ask him haltingly if he was OK. Beyond that, she was lost.

That small effort seemed to mean a lot to the man, though, who took a proper breath for the first time since his accident. Doug caught her eye, nodding at her approvingly. Cecily couldn't enjoy it until the man was safe.

He released his arms from the backpack loops. He tried to reach down to grab the straps, to save his equipment. But the pack shifted, sliding beyond his grasp, and was gone—disappeared into the depths.

That would be the end of that man's climb. He hung his head as Mingma gave him something to drink to abate the shock. But at least he had his life.

"Your turn now, Cecily," Doug shouted across to her. "Let's get up this thing."

Adrenaline pounded through her veins. But now she needed to put it to good use. She needed to tackle this wall. She craned her neck. It loomed even higher now.

She jammed the ascender as high as she could above her head and began to climb. With each step, she stabbed the points of the crampons into the ice until they felt secure. But even with the ascender holding her and her crampons digging in, it was much harder than she had anticipated. The ascender wasn't designed to withstand her full weight up a vertical wall, and the teeth kept skidding back down the rope.

Snow and chunks of ice rained on her, debris dislodged by the climber above.

She reached a small ledge in the wall and paused for a breather.

"Keep moving!" Doug shouted. *Easy for him to say.*

Some of the steps were taller than they had appeared from below. She managed to get her foot up to the next one, her knee huddled close to her chest. But pulling the rest of her body up to that height felt impossible. She heaved, clutching at the rope, but her foot slipped.

The teeth of the ascender bit into the rope and caught her as she fell, but she lost control, spinning on the line, scrabbling for purchase back on the wall. Her breath caught in her throat, but once she was secure again, she moved each limb in turn; she wasn't hurt.

The only thing she'd damaged had been her dignity.

She didn't dare register the people staring at her, judgment written across their faces. Her ice ax was strapped to her backpack, useless. She couldn't use it as an extra hold on the wall. All she had were her hands, her ascender and her crampons. She closed her eyes and took a deep breath. She was so close to the wall that her nose touched the snow, ice tickling the back of her throat.

"Fuck!" she muttered.

She was in almost the exact same position she'd found herself in on Snowdon. Crag-fast. Standing on a tiny ledge, no way up or down. She blinked, and she was back on the ridge on Crib Goch.

My name is Carrie Halloran. What's your name?

The voice of her rescuer, clear as day. Carrie had seemed so cool and confident, inspiring calm in Cecily when she'd been mired in panic. She remembered small details about the woman's face: the dash of freckles across her nose, the flecks of gold in her hazel eyes, the strands of dark red hair peeking out from beneath her waterproof hoodie. She'd focused on all those things to calm her racing heart.

Ce . . . Cecily.

Don't worry, Cecily. Did you come with anyone?

My boyfriend, but he's probably at the top by now. I'm sorry. I can't move. The tears had streamed down her face. Whenever she'd tried to move an arm, a leg, to try to find her own way off the ridge without having to be hoisted off by helicopter, her muscles shook. She couldn't control it.

I understand. I'm going to call someone to help. You don't have to move or talk. It's OK. You can just listen to me.

There's no signal! I tried already.

I'll send an emergency text. I'll wait with you.

The woman had dug a spare waterproof jacket from her backpack, passing it down to Cecily. She'd gratefully shrugged it on over her lightweight supermarket poncho. As they'd waited, the woman had talked, regaling her of stories of life in North Wales—jogging along the vast beaches on Anglesey, bivouacking overnight on Snowdon to start a challenge known as the Welsh 3,000s, dodging unruly sheep as the trail ran across the countryside. She said she'd come out to Snowdonia every week to climb the various ridgelines and challenge herself on the terrain, in all weather.

How can you do this all the time? Cecily'd asked, through chattering teeth.

What, climb mountains?

Cecily'd nodded.

The mountains are in my blood. But to be honest, I love the challenge. This environment will throw everything it has at you, testing all your faculties. Over the years, I've learned how to not just survive in this environment, but actually thrive. It makes me feel powerful.

How do you do that? she'd asked.

By staying aware and managing my risk. My dad would always say the same thing to me: "be bothered." So that's my mantra out here. Be bothered. Be bothered to check my equipment. To store my lipsalve in the same pocket every time so I know exactly where it is. To retie my laces the moment I notice they're loose. So often fatigue—mental and physical—will stop you from caring, and small issues quickly turn into life-threatening ones in the mountains. The moment you stop caring is the moment you've lost your ability to climb.

Her words had taken Cecily's mind off their horrific situation, the rain drenching through the jacket and the wind battering her back.

Now here she was on another tiny ledge, with people waiting above and below—and no one to encourage her. Ice chips fell into the neck of her jacket, and she shivered.

She tried to focus on the next level she had to reach.

She had to do it this time. *Do it for Carrie*, she told herself.

She took her heavy mitts in her teeth and pulled. They dangled from her sleeve, attached to her wrists with a piece of cord. Underneath were the thin merino wool gloves she wore for extra warmth. She removed those too, stuffing them in her pocket. She needed the dexterity and maneuverability of her bare fingers. It was the only way she was going to get up.

In one hand, she took the ascender, wincing at how cold the metal was beneath her palm. She pushed it up once again as high as it could go. With the other, she gripped a tiny hold in the ice with her fingers. She lifted her foot up one more time, digging her crampons deep into the step. Her muscles trembled, her lungs burning with the effort. One shot. That was all she was going to get. She had to make this count.

She wanted to be able to say that she had reached the summit of the mountain.

She wanted the exclusive interview with Charles.

She wasn't going to fail before even reaching camp two.

Make or break.

All of this drove her as she pulled her body up the wall, gripping with all her might, praying her crampons would hold. Her foot began to slip again but she continued to push the ascender up, willing it higher, willing the teeth to catch. Her nails clawed at the ice, and she prayed the hold wouldn't break off in her hand.

It was just enough. She managed to get her other knee up beside her foot before it slipped, and from there she was able to scramble to her feet. She stood for a moment on the ledge, panting. She'd done it.

After a tiny breather to celebrate, the pressure of other people waiting at the bottom kept her moving, even though her legs were trembling.

She tackled a few more steps, then finally she made it to the very top of the wall.

She'd passed the crux.

CHAPTER 26

SHE WAS GREETED AT the top by a huddle of other climbers as exhausted as she was. Irina was there, lounging on a patch of snow, munching on a granola bar. Irina caught her eye and held up her hand for a high five. Cecily was so tired, the action made her collapse down onto her knees, and then onto her behind.

Irina helped guide her down safely. After a couple of breaths, Cecily had the energy to swing off her pack and dig out some snacks of her own.

"That was a tough crux," said Irina, once Cecily looked well enough to handle some conversation. "Tougher than on other mountains. Well done."

"Oh, good to know. I thought I was making a complete idiot of myself."

Irina guffawed. "No, no. It is very difficult. The Sherpas have a name for it . . . they call it the 'Hanging Place.'"

Cecily shuddered. "I heard it was called the Hourglass?"

"That too." Irina nodded. "Whatever you call it, I just dread the thought of having to do it all over again in a few days. I'm not sure that I can. That's the problem with needing to acclimatize, isn't it? Constantly going up and down the same route. Knowing how hard it's going to be."

Cecily opened her eyes wide. She hadn't thought about it that way. Every time she came up the mountain, she would have to get up that wall.

"I might only do one rotation," said Irina. "Our plan is to go up to camp three tomorrow. What about yours?"

"The same."

"You have some people climbing without O²?"

"Other than Charles? Just one—Elise."

"Remarkable. I could never do it. But it is good to see a woman pushing the boundaries."

"Honestly, sharing a tent with her is like being on a mountaineering master class. And I can't wait for Charles to get here, to see him climb without the ropes."

To her surprise, Irina wrinkled her nose.

Cecily frowned. "You don't think what Charles is doing is impressive?"

"Ah, no—of course it is impressive. But there are so many big male egos here. Oh sure, it was fine to climb these mountains with ropes and climbing Sherpa support and oxygen when it was just men. But now women are starting to get a foot in, suddenly it's not good enough and you have to go 'alpine style' to be a real climber. Fuck them. We deserve to be here just as much as they do."

Cecily blinked. "I like your perspective," she replied, with a small smile. She clinked her water bottle against Irina's before taking a long draft.

As she tilted her head back, she caught sight of a huge serac hanging over the route. A chill spread in the base of her spine, the sight making her uneasy. It was undeniably beautiful, a vast sculpture of ice. It looked like a dancing bear, standing on two legs, one arm outstretched toward the sky. Just behind the bear, there was another that brought to mind the crooked tip of a witch's hat. Like imagining shapes in the clouds, only with blocks of ice that could fall with little warning.

She suddenly grew impatient to move, but no one else from her team—except Tenzing, who'd been in front of her—had yet climbed over the wall. Maybe that was for the best. She didn't want to be last to arrive at camp again.

"I think I'm going to keep going," she said to Irina. "Still have a long way to camp, and I'm as slow as a turtle. Can you let them know I went on ahead?"

"Of course. Slowly does it, that's the way. Don't let anyone get in your head, making you feel like you don't belong here."

Cecily acknowledged the advice with a nod, then started walking. She settled into a steady rhythm, and although she came across a few more steep walls that required the ascender, they didn't compare to the Hanging Place. She couldn't think of it as anything else.

Camp two arrived much more quickly than camp one, after only four hours on her feet. She picked up her pace as she approached the small cluster of yellow tents; now she had the rest of the afternoon to rest.

She was the first client to arrive. She helped Tenzing prepare lunch, shoveling fresh, clean snow into a large bag to boil for tea and cooking, glad to be useful.

She was also glad to have time to appreciate the view. It seemed to spread for miles. They'd climbed above the clouds, candy-white car-pets obscuring the ground below. The tops of mountain ranges rose in the far distance, and she couldn't believe that soon she would be standing higher than them all. The magnitude of what she'd over-come so far made her giddy. No wonder people like James, Ben and Charles were addicted to these challenges. She felt . . . unstoppable.

The different teams were more spread out at camp two than at camp one. The Manners Mountaineering tents were set up on a long, narrow ledge, barely the width of two tents, and the Russians were the only other team nearby.

The next person to arrive was Irina. Cecily rushed over to greet her, but Irina barely seemed to have enough energy to return Cecily's "hello." The woman shuffled toward an Elbrus Elite–branded tent and collapsed inside.

Cecily lingered, worried about how exhausted Irina looked. "Can I get you some tea?" Cecily asked, through the plastic.

She heard a grunt, but wasn't sure whether to interpret that as yes or no. She brought a steaming metal cup over anyway, hoping she was OK. When Andrej arrived and went to check on her, Cecily relaxed.

Elise was the next to come around the corner to the camp, easily recognizable in her brightly colored activewear. Mingma was a short distance behind her.

"I have some hot water ready if you want tea," Cecily said.

Elise beamed. "Thank you, chérie! I'll have you as a mountain buddy anytime."

Coming from her, the compliment was massive. She and Elise lounged outside Tenzing's tent, sipping tea and eating chocolate. The bright blue of the sky opened wide over their heads, and they basked in the warm sunshine, laughing and chatting. While she pushed her body to its limits, fears about the whistler were pushed back down to base camp. They were so high, so remote, so cut off from the world, that it felt like nothing could reach them.

Zak came next, then Doug and the rest of the Sherpa team, with Grant bringing up the rear. Doug had a look of absolute thunder on his face. Cecily sat up a bit taller, wondering what had gone on.

Doug strode toward Mingma. Under the pretense of getting up to find the bathroom spot, she crept closer so that she could listen.

"The absolute fucking nerve of that guy. I thought Galden was going to push him off the mountain. He wanted him to carry his backpack. On top of his own. It was outrageous."

Mingma inhaled sharply. Normally the most calm and measured person on the mountain, he was shocked. "He asked that?"

"He can fuck off. There's no way I'd allow that. I told him, 'If you can't carry your own backpack up the mountain, then you have no business being here.'"

She still didn't know who they were talking about. Doug was justified in being furious, however. She thought of how hard she had been on herself, how much she had judged herself for flailing about on the Hanging Place. But at least she'd never asked Galden to carry her backpack for her.

"Grant's down to his last chance. First the oxygen thing, now this. I didn't want him here anyway, but fucking Charles . . ."

"Cecily? Which tent is ours?" Elise's voice rang out. Doug and Mingma stopped talking once they realized how close she was. She scurried back to her tent, her heart in her throat. She was surprised that he would act that way, given how much noise he made about being strong. But then, he'd acted like he'd owned the mountain since he got here—she wasn't surprised he'd treat the climbing Sherpas that way.

Galden brought over her dinner: a rehydrated food packet. She had to agree with Zak—he was right about the freeze-dried spaghetti bolognese. It was palatable. She took each bite slowly—her stomach was so fragile at this altitude; it was hard to keep anything down.

The way Elise ate was reassuring, though. She inhaled her dehydrated meal, but she also loaded up on junk—chips, chocolate, gummy sweets. "We need all our energy for camp three," Elise said, as she offered Cecily a handful of salted peanuts.

They snacked together, while carrying on with their personal admin. Cecily tried to capture the details of the day for her blog on her notepad. Elise was on her smartphone, working on some of the images that she had taken. She was a whiz, her fingers flying faster than Cecily could keep up, cropping, highlighting, adjusting the image saturation and contrast—making the pictures social media–ready so she could post them as soon as she had a signal.

The look of concentration on Elise's face was intense, her tongue poking gently out of the side of her mouth. Some people might mock influencers, but the amount of work she put in to make her platform successful was impressive.

As darkness settled, Cecily nestled inside her sleeping bag, ready for sleep. Was everyone experiencing the same thing in the various tents dotted around the mountain? Were they all struggling to eat? Were they all feeling exhausted? Did they all have the same stuffed nose, the persistent throb of a headache? Elise sniffled beside her.

That's when she realized—those concerns, just the simple act of sleeping, eating and breathing, dominated her thoughts. She wasn't worrying about a mystery whistler, or someone dangerous on the mountain. She wasn't worried about her career, the enormous pile of debt waiting for her, the fact she hadn't got a home to return to.

Survival had taken over.

Maybe that's why Charles wanted her to experience the climb herself.

She thought of the Hanging Place again. How, if she'd slipped without her ascender, she could have been seriously injured. She couldn't imagine climbing without any safety ropes at all, and she'd only reached camp two. It put Charles's decision to climb without ropes into perspective.

But only if Charles is being honest about not using the ropes, she reminded herself.

Her eyes opened to darkness. Her digital watch face glowed: two a.m.

She stared up at the plastic roof of the tent, watching her breath stream out in front of her. She pulled the lip of her sleeping bag up to her nose. It was freezing.

Elise's breathing was calm and even beside her; she was asleep. But something had woken Cecily. A whistle. *The* whistle.

Fear pooled deep in her belly.

She shivered, her body tense and alert, her heart racing. She dreaded hearing the sound, the sequence of discordant notes. But there was only silence.

Now that she was up, though, she needed to use the bathroom. *That* she couldn't ignore. With great reluctance, she wriggled out of the heavy down bag, trying but failing to get her jacket on at the same time. The cold wrapped around her body first, making her gasp.

Elise groaned, but didn't wake.

Cecily pulled on her boots and slipped out into the dark. She fumbled with the button on her headlamp, cursing at the lack of dexterity in her cold, sleep-numbed fingers.

Then she heard the voices.

"Go *away*," said a female voice.

"You didn't seem to mind the other night. Come on . . ." A man.

"We were drunk. And I like you—but not here."

"No one has to know."

Cecily crouched down, moving toward the voices. One of them had a flashlight in their hands, although their fingers were filtering out most of the light. It was enough to tell who was talking. Irina was the female voice. And the man?

Grant. She was sure, this time.

"Don't you get it? We're on the mountain. I need to concentrate. Leave me alone or I'll scream—and then everyone will know what a fucking pig you are. Pig. Pig. *Oink, oink, oink.*" She threw back her head and laughed.

Grant backed away. If he turned now, he would see Cecily. She did not want to be in the path of that man when he'd just been brutally rejected. Irina was still cackling into the darkness; she wasn't calming down. "You've gone mental," she heard Grant say. In the intermittent flashlight, Cecily had to agree. Irina looked possessed. But then, if Grant was trying to force his way into *her* tent, Cecily would act out too.

When all was quiet, she snuck off to the bathroom and then returned to the comfort of her tent. She thought she heard a sharp crack and another cackle, but she put it to the back of her mind.

Irina could take care of herself.

CHAPTER 27

ELISE WAS PACKED UP and ready to go by the time Cecily's alarm went off.

"Are we going up to camp three?" Cecily asked, bleary-eyed after the middle-of-the-night disturbance.

She shook her head. "I just heard from Mingma. Bad weather is coming. There's a risk we'll be stuck on the mountain—without oxygen and little food, we'd be in trouble."

"I'm glad we're going back then," Cecily replied.

"I just hope I am acclimatized enough." Elise bit at the edge of her nail, and Cecily realized this was the first time she'd seen Elise properly nervous. But it was understandable, since Elise was planning her climb without oxygen—acclimatization took on extra importance.

"Doug will make sure you're ready." Cecily reached over and squeezed her hand.

When they got outside, Cecily was surprised to see other teams moving up the mountain. One climber waved back at them—it was Andrej. Irina must have been one of the bundled-up people following, but Cecily couldn't pick her out of the line.

"What about them?" Cecily asked Elise.

"Ah, each team has to make their own decision. I trust Doug and Mingma. They shared the forecast with me. I agree; I think going down is for the best. Sadly."

Cecily stood outside the tent, watching the Russians ascend until they disappeared into the upper icefall.

"You two can make a start if you'd like," said Doug from behind them. But they were distracted by an angry growl.

Grant burst from his tent, glowering, his fists curled at his sides. He had terrible sunburn across his nose and cheeks, and his eyes were bruised from lack of sleep. Hardly surprising.

"Everything OK, Grant?" asked Elise, her hands on her hips.

He snarled in reply, ignoring her and storming over to Doug. He was clutching his bright orange hard drive, which now had a giant crack in the center. "Look at what happened!" he shouted.

Elise ducked down to look in his tent. "Ben là, looks like a bomb went off in there," she said to Cecily, arching an eyebrow.

Cecily peered inside. Grant's sleeping bag was bursting from its compression sack, empty food wrappers and used tissue littering the corners. On top of his climbing gear, his camera kit was spread out all over the floor of his tent—some of it broken and cracked. She thought of the disturbance in the night. Getting rejected by Irina had cut him up.

"You took a hard fall on the ice yesterday," Doug said.

"And broke *everything*? No, someone did this."

"Come, Cecily." Elise touched her elbow. "Let's leave the men to argue. I want to be back in base camp by the afternoon . . . I've been dreaming of Dawa's food every moment I've been up here." Elise said, sliding wraparound sunglasses onto her face.

Cecily hesitated, torn. She was curious about the outcome of Grant and Doug's conversation, but she was also keen to get back. But as Grant kicked at one of the camping stools, she realized she didn't want to be in his path. She followed Elise toward the fixed lines. "I'm never going to take tuna pizza and vegetable soup for granted again."

"You're telling me."

Even though Elise was a much stronger climber, Cecily managed to stick to her side. Elise taught her how to wind the fixed line around her sleeve to "arm wrap" down the mountain. It was safer than holding the rope and faster than rappelling.

There was no doubt she felt closer to Elise now—the time they'd shared in the tent had helped them bond. But she wondered if perhaps it was more than that.

The mountain was dangerous—but with another layer, an extraspecial frosting, just for women. What she'd witnessed in the early hours of the morning had proved that. There was something so primal about this kind of expedition, constantly walking the line between life and death, being back in nature, living on the edge, adrenaline coursing through your body, your veins, your muscles. Everything seemed heightened. She'd seen the way that men on other teams looked at her. Like they were assessing which one of them was going to lay claim to her. She'd spent so long focused on getting her body mountain fit, she hadn't thought about how to fend off unwanted advances at altitude. That wasn't in any mountaineering manual.

That's because they're written for men, by men.

"So, last night was interesting," Cecily said, as they continued the monotonous routine of clipping in and out. "I saw Irina and Grant having a fight. He was being quite the prick."

Elise laughed. "Ah, you don't like him, do you?"

"I think he's a typical privileged public-school boy and a bit of a creep. From the day we met he's put me on edge."

"He's a man on the mountain. Trust me, I expect it."

"Don't you find it hard to deal with?"

"If I'm uncomfortable, I say: This life is not exactly a good match for having a boyfriend. I know how to stand my ground with the boys."

Cecily raised her eyebrows. "I doubt you have any trouble finding a man."

"Finding one, no—keeping one, much harder! I climb too much, always moving from here to there, spending too much time away. They think they like it—they always think they want an adventurous girl, and yet when it comes down to it they want someone to come home to who will be wowed by their adventures."

"Seriously? Even fellow mountaineers?"

"I have dated a few, and maybe we were happy for a while. Maybe they were even supportive of my dreams. But eventually we go off in different directions and I don't see them again." She shrugged again. "It is what it is. I prefer the mountains. This is my love. This is my love!" she said again, shouting it to the seracs.

Cecily laughed. Elise's energy was infectious, energizing. She was proud of herself for keeping up with the young mountaineer on the way back to base camp. A seed of confidence was beginning to sprout.

If only James could see her now.

"Do you have a boyfriend back home?" Elise asked.

Cecily shook her head. "That would be a big no," she muttered, her tone bitterer than she intended.

Elise's eyes widened. "Sounds like there's a story there . . ."

"Funny, my ex sounds a bit like what you were talking about. He was always the more adventurous one, with plenty of stories to wow me. He's a journalist too—he's been working for *Wild Outdoors* for a lot longer than me. I think he was the one who expected to get this gig."

She thought back to that evening at the Royal Geographic Society, after listening to Charles talk in person for the first time. She remembered the exact words he had said. They had made James almost choke on his champagne. *It's no coincidence you got the invitation. You're the 'Hero of Snowdon,' of course. But I also read 'Failure to Rise.' I'm very impressed by you.*

She'd blushed, shaking his outstretched hand. *Oh, you are? Kind of embarrassing next to your accomplishments.*

He'd grinned. *Not at all.*

Cecily told the whole story to Elise, ending with how Charles had chosen her to be the only journalist to get his exclusive story. Elise threw her head back and laughed. "I bet your ex was not happy about that."

"Not even a little bit. We broke up only a few days later." She waited for the accompanying pang of sadness, but in Elise's presence she could see the absurdity in the situation. It still hurt, of course. But she actually found herself smiling.

"What did I just say? Men . . . they can't handle a woman more adventurous than they are."

"Honestly, I didn't think I would say yes to Charles's invitation. James was probably in shock."

"No, no, don't make excuses for him. But tell me . . . why?"

"Why what?"

"You've told me how you got here. But why did you say yes?"

Cecily chuckled. "You make a better journalist than I do. I should be taking notes. I mean, why do *you* come to the mountains?"

Elise paused for a moment. "Because how could you not?" She threw her arms wide, gesturing at the view. She'd chosen an optimal moment for it. There was a break in the persistent cloud cover, and the sky was cobalt blue. From their position, they could see down the valley to Samagaun in the far distance. Beyond that, more peaks rose, their summits piercing the heavens.

"Funny, Charles said a similar thing in his speech at the RGS. During his talk, he said his most commonly asked question was: 'Why do you climb?' You know, whether he was like Mallory, climbing Everest 'because it's there.' And he replied that he did it 'because I can.'"

They took a couple of steps forward in silence. "I think there's more to Charles than that," said Elise.

"Like what?"

Elise came to a stop, at the very top of the Hanging Place. "Out here, the mountain decides who lives, who dies. Who summits and who has to turn around. Some people respect that. Others see it as a challenge. Something to overcome and conquer."

"How do you see it?"

"I've known enough good friends—some of the best mountaineers in the world—who haven't made it back alive, to know that nothing is certain on the mountain." Elise knelt down, examining the anchor point. Two ropes stretched away from it. She pulled on each one. "Ah, you tricked me! I didn't hear your answer to the question."

Cecily was about to reply, when she saw Elise's face. "What's wrong?"

"The rappel line is stuck," Elise said. "Allô?" She leaned out over the edge and shouted down. "Is anyone on the rope?" For good measure, she tugged the line, trying to signal to the person rappelling down it that they were waiting at the top.

"What should we do?" Cecily asked.

"We sit and wait."

"OK." Cecily dumped her backpack on the snow before perching on top of it. She grabbed a snack and her water, and they sat in companionable silence as they refueled.

After a few minutes had passed, Elise checked the rope again. It was still taut. She frowned. "Maybe the rope is stuck? That happens sometimes." She shouted down, but again—no answer. She shrugged. "I think it is clear."

Over her shoulder, Cecily saw Doug and Mingma were making their way toward them, minutes from catching up. She didn't think they'd be so happy to wait.

"There's a secondary rappel line here," said Elise. "I'll tie in and go down, then you can follow."

"Wait, Elise." Cecily chewed her bottom lip, reaching out to touch Elise's shoulder. "Can I go first, so you can check that I tie myself in properly? I don't want to have to ask Doug . . ."

Elise nodded. "Of course."

Cecily lifted the line, threading it through her figure-eight device under Elise's watchful eye. It took her a couple of tries, but Elise finally gave her the thumbs-up.

This side of the wall wasn't as hacked to pieces as the one used to climb up. Rather, it was a smooth, steep, vertical drop to a small ledge midway, before shearing off to the ground.

The rope ran smoothly through the device, curling like a snake around the metal; it was almost hypnotic.

She descended to the midpoint without incident. Below her, the yawning crevasse the Chinese man had fallen into was visible. She gripped onto the rope extra tight. But as she stepped backward over the ledge, she saw the reason the other rappel line was stuck.

All she could do was scream.

"Cecily! Dieu, are you all right?" Elise shouted from above.

She could barely hear above the ringing in her ears. She couldn't reply. The rope slipped from her right hand, and she tumbled backward. She just managed to catch herself again, but her legs wouldn't hold. It was only a short distance to the ground, and when she reached it, she turned over onto her stomach and retched into the crevasse.

She knelt there, quivering, not wanting to turn around. Not when she knew what was there.

But she had to. She looked up.

A body hung on the wall.

A long ponytail of blonde hair obscured the woman's face. Rope wrapped around her neck, digging into her skin. Her gloved hands drooped, lifeless and still, and her shoulder jutted out at an awkward angle. Horror clawed at Cecily's throat as she had a jolt of recognition—she could only hope she was wrong. She shouted as loud as she could.

"Help! Someone is on the other line! They're in trouble."

The rope she'd just rappelled twitched—someone was obviously tying in.

Doug's deep voice reached her. "Cecily, watch out! We're throwing another rope down so we can see what's going on."

She moved as far as the anchor would let her, crouching behind a small mound of snow. Behind her was the crevasse—but she wasn't going to cross the ladder without help, not until the shaking in her legs stopped. Another rope smacked the ground, and both Doug and Mingma appeared at the top of the wall.

Doug was the first to reach the woman, his mouth drawn in a firm line. He pulled the prone body toward him, but the rope was too tight. With Mingma's help, he clipped the woman onto his harness. Then he removed his knife and sliced through her rope, Mingma catching half the weight.

Slowly, they made their way down. Once they were on the ground next to Cecily, they started their rescue effort, untangling her from the rope, trying to clear her airway, seeing if they could revive her. Mingma got on the radio, calling down to base camp and camp one, asking for help.

Doug smoothed the woman's hair back from her face, and Cecily gasped.

"Oh my god. It's Irina."

CHAPTER 28

THE ATMOSPHERE WHEN THEY returned to base camp was grim. The Russian team's base camp crew had been quick to make their way up to help. Elise had escorted Cecily away, so that she didn't have to see Irina's body get wrapped in a bag and hauled like a sack of rubbish.

She was in a daze the entire route. Even when they made it back to the dining tent, she couldn't think straight. Elise encouraged her to eat from the spread that chef Dawa had provided for them. It was meant to be celebratory, congratulating them on their first rotation on the mountain.

Instead, Cecily felt sick just looking at it. Her hands trembled as she tried at least to sip sugary tea. The horror was too close.

"My god. That poor woman," she said. The first words she'd spoken since the wall.

As soon as she spoke, Elise placed her hand on her back, rubbing in circles. "I am so sorry you had to find her like that."

Cecily took in a shuddering breath. "I asked to go first—how could we have known? I just can't believe it. I thought she'd gone up to camp three with the rest of her team."

"It's such a tragedy."

Cecily's mouth was bone-dry. She couldn't rationalize what she had seen. She hoped someone with more experience on the mountain could explain. "What do you think happened?"

Elise played with her necklace. "I don't know. I couldn't really see from the top of the wall. But she must have slipped and got caught up in the rappel rope. It is possible that she was tired or confused . . . Maybe she was suffering from the altitude and that's why she was going down."

"Wait. Oh my god." Cecily's hand flew to her mouth.

"What?" Elise frowned.

"The argument. Between Grant and Irina."

"What was it about?"

"He wanted to join her in her tent."

Elise wrinkled her nose. "You're not serious? He wanted a hook-up at camp two?"

"She rejected him. It was quite brutal actually. She was very harsh . . . You don't think Grant could have had anything to do with this?"

"Merde," said Elise. She drummed her painted nails on the edge of the white tablecloth. "No, Grant was with us this morning at camp. I watched him climb yesterday—there's no way he could make it down to the Hanging Place"—she winced—"to the crux and back, in the night. You didn't see him fall—it was bad. He might be a creep but not more. It sounds like she wasn't herself? Sometimes that happens. Altitude can affect your behavior—make you act all crazy. Sounds like HACE maybe."

"But wouldn't she have started to feel better as she came down? And why was no one with her?" The unsettled feeling remained knotted in Cecily's stomach.

Elise shrugged. There were so many questions. Until Doug got back, they wouldn't get any answers.

A few hours later, Zak and Grant entered the dining tent, heads hanging low. Grant went straight for the food. Zak slumped down in a chair, rubbing his brow with his fingers. "That was intense," said Zak. "We were caught in that traffic jam behind the wall for ages. Took even longer than going up. Do you guys know what happened?"

Elise glanced at Cecily before answering. "A woman died while rappelling on the crux."

"Shit. You serious?"

"And it was someone we know," Cecily said. She looked up at her British teammate, watching for his reaction. "Grant, it was Irina."

"Irina's dead?" Grant dropped his half-eaten sandwich onto his plate. He looked genuinely shocked, but still, Cecily narrowed her eyes. There was barely a flicker of sadness on his face. Instead, he seemed more annoyed. "You're fucking kidding me. How? I needed to talk to her . . ."

Doug entered the tent, and his dark eyes went straight to Cecily. "Are you OK?"

She curled her fingers into fists to stop her hands from shaking. "Honestly? No. I'm not. I've never seen anyone like that before."

Doug nodded, gripping the back of a chair. "Of course. It was a shock. But I sent Galden up to let Andrej know what happened, since I couldn't get ahold of him on the radio. He's just come back with this report: Irina had been suffering with altitude sickness at camp two and decided to go down. Her group is on a one-to-two climbing-Sherpa-to-client ratio, so that's why she descended alone."

"Jesus. What do they think happened?" asked Zak.

"AMS and fatigue leading to an accident with her belay device. We think she had the figure eight over the locking mechanism of her carabiner, which then opened as she rappelled. She lost control, hit the ledge and then got tangled in the rope. Which is, unfortunately, how Cecily found her. Climber error causes most deaths on the mountain. The Elbrus Elite base camp manager is notifying her family and arranging a heli-evac of her body as we speak. When the weather clears."

"Do the rest of her team know?" asked Cecily.

"That's up to Andrej whether to tell them. They're at camp three acclimatizing, and they might be stuck there overnight because of the incoming weather."

"Will they be going home, too?"

Elise squeezed her hand under the table.

Doug coughed. "Her death is very sad, but she was an experienced climber—she wouldn't want the rest of her team to give up their dreams because of her. These are the high mountains. Accidents happen."

Cecily's entire body was cold, her mind blank.

"I'm going to check my cameras," said Grant. "I need to find out what the damage is."

"I don't know why you're so calm, seeing as you were probably the last person to see Irina alive," Cecily snapped.

Doug's bushy brows drew together. "What is she talking about?" he asked Grant.

"I have *no* idea," Grant replied, but he wouldn't meet anyone's eye. His face was red-raw and swollen, the skin on his nose already beginning to peel.

She stood up. "I saw you trying to get into Irina's tent last night."

"That's ridiculous. I was in my tent the whole night."

"Zak, you didn't notice him leave?" Cecily asked him.

Zak threw his hands up in the air. "Don't look at me. I asked for my own tent after getting no sleep at camp one."

Cecily blinked. "So you two weren't sharing last night?"

"Nope."

"It doesn't matter," said Grant. "OK, yes, I may have had a conversation with Irina. But only while I was on my way to the bathroom. Then when I got back my things were trashed—remember what I said this morning, Doug? She was out of her mind. She's cost me a fortune if this footage is destroyed. Look at the state of my hard drive." He pulled it out of the chest pocket of his jacket. It looked even worse than when Cecily had seen it at camp two. The center of it was smashed and splintered as if it had been hit by a hammer.

Or an ice ax.

Cecily's cheeks burned, her anger rising. "You're blaming her? Come on."

"Enough," said Doug. "Grant, we discussed this. Your hard drive took a beating when you fell on the crux. Cecily, no one on this team was involved in this."

"Except that I found her," Cecily muttered. She swooned, exhaustion hitting her. "I have to get out of here."

"Mingma will go with you."

"No, it's OK. I just want to go back to my tent for a rest. I'd prefer to be alone." She felt everyone's eyes on her back as she walked out through the dining-tent flaps into the waning afternoon light.

The weather front had moved in. Snow fell in thick flakes. She stood and stared up in the direction of the mountain. She couldn't see it—it was completely gray. She shivered, the cold seeping through her down jacket. She thought about Irina.

A second death. Already.

Coming here, to a place like this, put your life at risk. There was no getting around it. No matter how experienced you were, one false move, one slip, and you were dead.

The mountain was killer enough; no human could compete.

She made her way back to her tent, picking each step carefully.

It was then that she saw it. A piece of paper, pinned to the outer flap of her tent, close to the bottom.

She knelt down to pull the note free.

THERE'S A MURDERER ON THE MOUNTAIN. RUN.

CHAPTER 29

SHE DIVED INTO HER tent, throwing her belongings into her bag. She'd had enough . . . How could she stay on the mountain now?

She yanked the khata from the front of the tent, attempting to stuff it into the duffel. It snagged on the roof. "Come on!" she yelled at it, fear and frustration bubbling over. It fell into her lap and she twisted the orange fabric between her hands.

So much for the khata being a good-luck token. Two people were dead. Two people she'd known, spoken to. She might have been the last person to have seen them both alive. Her bad luck from Snowdon had stalked her here. Maybe *she* was the problem.

She closed her eyes, stroking the silky fabric, calming her breathing.

The note. *Someone left it for you. Someone wants you to feel this way. Who?* She opened her eyes and scrambled out of the tent, searching for the scrap of paper she'd dropped on the ground. She saw it, the letters feathering as the snow seeped through the back. She picked it up, taking it inside.

THERE'S A MURDERER ON THE MOUNTAIN. RUN.

She forced herself to think logically.

Whoever had left this hadn't signed it.

They wanted to be anonymous. Maybe that meant they were speculating. And unless others had received a similar note, it meant the warning was just for her. *Why?* And was it a warning . . . or a threat?

"Cecily?" She heard her name from outside.

She clutched the note to her chest. "Zak? What is it?"

He ducked his head and lifted her tent flap.

"Did you receive a note too?" she asked him.

He frowned. "Note? No. But you better come. That Dario guy's got some news—sounds serious."

"OK." She followed him outside, slipping the note into her pocket. Snow fell in thick flakes, dusting her jacket.

Zak put his hand on her shoulder. "You look pale. Must have been a shock coming across her like that."

"It was awful. But, Zak, do you think maybe it wasn't an accident?" She stopped outside the dining tent.

"You mean like the Alain thing?"

She glanced around, making sure no one could hear them. "What if there's someone dangerous on the mountain?"

"Honestly? I think that Ben guy *really* got in your head. Even if there was someone dangerous here—and it seems pretty far-fetched—we're a team, right? None of us is going to be alone, like Irina was. Everyone from our team was asleep when Irina died. You're safe with us."

"Except Grant," she muttered.

"You know I'm not his biggest fan either. He's a young guy, a bit of a jerk. But dangerous? I don't think so. No way he'd have the ability to pull off what you're thinking. Come on, kid," Zak threw his arm around her, bringing her close. "Let's go in." Zak swept aside the plastic vestibule of the dining tent.

Dario paced along the back wall. Seeing a man as confident as Dario look so uneasy was unnerving. A prickle rose along the back of her neck. This had to have something to do with the note, she was sure.

Elise entered behind them, with Doug following in her wake. "What are you doing here?" Doug asked Dario.

Dario ground his teeth. "While we were acclimatizing, our camp was robbed. Someone dug through our bags and took our team's tip money."

"You must be joking . . ." said Elise, her eyes wide.

"I wish I was. First the Russian, which is a suspicious death if I ever heard one. Now thousands of dollars are missing from my clients. Some of us had equipment stolen too. This isn't just some little hill. We are all supposed to be trustworthy up here. What, am I going to have to arm my Sherpas next time?"

"Calm down. You didn't misplace it?" said Doug.

"Don't be ridiculous. Are you calling my clients liars?" He squared up to Doug, and the atmosphere in the tent intensified. Dario was on *Doug's* territory here. Cecily noticed that Mingma and Galden had stood up. Dario spotted them and took a step back.

"Your team returned before us, did they not? They were all accounted for?" said Dario.

"I think you need to leave." Doug didn't speak much louder than a whisper, but there was steel in his tone.

"I am simply asking," said Dario, holding his hands up. "If the culprit was not from your team—and I'm not saying that he was—then it has to be someone else at base camp. We'll have a better chance at catching them if we band together."

"Wait, has anyone checked whether our money is still here?" asked Zak.

"Please, everyone—go and see if any cash or valuables you brought to the mountain have gone missing," said Doug.

Cecily had a sinking feeling as she approached her tent. Her eye caught sight of the boulder just beyond, and suddenly she thought of that lone tent she'd seen on the plateau. The domain of the mystery whistler. Whoever was living there could have raided their tents while they were all higher up the mountain. Biding their time.

The thought solidified her plan to leave. Her duffels lay across the entrance, the zips straining from her haphazard packing. She'd kept cash designated to tip her climbing Sherpa in a plain brown envelope at the bottom of her largest duffel bag. It wasn't particularly well hidden, but it was stuffed underneath unused dry sacks, bags full of snacks and books and spare notebooks.

To her relief, the envelope was there. But then her heart sank. It was floppy and flat in her hands. When she opened it, her suspicions were confirmed: empty.

There might not be a murderer in base camp.

But there most definitely was a thief.

CHAPTER 30

"HOW ARE WE GOING to handle this?" Dario asked Doug once they'd all returned to the dining tent.

"Fuck this. First my camera equipment, now my tip money?" said Grant. He punched the table. "This is a fucking joke."

"Did Dawa see anything?" Doug asked Mingma, their heads close together. Zak slumped over his coffee mug. Elise was on the verge of tears. Nausea stuck in the back of Cecily's throat. That was all the money she had left in the world. She'd allocated it for summit tips, but now it meant she couldn't pay for a helicopter back to Kathmandu to escape this place.

It wasn't just that. She felt violated. Someone had been in her tent, rifling through her belongings. She wouldn't have even known about it had it not been for Dario.

Mingma replied. "Dawa says no. But then he went to stay with friends in the Seven Summit team while we were at camp two."

She saw Doug's lips twitch—he was furious. Their camp had been left empty, totally exposed.

"We should get some of the other team leaders together, find out if it happened to anyone else," said Dario.

"Agreed," replied Doug. He pinched the bridge of his nose, pausing for a long moment before speaking. "First thing tomorrow, we'll get everyone together. This absolutely should not be happening on the mountain. Get the policeman from Samagaun here too. He'll hate coming up, but it's needed—before this gets out of hand."

The two team leaders left, and Cecily stared at the rest of the group, unable to believe what had happened.

Elise was distraught. "The Sherpas deserve that money. Otherwise I don't climb. It is as simple as that."

"You can't be serious?" Zak was aghast.

"It's not so easy for me! I don't have a thousand dollars I can pull from my pocket just like that"—she snapped her fingers—"or a successful job like you." She gestured at Cecily. Her lips trembled, her fingers fumbling at her necklace, rubbing it like a rosary.

"We'll figure it out once we're back in Kathmandu, Elise," Cecily said. "Don't worry—we won't let you go through this alone. I'll help any way I can. We're a team." She didn't dare admit that she was in no position to lend any money.

Elise nodded. "I think I'll go back to my tent now. I want to double-check that nothing else is missing." When she reached the dining-tent flaps, she turned around. "I know I'm young, but I've been climbing all over the world for years and never, never have I seen something like this. I just don't understand it. What kind of mountaineer would steal from the people who help us?"

Cecily collapsed into a chair, her legs shaking. The theft, Alain's death, Irina's . . . The whole expedition felt cursed.

"This better not affect our summit push," said Zak. "I paid a ton of money to be here."

"Charles won't let it," said Grant. "When he gets here, we'll be going up, I guarantee it."

It was suffocating, listening to them debate their summit attempt. The loss of money hadn't fazed either of the men. She needed to get out.

Back in her tent, she took a deep breath. She focused on packing her bags again, after the frantic search for her envelope of money.

There was a sharp cough from outside her tent. Doug appeared, crouching down inside the vestibule. "Anything else missing?"

She sat cross-legged on her mattress, dropped her hands in her lap and exhaled. "I've done a quick check but I don't think so. I carried most of my electronics with me on the mountain. Do you have any idea who took the money?"

He shook his head. "Not yet. The police will be here tomorrow, but don't expect much—I apologize in advance for that."

"At least it's not someone's life . . ." She sat in silence, thinking about Irina, Alain and the note. She wanted to tell Doug, but judging by how he had reacted to her theories last time, it wouldn't go down well. Plus, suspicion nagged at her. Something Elise had said and Zak had echoed: about how Grant lacked the physical ability to pull off killing Irina and get back to camp in time.

If any one of their team had the strength and ability to kill Irina and get back up to camp in time, in the dead of night, it was Doug.

"That's why I'm here." He shifted his weight, so he was farther inside her tent. "I wanted to ask you privately . . . After what happened to Irina, how are you feeling?"

Cecily blinked. She hadn't expected the question. Or the kindness in his tone. She didn't know if she could trust it. "To be honest? I don't know quite yet."

Doug nodded. "Between that and the theft, you must be feeling unsettled. But Dario and I are sorting it out."

"Is it OK working with him?"

"Why wouldn't it be?"

"I just thought . . . after what happened with you and Summit Extreme?"

He sighed and ran a hand through his silvery hair. "We disagreed about priorities when it came to guiding. They want to please the client. Me? I respect my client's safety and the mountain. Money doesn't even come into it."

"Even if that means knocking out a client?"

He stared at her from underneath bushy brows. "You heard that."

"I'm sure you had your reasons."

"No. I didn't. I was out of control. It won't happen again. I never want people to get hurt on my expeditions. I will do anything to prevent that. Anything." His voice was quiet but forceful.

An angry shout caught their attention. Another noise—this one lower. A growl. A telling-off?

Doug slapped his knees. "Mother of God, what's happening now?"

"I'll come with you." She wriggled forward to the vestibule, crawling out of the tent. Darkness had fallen, but there were specks of light from headlamps on the move.

She caught up with Zak as he came from the dining tent. Doug disappeared into the crowd.

"What's going on?" she asked Zak.

"I think they found the thief. The Sherpas are furious. That's their livelihood that was taken away. And a pissed-off Sherpa is not someone you want to deal with."

Cecily pulled her jacket tight around her body, hugging herself. "What do you think is going to happen?"

"I don't know. But I saw someone—Galden, maybe?—walk past with an ice ax. They might be about to dole out some real Sherpa justice."

"Oh my god, you can't be serious? What about the police?"

Zak shrugged. "We can't just stay here. We have to see what's going on." He jogged toward the commotion.

She didn't want to follow, but she had to know who it was. Maybe more witnesses would discourage anyone from doing something stupid and irreversible.

A stream of headlamps lit the way. It was a mob. They marched down to the entrance to base camp, where there was another cluster of lights.

As they approached, Cecily spotted a man—hog-tied with thick climbing rope—on his knees, surrounded by Sherpas. Dario stood over him, his jaw clenched with rage.

The man on his knees, in the middle of the group, was Ben.

And in front of him was a big pile of money.

CHAPTER 31

"OH MY GOD, BEN—WHAT happened?" She pushed through the crowd, kneeling beside him, but he flailed against his bonds, and she skittered backward.

"I didn't steal it!" he shouted. "I've been set up."

"Lie! We caught you sneaking away with the money," said Dario. He kicked at the earth, sending a barrage of pebbles and dirt in Ben's direction.

Cecily winced, watching Ben shield his head with his hands. She could feel tension rising in the crowd, pulsating, like it had its own heartbeat. It could quickly get out of hand. She turned to Dario. "Please—let's listen to what he has to say. I know this man from back home. There has to be an explanation."

"It's *mine*," Ben said, when the dust had settled. "I got a call from my wife. My daughter is sick. I need to fly home. I checked and tomorrow there's a break in the weather. I had to move down the mountain straightaway. It's the only chance I have."

"It's not true!" shouted someone in the crowd.

"I could kill him," Dario clenched his fists, pacing. "This is the joker we kicked out of our camp. His funds never cleared. Looks like instead of leaving, he has been stealing from other teams to survive." His eyes were wild. He really did look like he wanted to beat the shit out of Ben. And even though he might have fed information back to her ex, tried to scoop her story—and now potentially stolen her tip money—she still didn't want to see Ben hurt.

"No!" he protested.

"I know how to tell if he's telling the truth," Zak said, stepping into the middle of the circle. "I mark all my bills. If there are bills with red slashes down one side—those are mine."

"You mark your bills?" Cecily asked him.

"Of course. For situations like this."

"You don't mind us looking, do you, Ben?" Dario practically spat his name. Ben hung his head; he had no choice but to comply.

Everyone was watching as Dario's head Sherpa knelt down and counted the money in the snow. With everyone's headlamps pointing at him, it was as bright as daylight. So far, there were no red streaks. But while everyone watched the cash, her eyes stayed on Ben's face.

And she saw the truth even before they found that first red-marked bill. There was a tightness in his jaw and a hardness in his eyes. He had done this. And he knew he was about to be uncovered.

"Ben, why?" she asked.

The others turned to look at her. And then Dario shouted out. He reached down and grabbed a twenty-dollar U.S. bill, with the red streak on it.

Ben turned his head away, struggling against the ropes that bound his hands. It was futile. He had the entire Manaslu base camp watching him.

Dario stepped forward, and Ben scrambled away. "Fine!" he said. "I had to take the money. I had to get off this mountain."

"Ah, stop with your excuses." Dario threw his hands up in the air.

Cecily moved, trying to get in between the two men. "It sounds like he needed to get back to his daughter. He was desperate, not thinking straight. Right, Ben?"

To her dismay, he shook his head. "I had to leave because of that woman who died." Ben's eyes were wide, and the whites were bloodshot. His skin was sallow and his cheeks gaunt, as if he hadn't been eating. He looked ill. People had been known to get cerebral edema even at base-camp altitude. "Her death wasn't an accident. Someone killed her."

"Ridiculous," muttered Doug.

"It's not! I saw it happen."

"What did you see?" Cecily asked, her heart racing.

"It was too dark. I couldn't get a good look at his face. Everyone looks the same in their gear. But I watched him push her. There's a murderer on the mountain. I had to get away before I ended up being targeted next."

"This is bullshit. Let's get him!" came a cry from one of the Summit Extreme climbers. One of the climbing Sherpas lunged forward, his fist raised. Galden was next to him.

"No!" she cried out. She didn't care what Ben's motivations were for stealing, but she did know that he didn't deserve to be beaten to a bloody pulp—or worse, judging by the anger in the crowd.

She caught Galden's eye and to her relief, he stopped his companion before any damage was done.

Doug pulled his knitted hat from his head and wiped his brow. "You'll go down to Samagaun. The authorities can deal with you there."

"They're going to follow me and beat me up!" Ben protested, gesturing at the climbing Sherpas and Dario.

Doug surveyed the group. "Tenzing, go with him."

Cecily sighed with relief. She was glad he'd picked the mild-mannered and well-respected Tenzing to act as security for Ben. No one would dare to attack him while under Tenzing's watchful eye.

The older Sherpa unhooked a knife from his belt and sliced through Ben's wrist bonds. Dario collected the money (with the unenviable task of having to distribute it back to the clients—she'd let the guides figure that one out), and the crowd of angry people began to disperse. She shook with the aftereffects of adrenaline, her heart beating wildly. She stood stock-still, watching Tenzing and Ben disappear into the darkness.

"Come on," said Doug. "Let's get some sleep."

She followed the team back in silence, a weight hanging heavy on her shoulders.

She couldn't shake Ben's words from repeating over and over in her head.

There's a murderer on the mountain.

Exactly what the note had said.

CHAPTER 32

EARLY THE NEXT MORNING, she double-checked that she had everything she needed: food, water, her camera, laptop, phone and all her
chargers. She grabbed her passport and wallet too.

If she left now, she might make it to Samagaun before Ben was
whisked off to Kathmandu.

"Galden?" She stood outside the Sherpa's tent, saying his name
just loud enough so only he would hear.

There was a rustle inside the tent, and he appeared. "Didi—do
you need something?"

"I wanted to let you know—I'm going to Samagaun to use the
internet. I need to send some emails to my editor or she will—"

"I'll come with you," he said, without any hesitation.

She shook her head. "It's OK—the route is easy to follow. I won't
be long."

"I should ask Doug about this."

"I asked him last night." She felt guilty about lying, especially
to Galden, who'd been so nice to her. But she had good reason to
lie. She knew Doug wouldn't approve. He'd warned her last time
he would ask her to leave the team if he thought her paranoia was
growing.

It definitely was.

"He's fine with it," she continued. "I tried to tell him I was setting off but can't find him, that's why I'm telling you." She didn't
want to discuss anymore with Galden, or else he might find a reason

to make her wait. She started walking, praying that he wouldn't follow her.

She picked her way down the rocky moraine, following the small flags that marked the trail to the village. Some of the rock was slippery from the rain, freezing on the cold ground to ice. It was so early, most of base camp was quiet, and by the time she reached the trail she was alone.

She was beginning to regret her decision. She should have taken Galden up on his suggestion to accompany her.

Even on these lower reaches of the mountain, she sensed danger lurking. Not just the loose rocks underfoot, the damage that could be done by a slip or a fall. The mountain changed people. It tested all your faculties, the hardship and suffering stripping emotions bare. She'd been shocked by the Ben she'd seen last night. He was unrecognizable from the man she'd known back in England.

And there was another reason for her sudden unease.

She heard something, her heart racing. Her instinct was to crouch down, holding a boulder for support. She tilted her head back, in time to watch a drone soar high above her.

A videographer getting some dramatic establishing shots?

Or was the drone specifically out to look for her?

The drone lingered overhead, buzzing like a hornet. She wished she could swat it away.

She couldn't just stay where she was on the trail, paralyzed by the sight of the camera. She put her hands over her ears and picked up her pace down the moraine.

The drone stayed where it was, hovering.

Once she'd reached the village itself, she headed for the teahouse they'd stayed in. Shashi was in the dining room, clearing away the dishes from breakfast. Without the hordes of climbers, there was a different atmosphere—quieter, more contemplative. She paused as Cecily walked in.

"Oh no, are you injured?"

Cecily shook her head. "I'm fine. I'm actually wondering if you can help me. I'm looking for Tenzing? He would have brought down another climber last night . . ."

Shashi's face clouded over, the warmth of her initial greeting snuffed out like the teahouse fire. "No good business, that."

"I know. But I really need to speak with him . . ."

"They went down to the helipads to wait."

"Thank you," she said.

"Can I offer you tea?" Shashi said, but Cecily dashed back outside again. She was jogging now, terrified that Ben had been flown off the mountain before she could reach him.

But as she reached the landing zone she spotted Ben, sitting on the ground at the edge of the helipad, his head in his hands. Tenzing stood watch a few meters away. Everyone else gave him a wide berth.

Ben looked even worse in the bright light of day. How much weight had he lost in the week since they'd met in Samagaun? His face was badly sunburnt and peeling, his eyes wild.

She bit her lip. Maybe this had been a mistake. If he was in this condition, he was desperate. Desperate men lied. She was about to turn around when he lifted his head and caught her eye. She steeled her resolve and walked toward him.

"Cecily?"

At the sound of Ben's voice, Tenzing looked up. "Hi, Tenzing," Cecily said. "Can I talk to Ben for a second? I promise I'm not here to hurt him. I just want to ask a few questions. He's a friend from home."

Tenzing's dark eyes studied her, but then he nodded. He didn't seem bothered about what she did. His job was to get Ben on the helicopter, not to ward off nosy journalists.

For that, Cecily was grateful. She knelt down. "Ben, are you OK?"

She had to stop herself from grimacing as she got closer to him. His mouth was caked with yellow crud—from dehydration, most likely—and the skin around his eyes was puffy, swollen. He stank of stale sweat. "Thank god you're here. It's so good to see you. I'm so scared. I need to get off this mountain."

"Don't worry; the helicopter is on its way."

"I'm sorry I took the money . . ."

"That was a stupid thing to do, Ben," she said, softly. "But I'm not here to talk to you about that." She swallowed, then asked her question. "What happened to Irina?"

He picked at the dirt beneath his fingernails. "Someone killed her."

Hearing the words out loud again made Cecily's stomach churn with fear. "Go back to the beginning," she forced herself to say. "Why were you even on the mountain—hadn't Dario asked you to leave the expedition?"

He rocked. "Yeah, I was dumped from Summit Extreme. It was always a bit touch and go with money, and I couldn't get it together in time. But I'd come all this way, so I still wanted to climb. I hid out on the mountain and waited for everyone to start their acclimatization. I thought if I set off early enough, while it was still dark, I could get to camp two, past the crux, before it got busy. They'd never know I was there. I could acclimatize, get back down, while I waited for my paycheck to come through. Maybe I could beg my way back on the team . . ."

Ben had been hiding out on the mountain. Could it have been him she'd seen on the ledge? Cecily passed him some of her water as she processed his words. He took a swig. "Then what happened?" she prompted.

"It was all going OK, to be honest. I arrived at the Hanging Place about four a.m. and took a break, trying to figure out the best way to get up it. That's when I saw a headlamp at the top. Someone was tying in. At least—that's what I thought they were doing. I was surprised, because it was pitch-black and I didn't expect anyone else to be moving. Then there was a second light. They were acting strangely, like they . . . like they were dancing. A second later, one of the lights went out. The next thing I know, something comes flying down the wall. I turned my light on and saw her—but she was too far up for me to reach. I couldn't help her."

He seemed to spasm along with the memory, jerking out his legs in imitation of what he'd seen. She grimaced, but listened as he pressed on.

"I panicked. I knew I had to get out of there—as far away from that wall as possible."

"Why? Why not sound the alarm?"

"Because of the other light. Someone else—at the top of the wall, looking down at the woman. They were utterly still. Until they moved so the light shone directly at me. I ran as fast as I could after that."

"Who was it?"

"I don't know. It was too dark. All I could see was the bright light from their headlamp. But I know whoever it was saw me. And I knew I had to get away."

She swallowed. A second light. It could be something—or it could be nothing but his troubled imagination. Yet now there had been two fatal accidents on the expedition—Irina and Alain. She couldn't ignore the possibility that someone dangerous had been behind them. Even Dario had said Irina's death had seemed suspicious . . .

The pressure around them dropped as a helicopter approached. She felt the low judder of the chopper's blades in her belly, and she ducked as it flew overhead, spinning around to land on the helipad. She threw her arms over her head to protect herself from the debris disturbed by the landing.

"This is Ben's flight!" said Tenzing, over the noise.

A uniformed officer jumped out of the plane and approached Ben, leading him away by the bicep. Cecily jogged alongside them.

"Come with me," Ben shouted. "You shouldn't stay here either. You can't trust anyone on the mountain. You'll be safe back in Kathmandu."

"But who do you think it is?"

"Does it matter? If you're here, you're in danger."

He was right. It could be anyone, and that meant nowhere was safe. She put one foot on the helicopter skid. She could fly far away from the mountain. She could be back in London.

"A story is not worth your life," Ben said.

She lifted herself up, grabbing the handle on the inside of the helicopter door.

"Let's go!" Ben dragged her in by the hand. Looking into his face, she saw the reflection of her own failure. If she went with him, she'd be giving up, and everything she had sacrificed for this interview would have been for nothing. Then there was the note. If it wasn't a threat but a warning, then she had to stay. Someone had to find out what had *really* happened to Irina.

"No, Ben. I can't. I have to stay." She shook her hand free of his and took a stumbling step backward.

Ben lurched toward her, moving faster than she'd thought capable. He grabbed her upper arms and brought her close. She reeled back from the stench of his breath. "Be careful. You could be next."

Then the officer yanked him back, strapping him into the seat. The pilot shouted at her to move, and once she was a safe distance away they lifted up, taking Ben to his fate in Kathmandu. Her heart pounded in her chest.

"About to throw in the towel, were you?"

She spun around and found herself face-to-face with Charles McVeigh.

CHAPTER 33

THE HELICOPTER DID A loop of the valley over their heads, winging its way back to the capital city. She swallowed. Her mouth was dry, but she'd given her water bottle to Ben and now it was in the chopper with him. "Charles, you made it!"

"Arrived this morning. I was just about to meet Doug at the teahouse when I saw you. What was that all about?" He gestured to the helicopter.

"Um, the man they were taking away, Ben Danforth . . . I knew him from back home. He stole tip money and I wanted to give him a chance to explain why."

Charles squinted in the direction of the chopper with renewed interest. "You're kidding?"

She shook her head. "Tenzing brought him down. Bad things have been happening on the mountain, Charles. Really bad things. I'm so glad you're here." She broke down into tears, dropping her head into her hands. She had been so close to making the decision to turn around, to go home. She'd had one foot in the chopper. But she was still here. And she still had the mountain to face.

Charles patted her shoulder. "Talk to me . . ."

She inhaled deep into her lungs. "A woman died yesterday, below camp two. I was the one who found her."

"Cecily, that's terrible." He shook his head. "What happened?"

"Doug says that she got tangled in the rappel line. A freak accident. But Ben thinks something else happened."

Charles narrowed his eyes. "What?"

"He thinks someone killed her. He says he was there when she fell, and she wasn't alone. Someone pushed her off the wall. He ran away because he feared for his life." She pulled out the note from her pocket. "I think maybe he left this for me as a warning."

Charles clenched his jaw, staring at the note. "He could be right," he said, his voice soft.

Cecily's eyes widened. "What? You can't mean . . ."

"Well, where better for a killer to hide, than somewhere already known as the death zone?"

Cecily stopped walking. How could Charles know that? He was confirming her worst fears and yet he'd only just arrived . . .

He turned to her, when he realized she wasn't following. Then he gazed up to the mountain's summit. High above their heads, Manaslu stood silent as a sentinel.

"Cecily, up there, I've seen men's minds bend and twist. People with the most rational, logical brains, with athletic bodies to rival Olympians, with survival skills honed in some of the toughest environments on Earth—they are no match for the high peaks. They come undone. They make bad decisions. They see things that aren't there. Yes, I've seen the killer on the mountain. He's in all of us. He's up here." He tapped at the side of his temple. "The killer took that woman. He took Ben. But he won't take us. Because as a team, we will look out for each other."

She swallowed, her breath slowing as she understood what he was saying. Altitude sickness. It still wasn't a comforting thought. It meant everyone—anyone—could be a danger. "What if someone on the team succumbs?"

"You have me. I have faced that killer many times and bested him. If anything goes wrong, I will save you."

She tore her gaze from the mountain to look instead at this mountain of a man. She felt a rush of relief flood through her body. "I wish I had an ounce of your confidence . . ."

"I am experienced." He smiled, and she returned it. He slung his arm around her shoulders. "We should go and find Doug. He's lost many people to altitude. And yet he comes back every time. Soon you'll learn what we already know, that while danger lurks up there, so too does unimaginable beauty. I've tried to find it in other places but never succeeded. It's worth it."

They meandered back to the teahouse, slowed by a group of schoolchildren who streamed out of their classroom as Charles passed. They tugged at his sleeve, begging for autographs and photos. Cecily gathered them together at a nearby wall, Charles in the center, and took a big group picture. By the time they reached the teahouse, Doug and Mingma were waiting outside with Tenzing.

"Look who I found on my trek in!" said Charles, gesturing at Cecily.

Doug frowned. "What are you doing down here?"

She winced, preparing for his reaction. But Charles's arrival had emboldened her. "I came to speak to Ben."

Doug's lips drew tightly together. "And?"

She glanced at Charles. "He was obviously very unwell. He's on his way to Kathmandu."

"Let's forget about that now," said Charles, clapping Doug on the back. "We need to focus on the task ahead. What's the situation on the hill?"

She found herself once more awed in his presence. His height and long limbs gave him a looming, domineering gait, yet they were offset by his relaxed smile and sparkling blue eyes. She was drawn into his orbit, unable to tear her eyes away. When he stood, it was with a wide-legged stance, folded arms and straight back, like a military man. He exuded integrity, and she couldn't believe he would be involved in anything as paltry and scandalous as using lines and lying about it. Anyone who said that was jealous—and it was easy to see why. Charles was magnificent.

Doug scratched at his temple. "There's a window coming. Lines are fixed to the summit for the team. Should be good to go in a few days."

Cecily tugged at the end of her braids. She hadn't realized their summit push was happening so soon.

"Great news. Looks like I got here just in time, don't you think?" Charles winked at her, and she gave a tentative smile. "I want to catch up with the rest of the team, so let's make a move, shall we?" He gestured for Cecily to take the first step.

"Wait—I wanted to send a couple of emails first."

Charles adjusted his baseball cap. "We've wasted enough time down here. Come on—we're so close to the summit push now; you'll benefit from the lack of distractions."

"I really *won't* benefit from the lack of pay."

"You need to get your head in the game, Cecily. If you're worried about what your editor is thinking, your family, your friends . . . your mindset won't be right. Let's focus on that, shall we?" When she still hesitated, he sighed. "Think of it like this—would your editor rather some little blog now or the big interview with me later?"

"The interview," she said.

"Then let's go."

He walked off, brooking no more debate, and Cecily relented.

"Did you manage to get your permits and admin sorted out in Kathmandu?" she asked, as they walked the path to base camp. Suddenly the route didn't seem so difficult. She wasn't sure if she was getting stronger, or if she just felt more confident in his presence.

"Yes. All my summits have been confirmed. Not that that was in any doubt, but it's good to have it made official. I logged all the GPS tags and sent my photographs in, proof that I made all the true summits without the lines."

"So many hoops to jump through."

"I don't want there to be any doubt."

"Of course . . ." She thought about bringing up Dario's comments, but it didn't seem like the moment. The mood was so much lighter. There would be time for the serious questions later. "So once you've summited Manaslu, you'll have the record!"

He laughed. "That's right. But don't jinx it now."

Walking with the mountain guides was an education. Doug was deep in thought, walking up front with Tenzing. Yet even though his mind was clearly distracted, every step was taken deliberately, with not a single wobble. He could probably climb the mountain blindfolded and still beat her to the top.

Mingma nipped up the path with nimble grace, barely scratching its surface, despite carrying loads that doubled his body weight.

Charles, by contrast, was a beast. With every step the ground seemed to shake under his feet, the mountain submitting to him. He was cut from the same cloth as the early explorers, the ones who stalked the coldest, hardest corners of the Earth wrapped in layers of fur and wearing leather boots stuffed with straw. He was plucked from a different time.

A steady flurry of snow fell from the sky as they passed the first tent marking base camp. Even though the air was thick and soupy, word got out about Charles's arrival. Climbers emerged to shake his hand, and she felt more like a groupie than a team member. But she kept her head held high. She was here at his invitation.

"Charles! How were Shish and Cho this season?" asked a man in a lurid green down jacket.

"They say Shishapangma is an easier mountain, but I was breaking trail in snow up to my waist. Wasn't sure if I was going to make it. Cho—well, you guys know that story."

"What's been the toughest peak so far?"

"I thought I was going to say K2 or Annapurna, but you know what? Dhaulagiri really kicked my ass this year with the terrible weather conditions. One of the first on my list, but one of the toughest so far."

"At least Manaslu will be a breeze."

"It's a mistake to underestimate this mountain. Sounds like she's been tricky so far."

Charles talked to everyone who approached. How many were here out of professional curiosity—and who was jealous? She noticed that Dario wasn't anywhere in sight. No wonder, when he was the one who'd thrown the accusation out about Charles using the fixed lines. Of course she would give Charles the chance to defend himself. The fact that Dario wasn't here to make those wild claims in person made her doubt their veracity even more.

She could feel men's eyes on her wherever she went, and she huddled into the neck of her jacket. She'd been in a bubble up at the Manners Mountaineering camp, where she had Elise to buddy up with. Again, she noted how few other female faces there were.

"Charles, dai, we'd better keep moving if we are to make it for lunch," said Mingma.

Charles nodded. "I'm starving, so we can't hang around much longer. Onward!"

Eventually the Manners Mountaineering flag loomed out of the fog. She was amazed to find she wasn't nearly as out of breath as a week ago. Acclimatization was working.

Yet she wasn't happy to arrive at their camp. Despite Charles's reassurance that Ben and Irina had been victims of hypoxia, her paranoia returned, dragged in with the fog that lingered around the mountain like a blanket.

A shroud.

With every climber who followed them to their dining tent, she wondered: *Where were you when Irina died?*

She trained her gaze on Charles. The mountain legend in the making. What if he was wrong and there *was* someone dangerous here?

What if the killer was on their team?

Elise had been in the tent with her all night, she was sure.

Zak had been alone, but his company name was plastered all over this expedition. She couldn't imagine him jeopardizing that.

One of the Sherpas? Surely not. This was their livelihood. She'd seen how angry they were when Ben had taken the tip money. Killing clients would not be a good plan.

Doug, with all his anger-management issues, could be a suspect. He was obviously a strong enough climber to have pulled it off. Yet what Cecily had seen time and again was that he clung to his values—of respect for the mountain, and for the safety of the people on it—like a limpet to rock.

That left Grant. He had motive and opportunity, and she felt he had the ability—no matter what Elise had said. He could easily be faking his weakness.

But even Grant wouldn't be stupid enough to do something when Charles was around. Surely no one would.

CHAPTER 34

THEIR DINING TENT WAS packed to the gills. Doug hovered on the outskirts, his hands tucked under his armpits, but there was no way that he could talk to the team. It was so full, Cecily had to perch on a camping stool—all the chairs were taken.

Dario was still conspicuously absent.

Throughout the day and into the night, Charles held court. He dominated the table, sitting at its head. "We pushed through snow-fields up to here," he said, gesturing at the belt on his trousers. "It felt like we weren't going to make it. I've never been so exhausted in my life. I actually skipped two camps because the snow was so intense," he said, repeating the story of his time on Shishapangma.

"But you made it?"

"I made it. The *true* summit, crossing that knife-edge ridge à cheval, as they say. Not all my summits are glamorous! But I'm glad to be back here in time to summit with my team, on the final mountain of the whole project."

"The homestretch!" said Zak.

Charles smiled, lacing his fingers behind his head. "It's not over until it's over, but I'm feeling good."

"Tell us about the rescue on Dhaulagiri," said one of the men from Elbrus Elite.

He held up his hands. "Oh, I'm sure you've heard it all already."

"No, please." Cecily made her voice heard over the others. "I'm so intrigued. What actually happened?" Stories of Charles's rescues had been told over and over again in the press, but she wanted to hear how he told it to a group of his climbing peers.

He shifted in his seat, staring down at his hands. It was the first time she had seen him looking humble. A curious silence descended, everyone in the tent listening, rapt. "You know, I was climbing alone, trying to get to the top, fast and light. I left base camp in the evening, climbed through the night, reached the summit around midday, and it was glorious. But on the way back down, I came across two guys in trouble. They were sitting on the route, slumped on the snow. I knew instantly they were in a bad way. Hypoxic. Confused. One of them—Leonardo—had a leg injury. They'd tried to splint it, but he wasn't able to walk unaided."

"Shit," said Zak.

Cecily tore her eyes away from Charles. Looking around, the attention of the tent was firmly fixed on the bold adventurer. Well, no. Not quite. Doug was looking down at his hands, twisting in his lap.

"They needed more oxygen, but I wasn't carrying any. I radioed for someone to bring some up, but no one responded." He leaned forward on his forearms. "They both needed to get down the mountain, but while Leo couldn't walk, Marco could sit upright. I waited with them as long as I could, but if I stayed any longer, without any supplemental oxygen, I would have been a casualty too." He slid back in his chair and folded his arms, then rubbed the space between his thick eyebrows. "Only one of them was strong enough. Marco. Making that decision was the toughest call I've ever had to make. But something in his eyes told me he wanted to live. As for his brother . . . well, I looked in his eyes and saw defeat.

"We were well above eight thousand meters. I dragged Marco's arm around my neck and got him to his feet. Without oxygen my strength was deteriorating fast. But I got him down as far as camp three, carrying him on my back."

"Jesus," said Zak. "I've heard you tell that story before, but every time it gets me. You must have been exhausted."

Charles fixed Zak with his icy stare. "Up there I'm so focused, I don't notice exhaustion or fear or pain. I dial into that code-red aggression mindset, completing my mission no matter what. Then as soon as I see someone in trouble, it's like a switch. Someone needs me; I'm there. I access that hidden reserve of energy I hold back, just for those moments. From camp three, we were able to get him down to base and have him airlifted off. I then helped Doug arrange the rescue team for Leo. A group was already mobilizing to go when I arrived at base camp, but they needed me to give them a more exact location. Isn't that right, Doug?"

Doug grunted in response.

"But a location wasn't good enough. I picked up an oxygen mask and tank, ate some food, sucked down a Coca-Cola and then went with the rescue team, straight back to where I'd had to leave the guy. Unfortunately, by the time we made it back up to him, he was dead."

"Oh my god, that's awful," Cecily said.

"No one lasts long in the death zone," said Charles. "I wish I could have saved them both."

Death was so common in the mountains; it terrified her to think about it. And yet, without Charles, there would have been even more fatalities this year.

The chat moved on, and when she stood up to refill her water bottle, her stool was taken. She thought about asking for it back, but she'd been feeling a bit claustrophobic in the crowd. Soon she'd be able to ask Charles questions one-on-one, without people listening in. It was great hearing the way he told his stories to the group, but she wanted to get him alone, go deeper, tease out those *exclusive* narrative details that would make her article sing. She slipped outside, huddling into her jacket. The snow was still falling heavily.

Laughter and warm light from the cook tent attracted her attention. She made her way over.

"Come in, didi! Are you hungry?" Galden stood up as soon as she entered. He grabbed a metal plate from a tall stack.

"Thank you, Galden, but I'm fine." She was moved by how much the man cared for her, and grateful for his concern. "Just too many people in the dining tent."

"Everyone wants to speak to Mr. Charles," he said.

"Well, I would rather speak to you," she said, with a grin. "I'm glad I caught you here . . ."

Galden stiffened, interrupting her. "Wait—I am sorry for how I acted last night, didi. But when someone does what he did, it makes me so angry. To us, the mountain is like God. We must have justice."

She blinked. "Are you talking about Ben? Oh, I know what he did was very wrong. I couldn't let him get hurt but . . . he is in the hands of the authorities now. You will get justice."

Galden nodded.

She reached out and touched his arm. "Can I ask you a few questions for my article? Would you mind?"

"Sure, didi, sure." Galden grabbed her a foldout stool from behind one of the tables, and once she had a hot drink in hand and Dawa had placed a bowl of boiled potatoes and a plate of chili salt between them, the interview began.

EXCERPT FROM CECILY'S NOTES: INTERVIEW WITH GALDEN SONAM SHERPA

September 12

Without the Sherpas, there is no mountaineering industry in Nepal. Period. Once relegated to bit players in the alpinist history books, now the strongest climbers in the world are taking center stage.

The word "Sherpa" technically refers to a specific ethnic group of people from the Solukhumbu Valley high in the Himalayas, but has grown to become shorthand for a high-altitude climbing guide. All the Sherpas on Charles's team are from that region, handpicked and personally invited, just like the paying clients. We have four Sherpas on the team—Mingma Lakpa Sherpa, Doug's business partner and head guide, Tenzing Kasang Sherpa, Phemba Tenji Sherpa and Galden Sonam Sherpa. Their cultural traditions dictate that their first names are based on days of the week or taken from Buddhist scripture.

Yet while the Sherpa people have a global reputation for excellence in the high peaks, they also bear the greatest risk—and have suffered the most tragedies. Every year, hundreds of families are left without a primary breadwinner when another Sherpa is killed—just by doing his job. The money they can earn from the two-month Everest prime season, though, is life changing. And so they keep coming back.

Galden, 24, is from the village of Tengboche and walked to school in the shadow of Sagarmatha—Mount Everest. He is the guide I have grown closest to throughout the expedition, helped by the fact that he has referred to me as "sister" from the start and never lets me go an hour without making sure I've had a hot drink. He is the definition of calm and considered—yet with a strong sense of honor and justice.

I know that as long as he is with me on the climb, I will be safe.

CECILY: I'd love to know how you first got into climbing?

GALDEN: I was lucky. My uncle was a climbing guide, so he brought me into the business when I was very young. My first mountain was Lobuche East. Then I climbed Everest when I was eighteen. Once you have an Everest summit, you can say you are a true high-altitude guide. Tenzing worked with my uncle too. And so he is like an uncle to me. A great strong man on the mountain.

CECILY: A real family business!

GALDEN: With my father, brother and I together, we have over forty Everest summits, and many more on other eight-thousanders.

CECILY: Incredible. And each time you are taking such an enormous risk. Don't you wish you could do something else for a living?

GALDEN: It is the best way to make money for my family. Yet even though climbing big mountains is more popular, and demand is high, it is difficult for the younger members of my family. Too many people calling themselves "Sherpa" without any experience in the mountains. It is important to us that Nepal's climbing reputation is preserved as the safest and best.

CECILY: Tell me, what do you think about the people you climb with? The clients who travel all this way, and spend so much money just to climb?

GALDEN: Some, they become like family. Like you, didi.

CECILY: I'm honored, Galden. But surely not all . . .

GALDEN: If people do not come here to climb, then we would not have work. I would not be able to provide for my wife. It helps to grow our country. So I am grateful to everyone who comes. And we do our best to keep you safe.

CECILY: You are very diplomatic, Galden. Surely it must be difficult to risk your own life all the time?

GALDEN: This is my choice.

CECILY: But?

GALDEN: Sometimes, people, they come to the mountain and don't understand the risks. When that happens, they put us in danger. That's when I am not happy. But Doug does not allow that. That is why I am glad to work for him.

CECILY: It's so reassuring to hear you say that. You say you have a wife? What's her name?

GALDEN: Nima Doma. We have a baby on the way.

CECILY: Oh my goodness, congratulations!

GALDEN: It is hard to be away at this time, but after this mountain the climbing season is over for a while, so I can go home and meet my son or daughter.

CECILY: That is so exciting. Do you think your children will climb mountains?

GALDEN: My honest hope is that they do not have to do what I do. It is so dangerous. I hope they get a good education and grow up not needing to climb.

CECILY: I hope so too, my friend. So what do you think about Charles's mission and his record attempt? Do you think it should be a Sherpa at the center of the world's attention?

GALDEN: We are all very happy for Charles, dai. He is a great climber. It is part of our Buddhist culture to be happy for others. My youngest brother, he is training to be a monk. We have a beautiful monastery in my village, Tengboche. I would like to take you there one day.

CECILY: I would love that. My grandmother was Buddhist.

GALDEN: She would be proud—you are a strong climber, Cecily. The mountain will protect you. That is what we pray for.

There was a raucous cheer from the dining tent, interrupting them. With a belly full of potato and hot tea, Cecily yawned—the trip down and back from Samagaun, the fear ignited by Ben and the excitement of Charles's arrival—it had wiped her out.

"Let me take you back to your tent," said Galden.

"Thank you." She did feel a bit woozy and tired.

She put her jacket back on and took another mug of tea back to her tent. She and Galden walked in silence through the gently falling snow. "Can I ask you one more question?"

"Yes, didi. Anything."

"Why did Doug leave Summit Extreme? You were part of that team, weren't you? I only know some of the story—that he hit someone?"

Galden remained silent for a few steps. "It was our autumn Everest expedition. He got angry with a very rich, very powerful client.

There was a big hanging serac that threatened to fall on the route, so Doug said he wouldn't take us through the Khumbu icefall. All of us, the Sherpas, agreed with him. We lost so many in a serac fall in 2014, we never want to take a risk like that again. But this man tried to force us to go through. Doug refused. They had a fight."

"My god."

"Then Summit Extreme fired him."

"Is it normal for Doug to react that way?"

"I had never seen it before. But that same day, he had received a call from England that affected him badly. I think an incident with his family? But he never told us. Charles and Doug worked alone for a while. I was glad when I heard Charles was putting a team together for Manaslu and I could work with Doug again."

Cecily nodded. "So you respect him."

"Yes, of course. There is no man better at guiding than Doug Manners. He has the utmost respect for the mountain."

CHAPTER 35

SHE TOSSED AND TURNED through the night. The cold wrapped itself around her body, and yet her head felt as if it was on fire. Everything was tight, her muscles sore. Nausea rose in her throat, and her dreams were filled with darkness. She drifted in and out of sleep, but whenever she woke, her watch informed her that she still had hours before sunrise.

In the dark, she heard the creak of a rope. Behind her eyes, she saw Irina's body, gently twisting against the wall of ice. And always that discordant whistle in the background.

When she did wake up properly, she found herself inside a womb. All sound was muffled, and even though she was certain the sun was up, the light through her yellow-domed tent was muted. Even the air felt heavier, as if she were cocooned in soft cotton, a duvet thrown over the world. She unzipped her tent.

The sight of base camp took her breath away.

Almost half a meter of snow had fallen, blanketing the ground in a soft carpet of white. The sky by contrast was a piercing blue, the clearest it had been since they'd arrived.

She spotted Galden and Mingma nearby, going around to each tent in turn, shaking off the snow that had accumulated on the roof of each one. That's why it had been so exceptionally warm inside her tent. She'd essentially had another layer of insulation thrown over the top, a weighted blanket of snow.

A heavy weighted blanket. It was alarming how much some of

the other tents had caved in. She saw a couple of other sleepy faces emerge.

"What are you doing?" she asked Mingma, as they cleared Zak's tent.

"The snow can be heavy on the tent roofs. We had a big amount last night. Dawa—he had a problem, you know?"

She tilted her head. "What happened?"

"His tent completely collapsed."

Her mouth fell agape. "Oh my god, that's terrifying! Is he all right?"

"We got him out in time, but it was close."

"Thank goodness. Wow. I had no idea that could happen."

Mingma nodded, moving on to the next tent.

Cecily was amazed how the snow changed the atmosphere at base camp. It was a proper wintry scene now, so bright that it dazzled her eyes. She reached for her sunglasses and pulled her camera out of her down jacket. The blanket of snow in front of her was pristine, not yet marred by human footsteps.

She ventured to the kitchen tent to survey the damage. As Mingma had said, the cook's tent had caved in on itself, one of the poles snapped in half, the metal end poking up into the air. She saw the chef smoking a few meters off. "Are you OK, Dawa?" she asked.

"Look what the snow did! They had to dig me out."

"Are you hurt? I mean, apart from . . ." She gestured to his forehead, where a small cut was covered over by a small plaster. He still had dried flecks of blood in his eyebrow. "I have some medical supplies in my kit bag if you want a better bandage?"

He covered his wound with his hand. "No, no. I am OK. Do you want some hot water?"

Now it was her turn to shake her head. "I might head back to rest a bit longer." She cast her eyes over the tattered remains of his tent and felt a chill. To think that could've happened to any of them. Being buried in a cavern of snow or impaled by a snapped tent pole in her sleep did not seem appealing.

There were even more ways to die on the mountain than she had imagined.

She couldn't sleep, but she rested for a while in her tent, shivering beneath her sleeping bag. Eventually the time crept closer to eight o'clock, and her stomach rumbled.

"This weather is nuts, isn't it?" Zak said, emerging from his tent at the same time, stretching. "Shall we get some breakfast?"

She nodded. "I need coffee. And a lot of it."

A loud buzzing sounded over their heads, and Grant's drone flew overhead, taking aerial shots of their camp. This time she could see he was the one operating it, so the jolt of fear didn't come. In fact, she imagined it would look quite spectacular—definitely a cinematic moment for his film.

Grant was using the remote control topless, his shirt wrapped around his waist, showing off his toned chest. He wore his trousers tucked into the gaiters of his eight-thousand-meter boots, the laces loose, tongues lolling. She resisted the urge to roll her eyes and ducked into the dining tent.

The debris from the impromptu party the night before had already been cleared away. Elise was at the table, her chin in her hands, poring over a map of the mountain with Charles. He was pointing out the route he was planning on taking, adjacent to—but never touching—the fixed lines.

Cecily headed straight for the instant coffee. She'd just about stirred it thoroughly, along with large spoonfuls of powdered milk and sugar, when Doug walked in, looking grave.

"Everyone here?"

"Not Grant. He's filming," said Elise.

"Fine. I have an update. It might be bright this morning, but the bad weather front higher up the mountain looks set to stick." He showed the forecast on his phone—snow, snow and more snow. "We're stuck a few more days."

Zak groaned, but Doug's forecast proved accurate. The snow started again while they were eating breakfast and fell relentlessly throughout the day.

It killed any hope of Wi-Fi too. She had two more blogs written and interviews ready to send, but they weren't worth anything without a connection.

Zak kept tapping at his devices, changing from tablet to phone to laptop. "Is something up with the satellite signal too? I haven't been able to upload the footage from my camera for ages."

"It has been intermittent—"

"Sort it out, Doug. These people need to be connected," Charles interjected. He flexed his hands, cracking his knuckles. "Did you say Grant was outside?" he asked Elise. When she nodded, he strode out of the tent. Doug soon followed.

"Boy, am I glad Charles is here," said Zak. "Maybe things will start to pick up around here."

Cecily tilted her head. "You haven't been happy?"

"Are you kidding? No internet, no sign of a summit push—the camp was robbed! Doug let the standards slip. I'm paying a lot of money to be here, you know."

Elise packed away the map and instead shuffled a deck of cards. "Do you know how to play President?"

Cecily didn't, but it was easy enough to learn. A game of hierarchy and chance, where the game was rigged against the loser—who had to give his or her two best cards to the winner. It was perfect for a day trapped at base camp.

Mingma and Galden joined in too. After the number of hands topped twenty, and with Zak dominating as President, they got bored. Galden taught her how to make paper cranes, something he'd learned from his nieces.

"You're going to make a great dad, Galden," she said.

"Thank you, didi."

"I can't just sit around here anymore," said Zak. "I'm going to Wi-Fi mountain to check if there's any signal. Anyone coming with?"

"I'll come," Cecily said. Even if there was no internet access, she needed to stretch her tired muscles from the long hike the day before.

They traced the path that led downhill, toward Summit Extreme.

Zak nudged her arm as they walked. "Hey, I was thinking—I took some photos up on camp two. They should be ultra-high-definition, way better than that digital camera you have. I'd love for your editor to use some of the photos in conjunction with your blogs—if you credit me and TalkForward."

"I bet she'd love that! How should I tell her to access them?"

"I'll send you the link. The password is my favorite mountain, Rainier. I'd give you your own camera but I only brought two. I gave the other to Elise."

"Don't worry; I'm not jealous! I don't have an eye for photography."

"Just a nose for a story."

She snorted. "I suppose so!"

"You've had a lot to write about."

"That obvious?"

"I wonder what those lamas at the puja told the mountain," he continued. "They probably said something along the lines of 'make sure these assholes turn around and go home without summiting.' Maybe Doug didn't pay them enough for a good blessing."

She shivered, pulling the hood of her jacket tight under her chin.

"This snow is coming down hard, isn't it?" he continued. "I wonder how it's going to affect our plans."

"Is this even the way to Summit Extreme?" she asked.

The snow was falling heavier around them, almost blizzard-like now. A seed of fear planted itself deep in her stomach. They'd walked a long way from camp, and as she looked around now, she couldn't tell which way they had come. Zak had a stoic look of concentration on his face—but she wasn't convinced that he knew the way either. Their footprints disappeared quickly, covered in fresh snow. And all around them, the clouds had gathered in close, making them feel shrouded from the outside world.

She moved closer to Zak, grabbing the sleeve of his jacket. He stood a little straighter but his eyes darted about, trying to determine the right direction. "This way," he said. They took a few tentative steps, her foot slipping on the rock.

A heavy boot step crunched behind them. She and Zak pivoted around each other, but they couldn't see through the clouds and the mist. "Who's there?" shouted Zak.

No reply.

Only the steps continued, and the wobble of a rock close to where they were standing. The hairs rose on the back of her neck, her ears straining to hear every sound. She couldn't tell what direction the steps were coming from.

Every muscle was tense, her mouth dry, ready to run . . .

Then the fog parted and the Summit Extreme guide stepped forward.

Cecily released a long breath. A familiar face.

Still, the unease remained.

"What are you two doing out here?" Dario asked.

"We were coming to use the Wi-Fi . . . but I guess there's no chance of it in this." She laughed nervously, coming down from high alert.

He shook his head. "No, the signal is out. We are trying to get a technician in, but it is confusing everyone. You two have wandered a bit off course. Have a cup of tea with me and wait out the weather."

Dario started walking toward his camp. She shared a look with Zak, who shrugged and followed in the Summit Extreme guide's footsteps. Cecily jogged a few steps to keep up.

"Have you seen anyone tampering with the antenna?" Zak asked. When Dario shook his head, he continued. "I've been thinking on this, and I think one possibility might be a signal jammer. You can buy one off the internet for like thirty bucks nowadays."

Dario clucked his tongue. "What would a jammer look like?"

"Depends really. But a small black box, with lots of antennas sticking out one end."

"We have found nothing like that. But I will keep an eye out. Everyone on the mountain needs communication, though, so why would someone do that? I don't understand."

"Really wish I could get one of my guys out here. They'd sort it in no time. Maybe that Ben guy set up a jammer? Stop you from calling the authorities, that kind of thing."

Dario's shoulders tensed at Ben's name.

Cecily picked up her pace, so she was walking at Dario's shoulder. "Can I ask you something? I know you think Ben's a liar, but you both raised questions about Irina's death. What did you mean when you said it was as suspicious as they come?"

He stopped, his eyes searching her face. "Irina was a very experienced mountaineer. Very experienced mountaineers don't get rope wrapped around their necks during a rappel. Not even if they slip and fall."

"Wait, what?" said Zak. "I thought her death was a freak accident."

"So what do you think happened, Dario?" Cecily pressed.

Dario ducked inside the Summit Extreme dining tent and busied himself with making tea, loading his cup with mounds of sugar. "I don't know for sure. By the time our team got to the Hanging Place, there were so many footprints . . . It was impossible to tell what had happened or if anyone had been with Irina at the time. I asked one of the cooks on the Russian team. He said he had only seen one other person coming down off the mountain early that morning. But he could not tell what team he'd been from."

"That must have been Ben."

"How do you know that?"

Cecily swallowed, her mouth feeling dry. "I went to speak to him yesterday before he flew out. He said he'd been camping rough on the mountain. About a week or so ago, I saw a single tent, past our base campsite. It didn't seem to belong to any team on the mountain. Doug had no idea who it could have belonged to."

"Jesus, Cecily. Why didn't you tell us?" Zak said.

"Doug saw the tent?" asked Dario.

"No, when we went back the next morning it was gone."

"What did it look like?"

"It was red . . . with some kind of darker accents. And small. Much smaller than our base camp tents."

"Scheiss." Dario clicked his teeth. "I'm sure that's one of ours. Or was—on our last count, we noticed one of our high-altitude tents was missing. Dorje—my base camp manager—thought maybe we had miscounted. But Ben must have stolen it."

"Nightmare," said Zak.

"And now my team is more restless than ever, thanks to this bad weather. Looks like we might be grounded for a couple of weeks, or more . . . There might not be any summits this year."

"Really?" Cecily's heart pounded. "Why not? Why can't we just wait on the mountain until a window opens?"

"By October, the weather gets too cold and unstable and it is no longer safe for us to bring clients."

"That soon? What about Charles's mission?"

"He can stay as long as he wants. Maybe that is for the best. Trust me, I think Charles should be the only man on the mountain."

"What do you mean by that?" Cecily asked.

He sighed. "There is arrogance, there is ego, and then there is Charles McVeigh."

Cecily shivered. The idea of someone jamming their communications signals was a new horror Cecily hadn't thought of. But Dario hadn't seemed that surprised. And every time she spoke to him he found some way to plant seeds of doubt about Charles.

"I have got to speak to my team," Dario continued. "Stay and finish your drinks. Can you find your way back to your own base camp?"

"Sure," said Zak.

Cecily watched Dario as he put down his cup, his fingers curling into fists. His entire body seemed tense.

And as he swept through the tent doors, he let out a sound that chilled Cecily to the bone.

A whistle.

September 18
Manaslu base camp
4,800m

After what's felt like weeks of mostly gloomy clouds and heavy snow (but really has been five days), we woke to a welcome surprise this morning: bright sunshine and blue skies. Finally! By the time I got outside, it seemed like all of base camp had got up extra early to stare at the view.

The term "blue skies" hardly does what we are seeing justice. Up here, the air is thinner, but it is also more transparent, allowing us to see more of the darkness of space beyond. The result is an ultramarine sky that is a darker, richer, more intense blue than at sea level. "Rayleigh scattering" is the technical term.

Me? I am lost for words.

The break in the weather is also good news for us climbers, since it means we will be able to start our summit pushes imminently.

My mind is a blur. Although physically, I feel stronger for having acclimatized and rested, mentally I am in a rough place. All the dangers of the task ahead are racing through my mind. Although the mountain looks serene now, framed by that blue sky, I know too much to feel relaxed. Unlike on other mountains, there is nowhere safe to sleep on Manaslu.

I keep thinking back to 2012, one of Manaslu's deadliest years. An enormous serac broke free from the icefall above camp three, causing an avalanche that swept through the tents of the sleeping climbers, killing eleven people. It's the reason Manaslu has one of the highest death rates of all the big peaks.

And sadly, this was brought home last week. A climber passed away during our acclimatization routine—the second tragedy of the expedition so far. Her name was Irina Popova, climbing with Elbrus Elite. My thoughts and condolences go out to her friends and family, in Nepal, in London, Russia and beyond.

May she rest in peace.

I'm not writing this to psych myself out, to worry my friends and family, or to make excuses. But as the weeks progress, I've found myself thinking more and more about why we take to the high peaks. Is it simply for the achievement of a summit? Is that the only thing that would make this trip worthwhile? And the answer is: of course not. For those of you thinking, "Yeah, right. Of course she'd be disappointed if she didn't make it," maybe, before I got here, I would have agreed with you. But being here changes you. Each moment I spend on the mountain, every additional step that I take, feels like a win. A big win. Every day is pushing my limits—physically, mentally and emotionally. And I'm still going.

The truth is, I am physically the least experienced team member here—every step seems to take me just a bit longer. But I'm still taking steps forward each time. So if I don't make the summit, guys, don't be sad for me. I've already accomplished way more than I thought I possibly could.

CHAPTER 36

SHE CLOSED HER LAPTOP, leaned back, closed her eyes and took a moment to appreciate the warmth of the sun on her face. Writing the blogs, putting her thoughts down on the page, was therapeutic, but she wished she felt as optimistic and relaxed as she was aiming to come off to the reader.

Only a sliver of the doubts and fears churning through her body seeped into the text. She was still shaken after her experience at Summit Extreme a few days back. She'd waited to hear the tune in Dario's whistle, but Zak had started talking and the noise had been swallowed up by the fog.

And she still hadn't been able to send any of the reports over to Michelle. She knew she'd be in a lot of trouble. She'd just have to make sure she delivered an article that made it all worthwhile.

"Team? Dining tent," Doug called out. Butterflies fluttered in her stomach. He was about to make *the* announcement, she was sure. The one they had all been waiting for.

Zak stumbled his way into the dining tent, groggy after a nap in the sun. He wasn't the only one. Everyone seemed to have been lulled by the good weather.

The Sherpas were already gathered inside, standing along the far wall.

"What do we think this is about then?" asked Grant. He took another sip from a metal cup, balancing his feet up on the table. Since Irina had died and his equipment had been damaged, his mood had changed. The long snow days made any exercise impossible, he'd been engaging less in the games and conversations, his expressions clouded and brooding. Charles's arrival had perked him up a bit, and when he could, he'd been out filming establishing shots around base camp. But otherwise he seemed in a rough place.

Elise came in after, bopping her head to music playing through her headphones. She seemed totally unfazed by the long delay.

Finally, Doug entered with Charles. Doug leaned against the back of one of the chairs as Charles stood off to one side, his arms folded.

Doug coughed. "So, the time has come. The latest forecast says this window will last two days before turning again. We will make our summit bid tomorrow."

Cheers erupted in the tent. Charles smiled, the happiest she'd seen him, and the Sherpas clapped behind them. Doug, however, remained somber.

And so did she.

This was what these mountain guys lived for. The anticipation, the knowledge that all the training and waiting was paying off—that everything they'd been planning and preparing for was going to be put to the test. They were either going to succeed or fail over the next few days.

But she was still haunted by the thought of Irina's body. The dangers felt so real.

Mingma stepped up. "You will each be accompanied by a Sherpa, and you will climb together. They will carry your oxygen—except for you, Elise, of course. All our Sherpas are strong climbers, with lots of experience, lots of eight-thousand-meter summits, so you will be in good hands. We have prepared food for the mountain, so please take a look through and make sure you pack enough—at least three breakfasts, three lunches and three dinners. Zak, you will be with Tenzing. Elise, with Phemba. Grant, you'll be with me. And, Cecily, you will climb with Galden."

She caught Galden's eye and smiled. She was pleased. He was young and strong—more serious than Phemba, but more youthful and energetic than Tenzing, without the leadership worries Mingma had. Besides that, they had bonded.

Grant shifted back in his chair, his eyes fixed on the duffel bags filled with dehydrated food packets, but Doug put his hands up to stop him.

"Hold on. We have a few more things to cover. Practice with the oxygen masks so you get used to putting them on before we leave. Remember, the most important rule of all: My word is law on the mountain. If I tell you you're going down, you go down. No questions. I don't care if you're at camp three or a step away from the summit. Understood?"

She murmured her agreement, along with Elise. Doug cast his hard stare on the two who were quiet. She nudged Zak in the ribs. He glared at her, but then piped up, "Yeah, yeah."

"And you, Grant? Do you get it? This isn't a joke."

"You won't have to turn me around, so it doesn't matter anyway."

Doug was about to protest again, when Grant waved his arms in front of his face. "I get it."

"Good. And second only to me is your assigned Sherpa. If he makes the call, you listen. Getting to the summit is a great achievement. But the mountain will always be there. Getting back down alive is the priority."

"My turn now." Charles strode to the head of the table and all eyes turned to him. He caught the gaze of each one of them in turn. When he came to her, Cecily straightened in her chair. He smiled and gave her a nod. "This is it, team. We're climbing together, all the way to the top. This is what you have been waiting for. Don't fool yourselves. Climbing is more than one foot in front of the other. You have to *believe* you are capable of more." He paused.

"I've never told anyone this before, but I almost gave up on my first Everest attempt. It was so much harder than I had imagined. And I don't mean technically harder—I'd faced many bigger challenges than that before. But mentally? Climbing an eight-thousander is unlike anything else. I remember it as if it were yesterday. I was down on my knees beneath what used to be the Hillary Step. It was still dark; the sun hadn't risen yet. People were crawling over me on the lines—honestly, I think they'd given me up for dead. Objectively, I knew there'd be no chance at a rescue if I didn't move. I didn't pay for a climbing Sherpa, I didn't have good insurance—not that insurance means anything in the death zone.

"I'd never had that feeling before. That emptiness. That indifference for my own life. But when I thought it was all over, the sun rose over the horizon and hit my face. Warmth spread through my fingers, my eyes cleared, and I realized I had so much still to live for. I'd spent my entire life looking at the mountains, wondering what was up there. If I had it in me to take a few more steps, I'd finally know what it was like to have nothing more above me. No farther to go. To stand at the tallest point on Earth for a moment. What a privilege.

"I picked myself up and made it to the top. I knew who I was in that moment. The mountain made me.

"That's what makes these eight-thousand-meter peaks so special. These are the pinnacles of Earth. And reaching them tests you. They challenge you to be the very best versions of yourselves. So give everything you have to this opportunity, this moment, this mountain. Because if you do—trust me—your sacrifice will be rewarded with the most incredible gift, one that no one can take from you: knowledge of who you truly are. Appreciate it.

"And take your place in the history books, among the most valiant of people on Earth."

CHAPTER 37

AFTER DINNER, THE OTHERS fled the dining tent to get prepped. She knew she should go and pack as well. Yet she hung around, sipping at her hot tea with lemon.

Charles's speech had thrilled her and terrified her. Cecily could see now why Charles was a legend in the making. There was something almost supernatural about his will, and she wanted to absorb it.

But she *didn't* know who she truly was. Whether she had that capability. And she couldn't help it; paranoia still plagued her. Anxiety paced like a beast in her belly. She didn't want the fear to roar and bare its teeth, or she would be reduced to a quivering wreck, unable to move. Just like on Snowdon. She was doing so well at keeping it at bay, but she could feel it lurking around the corner.

"You good, chérie?" Elise had returned to the dining area, her arms open. Cecily stepped into the embrace, feeling the strength in Elise's body as she wrapped her arms around her back.

"I . . . I'm not sure I'm ready," Cecily replied. If she started talking about murderers and conspiracy theories, Elise would think she'd lost it.

"You've done everything you can. Now it's up to the mountain."

"The mountain hasn't been great to us so far. So much has happened. So much has gone wrong."

"Don't think about it. It only has to go right for the next couple of days. Then we'll be back in Kathmandu, and you and I can head to a spa for a well-deserved massage."

"You mean it?"

"I do. I'm so glad to have met you, Cecily. You're a good person. A good friend."

"I'm glad I met you too. My rock on this mountain."

They hugged again. Cecily sighed. She needed to get it together. When she finally gathered the courage to head outside, she had a welcome surprise: a sky wide, clear and full of stars.

She took a few steps away from the big water tank where they brushed their teeth and found a place that was far enough from the lights to really see the night sky. She almost never prayed in her real life. But in real life, she didn't surround herself with objective danger. She was about to trust her life to the mountain and to her own two feet. So she sent up a prayer to every god that could be out there, to every deity, ancestor or shooting star who might be able to lend her a hand on the journey.

Please let me make it to the summit.

Please let me make it back down.

For weeks now, the feeling she'd had at the temple—of being mixed up, vacillating between anxious and determined, fearful and courageous, wanting to stay and leave, had been tearing her in two. Now, though, she felt settled. She belonged on this team, and she was serving the memory of both Alain and Irina by remaining. If their deaths were tragic accidents, they wouldn't have wanted her to abandon her climb. But if someone dangerous had taken their lives? Well, it seemed she was the only person on the mountain determined to get some answers. She *couldn't* leave.

She had to admit that ambition had gripped her; she could feel the fingers of it around her heart. Not just for the summit, though she could picture the disappointment she would feel if she didn't make it, and the elation, the pride in her achievement, if she summited. But also for the story, the real story of the mountain, which was still eluding her and yet which she felt so close to understanding.

She looked up and spotted the constellation of Orion, hanging almost directly over the summit. In that moment, she knew where she was going.

Along the path that neither Irina nor Alain would ever tread again. She had to do this for them.

The wind blew, circling her, infiltrating the tiny gap between the exposed skin of her neck and the collar of her jacket, and again around her wrists and up underneath her waist. It sent a chill that wound its way down her spine, and she buried her hands deep inside her pockets, hurrying back to the confines of her tent. Her fears were never too far behind her, even when she tried to convince herself she was safe.

She set about packing her gear for the following day, then bundled into her sleeping bag. By the time she slept here again, she would have taken her final steps on the mountain. She'd better enjoy this night while she could. If she could.

Manaslu. I am coming for you.

DRAFT THREE

THE RISE OF SUSPICIOUS DEATHS IN THE HIGH PEAKS
By Cecily Wong

In 2012, despite a devastating avalanche that killed eleven people, over fifty mountaineers made the decision to remain on Manaslu and continue their assault on the mountain. Many of them reached the summit. Death—even in great numbers—is an accepted risk in alpinism. "Keep calm and carry on" is the preferred attitude. But should it be?

Irina Popova might have shone onstage as Miss Russia, but it was the mountains where she felt most at home. She completed the Snow Leopard Challenge—climbing the five peaks in the former Soviet Union above seven thousand meters—before her thirtieth birthday and had summited her first eight-thousander with Makalu in 2014. On the mountain, she was ready with packets of gummy sweets to hand out to anyone looking weary.

Alain Flaubert was a well-respected guide in his hometown of Chamonix, a place overflowing with proficient alpinists. He'd made numerous first ascents in the remote Karakoram, always chasing adventure. He loved wild swimming, embracing a life at one with nature, and his dream had been to leave a flag on the summit in honor of a friend who'd died on Everest.

Neither of these two alpinists lacked the right experience for a challenge like Manaslu, yet both lost their lives on the lower reaches of the mountain. Because danger is accepted, questions are ignored. Evidence is lost, the blame placed on the difficult terrain. No investigations are conducted.

Could accepting inherent risk mean that murder is going unnoticed? After all, with no regulation, the mountains are a wild frontier. Could they also be the perfect killing ground?

CHAPTER 38

SHE SQUEEZED HER EYES shut and stopped typing. She hadn't realized how late it was, and she needed to sleep. The words had niggled, gnawed at her all night, and it wasn't until she had them written down that she could see how paranoid she sounded. *The perfect killing ground?* She didn't have any proof.

Just the words of a man in the grip of altitude sickness, along with a drag deep in her gut, a lump in her throat—and the vision behind her eyes of Irina twisting on the rope.

But if her gut was right, she would investigate when she got back down from the summit. For now, she needed to keep her focus on the task ahead.

Low, low, high, low.

No.

There it was again: that mournful whistle, accompanied by heavy footsteps. It couldn't be Ben—he was back in Kathmandu. Was it Dario? Grant? Or someone unknown, who she hadn't even begun to suspect . . . ?

The whistler crept around her tent, doing a circuit.

She gripped the edge of her sleeping bag, tucking it tight under her chin. Cold sweat dripped down the back of her neck, and she pulled her elbows into her body, shrinking inside the down cocoon.

The whistle drifted away, passing her by, but the knot in her shoulders remained.

Then a shadow fell over the entrance, making the inside of the tent feel even darker.

She couldn't take it any longer. She pushed her laptop to the corner, pulled her boots on, and snatched her headlamp from the pocket of her tent.

"Leave me alone!" she shouted as she threw back the flap and stepped outside into the darkness.

A man stood outside her tent, his posture stooped.

Then he spoke. "Isn't this my tent?"

It was Grant. He took a stumbling step toward her.

"You need help." She sidestepped away from him. "Your tent is that way."

"Room for one more in there?" He slurred his words, and she reeled back from the stench of his breath.

"You're drunk . . ." She saw her opportunity. Maybe now his inhibitions were down, she'd get some answers. "Grant, where were you the morning Irina died?"

He waved his hands over his head. "I was in my tent . . ."

"You could have easily followed her down and back before morning. I heard what she said to you. Calling you a pig. That had to hurt."

His eyes flashed and he tensed his jaw. "Bitch had it coming. She was out of her mind."

Cecily's heart pounded in her chest. But she had to be sure. "And the lake. You were with Alain, weren't you?"

"That guy was crazy. He was throwing rocks at my drone . . ."

"Oh my god." Grant *was* the one. He was the murderer on the mountain. Her mouth gaped in horror, realizing how vulnerable she was. She needed to get away. She needed to get Doug.

She spotted a gap, a way around the man, and she took it.

Grant intercepted. He lurched forward, his hands outstretched. Cecily screamed. But he overreached, tripping over one of the lines securing her tent in the snow. He fell sideways into her tent, ripping the anchor lines out as he went.

"What the heck?" Zak was there first, bursting out of his tent a few meters away. Doug came running soon after.

"Nothing! I got lost. I didn't know which one was my tent." Grant rolled off her tent and stood up.

"You've been stalking my tent night after night," Cecily said. "I've heard you. Doug, this is what I've been talking about."

"So I tried to have a bit of fun before the summit. Big deal."

Doug stared between them.

"I don't want to be on a team with that man," she said. "He's dangerous! He has a motive for Irina and Alain's deaths . . ."

There was a stunned silence, all eyes turning to Grant. He rolled his eyes, his tone much more sober. "Oh, fuck off, no I don't. I said she had it coming. I didn't fucking kill her. Sounds to me like you're going mental like Irina. Not a surprise. You're not cut out for the mountain. If anyone is dangerous here, it's you. You're weak, Cecily." His eyes raked her body as he spoke, and she shuddered. Even though his eyes were glassy, it felt like he was seeing straight into her heart.

"Enough. Let's go," Doug jerked his head at Grant.

He stomped off, not looking back at Cecily.

"What an asshole," Zak said, stepping forward. "Don't listen to him. You OK?"

"I'm fine." She hugged her arms around her body.

"You don't really think—"

A scuffle came from inside Grant's tent. Doug shouted: "What the hell?" He dragged a bag from inside, clinking with bottles. "We talked about this. No more alcohol after the puja."

"I just had a couple of beers to relax before the summit. Nothing major."

"Nothing major," repeated Doug, pulling bottles of whiskey out of the bag, one after the other.

Grant's face drained of color. "Those aren't mine."

Doug shook his head. "Grant, pack your things. First thing in the morning, you're off the mountain."

Cecily heard a gasp from behind her. Everyone in the Manners Mountaineering camp was watching Grant and Doug. Elise had emerged, as had the Sherpas.

Even Charles had left his tent and was staring at the two men.

"What? You're joking. Because I had a couple of drinks? Like I said, those bottles aren't mine; no way I've drunk that much. This is absurd. Charles? Tell him he can't kick me off the team."

"Don't look at him. Look at me," said Doug. "I'm the team leader, not Charles. Mingma? In the morning, make sure Grant leaves our camp."

"Yes, Doug."

"What about our film?" Grant glared, still directing all his questions, all his energy at Charles.

To her relief, Charles folded his arms across his chest, widening his stance. "What Doug says, goes."

"No," said Grant. "You *know* why you need me on this team."

Now Charles took several steps toward the other man, who shrank back. "I don't think we have that issue anymore, do we? I suggest you pack up your stuff—before you really tip me over the edge."

"You can't treat me this way!" He pointed at Charles, raising his voice at the rest of the team. "This guy is a fraud. Those rescues he's so proud of? He faked them. I have it on camera," said Grant, gesticulating at Charles.

"You do? Then show us." Charles's tone was ice. "Go on, we'll wait. I have nothing to hide."

Grant clenched his fists. "I can't. That woman destroyed my hard drive at camp two."

Doug stepped forward. "You know what, I'm not going to take you throwing baseless accusations around. I don't think you should stay here another night. You should go down to Samagaun now. Mingma will take you."

"Don't touch me," said Grant, wrenching his arm away from Mingma. "This is all the fucking Charles show, isn't it? I bet you sent that woman to destroy my footage. You're all in on it." He gestured at Doug, the clients and the Sherpas, grabbed a backpack and stalked off, out of the camp.

She was relieved and yet her head spun with his accusations. She shook herself out of it. Grant was violent, volatile—a drunk, a liar. He'd throw blame wherever he thought it might stick. Anything to turn the attention from himself.

Zak hugged her. "He's gone now—you don't have to worry anymore."

In the meantime, Galden helped reshape her tent after the debacle. At least she knew she could sleep easy. Tomorrow she could start for the summit and not look over her shoulder worrying about Grant.

She opened the vestibule of the tent and yelped.

"Charles! Oh my god, you scared me. What are you doing?" she asked, when she realized what he was looking at.

He was staring at her laptop screen. "I came to leave something for you. But . . . what is this?"

She knelt down, trying to gather her laptop up, but Charles shifted so it slid farther out of her reach. Her breath went ragged, her ears suddenly ringing. Her words were her world, and that laptop contained every bit of it.

She never meant for anyone to read what she had written, at least not yet. These were her drafts, unedited, unfiltered. Her mouth was so dry she could barely get the words out. "It's just a rough . . ."

Charles frowned. "Of our interview?"

"Of *my* article," she said. She snatched the laptop away, and Charles didn't stop her this time. She closed the lid shut with a click. "I'm just writing what I see."

"'Killing ground'?"

"You know I'm worried. It's my journalistic duty to record what I'm seeing. Besides, I'm glad I'm doing it. Looking over everything, I think Ben was telling the truth. He was scared. He worried for his life after he saw the person who killed Irina. And after tonight, I'm more convinced than ever that person is Grant. He's been swanning around camp since the beginning, way overconfident. I heard Irina shoot him down that night. And he was at the lake when Alain died. Tonight, he came for me." She paused, her mind running through the possibilities. "I don't know what his motives are for doing your filming, but his intentions weren't good. What was he saying tonight . . . that you faked rescues?"

"He had no idea what he was talking about. He obviously thought he had something over me, but I can't see how that was possible."

"Of course not. So that leaves Alain and Irina . . ."

Charles sighed, tilting his head back so his headlamp faced the ceiling of her tent. "I was worried about this."

She halted in her train of thought. "What do you mean?"

"I'm worried about you. Doug told me that you were showing signs of altitude paranoia."

"What? No! It's not that."

"We've talked about this." He gestured at her laptop, which she clutched to her chest. "What happened to those people were accidents. I agree that Grant is not a good man. But this is insanity."

She swallowed. She took him in as he sat on her sleeping bag, surrounded by her things, dominating the inside of her tent. "Why are you in here, Charles?" she asked again, her voice quiet.

He lifted up a notebook, bound with a leather strap. "I wanted to leave this for you. It's my notes from previous expeditions. Thought it might help with the article. Then I caught sight of your laptop . . . I'm sorry, Cecily. Maybe this was too much for you." His tone was gentle, and he placed the notebook back inside his jacket pocket. "Being distracted by outside events, by other people, by conflicts and intrigues—that's why people fail in places like this. To succeed at high altitude, you must have an elite-level mindset. Complete focus. You need to be able to push away the petty concerns of everyday life because the concerns of the mountain are always greater. More immediate. Up there, it's life and death. Does it get bigger than that?"

Cecily shook her head. "This is life and death too. If Irina died and it wasn't an accident, that's an important story—not a petty concern."

"Then you're not the writer I thought you were." He crawled out of the tent, pausing in the entrance. Her heart sank at the look he gave her. It was something like . . . pity. And disappointment. Like she had already failed him.

"If I summit, you'll still give me the interview, won't you?"

He blinked. The light from his headlamp shone in her eyes, but she could still make out the soft expression on his face. "Of course I will. If you make it. But I'll give you one tip: you won't unless you let this go."

CHAPTER 39

WHEN SHE WOKE, THE camp was blissfully quiet. The sun was high in the sky as she packed up her devices to make her way to Wi-Fi mountain, hoping to finally send her blogs to Michelle, and to let her know she was leaving for the summit and that she would be out of communication range for a few days. She had to get a message out to Rachel, too.

Guilt ate at her. She'd promised to keep in touch, but she'd been so wrapped up in the events at base camp that even thoughts of her best friend hadn't broken through. The mountain was its own universe. It was hard to remember what it was like back home. She pictured Rachel on her daily commute, squeezing onto a packed Tube train, picking up a take-out coffee and sandwich. Cecily felt so removed from that life, even though that had been hers less than a month ago.

Wi-Fi mountain was deserted. She dropped into one of the camping chairs and opened her laptop.

"Anything?"

She looked up as Dario approached, wearing a Summit Extreme–branded beanie. She shook her head, shifting in her seat, suddenly aware she was alone with the mountain guide. Although she was pretty sure Grant was the culprit, there was a tiny seed of doubt in her mind.

"So frustrating. It's been out for a few days now," he muttered. "Never known it to be so bad. I'll have to go down to Samagaun today to get a forecast for my team. Not even my satellite devices are working as they should."

"Zak said the same. How is that possible? Have you found any jammers?"

Dario shook his head. "Nothing like what your friend described. It is highly unusual."

"Well, lucky for our team, Doug has a forecast. It's why we're going up."

The Summit Extreme guide stiffened, jerking his head back. "Seriously—you leave for your summit push today? No, surely not."

"Doug and Mingma announced it last night." She bit down on the edge of her thumbnail, Dario's reaction unsettling her.

"And after the drama you had last night?"

"You heard about that?"

"The mountain is a small place." He looked up at the sky, still shaking his head. "I'm also not so sure about that forecast. In my opinion, we need to wait a few days more at least. A week would be even better."

There *was* something charged about the air, something electric. But she thought that was her anxiety at work again.

"But I am glad I caught you here. It is about Irina—"

"Cecily?"

Doug stopped a few paces away from them. He crooked his finger.

"Please, take every precaution out there. Do not be alone," said Dario, hissing the final words as Cecily moved away to join her team leader.

Doug crossed his arms. "We don't mingle with other teams this close to the summit window. That's how viruses—and bad information—spread."

Cecily swallowed. "I was just seeing if I'd had any last messages from my family when he showed up . . . but there's still no signal."

"The team has to come first."

"I understand. But Dario said he hasn't had a forecast for a while and has to go down to Samagaun. He doesn't think the weather is right for a summit attempt."

Doug pursed his lips. "See for yourself." He passed his phone over to her, a screenshot of the forecast on display. A little row of suns hovered over the next few days, along with low wind speeds and temperatures around −20° C at the summit. It seemed to be exactly the window they'd been waiting for. Her face reddened. "Happy? Or do you want to stay behind?"

"No, it's not that. It's just . . ."

He stopped, bringing her to a halt. She felt chastised, like a child. "A team is only as strong as its weakest member."

"I understand. I'm here and I'm focused."

"Good."

She nodded. She knew Doug wouldn't let Charles down when it came to climbing logistics, so she had to trust him. Even though she didn't trust everyone on her team . . . if she was with Galden and took Dario's advice never to be alone, it was worth the risk.

Besides, she had her teeth in this story now. She wanted to see it through.

"The team is eating breakfast. You should join them. You'll need it."

After wolfing down bacon and eggs, knowing it would be her last proper meal for a long time, Cecily collected her backpack from her tent. Everyone was getting prepared now, and the excitement in the air was palpable. Elise was chatting with Phemba, discussing her harness setup and food choices.

Zak was lingering outside the dining tent, so she walked over to him. She gave him a brief hug. She could feel he was tense too, the anticipation of the summit push infusing them all.

Mingma gestured that they could start walking if they wanted. Cecily caught a whiff of juniper smoke as they passed by the puja site. She stopped, inhaling deeply, then reached into one of the small brass bowls to toss a handful of rice in the air—one last offering for safe passage on the mountain. The prayer flags fluttered in the gentle breeze overhead.

A perfect morning to be heading up.

Charles was setting off too, his backpack towering over his body. He was carrying his own tent, cooking supplies, down suit, rope—everything he would need to survive on his own on the mountain. Yet he moved as if he weren't carrying any weight at all. It looked so easy for him.

What must it be like to feel so at home in such a hostile environment? To stride along the line between life and death, rather than tiptoe? She tried to imagine experiencing a fearsome avalanche that killed your teammates, coming out as the sole survivor. It was high on the list of her questions to ask. She wanted to understand this man, who was so unlike any other.

So unlike any other . . . maybe it was too good to be true. Dario had accused him of using the fixed lines. Grant had accused him of faking his rescues. Was any of the myth Charles had built up around himself real? Or had she been blinded by James's hero worship, the esteem the climbing Sherpas seemed to hold for him, Doug's unwavering loyalty? Charles had brought her here, but Michelle was the one paying her (if she submitted an article worthy of payment, that is). And she owed it to her readers to get the real story.

Charles was compelling, charismatic, difficult and complicated. Getting to talk to him, unpack his motivations and dig deep into his history—that would be the only way to get a handle on any of the stories she had begun to draft.

Her goal was to write the most compelling article, focusing on the truth. And with every step higher, Cecily understood. The only place she was going to find out what that was, was on the mountain itself.

CHAPTER 40

THE SUN SHONE AS they walked to camp one, and she stripped off her waterproof jacket. She pushed the sleeves of her Merino wool undershirt up over her elbows and squeezed some sunscreen onto her forearms.

The climb was easier now that she had acclimatized. Her body felt strong. She leaped over the smaller crevasses with confidence, clipping in and out of the lines. Yet it was still a taxing mental effort, and she needed to keep her focus on the present.

A wobble on one of the ladders was a reminder of that. She was lost in thought, wondering how Charles could possibly cross these crevasses without using the ladders placed by the fixing team. It suddenly felt improbable that he *wouldn't* cheat.

Her concentration slipped and, with it, her crampon. Rather than place the front and back points carefully between the rungs, she had caught an edge, missing her footing. She slammed down onto her knees, the ladder juddering against the ice.

The clang of metal rang in her ears, her fingers clenched around the ice-cold ladder edge. She gritted her teeth and tentatively stood back up.

Only when she was safely on the snow on the other side did she breathe again.

A split second. A momentary lapse.

That was all it took.

She pushed all distractions aside for the rest of the walk.

When she stepped up to the camp, the view couldn't have been more different from last time. Whereas before the entire camp had been shrouded in cloud, now the sky was crystal clear. All around her towered the tops of other high peaks, layers of mountains against the horizon, and the vast plains of Tibet stretched out in the far distance. They were so high here that the other mountain summits were at eye level, looking across the jagged roof of the world.

Doug's forecast was proving right, the weather holding. Still, there weren't many teams around, and those that were seemed to be headed down the mountain.

She turned to Zak, who'd been climbing behind her the entire way. "Have you ever seen anything like this?"

But she was surprised. Zak's head hung low, his shoulders rounded. He was barely picking his feet up. They hadn't done much talking for most of the climb to camp, but she assumed that was because they had both been concentrating on the task at hand. The altitude must be affecting him more than she realized. She took his arm and helped guide him to his tent, fetching a cup of tea to revive him. He grunted at her gratefully, then disappeared inside.

She dumped her backpack in the tent she would share with Elise and dug around for her camera. She walked with it to the edge of camp, stopping to admire the view once more. She closed her eyes, breathing in the thin air, and when she opened them again, she tried to capture the image in her mind's eye: a memory that would last a lifetime.

Only then did she use her camera.

Already the sky was beginning to change color as the sun set, bright orange and red streaks stretching out overhead. A few more clouds appeared, clinging to the distant summits, but here the air was still clear. She could watch the sky all day.

She scouted the outer edge of the camp, trying to get photos from as many angles as possible—wanting to make sure she had footage to back up the images that Zak had promised her. There were a few empty tents, awaiting the teams who'd made the decision to stay down in base camp. The wind rushing through the plastic of these ghost tents created an eerie symphony.

Her boots crunched through a hardened top layer of snow, breaking a trail. Sometimes the snow came to the top of her boot, and her heart would stop for a moment—what if the next step she took was an unstable cornice that might crumble away, taking her with it?

She shuddered, deliberately moving away from the edge.

Still, she felt as if she were making a mark on the mountain in some small way. Pretending she was climbing alpine style for a moment.

She clambered over a small section of rock to look up at the route that they would follow the next day, trying to picture herself there, feeling as strong as she did today.

Then she saw something that pulled her up short.

A tent. Red, with dark blue accents.

It was across a chasm from where she was standing, on a small plateau farther around the mountain. There was no way for her to reach it. She waited, watching to see if the tent's occupant would show themselves.

She shivered, huddling into her jacket.

Darkness was falling quickly, and her heart skipped a beat when she remembered that she didn't have her headlamp. She had to get back, or else risk getting lost and slipping to her death—where no one would be able to find her.

Reluctantly, she retreated, following her footsteps until she saw the reassuring sight of the Manners Mountaineering flag. She ducked back into her tent.

"Ah, there you are. I was worrying about you." Elise leaned forward and grabbed her hand. "What happened? You look like you've seen a ghost."

"I saw . . . I don't know. It was a tent. On its own, on the other side of a crevasse from the rest of camp one."

"Oh?"

"It looked like one I'd seen at base camp too. I thought that one must have been Ben's—"

"The man who stole the money? But he is back in Kathmandu . . ."

"Exactly. But then who?"

"Could it be Charles?"

"I thought of that. But he wasn't on the mountain the first time I saw the tent."

Elise shrugged. "Must be someone else then."

It wasn't long before Galden "knocked" on their tent flap, with a covered bowl of fried rice in his hands. When she lifted the lid, the food was still steaming.

He crawled in while she ate, and soon Phemba, the Sherpa who was helping Elise, came by with her food too. Doug was next. Now there were five of them squished inside.

"So, how are you feeling?" Doug asked.

"Super!" said Elise, brightly.

"Good to hear. And Cecily?"

"First camp down, three more to go," she said, forcing a laugh. But she couldn't shake the unease from seeing that tent again. Who could it be?

"Unfortunately, the plan has changed. The weather window is tight, and we don't want to be on the mountain for long. So tomorrow we'll skip the usual night at camp two and head straight to camp three. Have one night there, then climb up to camp four. We'll have a brief rest, then start for the summit in the middle of the night. That would bring us back to base camp in three days. How does that sound to you?"

"Fine by me," said Elise. "That way I have less time walking without oxygen and no rest."

Cecily bit on the edge of her thumbnail. She was already nervous about tomorrow's climb. It meant returning to the Hanging Place. She remembered how exhausting she'd found it. But now it was layered, shrouded, in the memory of Irina's death.

This new plan meant she'd have to continue for hours more in order to reach camp three.

Camp three was the one she'd been dreading. They'd arrive there tired, late at night, potentially in the dark. She licked her cracked lips, her throat parched. "Isn't camp three the dangerous one? The one where . . . the avalanche happened?"

"We pitch on a different spot now," said Doug. "But I cannot say with one hundred percent certainty it is safe. It is the risk we take to climb Manaslu."

She hesitated for a moment. What choice did she have? "I trust you."

Then she heard a shout.

She thought she recognized the voice—and her blood froze in her veins.

"What's that noise?" Elise asked.

Doug shifted to the entrance. "I'll find out."

She wanted to know who it was, hoping her suspicion wasn't correct. She put down her bowl of food and scrambled to get her boots on.

"Cecily, didi, wait—you must eat!" Galden tried to stop her. But she couldn't miss this. She burst out into the semidarkness, fumbling with her headlamp.

Doug stood there, blocking her view. But the more yelling she heard, the more her heart sank.

Finally, Doug shifted position, and the light from her headlamp revealed the instigator.

Grant.

His face was red from shouting, but it looked like he had been caught sneaking around their tent with a camera. Tenzing was holding his arm, but he shook himself free.

"What do you think you are doing?" Doug's shoulders were tight, his fingers twitching, making her think he was surprised to see him too. "I told you to leave the mountain," he growled.

"Listen, mate, my footage from Cho Oyu was destroyed, you kicked me out, and I have to make money somehow. A spot was open on the Summit Extreme; they invited me on. I'm going to get another shot of Charles faking a rescue. I bet some networks would be very interested in that story."

"Why can't you just leave us alone?" Cecily asked.

"You here to play Charles's next victim, Cecily? That's got to be the only reason someone like you was invited on the trip."

"Dario," Doug called out. She hadn't spotted the other expedition leader standing behind Grant. "You gave him a place?"

"Yes. We saw him coming past our tents with all his gear and invited him onto our expedition."

"Your summit push was meant to be next week."

"It was. Yet when Cecily told me you were making a summit push today . . . and since we could not get our own signal, I thought we should come up too."

"Dario—you should send him down. He's dangerous," she implored. "He might have been involved in Irina's death."

"Go back to the tent," said Doug to her, cutting her off. "I will sort this out."

"But—"

"I said, go back! Unless you want to go down?"

Doug's word on the mountain was law. But she'd seen enough. She'd registered the change in Dario's expression. Maybe he'd heard her after all, and would send Grant down. She stomped back to the tent.

"Grant joined another team?" Elise asked her, once she'd ducked inside.

"Summit Extreme. God! I hate that he's here. Honestly I was finally feeling safe."

Elise gripped her hand. "You *are* safe with us. Grant is a wild card, yes. But he'll stick to his team, and we'll stick to ours. It will go well."

Cecily opened her mouth to protest, but then closed it again. Elise shared none of her suspicions about the people around them. Her entire focus was on the topological dangers of the mountain.

Elise nudged her knee. "Let's take a selfie. First night of our summit push!"

"OK." Cecily leaned forward, adjusting her beanie. Elise lifted her camera up above her head, angling it down, and took a snap.

They snuggled into their sleeping bags. Their wake-up call was five a.m., to begin their extra-long day to get to camp three.

But as much as her body wanted to sleep, her mind just wouldn't shut off. It kept whirring. Knowing a mysterious person was camped nearby, that Grant was only a few tents away . . .

Sleep wouldn't come easily.

CHAPTER 41

THE FOLLOWING MORNING, SHE stayed inside the tent as long as she could, delaying her start until she was sure Grant had gone ahead with the rest of the Summit Extreme team.

The way up to camp two was smoother this time, helped along by the better weather, but dread grew as they got closer to the Hanging Place. Would she see Irina twisted in the rope, her face blue and contorted in pain?

Galden tapped her shoulder, then pointed a little way up the mountain. She stopped and watched, her jaw slack.

It was Charles. This was the first time she'd seen him climb. He was more often out of sight of the fixed lines, carving his own way through the icefall. He was a master maze breaker.

"How does he do it?" Cecily asked.

"What do you mean?" Galden replied.

She paused, a million questions racing through her mind. She settled on an obstacle that had caused her the most concern. "Like the crevasses. How does he cross them without ladders?"

Galden laughed. "It is very difficult! Often, he has to find a way around. It can take much longer if there is no easy route, and climbers are often stopped in their tracks by crevasses too wide to cross. But alpine style doesn't mean he can't use *any* ropes—he just has to carry and fix them all himself. By doing that, he can find a way around most obstacles."

Charles seemed an alien creature, with incredible skill and a preternatural ability to read the mountain. He moved smoothly across terrifyingly steep cornices of snow, employing his ice ax like another limb. She thought that he would dominate the mountain, but he was far more graceful than that.

Plus, he was quick. While they were stuck on the lines, waiting to climb, he moved freely, nimbly. He moved with the confidence of someone attached to a line, even though she could see full well that he wasn't. Charles soon disappeared beyond view, among the great shards of ice.

As they approached the Hanging Place, she felt strangely numb. It looked different now. It had been so pummeled by climbers that the steepness of it was eased, steps now better defined and at more manageable heights. The section where Irina had died was closed off, the rappel moved so it came down a different route.

She swallowed, staring up at it from the base. But the anxiety over the difficulty of the climb never came. The steps made it much easier to haul herself up. Yet it also made it easier for her mind to wander.

Was this the place where Irina had taken her final breath?

How scared had she been?

Had someone wrapped the cord around her neck before pushing her off to die, terrified and alone?

Cecily threaded the rope, with its interlocking red-and-black design, through her fingers. Dark red, like blood.

She held back the scream that was building to a crescendo in her mind. Yet with the surge of terror came a burst of adrenaline, and, before she knew it, she had reached the top. She'd made it past the crux of the mountain for the second time.

After that, the only menaces looming were the seracs: the dancing bear and the witch's hat. They were the icy, glacial-blue sentinels of the mountain, standing guard over the wall. She bowed her head in honor of Irina, and then continued on, having no desire to linger.

They stopped at camp two for lunch and to rehydrate. Elise stood straight, hands on her hips, but she was quiet and unsmiling for once, conserving her energy for higher up the mountain. Zak, by contrast, lay on top of his backpack and sighed heavily when

Doug announced their rest was over. Mingma passed him a bottle of Coca-Cola.

"Is he all right?" Cecily asked Galden, keeping her voice low.

"Altitude," he replied, with a shrug.

"But he's been up this high before. Not just on our acclimatization routine, but on Denali . . ."

"Sometimes it hits you, even when you have experience."

She hesitated, wanting to go over to give Zak some encouragement but not wanting to put the spotlight on his struggles. He caught her eye and gave her a shaky thumbs-up, raising the bottle in her direction, and she nodded—feeling better about continuing. Tenzing would turn him around if he was really struggling, she was sure.

From that point on, Cecily was on new ground, climbing higher than she ever had before. Heavy snow drifted down, forcing her to add her waterproof outer shell layer. It was markedly colder too. Her down suit was buried in her pack; she needed to wait until camp three to change into it. Her only option to ward off the chill was to keep on moving.

The snow fell harder. Once again, the team separated, and she found herself on her own with Galden.

She was so busy concentrating on walking, on making sure that she kept clipped in and her safety lines secure, that she barely lifted her head to take in her surroundings. But when was she ever going to experience this again?

She paused for a rest and used it to take stock of the mountain around her. The snow obscured the view, but Manaslu itself was full of wonders. Eerie shapes loomed out of the half-light, ghostly sleeping giants of seracs. As she passed through the icefall, she spotted a shard of bright orange color embedded in one of the snowbanks: an old tent from a previous camp, swept down the mountain and buried. The victim of one of Manaslu's many avalanches. Seeing the remains of the tent, the poles jutting out of the side of the ice, sent a spike of fear through her heart.

Galden gave her a nudge. "Come on, Cecily. We must keep climbing. It is better not to stop for too long."

"Who did that tent belong to?" she asked, unable to tear her eyes away from the wreckage.

"I don't know, didi."

"Did they die?"

He didn't answer her. She didn't want to hear it aloud anyway, not if she was going to keep her resolve. She forced herself to look away and took another step.

The snow settled on her eyelashes—but the sky was too dark for sunglasses and her goggles were buried deep in her backpack. She wiped her gloves across her face and concentrated on the task at hand. Another wall—not as big as the Hanging Place, but still intimidating.

She pushed the ascender up the snow-covered rope and took a few steps forward. She dug her ice ax in above her head and pulled, at the same time pushing the ascender with her other hand.

But something happened that she didn't expect.

The ascender slipped, causing her to lose her footing and tumble back down the slope.

The safety line caught at the anchor point, but the force of the jolt caused her to lose her grip on the ice ax.

"Cecily, are you all right?"

She spotted the ice ax coming loose from the wall. "Galden, watch out!" she shouted. She threw her arms over her head.

A rush of wind passed her cheek, followed by a dull thud.

CHAPTER 42

GALDEN GROANED.

"Are you OK?" she asked.

He clutched at his shoulder. Her ice ax was planted in the ground a couple of meters away. "I am fine. It hit my arm."

"I'm so sorry, Galden."

"What happened?"

"I don't know. My ascender . . ."

Once she felt sure of her footing, she slid the device down the rope and unclipped it. When she showed it to Galden, he turned it over. The mechanism was completely clogged up with ice and snow.

She reached over to grab the ice ax. Galden tapped the ascender hard with the back of one of his carabiners, and chunks of ice fell out of the metal teeth. "You might have to keep doing that. Make sure that your ascender is biting the rope before climbing, yes? And maybe we will put the ice ax away for now. You should be able to climb without it."

She nodded, racked with guilt. She could have seriously hurt Galden. He looped the ice ax onto her backpack, using his uninjured arm, and prompted her to tackle the wall again. It was smaller than some of the ones she'd done already that day, but she was a lot more tired now, nervous about her ascender.

Without the ice ax, she needed her hands more. She wished she had practiced more on the bouldering wall, but somehow she managed to haul her body up. The ascender did slip a couple of more times, but since she was aware of the issue, she didn't hang her entire body weight off it, and so she was able to hold her position without causing any harm to herself—or to Galden.

Still, it took a lot more effort. When she reached the top, she was so tired she could hardly see straight. She looked back, but Galden seemed to be moving freely. It had been a close call, an accident that could have been so much worse. They'd been lucky, this time.

The path between camps two and three was the most undulating, and sometimes in the valleys between ice walls it felt like she and Galden were the only two people on the mountain. They were ants skittering over the surface of an icy pond, hoping it wouldn't crack. Apart from the steady opening and closing of the carabiners, all other sound was muffled by the snow. Under the muted gray sky, the mountain held its breath. Something big was sleeping, and they wanted to make sure that they didn't wake it up.

Every rise felt like a miniature summit, yet when she conquered one, another would appear in her way. It was monotonous, endless. And with every step she climbed higher, the oxygen in the air grew thinner. Her breathing became labored, her pulse quickening.

After a few hours, they stopped to rest. Galden passed her a slice of apple, but her stomach roiled.

She dropped her head in her hands. "I can't do this," she said.

"Didi, you are doing so well," he said, in that infuriatingly gentle Sherpa tone. "Not too far now. You are strong up here. We are moving fast."

"We are?"

He took another sip of tea and passed it to her. She raised her chin, staring up at the mountain.

Twisted columns of ice rose above them, like the ruins of a Greek temple. They sat directly opposite a large serac, and a tiny shard of that classic bright glacial-blue ice peeked out from deep inside. It was seductive. She almost wanted to walk into the crack in the ice and touch the blue, like a portal to another world. It was so much brighter than the murky gray around them.

Perhaps she was feeling a bit hypoxic, her mind losing its grip on reality. They were well over six thousand meters here, with still over a thousand meters left to climb over the next two days.

Galden didn't even have to speak anymore, he simply tilted his head and she knew to keep on moving. She stood up and stretched. They each added a final extra layer—in Cecily's case, her down jacket—as the temperature dropped further.

Not too far. Not too far. She focused on the promise those words held for her. Her energy was sapped—she was back to counting steps. As long as she could take ten steps forward, then she could take a little rest. Ten steps, then stop. Ten steps and stop. Not too far. Not too far. Too far. Too far. *Tofar.* Words lost all meaning.

And when she thought the next step might be her last, she looked up from her feet and saw a cluster of yellow tents half-buried in the fresh snow. She was so tired and cold that she couldn't appreciate the incredible surroundings. Her lips felt dry and cracked, her fingers frozen inside her gloves.

Galden led her to her tent, and she dropped inside.

Every movement took twice—three times—as long as it should. The signals from her brain to her limbs were sluggish, and even though she knew exactly what she needed to do—to get her outer layers off and her down suit on as quickly as possible—she had to think about every step. Unzip down jacket. Remove arm. Remove other arm. Her body fought her brain at every step. It didn't want the comfort of the down suit; it wanted the ease of the clothes she was already in. It wanted to curl up in the sleeping bag and not move.

She finally peeled off her outer layers until she was left in her thermals. She shivered, but dragged her brand-new bright orange down suit from its stuff bag. She would've done that first, had she been thinking straight. She barely had the strength to take it out, and her body temperature was plummeting.

She took a deep breath once it was ready, prepping her body for another push.

She pulled the legs of the suit on, then shuffled it up over her behind and shoulders. She took another deep breath. The effects of altitude were intense now.

She blinked several times, then she tugged on the zipper of the suit, bringing it up to her chin. The suit was like being wrapped in a duvet. She never wanted to take it off. She definitely didn't want to move. Then she heard a voice outside. "Hello, Cecily? Hot drink?"

"Yes, Galden—hang on." She glanced at her watch. It had taken her almost twenty minutes to put on the suit. How was that possible?

She rolled over and crawled to the front of the tent, taking the sweet, spicy, slightly peppery masala tea. The warmth spread through her body, making her feel human again. Now she was able to step outside and take in their surroundings.

It was spectacular—but also terrifying. A striated wall of ice climbed up ominously behind them, huge blocks hanging like bats in a cave, and in front there was a steep drop. There were far fewer tents here.

She was glad they'd moved the campsite, so they weren't sleeping on the grave of former climbers. This wasn't Everest, where walking past frozen corpses was almost part of the experience. But she had already encountered one, and she could only hope it would be the last.

She swallowed, feeling her paranoia rise again.

She wandered farther, taking pictures. "Don't go too far beyond where you're standing," Galden called out. His voice was calm as he spoke the warning, yet it filled Cecily with even more anxiety.

As she moved sideways along the camp, she heard angry voices. She ducked down, hidden by a snowbank as the pair came into view.

"Laisse-le!"

It was Dario and Elise. "You are telling me you trust him now?" asked Dario.

"Yes, I am. Leave it alone."

"What about Broad Peak?"

"Bof, I was hypoxic. You can't handle that he's a better climber than you!"

"You know it is not that." He reached out and stroked Elise's cheek. She leaned into the motion, tilting her head against his palm. It looked like a lover's tiff. Cecily's face reddened, and she hastily made her way back to their tent, pretending she hadn't overheard.

A few moments later, Elise crawled in. Cecily turned to allow her tentmate some privacy as she changed into her bright pink summit suit. But when she caught a glimpse of her face, Cecily had never seen the Canadian look so defeated. "Elise, what's wrong?" she asked. "Are you OK?"

Elise wiped a tear that had slid down her cheek. "It's nothing."

Cecily was dying to ask more questions—was she seeing Dario? Why wasn't she on his team if that was the case? What happened on Broad Peak? It seemed like Dario had also shared his suspicions about Charles with Elise, and Elise also didn't believe it.

Elise pulled out her phone, looking through the photos of the day. She sighed as she did so, turning her body away. Cecily took the hint and kept her mouth shut.

Galden and Phemba arrived at their tent with bowls of rehydrated chicken curry. Cecily couldn't bear to even look at it but Elise devoured her portion. Cecily forced the food into her mouth, where it lay on her tongue, a congealed lukewarm mass. She made herself swallow, then clamped her hands over her mouth to stop herself from hurling. There was no way she could eat it. She closed up the bag and grabbed a handful of nuts and chocolate instead. It might not be enough calories, but at least it didn't make her want to vomit.

Elise lay back in her sleeping bag and fell straight to sleep. Cecily wasn't surprised; she must have been exhausted.

But sleep eluded Cecily. Her mind raced over the events of the day—the Hanging Place, Zak's fatigue, the slip of her ascender, Galden's groan. How easily mistakes could be made up here—which could prove fatal. Her lungs rattled, her nose so congested she had to take every breath through her lips, drying them out. Eventually she gave up trying, and instead felt around for her notebook and pen. She might as well be productive, if nothing else.

As she wrote down her experiences of the day by the light of her headlamp, her mind settled. There was only one way that anyone ever got up a mountain: by putting one foot in front of the other. If she had a positive attitude, that would help too.

That was why she needed to write about it. She wrote what Galden had said to her: *You are strong up here.* She needed to see the shape of her goal in ink, watch the sentences unfold in front of her eyes and realize the truth.

She was going to get a great story. Because she was a mountaineer *and* she was a writer. She was brave and she was vulnerable. These things didn't have to exist at the opposite end of the scale, but rather they could be held together, one in each hand, and each could bear its own weight, just as the right hand is the mirror image of the left. She could be both.

Two more sleeps until the summit, then this experience would be over, and she wouldn't have to worry about death—accidental or deliberate, unintentional or premeditated—anymore.

She could hold on for that long.

CHAPTER 43

HER BODY WAS RIGID with terror, although she didn't know why. Then the sound came again, a roar like they'd camped in the path of a jet engine. Wind battered the tent. Elise groaned—the sound almost drowned out by the noise.

"What the hell is going on?" Cecily said.

"A crazy storm. We're not going anywhere today," said Elise.

Cecily cowered into her sleeping bag. The tent poles bent toward them, submitting to the will of the wind. She squealed as the plastic battered the top of her head. "This wasn't predicted, was it? Are we safe?"

Elise took a sip from her water bottle. "We are, but we'll need food and water. Merde, where is my camp stove?"

They didn't have one. They'd have to go without until someone came for them. Cecily tried her best to match her tentmate's calm exterior, but inside her every muscle clenched in terror at the sound of the storm.

The second the wind died down, they heard someone outside their tent. "Girls?"

Elise leaned forward and opened the zip from the inside. "Make room!" said the voice. Cecily drew up her knees and shuffled into the far corner of the tent, moving the bulk of her sleeping bag out of the way.

It was Charles, with Doug and Zak in tow. They were all blanketed in snow.

"Charles! Is everything OK?" Cecily asked.

"There's nothing we can do while we wait for the wind to die down. We will be warmer if we all stick together."

"This doesn't affect your mission?" she asked.

"Spending a few hours in a tent with my team while stuck in a storm doesn't stop this from being an alpine-style climb," he said. "Trust me, I take no risks on that."

"Good," she said. She felt much safer now that Charles was with them.

"Is it bad?" Elise asked Doug.

He nodded once. "Could be the end of our summit bid."

"What? You didn't tell me that. You're not giving up, are you, Charles?" asked Zak. "If you're not giving up, then we shouldn't either."

"It is my decision," said Doug.

Charles dominated the vestibule of the tent, folded up like a hibernating bear. "This storm wasn't in our forecast." He cast a dark glance at Doug, who didn't respond. "How such a stupid mistake could be made, I have no idea." Then he shook his body, dislodging snow over the bottom of the tent. "But it will clear. I know it will."

She swallowed. Charles might be a legend on the mountain, but even he couldn't control the weather—no matter how strongly he willed it. If Charles didn't summit, there wouldn't be a story to write about at all.

Doug dragged his backpack in front of him, brushing the snow off the top. He dug out two large thermoses, which he gave to Elise to distribute among their cups. Then he pulled out bags of dehydrated food.

There wasn't much else to do other than eat, drink and wait. Cecily's face was squished against the yellow plastic, her legs trapped underneath Doug's backpack, Elise on the far side with Zak, and Charles sitting in the entrance. The conversation—when they were able—turned to Grant.

"I never liked that guy," said Zak. "I guess he must be a pretty damn good filmmaker if you chose him, Charles, but I didn't get it."

Charles chucked a handful of roasted nuts into his mouth, crunching down. "Grant overstated his skill to me. But there you go. I've always been a better judge of the mountains than of people."

The storm buffeted the tent, and they heard a crack that could have been thunder—or another tent being destroyed—or ice cleaving from a cliff—and Cecily screamed. They huddled together as the plastic shook and the wind howled around them.

"It really doesn't sound good out there," said Zak, following up his understatement with nervous laughter.

Doug pulled out his phone. "Not good at all. I'm afraid this is the end of our summit push . . ."

Charles reached over and snatched the phone out of Doug's hand. He glared at the screen, but the force of his anger couldn't change it. "For fuck's sake. This is a screenshot, Doug. Where's the live forecast?"

"I haven't been able to get an update," Doug said, his voice calm. "Mingma is trying in his tent too. But look—there's a window in a couple of days. Too late for the team, but you can continue."

"Does this really mean we're going down?" Zak asked, his eyes widening.

"Yes," said Doug. "As soon as the storm breaks."

Cecily waited for an emotion to hit her: relief or frustration or sadness. But she felt empty—her energy levels depleted. She hung her head.

Elise reached over and squeezed her knee. "It will be all right. Maybe you can write about it anyway?"

"A sequel to 'Failure to Rise,'" Zak said.

"Oh, I don't know about that . . . ," she replied. She flicked her eyes up at Charles to catch his expression. If he didn't change his mind, a follow-up to her viral blog might be the only thing she had.

Charles rubbed at his beard, his lips pursed tightly together. He locked his ice-blue eyes on Cecily. "There's still time to see what happens. On the mountain it's not over until it's over." His voice was quiet. "Still, failure is sometimes not the worst consequence, isn't that right, Cecily? How about you tell us what really happened to you on Snowdon?"

Cecily blinked. She swallowed before replying. "What do you mean?"

"I think it would help to share."

"Yes, please, Cecily. Tell us. You know I loved your article," said Elise.

Doug shifted his position, grimacing. Zak smiled at her. Charles continued to stare, and she wilted under the intensity of his gaze. There was nowhere to hide.

She took a sip of tea. "All right. Well, Snowdon . . ." Even saying the word made her breath hitch—but another blast of wind helped her to cover it. She waited to see if the storm was going to rage and let her off the hook. But even Manaslu wanted to listen in, and the wind was quiet.

"I was doing the National Three Peaks Challenge with my ex, James—which involves climbing the highest mountains in Scotland, England and Wales in twenty-four hours," she explained, for Zak's benefit. "He was guiding me as he's got his mountaineering qualifications. It's really popular," she said.

"A gimmick. A stupid thing to try and do," muttered Doug.

Cecily nodded. "People definitely underestimate it. I know I did. It was last October, actually, just after you announced your mission, Charles. Weird to think that was the first time I'd heard of you, and now I'm here."

"A fortunate chain of events. Go on," he prompted.

"By the time we got to Snowdon, I was flat-out exhausted—not just from climbing Ben Nevis and Scafell but from driving all night, not getting any sleep crammed in the backseat of the van, not having a proper meal. The forecast for Snowdon was bad but not abysmal—I mean, it's Wales. Bad weather is what you expect. My boots had been soaked in the Lake District, so James advised me to swap out for my sneakers. We had to be at the summit in three hours to make the twenty-four-hour cutoff for the challenge. James was confident despite how tired I was. He turned us off at the sign for Crib Goch. He said it would give our attempt extra kudos."

"Crib Goch—what's that?" asked Zak.

"It's a famous ridge route to the summit," explained Charles. "It involves some scrambling, and you need to navigate a sharp arête. In normal conditions, it's not too bad. But it can be deadly in bad weather. You know all about that, don't you, Doug?"

Cecily glanced over at their team leader; his jaw was clenched, the muscles of his neck twitching. She frowned before continuing. "Right. And by the time we got to the ridge, we had all the weather—torrential rain, strong winds, hail. It was my first time doing a scramble like that . . . and, like I said, I was wearing these flimsy sneakers, with no grip. James moved a lot faster, so I told him to go on ahead while I turned around. I didn't want him to miss out on the challenge. I tried my best to pick my way back down the route, but I was so tired, and somehow I got myself into a position where I couldn't find a way to move up or down. I became crag-fast."

The wind against their tent took her straight back to the ridge. She closed her eyes for a moment before looking down at her hands. "I was frozen. Stuck. My palms were red-raw, from gripping the rock. The ledge I was standing on was narrower than my foot—I was basically balancing on my toes. Every muscle in my body was shaking. I couldn't move. I was paralyzed with fear. If I fell, I would die. I had no signal on my phone, and no one could hear my shouts because of the wind."

"What did you do?" asked Zak.

She paused. Most of the time she obfuscated the rest of the story, sped up to the end. But in the tent, surrounded by real mountaineers, she knew this was her moment to tell the truth of what had happened. All of it. "I was lucky. Thank god—there was another climber on the ridge. A woman. She spotted me and made her way over. When she saw I was stuck and in distress, she stayed with me, sending an emergency text message to the mountain-rescue team. I didn't even know there was an emergency text number, that's how unprepared I was. Then she lent me her spare jacket and waited with me for them to arrive. She talked to me for hours, all about mountaineering and her life in North Wales. She kept me calm, and I learned a lot from her.

"But the weather was getting worse and worse and darkness was coming. She grew more concerned. She scouted around and actually found a way for me to escape from the ledge. She gave really clear, simple instructions, moved so she could help me, held out her hand, asked me to make one tiny step to my right. But I couldn't. So she decided to move to me. But as she did it . . ."

She inhaled, her hands shaking. Now her emotions broke through the fog of her exhaustion: sadness, guilt, regret, yes . . . but also relief at finally telling the whole story. She owed it to Carrie to continue. Cocooned at camp three, they might as well be the only people on Earth. She needed to spit the words out, to make this confession.

"Cecily, are you OK?" Elise asked, reaching over.

She withdrew as far as she could. She didn't want anyone's comforting touch. Not yet. "But as she did it . . . the rock crumbled beneath her feet. I saw it happen, barely a few feet from me, but I couldn't do anything to help."

And then she'd heard the scream. Once the woman had started falling, there was no way to stop it. The sickening sound of Carrie's body colliding with the ground would stay with Cecily for the rest of her life.

All she had needed to do was take a single step. Instead . . .

"She died on impact. I was in shock. The adrenaline flowed through my body and I managed to move, scrambled down that route she'd pointed out to me like it was easy. I could have done it all along. I found a whistle in the pocket of the jacket she'd given me. I blew it, the only thing I could think to do. Just blew that whistle over and over. That's how the rescue team found our location. James wrote a story about it, framing me as a hero for staying near her and alerting the authorities so they could recover her body," she said, hanging her head in shame. "He had no idea I was the whole reason she died. I . . . I killed her."

Cecily buried her face in her hands. There *was* a murderer on the mountain.

It was her.

CHAPTER 44

CECILY TOOK ANOTHER RAGGED breath. "The woman's name was Carrie. Carrie Halloran. She was the real hero. I don't know where I'd be without her. Not here. She inspired me."

Zak shook his head in disbelief. "Jesus, Cecily. I can't believe you went through that."

Doug clenched his fists. "Let me get this straight"—his voice was hard as steel—"you and your so-called guide boyfriend decided to climb Snowdon via the hardest route—tired, rushing, with inappropriate footwear, in bad weather."

"I know. We were so stupid."

"You had no respect for the mountain!" His features contorted in pain.

Doug yanked his backpack out from where it had been trapped underneath her, and she tipped backward. By the time she righted herself, the anger was gone, replaced by cool detachment. "I have to check on the Sherpas."

"Wait, Doug . . ."

Moving faster than she thought was possible in the mass of bodies, Doug unzipped the tent and left.

Cecily wiped her face with her gloves. Doug was so angry with her. She felt like he'd seen inside of her, at what a bad climber she was. She shouldn't be on the mountain, no matter what opportunities or inspiration had brought her there. She was spiraling, all her doubt bubbling to the surface, her hands trembling with the force of it.

Charles was the one to take up her hands, clasping them between his own. "You did the right thing, confessing like that. But Carrie knew what she was risking when she went out on the mountain. It's what we all learn. Some in a harder way than others. Don't dwell on it. What's done is done—how you move forward is what counts. You will do this, Cecily. This is why I chose you to write my story after you summit. You understand the highs—and the lows."

She stared, transfixed by his gaze, and nodded.

He released her hands. "I'll go and check on Doug and send one of the Sherpas back with more water. You need to stay hydrated tonight."

In the next moment, he was gone, leaving the three of them in the tent.

"What's up with Doug?" asked Zak.

Cecily shook her head. She felt numb. Finally confessing had been a relief, but Doug's reaction had thrown her. "I have no idea."

"I'm so sorry you went through that," said Elise. She clucked the roof of her mouth with her tongue. "But it seems to me your ex is to blame. You said he is a guide, no? Taking you up there in bad weather and in running shoes?" She shuddered.

"No, Elise. It was my fault."

"It is no one's fault when someone slips. Me? I am proud of you. You are here, prepped, ready and facing your fear. That is very brave. To make that choice to return to the mountains: you are not a failure—summit or no."

Cecily felt tears prick her eyes. "You have no idea what that means to me, coming from you. I just . . . I can't believe we're turning around."

Elise shrugged. "The mountain will always be there. You can try again another time."

She envied Elise's composure. For her, things weren't so simple. She bit her lip. "If I don't summit, Charles won't give me the interview. It was his condition."

Elise scoffed. "As if it is your fault we don't summit because of a storm? If it is as bad as this, he won't be able to either."

"And if he doesn't, then there won't be a story for me to write about."

"What does it matter to you anyway?" said Zak. "It's just one story. You're a successful journalist. Think about me. All that sponsorship money down the drain."

"Look, I'm not a successful journalist. I've never written anything this big before. *Wild Outdoors* didn't want me on this story, Charles did. If I don't write it, my editor won't commission anything else from me. And if I don't get paid for this article, I won't have a job. Actually, I won't have a home. I put myself in a mountain of debt to get here . . ."

"You're joking? You kept that quiet," said Zak. He put his arm around her and squeezed her shoulders. "But something will come along. I have no doubt."

"Yeah." She gave him a weak smile and pulled the sleeping bag up to her chin. She wished she could share his confidence.

"Well, hey. Is it me or does it sound like it's getting better out there? Maybe that's why Doug left. Maybe he genuinely did need to check in with the Sherpas," he said.

The expression on Doug's face had told Cecily a different story. There had been real pain there. A tortured look she wouldn't forget in a hurry.

But Zak was right about the storm. It had quieted, and now another sound could be heard. Obscenities, shouting and a scuffle.

"What on earth?" she said.

"I'm going to find out what's happening," said Zak.

"But wait! The wind—"

"I won't go far."

Zak pulled on his boots and was out of the tent before Cecily could protest any further. She and Elise exchanged a look, wondering if they should follow. But then Zak's face appeared back in the entrance.

He clambered back inside. "You won't believe this, but Grant is going nuts out there. They think he's got severe altitude sickness. He's swearing at everyone, refusing to stay in the tent, stripping his jacket off, throwing his gloves off the cliff. They want to take him down but don't think they can in his condition. They might have to restrain him."

"You're not serious!" Elise said.

Mingma poked his head through their tent flaps.

"Please, everyone, stay calm," he said. His normally smiling face had a deep frown.

"Is it safe with him like that? What if he comes for us in the night?" Cecily asked, her eyes wide.

Mingma shook his head, and as he did, snow fell on her sleeping bag. "No, do not worry. Dario is sending him to base camp. He won't be making the summit push. However, we think maybe we can move up tomorrow. So we will need to be prepared. In a few moments, your climbing Sherpa will bring food. Then the three of you will need to get some rest. Don't worry about Grant. He is not our concern anymore," said Mingma.

But Cecily caught a whisper of worry on his face.

One rogue operator on the mountain, in such close quarters as this, meant it was dangerous for them all.

CHAPTER 45

ICICLES HUNG FROM THE inside of their tent, the heat from their bodies and moisture from their breath rising and freezing against the tent walls. Mini stalactites fell across Cecily's sleeping bag as she shuffled awake, disturbing them from the ceiling. At least the howl of the wind had died down. Cold air blasted her in the face, their tent opening. Panic struck. "What's going on?" she muttered, feeling groggy. What if it was Grant? What if he'd come for them?

She reached out, feeling around for her ice ax, ready to strike. But then the face registered: it was Galden.

Elise sat up next to her. "Everything OK?" she asked.

"Is it morning already?" questioned Zak, his voice muffled.

Galden's face was knitted with worry. "We must move quickly."

"Are we going down?" Cecily asked. She dreaded the answer.

But he shook his head. "No, we are going up to camp four. But . . ." he held his tongue, seemingly unwilling to say anything else. "Here. Eat your breakfast." He thrust a bowl into each of their hands, and was gone.

"That was strange," said Zak, as he wolfed down his porridge. Cecily held her breakfast of apple pudding in her palms, the smooth sludge anything but appetizing. She lifted it up in the spoon and let it drip on itself. Her stomach clenched, nausea rising. She quickly put it away, swapping for a granola bar instead.

When they emerged, fully dressed and geared up, Mingma was waiting for them. Doug was nowhere to be seen. "I have some news," Mingma said.

Zak groaned. "We're going down? But the weather seems to have settled."

He was right. The sun was out, the air fresh and clear, the wind calmed to a gentle breeze. Ideal conditions to continue up the mountain.

Mingma shook his head. "We are still climbing. But this is something different." He gestured for them to come closer. "It's Grant."

Cecily's heart skipped a beat. "What happened?"

"He is missing. He went to the bathroom in the night but never returned to his tent. They are looking for him now."

Cecily craned her neck in the direction of the Summit Extreme tents. "Where could he have gone? We're at camp three!"

"I know it's a shock, but we have to concentrate. I wanted to tell you so you can keep an eye out."

"Did he go down?" Zak asked.

"He wouldn't on his own, surely," said Cecily. She shivered, despite the sun. Grant was out there, somewhere.

"Why was no one watching him?" Zak scanned the Summit Extreme area, as if he expected Grant's head to pop up at any moment.

"I don't know. But they are looking, and we assume Doug has gone to help. We can only concentrate on keeping ourselves safe now. Do you have your oxygen mask ready? I will attach it to your tanks and get the flow started," Mingma said.

Where was Grant?

The straps of the mask were too tight against her cheeks, the rubber edge pressing the bridge of her nose. She couldn't breathe. She couldn't keep the mask on. It was a claw, gripping her face.

She ripped the mask off, gulping down the fresher air. Even though she'd be getting a higher concentration of oxygen from the mask than from the air outside, breathing felt easier without it.

She rested on her knees, even though she'd only taken a few steps. Then she made a second mistake: she looked up. Beyond the tents, on a clear, sunny day, with none of the snowy drifts that had clouded the view when she'd arrived, she could see the route leading to camp four.

Impossible. A never-ending uphill climb.

She turned to face the tent. She wanted to crawl inside and wait for the rest of the team to return from the summit. Her resolve vanished. Melted, like the top layer of snow under the heat of the sun.

An arm wrapped around her shoulder. Galden.

He placed the mask back over her mouth. "Take a deep breath, Cecily."

She shook her head. *I can't do it*, she wanted to say, she *would* say if she could speak with that mask over her mouth.

He could tell.

"You *can* do this. Just breathe. Take your time."

Her heart pounded. Her stomach roiled; she thought she was going to be sick. *Is this what you wanted me to write about, Charles? Is this the joy of the mountain?*

What was the joy? Was it in surviving where other people perished? The problem was, she *hadn't* survived yet. She was still in the middle of the ride, heading up into the most dangerous part of the mountain, into the death zone. Like Charles had said after Ben's departure, her "inner killer" could take over.

She could die if she didn't learn to breathe with the oxygen mask, if she took a wrong turn and got lost, if she forgot to clip in, if she didn't have enough to drink, if her ascender slipped, if her crampon caught in her boot, if her brain started swelling, if the storm returned and blew her off the mountain . . . or if Grant was hiding somewhere on the mountain, waiting to attack. There were so many ifs where the consequences would be fatal.

The sun beat down, reflecting off the snow, and beads of sweat formed on her brow. The hill rose in front of them, the huge sloping back of the mountain beast. Some climbers were making their way down, tiny ants in her vision. The oxygen tank in her backpack pulled at her shoulders. She was steaming inside her down suit, so she unzipped the vents at her side and under her arms to allow air to circulate.

"Come on; let's move. One step at a time," Galden said.

She noticed as he took a step away that he was holding his arm strangely, keeping it close to his body. The arm she had hit by accident with the ice ax. She wanted to ask if he was OK, but the mask and his speed prevented her.

She walked on. Even though this wasn't a technical section of the mountain, it was one of the slowest. Everyone was tired, and the heat sapped their energy even more.

Elise was behind Cecily, her camera held out on a selfie stick as she narrated her way up the slope. She flipped the camera so that it faced a small speck on the mountain, farther up and to their left. Cecily squinted, watching the dot as it climbed ever higher. Charles. He was moving at pace, with a liquid ease.

As much as watching him was blowing her mind, made all the more impressive by how hard every other mountaineer was having to work just to take a step while attached to the fixed lines, she had to concentrate on herself. She scooped snow from the ground and doused her wrists, the back of her neck. Even on a snowcapped mountain, approaching seven thousand meters above sea level, she was melting, hotter than if she'd been on a beach in Ibiza. Her down suit was doing its job too well. She didn't dare remove her oxygen mask, but she opened all the zips on her down suit so it was almost hanging off. Underneath the suit, her layer of black merino wool thermals seemed almost scalding to touch. Whenever she lifted the mask to take a drink, she wiped buckets of sweat from her lips and nose.

At least her ascender held today, and she didn't worry about sliding back. The route grew steeper, but they had left the main icefall, so there were no more big walls to tackle. The heavy banks of snow around them were the risk now, which is why she stuck to the path carved out by the rope-fixing team. Any deviation risked disturbing the snowfield and triggering an avalanche.

She and Zak climbed together most of the way as Elise fell behind. Zak stood out in his silver top-of-the-line custom-made down suit. More astronaut than mountaineer.

At the top of the slope, but still hours from camp four, they sat to rest and refuel, looking back at the huge slope they'd just climbed. It was an incredible view back down to camp three and even camp one, now a tiny smudge in the distance. No words needed to be spoken. They simply looked out and breathed.

By unspoken agreement, after a few moments, they continued. The weather turned as they entered the fourth hour of climbing. The sun disappeared behind a thick cloud, the temperature dropping. Her down suit—with all the zips done up now—came into its own. The mask was still desperately uncomfortable, and she swapped wiping sweat from her upper lip to dislodging icicles from around her neck. Frost built up around the collar of her orange down suit, coating it in a crust of white. She pulled her buff so that it covered the exposed skin around the mask, replacing worry about sunburn for frostbite. The variety of life-threatening conditions she had to deal with was dizzying.

After another hour of walking, she saw the fluttering yellow of the camp four tents. One night here, then the last major push for the summit. It was about three p.m., and at midnight they'd be walking again. By this time tomorrow, she could be back in base camp—if everything went to plan.

Zak was a few steps ahead. He stopped so abruptly, she almost plowed into his back.

"What's going on?" she asked, tugging down her mask.

"Can you hear that?" he said.

She listened too. Shouts were coming from the tents. Shouts at over seven thousand meters? Her thoughts jumped to Grant. Had they found him? Was he causing more havoc?

"I think that's Doug's voice," said Zak. "It's good he's here at least . . ."

They exchanged a look of concern and picked up the pace. If it were possible to run while attached to a line, wearing a mask and with crampons on their feet, they would have.

Dario was gesticulating wildly at Doug and Mingma. As they approached the tents, they could see why he was so angry. The Summit Extreme tents were ripped apart, the plastic flapping in the wind. They'd been destroyed.

CHAPTER 46

A FEW METERS BEHIND, the Manners Mountaineering tents were intact. Her relief was mixed with shock for Dario's clients. Who would do this? What kind of person would sabotage an entire team, putting lives at serious risk?

"You have ruined us!" said Dario. "Are you really so desperate that you endanger innocent people?"

"Dario, calm down. It wasn't us," replied Doug.

"How did this happen then?" He gesticulated at the tents again.

"How should I know? The winds have been strong up here the past few days."

Dario threw his hands up in the air. "The wind? The wind I suppose chose only our tents to destroy. You would know, since you were the only one up here before us."

Doug narrowed his eyes. "Don't provoke me, Dario. Other teams have been on the mountain too."

"What are you going to do? Punch me as well? That would well and truly bury your company, no matter what Charles is doing to prop it up."

Behind Dario, the Summit Extreme clients sat on the ground, heads in their hands. Cecily couldn't blame them. They'd done the hard work to climb to camp four, and now their summit plans were in tatters along with their tents.

Mingma stepped in. "We can help prepare food for your climbers."

Dario reeled back. "You're not going to stay on the mountain after this? There's obviously someone dangerous out here. With the satellites down, you cannot be sure of the forecast. Going to the summit is foolish! You have to return to camp three, along with us. Doug, you know that is the only option. You are the most safety-conscious man I've ever known!"

Return to camp three? After everything it took to get here? It was unthinkable. She knew she wouldn't have the energy to turn around.

"I understand you need to go down, Dario. But our tents are fine. We are staying," said Doug.

Dario stared at him in utter disbelief.

"Thank God for that," Zak whispered to her, pulling down his mask. "I thought our summit bid was finished."

Cecily took a deep breath of the oxygen filtering through her mask, trying to calm her racing heart. Dario was right. Doug was the most safety-conscious guide on the mountain. But here they were, in the aftermath of a storm, with sabotaged tents and a mad man potentially at large, and he was asking them to stay.

She wanted to make the summit. But it didn't feel right.

When it was clear that Doug and Mingma weren't going to change their minds, Dario stalked off, shaking his head.

She edged toward Doug, wanting to ask if there had been an update about Grant. But he moved away from her the moment she took a step.

Snow fell thickly, and they were buffeted by a strong gust of wind. She prayed the storm that had kept them inside the tents at camp three wasn't returning.

Galden appeared at her shoulder, gesturing for them to follow. She and Zak shuffled in his wake. She clenched her fists inside her thick overgloves. She tried to keep her eyes away from the Summit Extreme tents, not wanting to feed the already unsettled feeling lodged in the pit of her stomach.

He guided them to a tent. "Here, go inside." Without questioning, they shuffled in, collapsing. Galden ducked in after. "You two and Elise will share again tonight. Will be easier to stay warm."

She nodded, no energy to talk. Elise arrived a few moments later, after they'd arranged their sleeping mats and bags. "I passed some of the Summit Extreme team on their way down. They told me about their tents. Terrible."

"Dario thinks someone did it on purpose," said Zak.

"No, no, no. Surely not." But her horrified expression didn't mirror her words.

Their tent was unzipped. "Elise?" came a strong Austrian accent.

"Eh? What are you doing here?"

Dario reached out a thick-gloved hand. "You have to come with me." His eyes were wild. "Please. I have to go down with my team, but I couldn't leave you." Dario glanced at Cecily and Zak, but then returned his focus to the young French Canadian. "Let's go. It's not safe."

Elise drew back. "Dario, no . . ."

Someone pulled back on Dario's shoulder. "Leave her alone. This is my team. I make the decisions."

There was more commotion, and Dario shouted Elise's name one more time. But then he left, and Doug ducked inside their tent instead. His dark eyes studied Elise. "I didn't realize you were involved with him. You never disclosed that." Elise avoided his gaze, and he grunted. "Anyway, you're moving tents again."

"You're fucking kidding me!" Zak exclaimed.

"It's the best option. We have plenty of tents, and you and Cecily will get better sleep with your own supplemental oxygen supply. Elise wants to climb without O_2. This way, she can't be accused of any wrongdoing."

Elise stared down at the floor of the tent, clutching at her necklace. She looked spooked by Dario's intervention, and Cecily couldn't blame her—she felt it too.

Elise's fear was contagious. Cecily felt the strands of it tugging at her throat. She thought of what Dario had said back in base camp: *Do not be alone.* Now she was being ordered into her own tent. Exposed. Isolated. But they were part of Doug's team, and Doug had made it clear his word was law on the mountain.

"Zak, let's go."

"OK then," said Zak. Because they were staying in their down suits, there wasn't much for him to pack up. He crawled to the front of the tent.

"I'll be back for you in a moment," said Doug, looking directly at Cecily.

She shivered.

When Doug and Zak were gone, Elise grabbed Cecily's hand. "Please be careful. Maybe Dario was right. Something doesn't feel right here."

"Then why didn't you go with him?"

"The summit . . ."

Cecily hadn't thought about it much before, but no matter how casually Elise talked about the mountain always being there, she was under so much pressure—from her followers and her sponsors—to make it to the top. Cecily wasn't the only one afraid to give up and afraid to go on. Elise lowered her voice. "But I don't like what I see in Doug right now. You know about his temper, right? Plus, there's something else. Cecily, I haven't been totally honest about the real reason I'm here."

"What do you mean? Didn't you come along to boost Charles's social media presence?"

"Officially I did, but unofficially . . . Merde." She blew out a sharp breath. "I am the one who told Dario I saw Charles use fixed lines on Broad Peak. My GoPro was broken, so I couldn't get video. But I thought I saw him do it."

"Seriously? What did you think you saw?"

Elise hesitated. "Because I wasn't using oxygen, I was moving very slowly—even Phemba had gone on ahead, so I couldn't see him. There was so much snow this year; the risk of slab avalanches was immense. I didn't blame Phemba for moving fast. I tied into an anchor point to rest, and my biggest fear came to life: just behind me, where I had stepped, I triggered an avalanche. I was safe, but I shouted a warning for anyone below me. I didn't think anyone was there, but then I saw a dark red summit suit, and I thought, Oh no! Charles! But when the snowdrifts cleared, he was still there, flat against the mountainside, safe. I was relieved, but then I thought I saw our fixed line wrapped around his arm. I was too far away to be sure. I told Dario what I saw, and he was outraged."

"Even if grabbing the rope had saved Charles's life?"

Elise nodded. "Charles is making a big claim on his mission, so, yes, it matters. It wasn't the first time Dario had heard something about it . . . so we hatched a plan to get proof this time. Manaslu would be our last chance. Dario wanted me to join Charles's team to catch him cheating."

Cecily blinked rapidly, hardly able to take in what Elise was saying. But she knew Doug would be returning for her at any moment. She had to find out more.

"So you and Dario are . . . ?"

"He is my boyfriend."

"Why were you two fighting yesterday?"

Elise blinked in surprise. "You saw us?"

Cecily nodded.

Elise sighed. "We argued because since I've been climbing with Charles, I haven't seen anything wrong. I don't think he's a cheater. I must have been mistaken. And I think Dario is jealous. I was worried he might do something to sabotage Charles." She dropped her head into her hands. "But now, with Doug so angry, I am scared . . ."

Cecily touched her shoulder. "What do you mean?"

Elise caught her gaze and held it. "I am afraid of what he might do now that he knows I came here to ruin Charles's mission."

"How could he know that?"

"Because I told him. At camp three this morning, before anyone else was awake. I told him because I was wrong and I wanted to apologize, but he stomped away from me, faster than I could keep up. Now the Summit Extreme tents are ruined and—"

"And you think Doug was responsible?"

"There's no other explanation."

"Oh god. I thought *I* had pissed Doug off. With my story about Snowdon. He seemed so angry." Cecily paused. "But Charles doesn't know that's why you're here?"

Elise pursed her lips and shook her head. Her lipstick had rubbed off, and beneath it her lips had a tinge of blue. "I wanted someone else to know. I want you to be careful. In case . . ."

"Your turn," said a gruff voice. Cecily jumped in her sleeping bag—she hadn't even realized that Doug had returned. The snow muffled all sound. "Let's go."

"Good luck," Cecily said to Elise, once she'd gathered all her things in her arms.

"You too," Elise said. "I'm sure it will be OK." She clutched at her necklace.

Cecily followed Doug out into the night. It was pitch-black, snowing, and it was all she could do to follow in the light of his headlamp to the right tent. He lifted the tent flap and she stooped inside. What else could she do but trust him? She was helpless.

Doug was framed in the tent's entrance. "At midnight, I'll wake you, then it will be time to go. Don't worry about packing up your sleeping bag and mattress—just have what you need for the summit in your pack. Food, water, extra gloves. Travel light."

"Will Galden be with me then?" she asked.

Doug sighed, rubbing the space between his brows. "Cecily, you were a fool to come here."

"What?"

"After what happened on Snowdon, you have no business being on the mountain. If I had known, I would have refused your place. You're unprepared, reckless and lack willpower. But since you're here now, you are under my care. I will keep you safe. I haven't lost a single person under my watch yet."

Her mouth felt dry; she couldn't find any words. He started closing her tent flaps when finally she found her voice. "Did you do it?"

There was a pause. He opened the tent again. "Do what?" he asked.

"Destroy the Summit Extreme tents so they couldn't stay here."

He reached down and pulled the oxygen mask up onto her face. "Get some rest," he said gently.

He left her in the darkness. Without Elise beside her, she felt so alone. Wind battered the tent, though not as strongly as the day before, and she hunkered down into her sleeping bag.

Camp four. The summit attempt was only hours away. She'd already accomplished so much and overcome so many obstacles just to get here. But sleep was impossible.

Tomorrow was the day she'd been waiting for, building up in her mind. She tried to break down the task ahead to make it seem more manageable. First, she had to sleep—only four hours maximum. Alarm set for midnight. Wake up, pull on boots and crampons, fill water bottles, eat.

Find Galden. Start walking in the dark. Follow the fixed lines for eight hours, treading carefully. Then along a narrow ridge to the summit itself.

Her mind raced. If only getting to the summit was all she had to worry about. Now she had so many questions—about Grant, Dario . . . and Doug.

Then there was the urgent press of her bladder.

With reluctance, she removed her mask, left the tent and scooted around the back, finding a spot a few paces away from camp to relieve herself. She had to be quick—the air was frigid, and without her oxygen she could feel every breath in her lungs, short and shallow. She could only move a few steps before needing a rest. Her legs felt like dead weights. How Elise and Charles were able to do this entire climb without oxygen was unfathomable.

She stood up. The sky was dark and clear—the snow had stopped, and it seemed like Doug had been right about the forecast all along. At least Charles would be able to complete his mission.

But something else attracted her attention.

It was the whistle.

She heard it again. Now she knew she must be imagining it. She must be hypoxic, and this was the result. *Unless Grant was nearby.*

"Cecily?"

The sound of her name spooked her. A looming figure stood in the dark, standing by her tent. It was Charles—and to her surprise he was smoking. "You'd better get some rest. We'll all need our energy for what is to come tomorrow."

"What about you?" she asked.

"A pre-summit ritual. One smoke." He took a long drag. "You can write about it, if you want."

"Are you camped nearby?" she asked. She hadn't seen Charles's tent yet, as he'd packed it away at camp three before she could look. She was curious whether his alpine-style tent was much different from theirs. She was about to ask when Charles answered her.

"Just over there. There aren't many other safe places to camp on the mountain. But I'm confused. Where is everyone?"

"What do you mean?"

"Dario's team, the Russians . . . none of them are here. Only our team."

"The Summit Extreme tents were ruined; they had to turn back. I don't know about Elbrus Elite."

"What?" Charles's head snapped around, staring at the Summit Extreme tents. He hissed a long exhale through his teeth. Then he dropped the cigarette butt in the snow, extinguishing it with the toe of his boot. "But you . . . are you all set for the summit?"

"Yes. I leave at midnight."

Charles nodded. "Good, good."

"When will you be heading for the summit?" The sentence came out slowly; she needed more time between words to catch her breath. Charles raised an eyebrow. He was right. She needed rest.

"Soon," he said. "Before you, most likely. Maybe I'll see you up there."

"Charles?" She debated telling him her suspicion that Doug had destroyed the tents, but something stopped her. "Good night."

"Good night, Cecily."

She scuttled back to the tent, but before getting in she paused, looking over her shoulder. The light from Charles's flashlight still shone a distance away.

This was her chance to get a look at his tent. She ducked, keeping low to the ground, one hand on her tent so that she didn't get lost. She moved carefully, stepping over the anchor lines, moving around the circumference.

As Charles had said, there was the outline of his tent, just behind

hers. The tent was red, with navy blue accents. There was an X of
duct tape in the corner, showing how well it had been used.

Cecily gasped and snapped off her headlamp.

Her heart raced inside her chest. She scrambled back to the front
of her tent, rushing to crawl into her sleeping bag. She grabbed the
oxygen mask and pulled it over her head, taking deep breaths until
she felt calmer again.

It had been Charles's tent she'd seen that night at base camp.

He'd been lying to them.

Charles had been on the mountain for far longer than anyone had
realized.

CHAPTER 47

MIDNIGHT, AT CAMP FOUR.

She woke to the bleeping of her watch, muffled through her hat pulled down low over her ears.

Her first thought: *no*. She didn't want to move. She was surprised she'd slept at all after the revelation the night before. She half wondered if it had been an altitude-induced hallucination, some twisted dream. The reality—that Charles had been lying to them—was far more terrifying. Why would he do that?

You're a journalist, Cecily. When you get back down to base camp, you can ask your questions, demand answers. There was nothing she could do now at camp four.

On summit push.

She'd been waiting for this.

This was different from Snowdon. She'd done all the hard work. She'd prepared. She'd trained. She was about to summit one of the highest mountains in the world.

She'd come so far already. What were a few more steps?

She sat up, suddenly panicked. *What's on my face?*

Her mouth and chin were soaked with condensation beneath the oxygen mask. She wiped it away with the edge of her sleeping bag. Her head pounded. She emptied her bag of anything she wasn't going to need on the summit. All she had were a few granola bars, two half-liter bottles of water, energy tablets, her down mitts, some artificial hand warmers, her wonky flag, her oxygen tank, her camera, phone and some spare batteries. Everything else was surplus. She crawled out of the tent and stabbed her ice ax into the ground.

Doug trudged toward her. "Good. You're up. Plans've changed."

She pulled down her oxygen mask. "A-again? What do you mean?" she stuttered, feeling woozy.

He didn't answer straightaway. "You'll need water. Pass your bottles to me," he said. He filled up her small half-liter Nalgenes with hot water, and she dropped some fizzing energy tablets into them. She tucked one of them into the breast pocket of her down suit, along with her camera and phone. It would help keep her batteries warm.

"Where is Galden?" She hoped the fuzziness in her mind would clear once she started moving. She noticed that Doug had been talking to her while she'd been distracted by her water bottles, her mask and headache. She tried to tune her focus back in.

". . . will be right behind you. You'd better move. The storm is returning. Follow the rope and you'll be fine."

"Wait, Doug—" she paused, swallowing down air, trying to catch her breath. It was so much effort to talk, but she had to ask. "Has there been any sign of Grant?"

He shook his head. "No. Nothing yet. But don't worry about him—"

Cecily cut him off, interjecting with her next question before she could stop herself. "Did you know Charles has been on the mountain since the beginning?"

His eyes widened by the tiniest fraction. "Of course I knew," he said softly. "I will explain everything. Let's talk at base camp."

She nodded and replaced her mask. Galden was going to follow; she was going to get her answers. Doug reached into her backpack and replaced her oxygen tank with a fresh one, adjusting her flow rate. There was no more technical climbing now—as long as she could put one foot in front of the other, she would make it.

She turned on her headlamp, and Doug pointed her in the direction of the fixed lines. "Step carefully," he said. "See you down there."

She couldn't speak through the mask, so she gave a thumbs-up in her gigantic mittens. She trod through the snow toward the fixed lines. She reached the anchor point, where two ropes lay twisted. One, leading up toward the summit. The other, down to camp three. She clipped into the summit line.

Her watch showed it was half past midnight. Her headlamp only illuminated the next step in front of her, and the thin rope was her guide. She walked steadily. When she stopped for a sip of water from her bottle, she looked up at the clear night sky, full of stars.

Orion hung over the route. It was like she was climbing toward him, reaching to the heights of the gods. She was currently one of the highest people on Earth. No other teams were currently climbing other eight-thousanders. She was as close to the heavens as it was possible to be on two feet.

She felt strong. Stronger than she had the entire time on the mountain. She thought maybe she was moving *too* quickly. Galden hadn't caught up yet. There was no sign of the sun on the horizon. She had never imagined reaching her first proper summit under the cover of darkness.

She looked for a telltale headlamp bobbing her way that could be Galden or one of her teammates. But she couldn't see a thing. Only the thin strand of rope guiding her way. A wrong step would result in a steep drop, and if she wasn't clipped in, she could easily fall to her death. But fear seemed to have shrunk down to the tiniest speck in the deepest crevasse of her mind. All emotion was gone, but the intellectual knowledge of the danger was there. It was present, and yet she didn't care about it.

Was this acute mountain sickness, this apathy? It was the strangest feeling.

She used the endless walking to mull over the events of the night before. Why had Charles pretended to arrive on the mountain late? The simplest explanation was that he wanted time on the mountain without the team. Doug had known, so maybe Charles had needed time to plot his route through the icefall and around the crevasses, so he could show up and race to the top, making it appear effortless.

But there was also the note. Alain and Irina were dead. If their deaths were not accidents, as she suspected, that still left someone dangerous on the mountain. And Grant was missing . . . He could still be a threat.

Put one step in front of the other, Cecily. Don't be so concerned about dying.

But dying was all she could think about. Nothing lived up here. Not for long. The fact that she dared to breathe here at all was in defiance of what was natural.

She touched her hand to her face. She'd removed her oxygen mask for some reason. Oh, right. She needed to drink. She fumbled for the bottle tucked away in the inside pocket of her suit, her huge down mittens making ordinary movement difficult. The tepid trickle of water felt like a dream as it slid down her parched throat. But then she shivered. She put the now-empty bottle back and redid the zipper again. Stupid of her to leave the zip open—the cold had rushed into her suit like floodwater.

Her decision-making was skewed. She was likely hypoxic. It felt like time was melting away, and she wasn't aware of it passing. Only that she was moving forward and up, stepping, stepping, stepping.

The sky around her had lightened. The sunrise was unlike any she had seen before. Golden light spreading across the blankets of snow turned the fearsome landscape into an enchanted wonderland.

She was aware of the vast expanse around her, of the clouds like opaque bubble wrap, far below her feet. Tips of other far-off peaks glowed orange in the early light of the sun. Minute snowflakes gathered on her eyelids. Gigantic and tiny. There were no mediums here, no balance. Nothing but extremes. She was sure Galden was catching up behind her, his steady pace, his rhythmic breathing, his dark eyes boring a hole into her down suit, willing her to keep going. Even her hypoxic brain knew that if she stopped for too long, his life would be in danger too. Kill herself, kill him. With more than just her own life in her hands, she found her focus. She willed herself to move. She lifted her feet, so heavy inside the triple-layer boots.

She licked her lips, which were completely dry. Come to think of it, her mouth was parched. Again. So soon. Hadn't she just stopped for water? What had been left in her Nalgene hadn't been enough.

Did she have another? Maybe in her backpack. Could she be bothered to remove it? She thought if she did that, she might not put it back on again.

She adjusted the mask on her face, taking an extra-deep breath.

She stepped forward.

Then she heard a loud pop, followed by a hiss of oxygen escaping. She stopped, clasping the mask to her face, fumbling along the hose with her other hand to try to stop the leak. As if that would work. Her supplementary oxygen tank was malfunctioning. A nightmare come to life. Had she broken it? But she hadn't touched the tank or its connecting hose since camp four . . .

Only one person had even been close.

Doug.

"Galden!" she shouted, though her mask muffled the sound. He had to be close. She needed his help. But the reassuring tap on her shoulder never came. Her peripheral vision was bad, blocked by her goggles and the hood of her down jacket. She had to move her entire body to see behind her.

She turned.

But Galden still wasn't there.

She was completely alone on the mountain.

CHAPTER 48

SHE SHOULD GO BACK down. Her oxygen tank was broken. With every step, from this moment on, her body was deteriorating. Her cells were dying, her brain and lungs starved of oxygen. Her body would be declining rapidly at this point. But she was so close.

She could see the summit. No one else was up there—just the colorful array of prayer flags marking the top of the mountain, fluttering in the wind. She thought with all the people there had been at base camp, she'd be waiting in some kind of queue. But no.

Was her mind playing tricks on her? She took another step forward. She took in a breath. A few more steps like this, and maybe she could do it . . .

The way up to the summit was steep, a knife-edge ridge with a path the width of her boot and sheer drops either side. She waited for the panic to come, but fear belonged to someone else now. She felt detached, her body moving of its own accord, closer to the summit. Her brain caught up; her legs were right: she couldn't stop now. She clipped into the next fixed line and fumbled with the ascender to make the last few steep meters. One step at a time.

One step, one step.

And then there she was: on the top of the mountain, at the jumble of prayer flags marking the summit. Three weeks after setting off from the UK, and only three months since agreeing to join this expedition, she'd made it. She'd succeeded.

Relief, joy, disbelief—all the emotions flooded her senses. She marveled at the view. She was high above the clouds, in a fairy tale, in a floating castle looking down upon the world. The path she'd come up was empty, not a soul to be seen.

She removed her phone from the zipped pocket of her suit, grateful it still had battery power, and angled her arm to take a good selfie—difficult when she was basically wrapped in a duvet and weighed down by her useless oxygen tank.

She managed to get a shot—but in her huge goggles, she was hardly recognizable. She lifted them onto her forehead. Then she took off her gloves to get a better grip. She took another photo.

As she put her camera back in her suit, a gust of wind almost knocked her off her feet. A tiny ember of fear blew her back to life, and she felt exposed, all alone on the tiny summit plateau. Dark clouds loomed in the distance. Maybe the storm was returning. The cold had buried itself deep into her bones now, her fingers cramping. That's when she realized she was still not wearing her gloves after taking a photo. She shoved them back on, clenching her fists inside the down, wiggling blood back into her fingers.

She almost forgot about her summit token. She fumbled in her pocket for her wonky British flag, unfolding it on top of the others. She knelt down to tie it in; she was part of the mountain now. She held it under her palm and closed her eyes. *Thank you.*

When she opened her eyes again, she felt disoriented. Had she merely blinked, or had she passed out for a moment? Longer than a moment?

She heard a voice.

"Caroline."

She gripped her down suit over her heart, turning her body to the sound. Doug appeared on the tiny summit platform, digging his ice ax into the snow with every step.

"Doug! I didn't know you were so close; I couldn't see anyone behind me." Her words came in gasps. She'd been in the death zone now for—well, she didn't know how long, but too long, without supplementary oxygen. She staggered back to her feet. "I made it to the summit. Can you believe it? I did it. I actually did it."

The expression on his face was pained, his brow furrowed. "You're not supposed to be here. I told you to go down, with the rest of the team and the Sherpas. When I realized you'd gone up, I had to come and get you."

"You did?" She frowned. She couldn't remember. She'd missed some of his instructions but had he really told her to descend?

"You've made a big mistake by coming here." he said. "Your carelessness is going to cost you. Caroline—"

"No, Doug. It's Cecily." Was *he* confused? He didn't have an oxygen mask on either, but his eyes were sharp and clear.

"Cecily, yes. But Caroline is dead. It was because of you."

She stepped backward as he stalked toward her. The summit plateau shrank beneath her feet.

"Caroline was my daughter," he said, moving ever closer.

"I didn't know her, Doug. I think you're mistaken." She couldn't tear her eyes away from him.

"You didn't know her. But you killed her."

His words hit her with the force of a hurricane. "What?"

Tears shone in his eyes. Her back pressed up against the mound of prayer flags, and she gripped them in her fists, clinging onto the summit for dear life.

"The story you told about Snowdon. Your reckless, idiotic decision-making. The woman who tried to help you . . ."

Carrie.

Caroline.

It couldn't be.

"N-no," Cecily stuttered. "Her last name was . . . was Halloran."

"My wife's maiden name."

Cecily's heart skipped a beat. She thought of the woman's reassuring smile, the hours they had talked. The mantra she'd relied on, on the mountain: *Be bothered.* Then the scream. The accident that could have been avoided. If she'd only moved.

You called for help, Cecily. You're a hero. James's voice, so assured. Yet she carried the guilt, the shame around with her. And now to learn that Carrie had been Doug's daughter?

October. When Doug broke down and hit a client from Summit Extreme. The bad news . . . it had been his daughter's death.

"Doug, I'm so sorry. She slipped. I'm sorry," she repeated. She swooned, her vision swimming. She tried to breathe but she couldn't focus on any single action.

Doug wasn't even looking at her anymore. His gaze was focused out across the sunrise, staring at the gentle bubble of pale pink clouds, the shards of golden light reflecting off the mountaintops, a child's drawing of Heaven made real. "And now you're going to die just like she did." He clenched his fists inside his gloves, the down balling up.

Her heart caught in her throat.

One thought crystallized, cutting through the hypoxia fog of her mind: Doug was dangerous. She had to get away. "Doug, please . . . don't do this." She fumbled at her harness, searching, searching. "I don't want to end up like Irina."

Doug shook his head. "You have no idea at all, do you? No one can save you from what's coming."

He launched forward, his arms extended, and Cecily screamed.

CHAPTER 49

SHE FOUND IT. HER fingers gripped the handle of the knife Doug
had given her before their training. It was clipped with a nonlocking
carabiner. All she needed to do was find the release and squeeze . . .

The scream threw Doug off-balance, and that was what she needed.
She lunged with the knife in her hand.

It worked; he wasn't expecting her to fight. He jumped back,
the blade scraping across his suit, and it bought her enough time to
scramble the first few steps off the summit plateau.

She wasn't clipped in, but, frankly, versus the nightmare that was
above her, she took the risk.

Then she glanced down at the precipitous drop beneath her feet.
She changed her mind.

A jumble of ropes was tangled at the anchor point down from the
summit, and she clipped into the first one she grabbed. She dared a
glance back up at the tiny plateau; Doug hadn't followed her yet.
She had to trust her own instincts, which currently felt wrapped in
eight thousand meters' worth of heavy cloud.

She sidestepped down the mountain, clinging to the rope. Her
heart raced from adrenaline, her vision hazy from the lack of oxygen.
Her hands were numb from fumbling with the carabiner.

Her concentration on the rope, she didn't realize that a prong
of her crampon had caught in the gaiter of her opposite boot. She
tripped, and before her brain could process the mistake, she was falling. Her shoulder pounded against the mountain. She was out of

control, at the whim of the slope. Her training took over, and she tried to self-arrest with her gloved hands—but she couldn't. Her ice ax was back at camp four. Her poles too. Her hands were too weak to stop her body or make any kind of meaningful grip in the ice. But she didn't feel afraid. If she was going to die, there was nothing she could do to stop it now.

She felt a jolt as her safety line caught on the fixed rope. She slowed enough to dig her fingers and knees into the snow, bringing herself to a halt. Her heart pounded in her chest, a jackhammer.

She lay on the slope, just breathing. Her eyes were squeezed tightly shut. She didn't want to face the reality of her situation.

She didn't know how long she lay there. Time slipped by in the death zone—minutes felt like hours, yet it also seemed like only a few moments ago that she had been in the tent, packing up her bag.

She blinked her eyes open, wincing against the brightness of the snow. She'd stopped on a tiny ledge, barely the width of her boots. Gingerly, she put pressure on her legs, digging the crampons into the snow to try to create a more secure base.

She yelped as pain shot through her left leg, her knee protesting the movement.

"Help!" she cried out, but it barely came out a croak. There was no one to hear her anyway, except for Doug. And he wanted her dead.

She felt a pull on her safety rope. She tugged back, showing that she was still alive. She thought she heard her name, carried to her on the freezing wind. Although the fall had seemed like forever, now that she had stopped, it didn't look like she had too far to climb to get back up to the route.

But as she pulled again, the end of the fixed line tumbled down after her. It was frayed. She stared at the end of it. Had it been cut? Or had she tied into a rotten line and it had snapped of its own accord?

She wished she was experienced enough to know the difference.

For a moment, the wind was quiet. She heard a voice high above her, the crackle of a radio. "Cecily's fallen," she heard. "Couldn't save her."

Doug wasn't coming to her rescue. He wasn't even going to try. He'd watched her fall, and then he left her here to die.

But she wasn't dead yet.

She swallowed down her pain.

She couldn't stay here, stuck to the wall of snow and ice, arms and legs splayed, desperate not to fall any farther. Crag-fast, again—but this time in the death zone, where every minute she didn't move, she was dying.

"Are you OK?"

She heard a voice. A woman. She looked up and then winced, the bright sunshine searing her eyes; her goggles had been knocked askew in the fall. She fumbled in her pocket for her sunglasses, clawing them onto her face.

"I can't! I can't move!" she tried to shout, but her voice wouldn't work. The sound came out a garbled mess, every word interrupted by a straggling breath.

"I can see the route—just a few steps. You can do it!"

Cecily's head rang. As she dared another glance up, toward the voice, the mountain was as empty as ever. Was there someone above her?

It didn't matter. This time, she had to move.

Stand on your own, Ceci. She heard her grandmother's voice.

She tentatively wiggled her uninjured foot. She dragged it underneath her, then staggered to her feet. She shuffled sideways, digging in the points of her crampons as deeply as she could, then moved the other foot over. With this painstakingly slow movement, she somehow edged herself across the mountain.

"I'm coming!" she cried out, or maybe she didn't; she couldn't tell. She was moving, though. That was the important thing.

Whenever her brain remembered that she was unsecured, in the death zone, without supplementary oxygen and no one coming to save her, she stopped and allowed the panic to wash over her. When her injured knee wasn't strong enough to push through the snow, she had to use her arms. Her gloves were soaked through from the effort of shifting snow, but she had no choice but to keep at it.

One small step at a time.

She nearly lost it when she saw a bright blue fixed line poking out of the snow, and a trail of footsteps. She flung herself toward the line; she could have kissed it, if her face hadn't been covered by her buff. She clipped in, and then she really did collapse down onto her knees and cry.

She knew she had to stand again. And at least it was easy to know which direction she had to go: down.

Doug was on the mountain somewhere. He thought she was dead. Fallen. He'd told her to go down. When she hadn't, he'd followed her up here.

To save her? Or to take the opportunity to kill her where no one could come looking? Her head swirled. Nothing made sense. After all, she'd heard Carrie's voice calling down to her, clear as a bell, urging her to move. Her mind had obviously been playing tricks on her. What if Doug hadn't been at the summit? She carried so much guilt and shame with her, and telling the story at camp three had dragged it all right to the surface. Of course her mind would conjure up a person close to Carrie in that moment, her worst fears of being accused of her death brought to vivid life.

But then what about the fixed line?

She didn't know. But she knew the fear was real.

The pain in her leg was real.

The approaching storm was real.

She could feel it building behind her, the wind growing stronger as it buffeted her back. She had to get back to base camp before it hit. She needed to find Elise and Zak, and make sure they were OK. And if she *hadn't* been hallucinating, then she needed to be somewhere Doug couldn't get to her alone.

She looked from side to side, up and down the trail, but there was no sign of Doug—or of anyone else for that matter. More proof that she had been imagining things. The wind picked up again, blasting her.

Breathe, Cecily.

Cold air filled her lungs. It was strange. When she'd pictured breathing up here, she'd assumed it would feel like suffocating. Choking. Maybe, in a way, like drowning.

But it didn't.

She could feel the sting of the wind on a tiny bit of exposed skin on her cheek, between her buff and her sunglasses, and then a stronger gust against her body, threatening to bring her to her knees.

The air was there. It just wasn't doing what it was supposed to.

She was so tired. Her muscles struggled to work as she pushed through the snow. Not just her muscles. Her blood. Her lungs. Her brain.

It was simple, really—there wasn't enough oxygen in the air, less than a third of what her body was used to. The altimeter on her watch read that she was still up above eight thousand meters. In the death zone.

Her heart raced. She looked over her shoulder. *Was he following?* She stopped in her tracks. A hulking silhouette, a few meters above her, his ponderous steps breaking fresh snow, stalking her, chasing her. But no . . . She blinked and realized it was only the shadow of a cloud on the mountainside.

Without enough oxygen reaching her brain, not even her eyes could be trusted.

So is he coming? Or is he waiting below?

She didn't think it was possible for her heart to beat faster, but it did, galloping inside her chest. Her breathing sped up too as she gulped down the thin air. She swooned, her head spinning.

What did it matter if he was above or below her?

Worry about *him* later. Worry about survival now.

She moved as fast as her body would let her. A thousand-meter drop was one misstep away. Meanwhile, phantom footsteps haunted her from behind.

She had to get down the mountain.

And she was going to have to do it on her own.

Then her eye caught on a bright pink summit suit sitting a little way off the path. Elise. Thank God. Elise was so experienced on the mountain; maybe she could explain what was happening to her. Maybe she was the voice she'd heard, telling her to move.

She stumbled through the heavy snowbank, following the foot-steps that led to her teammate. She pulled down her buff. "Elise! Elise!"

The woman turned toward her, just as a gust of wind smacked Cecily in the face. She threw her hands over her head, coughing and spluttering, driven down into a stoop.

She crawled the last distance, gripping onto the pink material of her friend's suit as she waited for another gust of wind to pass overhead.

"Elise? It's Cecily. Are you OK?" She shook the woman's arm, but her body was still underneath her fingers.

Elise was dead.

CHAPTER 50

A STRANGLED CRY ESCAPED her lips, despair rising in her chest.

She shook Elise's body again, unwilling to admit what she knew to be true.

"Elise, wake up. Please." She was desperate for her friend to flash her trademark smile. Her lips were freshly painted red, yet against the frozen white of her skin it looked gruesome, like a slash.

How was this possible? Tears streamed down her cheeks, freezing there. She tried to move the body, dragging her lifeless arm around her neck and lifting. She wanted to take her down as far as she could. But she'd spent hours without supplementary oxygen and she didn't have the strength.

She had to leave her.

Elise had been the strongest among them. She deserved so much better than this.

As she placed Elise back against the snow, the hood of Elise's suit slid back and Cecily saw a trickle of dark red blood on her neck. Cecily's heart pounded as she gently turned Elise's head. A wound gaped in the back of her skull, her hair matted with frozen blood.

Cecily drew back her hand in shock.

Had Doug done this too?

She curled against Elise's body. She couldn't stay long, or else she would die of exposure next to her friend. Her heart broke at the thought of leaving Elise. She wanted to take something for her family, in case the body was buried by the storm.

Her head pounded. Confusion, nausea, a headache. Hallucinations. All classic signs of HACE. Her knee throbbed inside the down suit.

But then a brain wave hit her: Elise's camera. She felt like the worst kind of scavenger, unzipping the top of her down suit to rummage inside. But she couldn't find it in the pocket where Elise normally kept it, and she couldn't bear to look any further. Then something else caught her eye. The necklace, with its Lucite pendant. She unclipped the chain and slid it into her pocket.

She kissed Elise's hand through her glove. Then she rolled over and started shuffling away, staying low beneath the fierce wind.

She didn't know how long she walked, but she screamed into her buff as the first tents of camp four peeked out of the snowy fog. It meant two things: that, one, she was out of the death zone now, and with every step she'd be getting stronger. And, two, that maybe— just maybe—she'd find help at last. She wasn't sure she could make it much longer on her own.

She unclipped from the final fixed line before the camp and stumbled into the closest tent, the wind howling against the plastic, hardly offering any respite. She held her knees to her chest and sobbed. She was so cold now, shivering, crying, her head and lungs burning. She wanted to be home.

Then she heard a terrifying sound.

That whistle again. Low, low, high, low. If this was another hallucination, she wanted it to stop.

Doug. It had always been Doug.

Alain. Irina. Elise.

And now he was in the camp, coming after her.

The sound snapped her out of her stupor. Her watch was cracked and lifeless from her fall. Her phone and camera were dead too. She had no devices; no way to call for help, nothing except the knowledge that Doug had told everyone over the radio that she was dead.

No one was coming.

She crept outside, keeping low to the ground.

She saw a flash of Doug's navy-blue down suit stalking the camp. He moved toward her, opening tent flaps along the way. She moved behind the tent, closing her eyes, barely able to breathe. If he saw her, she didn't know what she could do to protect herself. But he simply flipped open the front of the tent, saw it was empty, and walked away.

She breathed a sigh of relief.

And then her heart jumped out of her chest, as someone reached out and grabbed her arm.

She wanted to scream, but the sound was muffled by her buff. She stumbled backward, pulled by the hand on her arm into another tent.

Once in, she was let go of. She veered around and found herself staring at Zak.

"Cecily, Jesus, thank fuck it's you." He pulled her toward him, and hugged her so tightly she felt every bruise from her recent fall. She cried out in pain.

Zak didn't seem to notice. "Doug woke me up and told me to go down. I was a bit pissed off at him, to be honest. But I started packing up my things and look . . ." He opened his palms, showing off his GPS communications device. It had been smashed to pieces, along with his camera. "I ran outside to find Doug, but everyone was gone. No Sherpas, no teammates . . . You'd all gone. And without my devices, I couldn't send a message for help. I tried to find the fixed lines to go down, but then the weather got bad and I couldn't. I tried to get back to my tent. I must've gone into about four before I found mine. I didn't know what else to do." He shook. "You have no idea how glad I am to see you. Is there anyone else out there?"

"I think maybe Doug . . ."

"Great! Let's go get him and get off this fucking mountain."

But Cecily grabbed his arm before he could exit the tent. "No. We have to be careful. Doug is dangerous. He came after me on the summit. He . . . he attacked me."

"Shit." Zak's voice was quiet. Unexpectedly so.

"You don't seem surprised," Cecily said, thrown by Zak's calm reaction.

"No, god, I am surprised. It's just . . . something makes sense now." He reached behind his back and pulled out a small black rectangle, with about a dozen pointed antennae sticking out of it. "I found this in Doug's tent when I was trying to find mine."

"Is that . . . ?"

"A signal jammer. Motherfucker. I didn't want to believe it. But he must have been doing this the entire expedition. We never stood a chance, did we?"

"He thinks I'm dead." Her voice cracked as she spoke, her throat closing in.

Zak dropped the jammer and grabbed her hands. "Cecily, it's OK. We'll get out of this together."

"It's not just that. It's Elise. Zak, she *is* dead."

"What?" He reeled back, clawing at his cheeks.

"I saw her lying in the snow. The back of her head was covered in blood."

"No, no, no. Doug would never do that. He wouldn't hurt you."

Cecily lowered her voice. "He thinks I killed his daughter."

"B-but that doesn't make any sense!" Zak stuttered.

"Remember that story I told you? About Snowdon? The woman who died—that was her."

"Oh my god, Cecily . . . But you know that wasn't your fault, right?" He pulled her close as the storm battered their tent. He rubbed at his brow. "I can't believe this. And what about Elise?"

"He thought she was spying on Charles, trying to catch him cheating. He owes Charles his career, Zak. He doesn't want anything—or anyone—to get in his way."

The tent shook with the wind, the poles bending inward. Cecily caught Zak's eye and they stared at each other for a moment.

"What do we do now?" Zak asked.

Cecily swallowed. "We have to do exactly what you said. We have to get off this fucking mountain."

CHAPTER 51

"WE SHOULD ROPE TOGETHER," she said. "There's no point worrying about Doug and the storm if one of us is going to fall down a crevasse and die anyway."

"Good point. Do you have extra rope?"

"No. Do you?"

"No."

They stared at each other. Then slowly she shook her head. "We shouldn't be on this mountain. We're not prepared. We're not true alpinists. We're . . . tourists up here."

"Well, I didn't count on the Sherpas abandoning us! I didn't expect our so-called team leader to be a psychopath! What the fuck are we supposed to do? We can't leave; we can't stay. We're completely screwed."

She locked eyes with him. They might not be roped together physically. But they needed to be in this together. As a team. If they had any chance of making it at all.

He stared back, hysteria visible in his irises. She knew their roles were going to alternate and shift—at some points, he would be the steady one, the rock, but in this moment she needed to be his.

"Listen. The wind has died down. Doug is out there, and he's moving—that must mean he's not urgently seeking shelter. Maybe that means we can move too. We need to travel as light as possible. My oxygen mask is broken—so there's no point in carrying the tank around anymore."

"Mine is busted too. Another coincidence, or . . . ?"

She didn't want to think about it.

"What time is it?" she asked.

"Ten."

She swallowed. They'd been over seven thousand meters for over twenty-four hours. It was too long.

"Let's move," she said.

They stepped into the bleak whiteness, keeping low to the ground. Their first challenge would be finding the fixed line. If they could do that, then maybe they stood a chance.

She took the lead since Zak was hanging back, tentative in every movement. Fine. She would do this. She traced the line of tents, but there were so few now—she had no idea where the fixed line might have ended. Then she spotted something she recognized: her ice ax, sticking up out of the snow in front of her tent. She grabbed it, hooking it onto her harness. She felt stronger with it on her.

Finally, she spotted a cluster of brightly colored rope. "Over here!" she shouted. She fumbled with her carabiner and attached herself to the line. It led downhill, so it must be the right one.

"Come on, Zak," she said through her buff. He gripped the arm of her down suit, and she made sure he was clipped in before they continued. In this way, they shuffled down. She remembered how steep it was from the journey up, and they had to keep a tight grip on the rope in order to stop from slipping. Her knee cried out in agony now, every step a punch in the gut. But she didn't want to die. She wasn't ready for it.

The rope dug into her arm, but she didn't loosen her hold, sliding down. She'd watched the Sherpas flying down these ropes, using momentum to propel themselves. She didn't have any of that speed or confidence.

As they descended, Zak grew impatient. At the next change point, he took the lead.

They made good time. The thick soup-like clouds hid the steep drops around them, condensing their vision, so there was nothing compounding the fear of what they were facing. She half hoped Doug had left them for dead and was making his own quick way to base camp. How was he planning to explain the loss of his team? She simply couldn't understand.

Zak pulled up to a stop, and she was forced to halt behind him. Her knee buckled beneath her, and she stumbled. The rope dug into her arm, but it held. "What's happening?" she tried to shout above the sound of the wind.

"Shit. The lines have been removed."

She paused, his words sinking in. "What do you mean?"

"See for yourself . . ."

The anchor for the fixed line was buried in the snow, but the rope itself was not there.

"Oh my god." She couldn't believe Doug had done this. There was an unwritten rule of the high-altitude peaks: no one touched the fixed lines. What was good for one team was good for the others. By sabotaging the lines, he'd gone against everything he'd stood for his entire life. He was determined to make sure they didn't make it off the mountain.

The route ahead didn't look *too* bad. If they were extra careful with their steps, and used their ice axes to dig in, they could descend without the lines.

They didn't have a choice.

"Come on. We can do this anyway. We can't go back up now," she said to Zak. "The only way is forward."

He quivered in his suit, the fear in his eyes raw and primal.

"Stay calm. Breathe." She appealed to the man beneath the wild animal. He needed to maintain control or else he was doomed. This was what Charles had talked about. The killer inside. Zak would kill them both if he allowed fear to take over. One false step, a slip of concentration in this weather, under these circumstances, and he would be gone—likely taking her down with him.

She gripped his shoulders, guiding him to a mound of snow, still clipped into the previous line. His eyes were blank. Maybe his shaking was more than fear. He was dying, his body breaking down.

She kept her toes warm by wriggling them, moving her fingers and bashing her hands together, but Zak just sat there.

"Come *on*, Zak!" she shouted at him. She rubbed his hands with hers, trying to reignite some fire inside him. "Stay with me."

He needed water. She fumbled in the breast pocket of her suit, daring to open her zipper a tiny way. The cold rushed in like seawater on a beach, freezing her to the bone.

She took out her half-liter bottle, but it was empty. The second one had only a few sips left.

Still, if Zak died on her, she would well and truly lose her mind. Keeping him alive was the only thing giving her focus. She cupped his face with her hands, forcing the liquid down his throat. To her relief, it worked. He blinked, and she saw some of the light return to his eyes.

"Cecily?"

"We're going to make it, Zak. But we have to keep going."

She dug around in the snow with her glove—the down soaking through with moisture—but it was worth it: she found the rope. It hadn't been removed after all. Small mistakes. Errors in judgment. That would be their downfall if they weren't careful.

"Look, Zak!" she cried out, almost delirious with glee. But he was swaying. She reached out and clipped his safety line to the previously hidden rope. Then she took his second safety and clipped it onto her harness. It was far too short to comfortably rope them together, but it was the only thing she could think of in these circumstances. She placed him in front of her, because there was no way she would be able to stop them both from falling if he stumbled into her from behind. At least this way she could brace herself, and if he did fall, then she could cut the line connecting them. Maybe.

"You're not going to die on me," she said, but more to bolster her own confidence than for him. He wasn't listening to her anyway. She fumbled with the rope in her hands, coaxing Zak down the slope. There were a few hairy moments where it seemed like Zak was going to slip, but her sheer willpower—and the dig of her crampons into the snow—kept him glued to the mountainside.

She knew that every meter they descended, the stronger he'd get. Every step they took, they'd be nearing camp three. That was what drove her. The fact that safety could soon be at hand.

She could picture the climb in her mind's eye. The long, straight slope of the mountain. This wasn't an area riddled with crevasses, so her confidence built. Camp three would come.

The weather—by some miracle—calmed, slowly, slowly. Yet that gave her a chance to register her pain and fatigue. The ice ax felt like a dead weight in her arms, but she thrust it into the ground with all the energy she could muster with every step. She resorted to sidestepping, not trusting her knee to hold facing forward. At the next anchor point, she unclipped herself from Zak. He was holding his own again.

She nudged his shoulder, and without a word, pointed to a flash of yellow not too far below. They were almost at camp three. He nodded.

Her hands were numb. The damp in her glove had frozen, and she wondered if at the end of this she would keep her fingers.

Manaslu. This was supposed to be one of the least difficult mountains, the achievable one, the one that Charles could breeze his way up and take his place as one of the world's greatest mountaineers. Where was Charles, anyway? Had he summited? Would his visions of worldwide recognition and history-making glory be overshadowed by so many bodies piled up?

When they made it to the first tent, they dived in. The respite from the wind and the cold was a relief, but it was temporary. They still didn't have any supplies.

She ripped her pack off her back—it was no longer blue but white, covered in frost that cracked as she broke into the straps. Her fingers struggled to work the zips, and she cried out with frustration. She knew she had another pair of gloves in there, and she needed to get them on her hands.

Zak tried to help, and between them—each one pushing a side—they got the zip open. It was enough for her to rip into the top and grab the gloves.

She also sent up a small prayer of thanks to the preparedness gods—as she had some artificial hand warmers in the top zipper of her backpack. She shook them open.

She popped them inside her gloves, praying that they'd bring life to her fingers before it was too late. She didn't even dare to look at her gloveless hands; she swapped the gloves as rapidly as she could.

"We're fucked," moaned Zak.

"Do you have anything at all in your backpack that we can eat? A cereal bar or something?"

He shook his head. So much for *his* preparedness.

She thought she had something, but it took forever for her to search in her bag, even with the hand warmers in her gloves. When she found the bar of chocolate, it was a frozen block of chocolate mush. It was nearly impossible for her to bite into, and in terms of nourishment it offered almost nothing at all.

She heard a sound outside, different from the wind. A crunch of snow.

She gripped Zak's hand so tight, he grunted awake. She hadn't realized he'd fallen asleep.

"What is it?" he asked, groggily.

"Zak. There's someone outside the tent."

Her voice was barely a whisper as she spoke. Zak's eyes were wide now, as the reality sunk in. But there was something different about these footsteps. They were different, lighter than Doug's, the quality of which she felt was etched into her brain.

It gave her hope. But she wasn't taking anything for granted. Her fist wrapped around the handle of her ice ax, and she crept toward the opening of the tent. Zak shook his head furiously, but she locked eyes with him until he calmed. Then she nodded, and he mirrored her.

She didn't know why he trusted her, when she barely trusted herself.

She carefully pulled back the tent flap, raising the ice ax in her other hand.

CHAPTER 52

"WE'RE SAVED! WE'RE SAVED!" Zak shook her arm. "Galden, we're over here!" he cried out.

Galden's head swung around at the noise, and Cecily saw his eyes light up as he saw her. She felt the same rush of relief.

He jogged through the snow toward them. Cecily noticed he held one of his arms close to his body, a makeshift sling holding his wrist around his neck. "Zak, Cecily, you're alive!" He dropped to his knees, embracing them both. "Last night, Doug ordered us to go down with the Summit Extreme team. They needed extra help to get their clients to base camp. Doug said our team's summit push was over, and he would lead you all down in the morning when you had had a chance to sleep. The others made it to base camp with the Summit Extreme team this morning."

"You didn't go with them?" Cecily asked.

"My arm was bad, so I needed to rest at camp two while they went all the way down. I heard over the radio that you had fallen, Cecily." Galden's voice broke, his head dropping into his good hand. "I had to come back up. I had to see if I could find you. I shouldn't have left you in the first place . . ."

"You didn't know," she said, gripping his gloved hand. "But you're here now. We need help."

"Let me radio that you are all right." He fumbled at his side, then he sent a message down the mountain that he'd found them and they would be leaving camp three. He waited a few beats to hear some confirmation back, but all they heard was static. A strong gust of wind blasted the tent, forcing them to huddle together against its power. "We cannot stay here. It's too dangerous. We have to get down."

"Come on, Zak—one more push?" she said, trying to inject some positivity into her tone.

Zak closed his eyes, and she feared that they weren't going to open again. But then they did, fixing her with a fierce stare. Her heart lifted. He'd found strength, from somewhere, somehow, and now she had to find it too, dig down deep within herself and anchor to that tiny part of her that was screaming out for survival.

"Wait, Galden—we've had nothing to eat or drink for hours. Do you have anything?" she asked.

"Let me see." Galden pulled a couple of snack bars out of his jacket, along with a thermos of tea from his backpack. She'd never been so grateful for anything in her entire life. She could barely drink the tea; her lips were so cold they could hardly create a seal around the thermos rim. She was in much worse shape than she thought. Although she bit down on the granola bar hungrily, her teeth struggled to break through the firm mixture. Once she managed it, her mouth was so dry that the food sat there without dissolving, solid. She swallowed it anyway; her body needed it.

Zak was doing even worse than she was. The tea spilled down his chin, more of it on his down suit than in his mouth.

"Time to go. I can't carry you both. We'll have to rope together and maybe we will find some help." Galden unhooked a coil of rope from his backpack. He put Zak in between them. That meant he thought she was the stronger one. The thought wasn't that comforting.

Once he was confident they were secure, he headed back outside, and they had no choice but to follow.

Without him, they wouldn't have stood a chance. The snow—though falling more softly now—had completely obscured any of the footprints that would lead them to the route.

The sky cast a gray pall over everything. It obscured all sense of time, all sense of perspective—or maybe that was her own hypoxia. They crept perilously close to a drop, but she could not even summon fear.

They moved fast. Zak struggled, but between Galden, her and the fixed line, they managed to keep him on his feet. She was terrified of Doug stalking them on the mountain, but with Galden there she knew they had a better shot.

They just had to keep moving.

There were parts of this descent where they had to rappel down steep sections. Zak tumbled down the first rappel and Galden struggled to belay him, which meant she was almost pulled over too. Suddenly she wasn't so comfortable with being roped to him.

Galden agreed. At the next rappel point—one where the consequences of falling would be much worse, he stopped and unhooked them. She sat down in the snow, clinging to the fixed line, willing energy into her body and hoping that camp two was near.

The temptation to curl up in the snow and sleep was strong. Would it be so terrible?

Galden concentrated hard on rigging a setup that would allow him to lower Zak to the next level. He saw her drifting and gave her arm a shake. "Cecily. I have to go down with Zak. You rappel after us. Got it? I'm going to get you both down alive."

She nodded, then readied her figure eight to attach to the rope. He seemed satisfied and returned to help Zak.

When it was her turn, she took extra time descending. Her knee screamed in agony, but somehow she made it. They'd reached the upper part of camp two. There was a tent off to the side, half-buried in the snow. Beyond that, a large crevasse.

Galden waved her over. "Zak needs shelter. Let's try and move him into the tent." She nodded, and braced Zak's arm over her shoulder. But she wasn't strong enough to pick him up. Her own knee buckled.

"It's no good!" she said, collapsing. Zak fell into the snow too. She saw the wince of pain on Galden's face that he was trying so hard to conceal.

"Don't worry," he said. "I will stay with Zak here. But we both need water. Check the tent. Bring it to us."

"Got it." She staggered over to the tent, dropping her pack and ice ax outside.

But when she opened it—someone was already inside.

CHAPTER 53

"OH, CHARLES, THANK GOD it's you." She collapsed, half in the tent, and Charles helped pull her the rest of the way in.

"Cecily! Are you OK? What's going on out there? I heard over the radio that Galden found you alive . . . I'm so relieved."

"He's with Zak outside. They need help. Zak's not doing well, Galden is injured and they urgently need water."

"Yes, I saw you coming down so I put some snow on to melt." He gestured to a small canister over a gas flame, next to his enormous backpack. "Have you seen anyone else? I haven't been able to get ahold of anyone on the radio. Doug? Or Elise?"

"Elise . . ." She barely managed to get the name out; it stuck in her throat. "She's dead. Above camp four. She'd been hit in the head. And as for Doug, he . . . he tried to kill me. I think he might have messed with my oxygen tank, and then he lunged at me on the summit and I only managed to get away because he thought I'd fallen."

Snow clung to Charles's facial hair, the beard grown while at base camp and those bushy eyebrows, turning them white. It made his eyes even more piercing, like she was staring into the heart of a glacier. "The mountain does strange things to men. Especially to desperate, grieving ones. Doug is all of that."

She buried her face in her gloves. "He thinks I killed his daughter." She sobbed, the shock of what she'd been through coursing through her veins, the relief of finally being rescued settling in. She was with Charles, Galden and Zak now. Doug couldn't take all of them.

"Well, didn't you?"

She blinked, sitting up straighter. "What? I didn't mean to get in trouble on the ridge. I was following James on a route he had no right taking me on. I got stuck . . ."

Charles tutted. "See? Still making your excuses. You represent to Doug everything that is wrong with mountaineering at the moment. So thoughtless, so reckless. No respect for the mountain."

"That's not true. Well, maybe then it was, but I've learned."

"Have you?" he said, softly. "Looks like you're in need of rescuing once again."

"Please, Charles . . ." Cecily took a shuddering breath, trying to keep her focus on the present dangers—not the past. The wind blasted through the tent, and she thought of the two men huddled outside in the cold. "It's not just me this time. We should go and help Galden bring Zak inside." She scrambled back toward the entrance, knocking over Charles's backpack in the process.

In turn, it knocked into the canister, and Charles hissed with frustration as he tried to keep the gas flame lit.

The lid of his backpack tipped open, and some of the contents tumbled out.

That's when she saw it: a TalkForward camera.

Elise's camera.

She looked up and met Charles's cold stare. He knew she'd seen it.

She swallowed, not wanting to ask and yet unable to stop herself. "Why do you have that?"

Charles sighed, extinguishing the gas canister flame. "It didn't have to be this way. This wasn't the plan."

Cecily's gaze darted between the camera and Charles's face, putting the pieces together, terror rising as the truth dawned. "It . . . was you?"

Charles continued as if he hadn't heard her. "I wanted you all to make the summit so we could come down together. Triumphant. Only Doug had other plans.

"He knew the forecast was wrong all along. He'd been blocking the signal to keep me from realizing that the storm was coming. He wanted me caught up in it, but concealed his lie by bringing the team along for as long as possible. He tried to turn you all around at camp three, remember? I was not going to let that happen. I had to distract him. That's why I asked you to tell the Snowdon story. I knew you were responsible for his daughter's death."

"But . . . I don't understand? You invited me here."

"I did. For that exact reason. Oh, you should have seen him when he got the call. He was distraught. He didn't want to know what happened, but I did. I read all the articles about her death, the ones calling you the 'Hero of Snowdon' for helping. When you published 'Failure to Rise,' I took note of you. I knew there was more to that story. And when I thought Doug was growing suspicious about me, after Broad Peak, I thought of a plan. I'd take a team to Manaslu. Make him too busy to thwart me.

"It didn't work, though. He still tried everything in his power to keep you guys *off* the summit."

"But why?"

"Foolish man. He actually thought the storm would stop me. Maybe even kill me." Charles detached his ice ax from his backpack, moving at a menacing pace.

Fear gripped her throat, making it hard for her to talk. "Why did he need to stop you?"

"He knew I'd found something that gave me even more of a rush than summiting mountains."

"I don't understand . . ."

"No?"

She edged backward, her shallow breaths picking up pace. She wasn't safe here. Her body knew it, even though it took time for her mind to catch up. Doug had tried to turn them around. *You have no idea at all, do you* . . . He hadn't wanted them on the mountain with Charles.

There was a dark stain on the end of his ice ax. She didn't want to know where it had come from.

Except that she had seen his victim with her own eyes, touched the blood with her hands.

"*You're* the murderer," she whispered. "But why?"

Charles ran his finger along the curved metal edge of his ice ax's blade.

Cecily's mouth went dry.

"Because I can," he said, his voice quiet. "I've always known I was different. When I was a kid, Doug thought the challenge of the mountains would be enough to satisfy me. But even that became too easy.

"Then Peak Lenin happened. Nature threw everything it had at me, and I survived. Could someone like you even understand that? The strength of will it takes to absorb the greatest force the mountain can throw at you, to climb out from under the weight of that snow, to feel the sun on your face and know that you have been chosen? I had been climbing with two guys I thought were strong, but they were taken. No. I am different, and I want the world to know it."

He paused. "But the world isn't ready for me. I announced this mind-blowing challenge, my Fourteen Clean, and did anyone care? People are so shallow, these armchair warriors, daring to criticize those of us out here pushing the boundaries of what it means to be human. No one would support me, saying that what I was attempting was too dangerous. Then came Dhaulagiri. When I came across those two guys collapsed on the side of the route, blocking my path, hypoxic, I was angry. I placed my hand on the first man's neck to check his pulse. It was there, but it was faint. If he descended, he might have survived. His brother was moaning, near death as well. Both of them so pathetic. They didn't belong up there.

"I returned to the first man and placed more pressure on his neck. He struggled then, oh yes—the fight returned, the fight to live, to survive. It had been in him all along, his mind had given up, but his body could have gone on, if he'd chosen to. But it was too late . . . the light disappeared from his eyes. Mine was the last face he saw. No summit has ever made me feel so powerful." As he spoke, he made the gesture, wringing an imaginary neck between his fingers. Bile rose in Cecily's throat. She didn't have a weapon at hand, and her knee still ached. She had only one hope: to escape to Galden and Zak. Maybe between them they could overpower him.

"That man was weak. Too weak to be where he was. I did what was right. I could decide which man would live and who would die. I took his brother down. When I went back the next day with the rescue team, there the other man was. Sitting, dead, exactly as I had left him. And no one knew my part in it. When people die in the death zone, no one bats an eyelid. And by rescuing his partner, I became a hero."

"They'll know this time," Cecily said. "What's your plan, to kill the whole team? No one will think you're a hero in that case. Your reputation will be ruined."

"My reputation is secure. Like I told you, there is no more perfect place to kill than up here. On Everest, it took the smallest shove—no, not a shove, a nudge, barely anything at all—and a man fell to his death. A man who thought he saw me touch the fixed lines, starting a vicious rumor. The audacity! To presume I'd use the crutches and props ordinary men need to climb these peaks."

Tears swelled up in Cecily's eyes. "But your rescues? You . . . you save life, not take it."

"Even the greats need good press." He laughed at his own bad joke.

"So Cho Oyu. Grant *did* have footage of you faking a rescue?"

Charles sneered. "I have no need to fake a rescue. I wanted to kill that man—but when I saw the drone, I had to save him instead. Grant thought I was staging it, thought he could use the footage to threaten me. Blackmail a place on my team, the film rights to my story. Ridiculous. Still, by inviting him here, I could deal with him and whatever film he thought he had. You were all selected so carefully. Elise, with her social media—she could quash any niggling cheating rumors. Zak—so rich, he funded my entire mission and more, in exchange for this climb, so money became no object. And you. You were my secret weapon against Doug. A bomb to set off at just the right moment—like when he wanted to turn you all around at camp three. I needed you on the mountain. For one final, dramatic rescue that would secure my place in the history books. Last night, when you left your tent, I tampered with your oxygen. I knew it would break sometime on your summit push. You'd be helpless and I'd be there for you. But you've almost impressed me. Doug tried to turn you around and you went for the summit anyway. Look how far you've come without oxygen."

Cecily blinked. All along, she'd thought Charles had chosen her because she was strong. But he'd chosen her because she was weak. "This was all planned? Oh my god . . . Irina? Alain? Did you kill them as well?"

"It took me a long time to figure out who the Everest man had called from the mountain. But when Alain posted on that forum, and I saw he was coming to Manaslu, I knew I had to take my opportunity. As for the Russian woman, she got in the way. I had to destroy Grant's footage so nothing incriminating would remain on film. I snuck into his tent on camp two and smashed the hard drive, but she saw me—so I had to take her out before she reached base camp."

Cecily clamped her arms over her head, as if she could block out the horror. But it was right in front of her eyes. "Why are you telling me this?" she whispered.

The answer was obvious: he didn't intend to let her live. So to survive, she had to do something drastic. Her eyes were wild, flitting around the tent. Charles saw what she was trying to do; he didn't seem worried.

"Instead, Zak will be my rescue story. I'm sure his company will reward me generously for the effort."

"But why Elise?" she whispered.

"She came to me on summit push night, told me Doug was sending her down. She confessed to me the real reason she'd come to the mountain—to spy on me—and she apologized. Well, I convinced her to go for the summit with me. But when I found my moment . . ." He didn't need to finish the sentence. "I took the camera with me, so I could destroy it later." Charles shifted his body toward her and she flinched, but he didn't strike her. Instead, he grabbed the camera from the floor.

"I can do it now."

He took the ice ax, twirled it in his hands and smashed down on the camera with all his might. Despite herself, she screamed.

Then she moved. She scrambled on all fours to the edge of the tent and burst out into the storm.

CHAPTER 54

"GALDEN!" SHE SCREAMED.

The wind blasted her body, stealing away her words and driving her to her knees. She threw up her hands to protect her face.

That was when she heard it. A whistle. Casual. Relaxed. From the tent behind her.

Low, low, high, low.

Fresh terror reared up within her, chilling her far more than the fierce storm howling outside.

With his one good arm, Galden had managed to drag Zak closer to the tent. The American looked in terrible shape, his head lolling and eyes closed.

She grabbed Galden's down suit, pulling him away. "We have to get out of here!" she said. "You take Zak's other arm . . ." She knelt down beside Zak, trying to get her shoulder underneath his armpit to support his weight.

"Did you get the water?" Galden asked, still standing, gesturing to the tent.

"No, Galden, come on!"

Charles swept through the tent door. Galden let out a cry of shock, raised his arm in greeting, then turned back to Cecily with a big smile, his voice was full of hope. "Charles is here, didi. We can move faster now. We can—"

Charles swung the ice ax and she just about had time to let out a strangled cry of despair as it hit Galden square in the back. She fumbled at the carabiner on Zak's harness, still connecting him by a loose length of rope to Galden. She couldn't leave him. She had to at least try . . .

Doug had known. If it hadn't been for the Snowdon story, he would've turned them around at camp three. She wouldn't have made the summit, but she would have had her life.

That was as far as her thought process got. Charles removed the ax from Galden, who was on the ground, bleeding, groaning, dying. She wanted to go to him, but Charles stepped toward her and Zak. She clambered away, her bad knee buckling underneath her.

The slow, cold, methodical way he moved terrified her. As did the smile on his face. He was enjoying this. Every second of it. The power he had over them. She was on his territory, where he was king.

He didn't even bow to the wind.

"Don't run, Cecily. If you run—I will kill Zak."

She was torn. She didn't want to leave him. But if she got away, she might just survive. Then she could send help for Zak . . .

Another groan from Galden reached her ears, a guttural cry of pain, and her thinking reversed. Something else took over, something deeper and more primal, and she surged forward. She wasn't about to lose another of her teammates on the mountain. She ran at Charles. He wasn't going to take another life. Not if she could help it.

Her choice surprised him. He hesitated, still hovering over Zak, who was finally beginning to stir. That indecision was enough. She launched herself at him, not having any weapon other than her body—and the element of surprise. Yet the topology of the mountain was in her favor. The crevasse swung to his left, and although he thought she was going to push him backward—and that was how he braced himself—instead, she grabbed his arm and pulled him to the gaping hole in the ice, using the entire weight of her body.

Seeing as he was braced in the wrong direction, her plot worked. It took him a few stumbling steps, but one of his legs disappeared through the crack, throwing him wildly off-balance. She rolled over, out of his reach, as he scrabbled around to try to take her down with him.

He disappeared over the lip of the crevasse.

She didn't have a lot of time. It might have worked to get Charles down, but he wasn't out. If anyone could crawl their way out of a crevasse, he could.

She rushed over to Galden. She knew just by his posture that he was gone, and she reached over and closed his eyes, which were open and staring up at the sky. She moaned, an involuntary sound from deep within her belly.

"What's happening?" Zak's words garbled together, but they brought her back from the brink.

He was still alive. They could get through this together. "We have to go." She grabbed her backpack and ice ax from outside the tent.

"What about Galden?"

She couldn't answer him. Besides, they had something else to worry about. Darkness was falling. If it got dark before they reached the tents at camp one, not only would the temperature drop even further, but they wouldn't be able to see. They didn't have flashlights and no time to hunt for one. She didn't think Zak would survive a night exposed on the mountain. She didn't think *she* would survive either, but that voice she tamped down and buried. There was no point thinking about her survival. She had to keep Zak alive. Keep him alive. Get him down. If she could do that, she would save herself too.

She threw Zak's arm over her shoulder, lifting him to his feet. She kept imagining Charles crawling out of that crevasse; every shadow threatened to be him. Zak swayed on his feet, but to her relief he stood on his own. She held him for good measure. They floundered toward the fixed lines and started making their way down once more.

Mercifully the deep valleys of the icefall kept them sheltered from the fierceness of the wind. Cecily kept looking over her shoulder, willing Zak on faster, but she didn't see a soul. Zak wanted to duck into one of the tents and rest, but she urged him on. Charles was after them, and Galden had already paid the ultimate price.

She didn't want to tell Zak the whole truth, in case fear paralyzed him as it was threatening to do to her.

After all, they had one major obstacle left: the Hanging Place. Once they were past that and down to camp one, it was a straight shot to base camp. If they stayed on the fixed lines, they might be able to get back even in the dark.

She didn't even feel pain in her leg anymore—her mind blocked it out, discarding anything that wasn't necessary for her survival.

Anger had replaced it. Anger was what was going to keep her alive. Anger powered every step, gripped the rope. Anger for what had happened to Galden, to Elise. It wrapped around her body, and she leaned on it with everything that she had.

Even though her hands were so cold they burned, she gripped her orange-handled ice ax for dear life.

She dared a glance behind. In the distance: a figure in a red down suit with navy blue accents. Charles. He'd emerged already.

She picked up the pace, so she practically dragged Zak down the fixed lines, moving so fast they arrived at the top of the Hanging Place in record time. A race against the night—and the killer stalking them.

She tied Zak's rappel device onto the line. "Can you do this, Zak?"

"No, Cecily . . . What about you?"

But she didn't want to waste time arguing. Zak was in rough mental shape, but physically he was fine, and getting stronger as they descended. She wasn't going to leave him to Charles's mercy. Her knee was in agony; she might not make it far. But she had her ice ax. That was something.

She handed him the brake line, wrapping his fingers around it. "Don't let go of the brake, OK? Lower yourself slowly. You can do this. And when you get to the bottom, get to base camp. Don't wait for me. I'll catch up if I can."

"Cecily, be careful," he said.

"Go."

She watched him disappear over the edge of the wall before turning back around to face her fate.

She dropped to her good knee, clutching the ice ax in her hand.

Charles approached, not changing his pace, his heavy boot steps crunching the snow beneath his feet.

"Giving up again, are we, Cecily?"

She threw down the ice ax at his feet. The lamas had blessed it. Fat use that had been. "This is what you need, isn't it? You need your victims to be weak. No weapons. Defenseless. That's *really* why you like killing in the death zone. Because your victims are already half-dead." Despite everything, she laughed. "You're no hero. You're a coward."

He snarled, springing toward her.

But something stopped him. From behind a mound of snow Doug launched up, grabbing the hood of Charles's down suit, yanking him back.

Charles's eyes narrowed. He pivoted around, dislodging Doug's grip.

While he was distracted, Cecily leaned forward and grabbed the ax. Then she stood, hauling herself to her feet. She winced, inhaling a ragged breath, lifting her head. She took a step backward. Now she was balanced half over the cliff edge of the Hanging Place—and she wasn't hooked into a line. She glanced over her shoulder and down. Zak was making his way—he hadn't slipped. Maybe she could give him some time to escape, so he could live.

"Enough, Charles," said Doug. "I know what you've done. I didn't want to believe it. I couldn't. I told myself that what I suspected— Marco, Pierre, that Sherpa on Broad Peak—couldn't be true. But I saw what you did to Grant at camp four. And so it ends here."

Charles laughed. "Don't you get it? It only ends here for you. If you kill me, you will never work in the mountains again."

"I don't care about that. My life was over the moment Caroline died."

"But I wasn't responsible for that," Charles said. "She was." He pointed back at her, and Cecily froze under the force of it. Worse still was the pain on Doug's face. The torment her incompetence had caused.

"I know," said Doug. For a moment, the wind died and the snow halted.

Doug raised an object in his hands, pointing it directly at Cecily.

A gun. Her heart seemed to stop beating. Time slowed, and all she could see was the impossibly black hole at the end of the barrel.

"I'm sorry," he said, staring at her. "I didn't want you to get caught up in this."

He pivoted, until the gun faced Charles. Then kept on raising it, until it pointed at the sky.

Charles's voice trembled; it was the first time Cecily had heard a hint of fear. "Don't do it, Doug. You'd disrespect the mountain like that?"

"The mountain will always be here. I need to protect the people who are climbing it."

"If you do, you'll kill us all. Me, Cecily and yourself."

Doug's voice was quiet. "I already died." His eyes flicked to Cecily. "Jump," he said.

Charles shouted: "No!" and ran at Doug full sprint, his ice ax extended.

Doug pulled the trigger. A flare shot out of the end of the gun, aimed at the sky.

No, not at the sky.

At the dancing bear serac.

Charles swung the ax.

It was too late. The flare entered the bear's heart. There was a rumble, deep and dark as thunder, as the enormous block of ice tore from the mountain.

Cecily was paralyzed. She couldn't follow Doug's command. She could do nothing but wait. She could see what was coming for them. And she didn't feel fear. It was . . . inevitable.

The mountain was going to kill her. Not Charles.

She closed her eyes, gripping her ice ax with both hands.

And then the snow and ice came to drown her.

CHAPTER 55

COLD, THEY SAY, IS good for the body.

Take a dip in icy water. In small doses, it can sharpen the brain, halt—or even reverse—dementia. Boost the immune system. It was supposed to be numbing. Painless.

But for Cecily, the cold was an embrace of needles. A thousand tiny sharp shooting pains.

So when the numbness came, it was a welcome relief. Her pain disappeared, and all became dark.

But the darkness didn't scare her anymore.

There was nothing as scary as the wall of white that had plummeted toward her.

In darkness, there was always the hope of a flashlight to scare the shadows away.

But a whiteout was all-encompassing. It engulfed her senses. It shattered her bones.

And it swept her over the Hanging Place and into oblivion.

CHAPTER 56

She lay in a bed, surrounded by pine walls. Blankets and sleeping bags weighted her down, a cocoon of warmth.

Out of the corner of her eye she saw Mingma asleep in a chair, a few meters away from her. She tried to turn her head, but every movement sent a shudder of pain through her body. She groaned, inadvertently and almost inhumanly. Pain caused her vision to white out. The noise she made jolted him awake, and he reached over and gathered her hands in his own.

"Don't try to move."

"Where am I?"

"We are back in Samagaun. We're keeping you still until we can get you airlifted to a hospital, as we don't know your injuries. The helicopter is on its way. It shouldn't be long."

"What happened?"

"There was an avalanche on the mountain caused by a serac fall. A terrible one. Many lives were lost. You were protected by the steepness of the Hanging Place. Your ice ax caught against a solid piece of ice, thank goodness. Using it saved you."

She sat up—or she tried to. "What about Zak? Did he make it down?"

"Yes, he did. We found him in a crevasse near the crux."

"Is he OK?"

"He has a broken leg and a bad blow to his head, a concussion. He doesn't remember what happened."

"What about the others?" she asked.

"Doug and Elise are still missing. They are searching for them." Mingma bowed his head. "Cecily, I am so sorry. Doug sent us down to base. He convinced us that he would bring you down. The storm was too bad for us to turn around. Only Galden was left at camp two. We should have questioned Doug. This is my fault." His voice choked. She wished she could turn and look at him, but she couldn't move.

"No, Mingma. It wasn't Doug. It was Charles . . . He murdered Elise, Galden and Doug. He tried to kill me too, and he told me about many others. Doug set off the avalanche to kill Charles. To stop him."

There was a long beat of silence.

"Cecily—you are confused," Mingma said, his voice soft.

"No, I'm not. I watched him kill Galden with my own eyes. He admitted to me that he killed Elise—not only her, but Irina and Alain and probably Grant too. Doug knew Charles was a killer. That's why he tried to get us all off the mountain. That's why he sent you away . . . He was trying to keep people out of his path. But now Charles is gone. Thank God."

The door to the room opened, and bright light flooded into the room.

"Is she awake?"

A shudder of fear shot through her body. She groaned again. The weight of her mattress shifted as he sat down.

"Cecily, can you hear me?" he asked, squeezing her leg through the blanket. It was Charles. He'd survived.

She whimpered.

"What's she been saying?" Charles asked Mingma.

Her heart momentarily stopped.

"Nothing, Charles, sir," Mingma replied. Maybe there was a part of him that did believe her.

"How long until the helicopter gets here?"

"Within the hour," said Mingma. "Mr. Charles . . . you should go back and rest too. Your arm needs to heal."

"OK, OK. I just had to check on our little survivor." He leaned down to whisper in her ear, so low Mingma couldn't hear. "The mountain will never kill me."

The sound of his voice made her stomach clench. Her teeth ground together as he stood up and walked away. She waited a few beats until she was sure he was gone.

"Mingma, I'm telling the truth, I promise you," she said.

"Do you have any proof?" he asked, barely a whisper. When she didn't reply, he patted her hand again. "I have to go check on the helicopter. Please, try to rest." And then he left her in the dark.

She couldn't prove anything. Her head spiked with pain, and behind her eyes all she saw were stars.

No. Elise, Galden, Doug, Irina, Alain. Their lives needed to be honored. The mountain hadn't taken them. Charles had. But who would believe her?

EVIL ON EVEREST: THE REAL STORY OF CHARLES MCVEIGH
By Cecily Wong

On September 23, a serac fall caused a monster avalanche on Manaslu, the eighth-highest mountain on Earth. The avalanche was blamed for killing four people: veteran mountain guide Doug Manners, experienced guide Galden Sonam Sherpa, elite French-Canadian climber Elise Gauthier and British filmmaker Grant Miles-Peterson—and injuring three others: TalkForward CEO Zachary Mitchell, international climbing sensation Charles McVeigh . . . and me.

But the mountain was not to blame.

These deaths, and at least four others before, came at the hands of one man, on a mission he dared to call "Clean."

Charles McVeigh.

The embodiment of evil on the mountain, he took advantage of climbers in a weakened physical state to commit his heinous acts. He used the inherent dangers of the terrain—the lack of oxygen, the yawning crevasses, the steep drops—to cover up his crimes. Who knows how many others may have been his victims? It is near impossible for officials to investigate deaths that happen above eight thousand meters.

Charles said it to me himself on his arrival in Samagaun: "Where better for a killer to hide, than somewhere already known as the death zone?"

But the time for hiding is done.

His reign of terror in the mountains is over. Charles is about to be exposed for the villain he is, and his victims will finally find peace.

CHAPTER 57

It would never be published. But she had to write it, to get the words down, if for her eyes only.

She'd already spent too long in the hospital in Kathmandu. Incredibly, she'd survived with minimal injuries—the worst that she'd suffered were to her left knee and her right hand, and some snow blindness scarring on her retina. The knee and vision would recover. But the tip of her ring finger? That, she wouldn't get back. It turned out that when she'd dug into the snow with her glove, the tissue hadn't been able to recover from such frigid cold. But if that was the only casualty, she knew she'd got off lightly.

Zak had a severe concussion and a broken leg. He'd made it to the base of the Hanging Place by the time the avalanche had hit, but he hadn't made it across the crevasse. The ladder had tipped in and caught against the icy wall—saving his life but breaking his leg. He was still recovering from surgery and preparing to be transferred back to the States.

She'd gone to visit him in the hospital, of course. He couldn't remember what had happened on the mountain—everything from summit night onward was a dark blur. But they gripped hands anyway, bonded for life by the experience they had survived together.

Dario had visited her, in despair. He'd believed her story instantly, but there was nothing he could do to incriminate Charles without proof. "I knew I should have convinced Elise to come down with me. I knew I was sending her into the lion's den. I should have saved you all. I'm so sorry."

Worse had been the headlines. The interviews on all the major news stations. They universally praised Charles, the hero, who'd announced that he'd completed his record and then risen from the avalanche to rescue her. He was more than Charles the conqueror. He was Charles the savior. The hero of Manaslu. The danger turned people on, the horror and the terror. It only added to his mythology.

But whenever she saw his name and face in print and on-screen, her bones turned to water. She was the only one who knew the truth: Charles was a killer.

She wished she knew why the mountain had spared him. Apparently he'd been able to self-arrest with the ax he'd swung, riding the wave of the avalanche and surviving with only a broken arm. Once they'd dug him out of the snow, he'd insisted on staying on the mountain to "help" with the recovery of the bodies.

Or, more likely, to cover up his crimes. They'd not yet found Grant or Elise, and Cecily knew for a fact that Elise's body had been nowhere near the avalanche site.

Her parents wanted her to come home straightaway. Rachel said she'd jump on the next plane to Kathmandu.

But she said no to both. They hadn't experienced it. They hadn't found Elise's body, held hands with Zak, seen what Galden sacrificed.

Her survival meant little if their stories were lost, buried beneath the ice.

Before she could return, before she could see anyone, she had amends to make.

Galden's village, Tengboche, was high up in the Khumbu region of the Himalayas, far from Manaslu, and home to the better-known giants, like Mount Everest. It took her a few days to get there. She flew on a rickety plane to the world's most notorious airport in Lukla and then took a bumpy Jeep ride to the village—probably no better for her knee than trekking, but Mingma had insisted that was how she traveled.

She'd arrived with him over the Nepali holiday of Dashain. It was meant to represent the triumph of good over evil, but she couldn't help but feel that evil had won the day.

It wasn't a joyous occasion. Yet Galden's family were so welcoming to her. They invited her to share in a Dashain ritual, which she was honored to do.

She sat across from Galden's mother, who chanted and burned incense. It reminded her of the puja and her grandmother. Tears welled in her eyes as she thought of everyone she had lost.

His mother leaned forward and pressed a blessing into her forehead, a bright red spot mixed with rice. Cecily bowed toward her, and his mother bowed back, her hands pressed together in prayer. There was no blame there, but Cecily couldn't help but feel overwhelmed with grief. She knew that by losing Galden their whole family would suffer. She knew she would do everything she could to support them.

On her way out of Galden's family home, she passed beneath the monastery that she'd heard him speak about. It felt like a good opportunity to leave something for the people who'd died at Charles's hands—memories, and an offering.

Inside, the monastery was a riot of color, vivid reds and blues, accented with sparkling gold leaf. The vibrancy reminded her of Elise. She knelt down and bowed her head, thinking of the dead.

There was a small shrine of prayer flags surrounding a statue of the Buddha. She asked the lama for permission, and he nodded. She didn't have anything that belonged to Zak, Doug or Galden, so she took her notebook and wrote their names, then folded the paper up into a tiny crane that Galden taught her during the long days at base camp. She placed it on the shelf next to the Buddha. Then next, she took out Elise's necklace, the one she'd removed from her lifeless body. The proof that she hadn't died in an avalanche.

The proof that the mountain hadn't killed her. Charles had.

She stared down at the pendant in her palm. Cecily thought Elise would want it to be left here in Nepal, where she had felt so at home.

As she lifted it to hang it on the shrine, she thought of the camera.

Specifically, the TalkForward cameras. They beamed satellite footage directly to cloud storage.

What if . . . ? She didn't hold out much hope—Zak hadn't been able to make it work even at base camp. But Doug had been jamming the satellite signals at the camps.

Closer to the summit, the signal might have connected.

It was a long shot, but it was something.

"Thank you, Elise," she whispered. She kissed the necklace before hanging it on the shrine.

She walked outside the monastery. "Mingma?"

He stood with his hands clasped behind his back. There was sadness in his shoulders that hadn't been there a month ago. "Yes?"

"Is there somewhere I can access Wi-Fi? It's urgent."

"Of course. I will take you."

She limped down to the Everest View teahouse, leaning on his shoulder. They stepped up to the roof terrace, where she sat in the sunshine and Mingma brought over strong sweet masala chai. She removed her laptop from her backpack and connected to the Wi-Fi—ironically there was a strong signal up here.

She typed in the link to Zak's private server. There were two folders, both locked with a password. She tried Zak's first: *The password is my favorite mountain.* Rainier.

But her heart sank as it opened.

There was nothing from the final day.

Elise was her last hope. She clicked on the folder.

The password-protection box popped up. But she knew Elise's favorite mountain: the Eiger. She typed it in and watched as the files appeared in front of her eyes. She carefully noted the time stamps.

She clicked on the most recent file and gasped. Elise's smiling face appeared on the screen, the sensitive camera lens able to pick up her face even in the dead of night. She was wearing her summit suit, and Cecily recognized the small mound of tents in view behind her: camp four. "I'm going up to the summit, guys!" said her voice, so full of hope and excitement. "Charles has convinced me."

There was a shaky moment as Elise pinned the camera onto her pocket, and footage of her walking slowly away from camp.

Cecily watched on, unable to tear her eyes away, nausea rising. Her scalp prickled as Elise turned toward her killer, capturing his face on the screen.

Elise had realized in the last second what was about to happen. The last few seconds were of her running—or trying to—through the snow.

Then the screen shuddered and went black.

Cecily clamped her hands over her mouth. But this was it. Elise's final gift.

Video proof that Charles was a murderer.

She had him.

This would be the new biggest story in mountaineering history.

Beside her, Mingma inhaled sharply.

"Now do you believe me?" she asked him.

"I must go." He stood up from the table abruptly, knocking his chair over so it clattered on the tile floor, and hurried out of the teahouse. She didn't know what he was going to do. But she knew she wouldn't want to be Charles when Mingma and the other Sherpas found him.

She composed an email to Michelle:

If you want the real story, I have it.

She attached a still from the video as proof and the draft of her article "Evil on Everest."

It would be enough.

Outside the teahouse, there was a bamboo swing set up for Dashain, swaying in the afternoon light, and in the distance there was Everest, Sagarmatha, Chomolungma, goddess mother of the world.

She sat on the swing, staring up at the closest place to Heaven on Earth, and she breathed.

ACKNOWLEDGMENTS

JUST AFTER SUMMITING MANASLU in September 2019, while still in the death zone, I sat down in the snow, took out my notebook and started to write. What I wrote up there won't see the light of day—I was hypoxic, exhausted and my handwriting is almost impossible to read! But I knew even then that I had to write a novel about my time on the mountain. Thankfully, my expedition was far less eventful than Cecily's, but it was still one of the most powerful and transformative experiences of my life.

So my first thanks goes to the incredible leaders of my eight-thousander expedition: Nimsdai Purja and Mingma Gyabu "David" Sherpa of Elite Expeditions. Their guidance and mentorship on Manaslu (and on Aconcagua before that) gave me the confidence to tackle challenges I never dreamed I could attempt. The Manaslu expedition formed part of Nims's Project Possible world record–breaking achievement, and it was an honor to share the mountain with him, one of the greatest mountaineers of our generation. I also have to thank Tensi Kasang Sherpa, who was my personal climbing guide on the way to the summit (feeding me much-needed slices of apple on the way). I had the best tentmates—Deeya Pun and Stefi Trouget—who lifted my spirits when I needed it most, and incredible teammates in Steve Davis, Sandro Gromen-Hayes, Avedis Kalpaklian and Khodr Ghadban. The memories we made together are some I will never forget.

My journey into mountaineering began only the year before, when

I summited my first-ever peak: Mount Toubkal in Morocco on New Year's Day 2018. I owe so much of my passion and knowledge about mountaineering to the guide on that trip, Jon Gupta. It was Jon who taught me to "be bothered" and who believed I could climb Everest if I wanted to—little did he know, he shattered a lot of the limiting beliefs I held about myself in that moment. Thanks also to Éric Bouvant, my guide on Mont Blanc, whose lessons in breathing and pacing myself at altitude were integral to my success on that peak.

However, while many people have helped me on my alpinism journey, any errors when it comes to the technical mountaineering sections of this novel are my own.

Writing a novel is a lot like climbing a mountain, and I needed all the support I could get for this process too! I couldn't ask for a better agent and friend than Juliet Mushens. She believed in this book long before I did. She is a visionary, one of the most inspiring people I know, and there is no harder-working person in publishing. Her team—Liza DeBlock and Kiya Evans—are simply the best. Across the pond, my North American agent Jenny Bent is an absolute rock star. I'm so grateful to have them all in my corner.

Thankfully, they placed the book in the hands of some of the best editors in the business. Joel Richardson at Penguin Michael Joseph, Edward Kastenmeier at Anchor Books and Lara Hinchberger at Penguin Canada worked so hard to whip this book into shape. Their advice and support went above and beyond what was required, and I'm so thrilled to have them with me on this journey to publication. They've made all my wildest dreams come true.

Alongside Joel at Penguin Michael Joseph, I have to thank Grace Long, Clio Cornish, Lucy Upton, Ellie Hughes, Liv Thomas, Lee Motely, Emma Henderson and Jennie Roman. Together they form the most brilliant editorial, marketing, publicity, design and sales team an author could ask for.

Writing can be a lonely business—especially during the pandemic, and when pivoting to a completely new genre. I particularly have to thank Kim Curran, the very first person to read a draft of *Breathless*. She is also my climbing-wall buddy, though we probably solve more plot problems than boulder problems, for which I'm end-lessly grateful!

Everyone needs a friend like Amie Kaufman, who barely batted an eyelid when I told her about this opportunity I had to climb an eight-thousander, and she had these wise words for me: I absolutely had to write this book. While I was at base camp, I had a WhatsApp group for friends who wanted updates on my expedition, and they ended up being a lifeline to me while I was away. To Juliet (again), Sarah Woodward, Adam Stratford, Tania Stratford, Maria Felix Miller, Natasha Bardon and James Smythe—thank you for being the first to say my wild mountain stories would (with small tweaks!) make for a great murder mystery! Laura Lam, Juno Dawson, Tanya Byrne, Zoe Sugg, Sarah Jones, Stacey Halls and Katie Ellis-Brown provided much-needed encouragement, laughter and advice throughout lockdown.

None of this would be possible without my family, immediate and extended, who always root for me while I'm writing and while I'm climbing! Thanks to the McCullochs, the Barneses and the Liveseys for your unwavering support. My sister, Sophie, and my brother-in-law, Evan, constantly inspire me with their creativity, passion and focus. And my parents, Maria and Angus, are always my most enthusiastic first readers, my loudest advocates, my pillars of strength. I couldn't have written this book without the courage and resilience they've instilled in me.

Finally, a special thanks to Chris—who invited me on my very first mountain trip. You push me to grow and become the best person—and writer—that I can be. I can't wait to see what other adventures await us . . .

ABOUT THE AUTHOR

AMY McCULLOCH is the author of eight novels for children and young adults, including the internationally bestselling YA novel *The Magpie Society: One for Sorrow*. In September 2019, she became the youngest Canadian woman to climb Manaslu in Nepal—the world's eighth-highest mountain. She also summited the highest mountain in the Americas, Aconcagua, in −50°F temperatures and 55 mph winds, and has visited all seven continents. *Breathless* is her adult fiction debut.